D0187235

Praise for the novels
of Michael Farmer

War Dogs

"A thrilling military adventure . . . exciting from the first word to the last . . . and just good old-fashioned fun to read."
—Ralph Peters, author of *New Glory: Expanding America's Global Supremacy*

Iron Tigers

"Fans of tank action who didn't get enough in Farmer's *Tin Soldiers* will be delighted with the many vividly described battle scenes in his latest."
—*Publishers Weekly*

Tin Soldiers

"*Tin Soldiers* is a gripping and potentially prophetic thriller."
—W.E.B. Griffin, *New York Times* bestselling author of *The Corps* and *Brotherhood of War* series

"Authentic, muscular, and swift. A remarkably timely novel . . . destined for well-deserved success!"
—Ralph Peters

WAR DOGS

Michael Farmer

AN ONYX BOOK

ONYX
Published by New American Library, a division of
Penguin Group (USA) Inc., 375 Hudson Street,
New York, New York 10014, USA
Penguin Group (Canada), 90 Eglinton Avenue East, Suite 700, Toronto,
Ontario M4P 2Y3, Canada (a division of Pearson Penguin Canada Inc.)
Penguin Books Ltd., 80 Strand, London WC2R 0RL, England
Penguin Ireland, 25 St. Stephen's Green, Dublin 2,
Ireland (a division of Penguin Books Ltd.)
Penguin Group (Australia), 250 Camberwell Road, Camberwell, Victoria 3124,
Australia (a division of Pearson Australia Group Pty. Ltd.)
Penguin Books India Pvt. Ltd., 11 Community Centre, Panchsheel Park,
New Delhi - 110 017, India
Penguin Group (NZ), cnr Airborne and Rosedale Roads, Albany,
Auckland 1310, New Zealand (a division of Pearson New Zealand Ltd.)
Penguin Books (South Africa) (Pty.) Ltd., 24 Sturdee Avenue,
Rosebank, Johannesburg 2196, South Africa

Penguin Books Ltd., Registered Offices:
80 Strand, London WC2R 0RL, England

First published by Onyx, an imprint of New American Library,
a division of Penguin Group (USA) Inc.

First Printing, January 2006
10 9 8 7 6 5 4 3 2 1

Copyright © Michael P. Farmer, 2006
All rights reserved

 REGISTERED TRADEMARK—MARCA REGISTRADA

Printed in the United States of America

Without limiting the rights under copyright reserved above, no part of this
publication may be reproduced, stored in or introduced into a retrieval system, or transmitted, in any form, or by any means (electronic, mechanical,
photocopying, recording, or otherwise), without the prior written permission
of both the copyright owner and the above publisher of this book.

PUBLISHER'S NOTE
This is a work of fiction. Names, characters, places, and incidents either are
the product of the author's imagination or are used fictitiously, and any resemblance to actual persons, living or dead, business establishments, events, or
locales is entirely coincidental.

The publisher does not have any control over and does not assume any
responsibility for author or third-party Web sites or their content.

If you purchased this book without a cover you should be aware that this
book is stolen property. It was reported as "unsold and destroyed" to the
publisher and neither the author nor the publisher has received any payment
for this "stripped book."

The scanning, uploading and distribution of this book via the Internet or via
any other means without the permission of the publisher is illegal and punish-
able by law. Please purchase only authorized electronic editions, and do not
participate in or encourage electronic piracy of copyrighted materials. Your
support of the author's rights is appreciated.

War Dogs is dedicated to my father, Kenneth Farmer.

Dad . . . thanks for the love you so freely gave the boy and for the example you passed on to the man.

A book cannot come close to letting you know how much everything you've done for me in this life means. Nonetheless, this one is yours.

Oh, and despite the substantial body of evidence to the contrary, I *was* listening all of those times, but had to learn a few things on my own . . . the hard way, naturally. My frequent blunders throughout life are no fault of yours, so sleep well.

With love, Michael

ACKNOWLEDGMENTS

I speak from experience (that has cost me many beers) when I say I realize I'll never remember all of the friends who helped make *War Dogs* come to life. But once again, I'll try. At least the Class VI store is tax-free. . . .

To Vicky, my best friend and biggest fan. Vic, without you this book wouldn't be what it is. Thanks for helping me tame my demons and tone down the Farmerisms in the book as necessary. You know I love ya.

To my CENTCOM buddies in Tampa: Mark Stoller, Matt Wloczewski, Julie and Pat Hartman, et al, particularly for their help with the contest. Sorry I had to veto the colorful suggestions.

To Frenchy Fortin for his assistance with the Urban Recon LIDAR piece of the story. This is a real-world tool, folks. It's going to do wonders for combat-mission planning, which leads to more dead bad guys; that's a good thing. Hats off to Scott Forman and his Urban Recon ACTD team at Fort Bragg for a job well done.

To Brent Howard, my editor extraordinaire. Admittedly, when we met and I realized he could be my, uhhhh, younger brother, I had a moment's hesitation. As it turns out, Brent, you're a true professional and it's been a pleasure doing business.

To Jake Elwell, my agent and good friend. As ever, Ice Cream, thanks for the sage counsel. But I'm still cutting your percentage.

To Joe Davidson, aka Mike Stuart—many thanks, brother. If the plasma cannon defense system has any holes, it's all his fault.

To Kris Milner—thanks for the read-throughs, and thanks for the ear when times weren't so hot. You're a sweetheart and Mike is luckier than he'll ever realize.

To the boys of Bad Monkey—Chris, Danny and Brian. Your cover of "Interstate Love Song" truly rocks, as do you guys.

To any of the people I've forgotten—apologies. As ever, beer to follow on receipt of undeniable proof.

Chapter 1

Triangle of Fire

24th Marine Expeditionary Unit (24th MEU)
Sunni Triangle, Northern Babil Province, Iraq

Twenty-four Toyota four-wheel-drive trucks roared to life in the evening twilight. Each had the same insignia—a black scorpion with an overlaying dagger. In each vehicle were six hardened men, all members of the newly formed Iraqi SWAT commandos, or _Al Hillah_. Their clothing was uniform—one-piece khaki assault suits with an Iraqi flag stitched to the shoulder. The only area of wardrobe in which they varied was their headdress: some wore khaki balaclavas, others black. The soldiers preferred to hide their faces, as a veiled countenance tended to instill fear in the hearts of their enemies. Metallic sounds issued from the vehicles as the soldiers performed function checks on a wide variety of weaponry: 7.62mm Russian AK-47s, 5.56mm SIG Sauer assault rifles, ever-reliable pump shotguns—all carrying heavy loads—and 9mm and .45 caliber pistols and grenades. Slowly the weapons were holstered or brought down into combat-ready positions.

A U.S. Marine Corps colonel turned to his Iraqi counterpart. "They ready, Colonel?"

The foreign officer nodded, a thin yet proud smile playing along the edge of his lips. After more than a decade of disgrace following Desert Storm, he had been given the opportunity to do once more what he loved most: the chance to lead troops in combat. Admittedly these weren't ordinary troops, but by Allah, they had turned into soldiers in the past few months.

Following the fall of Iraq to U.S. forces, Iraq's army had fallen into a shambles. When the Saudis and Russians had invaded his country a year ago, it had been the Americans and their allies, the British and Australians, who had ultimately smashed the foreign forces in the sands of western Iraq. Over the past years, however, the Iraqi army, had been slowly rebuilt, one piece at a time. Now, when Iraq faced a significant threat from within its own borders, his commandos were ready. These men had been picked with unique qualities in mind. None had military experience. The average age—unheard of for military shock troops—was forty-one. They were the men who'd raised families and endured under the shadows of Iraq's regimes. Most important, these men had recognized they had an opportunity when the United States liberated their country; that for the first time, they had a chance to be part of something their children, and their children's children, could be proud of.

But there were always those who did not want to see a people rule themselves. These individuals and groups had many names: al-Qaeda, Islamic extremist, and insurgent among them. The only thing the majority of them had in common was that they came from countries other than Iraq. These terrorists hid behind Iraq's people, lied to the world press about their aims, and hindered the democratic process that Iraq yearned to see come to fruition. Many of the terrorists in the town the colonel's forces would be attacking had fled from the most recent allied assault on Fallujah. What the unsuspecting foreigners had no way of knowing was that *this* day, a day of atonement, it would be native Iraqis, backed by U.S. Marines and British Black Watch soldiers, who would put the sword to them. After the commando forces rolled into the town, the Marines and Brits would follow with heavy weapons in support. But the colonel's commandos would be the hammer that crushed this piece of cancerous insurgency threatening Iraq's quest for freedom. Once they finished their work in the town, they'd move to the next viper nest, and so on, until the mission was complete. *En shallah.*

And so they waited, in the hour before nightfall, ready to attack the town to the east. The call to prayer could now be heard from the settlement's single mosque, a siren call to the attackers carried on a warm desert wind. One man, a black balaclava shrouding his features, looked toward the colonel with piercing eyes. The Iraqi officer nodded. The man's hand went to his temple in a rigid salute. Clear on his forearm was the tattoo of the black scorpion and dagger of their unit.

The colonel looked to the Marine ground commander and at last answered his question. "Yes, Colonel, they are ready."

The American nodded in the direction of the tattooed commando. "Who is he, Ibrahim?"

The Iraqi officer smiled. When they were alone, he and the American commander spoke on a first-name basis. "That man, Matthew, is quite special. No . . . more than that, quite *remarkable*. And yet, he is not unlike my other misfits."

"What do you mean?"

"Before the invasion of Kuwait, he studied medicine in America. At Columbia University, in New York. While there he even participated with the university's sports teams. He was a decathlete." The colonel paused. "He saw the souring of relations between the United States and Iraq following Saddam's use of chemical agents on his own people in Halabja in 1988. He had the opportunity to remain in America at that point, yet he chose to come home to serve his people."

"What is this man's name?"

"Sayid," replied the Iraqi officer. "Sayid Bakr. He is the grandson of General Ahmed Bakr, the fourth president of Iraq and the man who appointed Saddam his vice president after the coup that put Bakr in office in 1968." The colonel shook his head. "Talk of allowing the fox into the henhouse. Within a few years, Saddam Hussein for all intents and purposes ran Iraq. By 1979, it was official."

The Marine colonel looked at the Iraqi in the lead Toyota. He would not in a million years have guessed the commando to be a physician trained in one of the top ten medical schools in the United States. The American officer would have used one word to describe the man: warrior. "What made Bakr decide to turn away from medicine to . . . this?"

The Iraqi shook his head. "You have to realize, many Iraqis had high hopes for our country following Desert Storm. We thought the United States and its allies would continue north and remove Saddam from power." A shadow crossed the officer's face. "If only you had. When the embargoes began, things turned bad for the common Iraqi. Saddam and his acolytes lived high, while the rest of the population suffered. It came to the point where trained men such as Sayid, men who could make a difference, were hamstrung—lack of medical supplies and equipment, lack of trained assistants. You understand what I am saying?"

The American nodded.

"Finally, in early 2003, just before the American invasion, Sayid's own father was presented to him on the operating table."

"Jesus."

"Yes." The Iraqi smiled. "And praise *Allah*." The smile disappeared. "It was the old man's heart. He needed a transplant. Normally, a son would never be the primary caregiver for a parent, but Sayid was by far the most qualified to handle the situation. It was his specialty."

"He was a heart surgeon?" asked the American incredulously, looking once more at the fighter leading the commando column.

His Iraqi counterpart nodded. "A very good one.

And a suitable donor was found, killed the same day in an auto accident in the capital. But as the heart was being loaded on a helicopter in Baghdad, a government official intercepted it. Apparently someone high in the Baath Party needed it worse."

"Christ."

The Iraqi nodded sadly. "Yes, and praise Allah once more. Bakr's father, of course, died within hours." The colonel paused, silent a moment, not knowing quite how to put what he was about to say. Finally he shrugged and continued. "Something in Sayid . . . snapped. He disappeared into the desert for over a month. When he reappeared, he was changed. Sayid had always been burly, athletic. He returned gaunt and burned by wind and sun. While his skin has since healed, he has never returned to his prior robust form. Do not misunderstand me, he is still strong, but strong like a thin piece of Damascus steel." The Iraqi looked to the sky and sighed deeply. "But the physical changes were not the worst of it. Sayid had formerly been a man quick to smile, a man with a ready wit. He was outgoing and compassionate. Since his time alone in the sun and sand, he seems somehow . . . hollow. And yet, driven." The Iraqi nodded. "You can see it in his eyes. They burn for an opportunity to make up for what happened to his father, a crime he blames on the former regime and its minions. Once that pig of an ex-president of ours was captured, I thought perhaps the Sayid of old, he of the quick smile, would return, but . . . he has not. Instead he has simply shifted the focus of his retribution onto our ex-leader's Baath Party followers, many of whom are in that township to our east."

The American chose his next words carefully, seeing that his counterpart had some personal feelings for Sayid Bakr. "Colonel al Hadi, are you certain that Bakr can be counted on now, after all he has been through? That he's *stable*?"

The colonel shrugged. "You have seen him train?

What do you think?" The Iraqi smiled a small smile, the smile of someone finding some bit of light in the darkness. "Praise Allah for Sayid's wife and daughter. Yes, he's stable enough, Colonel. Those two women kept him from going over the brink and into madness on his return from the desert. He will be fine. And one day, I hope, he will find peace."

"Family often is all that holds a man together when the rest of the world goes insane," the American officer observed.

"Yes," said the Iraqi simply. He then pointed toward the town. "And Sayid's is there."

The Marine colonel grunted. "No wonder he's champing at the bit to get going."

The Iraqi officer's face turned grim. "Yes. Sayid and his men cover their faces not only because the sight inspires fear in their enemies, but more importantly, to protect their identities. If the insurgents in the town knew that families of my SWAT commandos were present . . . it would not go well for them." The officer didn't elaborate further. There was no need. The world had seen time and again, through grainy videos delivered via Arab television networks, what happened to those the fanatics accused of being traitors to their cause.

"What do you say we get going then, Colonel?"

The Iraqi nodded and cried out in Arabic. *"Roah! Roah!"* Go! Go!

The Marine smiled as the contingent of Iraqi fighters assigned to him screamed in response to their commander and rumbled east in a cloud of dust and roaring engines. The commando captain, Sayid Bakr, stood tall in the rear of the lead Toyota, a Benelli 12-gauge automatic shotgun in his hands and a .45 caliber automatic on each hip.

"Is the support force ready to launch?" asked the Iraqi, turning to his American compatriot.

The Marine nodded as he listened to the radio chatter of his units over the command and control net in the vehicle parked next to him. He pointed to the left. A small series of hills ran east to west. Over their crests, mountains of dust began to rise into the sky, transformed from white-gray to crimson by the sun's last dying rays. From behind the easternmost hill burst a screaming sound, a bansheelike shriek that was familiar to mechanized warfare professionals around the world—an Abrams tank's fifteen-hundred-horse-power turbine whine. The Marine M1A1's 120mm gun tube emerged into view like a javelin announcing its knight and his mount. Behind the long metal tube rose not a steel-visaged warrior atop his steed but an eight-foot-high, seventy-ton monster spitting rooster tails of sand in its wake as it sped at over thirty miles an hour in the direction of the town. The remaining tanks of the supporting company and the unit's various support vehicles followed close behind. Within moments over a dozen Abramses spread across the desert floor in line, headed east.

Hearing the sound of numerous vehicles rapidly approaching from the west and knowing that the engine noises could not bode well, insurgents scattered from the town's outlying buildings, pulling their *shemaghs*— a mixed collection of checkered red and white, along with the ever-popular black—around their faces and adjusting their weapons, for the most part 7.62mm Russian AK-47 Kalashnikov assault rifles and a smattering of RPG-7 rocket-propelled grenade launchers.

At the town's first intersection, an insurgent leader stopped at a checkpoint manned by two men. He bent slightly at the waist as he panted from the exertion of the run from his group's makeshift headquarters. "You . . . ," he began, and then paused, bending over again and sucking in deep lungfuls of oxygen as he attempted to recover. To the west he could hear— louder now—the approach of the vehicles his men had radioed in only moments ago. "You will stop anything coming through this intersection! Do you understand?"

The men—boys really; one a Saud, one an Egyptian, both recent Iraq "immigrants" who'd infiltrated into Iraq via the porous Syrian border—nodded.

"Good! I am bringing more men forward. Until they arrive, you will—"

At that moment all hell broke loose. Earlier in the day allied intelligence had pinpointed the insurgents' headquarters. Now the three men at the checkpoint listened as a whistling sound preceded the impact of a series of 155mm howitzer rounds fired from the west.

"Artillery! Get to cover!"

The day's last rays blinded the men as they looked skyward in the direction of the incoming artillery. Their search of the sky was of no use; they never saw the rounds impact the building housing their headquarters. The senior man at the checkpoint then realized that all three of them had turned their backs to the west as they watched the headquarters burn. "Keep your focus on the road!" he screamed, recalling too late why he had moved to the roadblock to begin with. They saw a cloud of dust materialize from nowhere, saw the silhouettes of trucks full of men and bristling with weapons.

The leader stepped forward and began swinging his rifle to his shoulder. "Stop! This town falls under the jurisdiction of—"

Sayid Bakr's roaring shotgun interrupted the directive in mid-sentence. The blast caught the insurgent leader, the son of a local Baath Party mainstay, square in the chest, lifting him a foot off the ground and throwing him backward, a gaping hole now his torso's major feature. The body ended up splayed atop the three-foot-high stack of sandbags surrounding the guard post, the man's eyes staring skyward as if asking if what they were seeing could really be the reward for his efforts.

The two checkpoint guards, their eyes wide above the folds of their *shemaghs*, had just begun lifting their own weapons as the Toyota closed the final few feet to the checkpoint. Bakr's shotgun roared twice more in rapid succession, long tongues of flame announcing each shot in the deepening twilight. Sayid Bakr did not celebrate, but instead raised his right arm and motioned the first group of vehicles behind him toward the mosque visible across a courtyard five hundred meters to their front.

Three of the Toyotas continued forward in the direction of the mosque as the remaining vehicles followed Bakr's truck toward the smoldering headquarters building. Bakr intended to close off the area surrounding the building before the rats could escape, as they'd done in Fallujah, and to then methodically clear the rooms in each building once American Marines were in place to back his team's play.

The commando captain thought about the vehicles he had diverted from the mission and hoped his commander would understand. He smiled wryly— something he had not done often since his return from the desert—as he thought of the man who had attempted to give his life focus once again. Other than his wife and daughter, Colonel al Hadi had been responsible for keeping him from going over the brink. Bakr was a man who believed in being honest to oneself. He knew how close he had come to falling over the edge of sanity into the black limbo beyond.

He thought the colonel would understand; no, he *knew* al Hadi would understand. Their contacts in the town had passed word to their team that the mosque was the location of the insurgents' ammunition depot. The commandos also knew it to be the fallback position of the insurgent leadership if they were forced to abandon their headquarters. Again Bakr smiled to himself, this time grimly, as he saw the roof collapse through the building's two floors, flaming debris exploding a dozen feet into the street. Yes, he could safely surmise the headquarters was abandoned at this point. But the commandos' local informants had given them a new piece of intelligence this morning. The village cleric, a godly man who disagreed with the methods of the fanatics in his country but who was not in a position to deny those who had descended upon his village, had directed that if hostilities erupted, the town's faithful should gather in the mosque until it was safe to go into the streets once again. Bakr spit in disgust. *Holy men.* Despite the fact that the foreign swine intent on turning Iraq into another Beirut had shown their colors over and over, the Islamic religious leaders still could not envision "believers"—no matter what country they hailed from—using religious sites for anything other than purposes of worship.

Sayid Bakr nodded to himself. Yes, Colonel al Hadi would understand the necessity of securing the mosque before the insurgents could fall back on it. More, he would understand that the families of the commandos in the town, including Bakr's own family, must be safeguarded from the hell storm that was descending on them as rapidly as the night.

As fate would have it, at the moment the warning went out over the insurgents' radios that trouble was arriving from the west, two of their numbers were in the process of downloading the latest delivery of arms and ammunition from their contacts in Syria. The elder of the two, an experienced terrorist with a year of fighting in Afghanistan under his belt before following so many of his brothers to Iraq six months earlier, grabbed the 7.62mm Russian sniper rifle that rested against the side of the mosque. He pointed to a light machine gun and several belts of ammunition as he yelled at his partner, "Grab the weapon and ammunition and follow me!"

The men ran into the building, narrowly avoiding the local mullah as he directed families to gather in the mosque's worship area. The old man's eyes, looking twice their natural size behind his thick glasses, grabbed the man carrying the rifle. "Do not bring these weapons into the house of Allah! You will leave here at—"

The Saudi sniper cuffed the cleric across the mouth hard enough to draw blood. "Get *off* of me, old man. I do not have time for your babble."

The mullah stood dumbfounded, his glasses askew, as he watched the pair run up the stairs and into his church's upper level. He raised his hands and eyes to heaven. "Allah be with us."

The Marine gunnery sergeant commanding the lead Abrams on the outskirts of the town looked through his sight extension at the green thermal image his gunner had described. "What the *fuck* are those guys doing? It looks like they've split off and are heading to the mosque."

Though he couldn't see it, the tank commander felt his gunner's shrug. "Beats me, Gunny. That's why I told you to take a look. You get all the big bucks, so you figure it out."

"Fuck you, devil dog," replied the NCO, but in such a distracted voice that he might as well have been talking to himself. "All right, Riley, listen up. The rest of the company's arrived and are overwatching the main body of the commandos. I'm going to let the company commander know what's going on, but I want *you* to keep an eye on that mosque. Whatever those guys are up to, they may need some help."

"Aye, Gunny," replied the gunner. Putting his face to his sight, Riley began a scan of the area surrounding the mosque.

The elder of the pair in the mosque's tower watched through his rifle's scope as the squad of Iraqi commandos dismounted and began moving toward the church. Without taking his eye from his sight picture, the senior man spoke quietly to his accomplice. "Listen carefully," he said as the younger man finished loading a belt of 7.62mm rounds into his machine gun. "Do not fire until I do. I'm going to wait until most of the team is in the courtyard. My first shot will take out the leader. That is your signal to open fire on the remaining members of the squad. Work your way from the back to the front so as few as possible have an opportunity to escape the kill zone. Do you understand?"

This was the machine gunner's first brush with actual combat. Sweat broke out across his forehead and he had to wipe his suddenly damp palms on his clothing.

The sniper turned and hissed at his partner, "I said do you *understand*?!"

"Ye . . . yes," the gunner replied. He slowly brought his machine gun up and laid the barrel across the tower's balcony, keeping his head low so the approaching enemy soldiers would not see him. He turned and looked into the withering glare of his superior. "I understand. Praise Allah, we will strike a blow at the Americans' lapdogs and rejoice in paradise tonight."

The sniper turned back to his rifle and picked out his target. Just a few more steps. He smiled. "Do not be in such a rush to die, young fool. Paradise can wait a bit." He laughed harshly. "But I promise you this . . . botch this ambush and *I* will send you on your way to paradise."

"Gunny! I've got activity in the mosque tower!" yelled the Marine gunner over the M1A1's intercom.

The tank commander, who'd been observing the area with his night-vision goggles from the turret, dropped into the commander's station. "What have you got, Riley?"

Again the invisible shrug. "I'm not sure. It's gone now . . . but it looked like something was propped on the ledge of the tower."

"Give me a crew report," growled the gunny.

"Driver up," came the metallic voice of Lance Corporal Dunn from his position in the tank's forward compartment.

"Loader up, HEAT loaded."

"Gunner up, machine gun indexed," said Riley, indicating that his selector switch was in position to send 7.62mm coax rounds downrange if he squeezed his triggers.

The tank commander put his face to the sight extension. He could clearly see the warm bodies of the Iraqi squad as they entered the mosque's courtyard. The tank's thermal imaging system picked up the Iraqis' body heat, distinguishing them from the darkness as white figures moving across a green landscape. He looked to the mosque's tower. Nothing. "What's your range to the mosque?"

The range indicator in the lower portion of his sight picture flicked to display fourteen hundred meters as the gunner lazed and replied, "Range one-four-hundred."

"Shit," replied the gunnery sergeant. "Too far for coax. Switch to HEAT."

The gunner flipped one of the many switches above his sight and then returned his face to his scope. "HEAT indexed."

"Now don't you . . ."

"I know, I know," replied the gunner in a weary voice. "Don't shoot the freakin' mosque."

"Right," replied the tank commander. "Just keep your eyes peeled." And with that the NCO pulled himself up and back into his turret's cupola.

In the main room of the mosque, Fatima Bakr held her five-year-old daughter closely. "Do not cry, little dove," she cooed. "We do not know that anything is wrong, now do we? And we are in a safe place, a holy place."

The little girl wiped a hand across her eyes and

sniffed into her mother's shoulder. "Those men frightened me, Mother," she said quietly, looking upward toward the tower above them where the pair had disappeared minutes earlier. "They have guns. And one of them struck the mullah. I did not think anyone was supposed to do that," she said in the innocent voice of a child.

Fatima rocked her daughter. She looked around them to see if anyone was within hearing range. "It will be all right, little dove," she whispered into her daughter's hair. "I received word today that your father will be with us soon." She spoke the words to reassure, but they sounded hollow to her own adult ears. And then a troubled expression crossed Fatima's face as she, too, looked upward.

"On my mark," breathed the sniper. "One, two . . ." The crack of the 7.62mm round exiting the rifle broke the night's silence. Fast on its heels came the chatter of the light machine gun.

Riley jumped back momentarily from his sight, as if the brow pad had burned his forehead. He quickly bent forward to his sight again as he yelled into his boom mike. "Shit! Gunny, the tower! I've got two men, one with a machine gun! Half the Iraqi commando squad is already down."

The tank commander had zeroed his night-vision goggles on the scene as soon as he'd heard the rifle shot. *Fuck, fuck, fuck,* he thought. *I'm going to get in big trouble for this.* But he couldn't keep watching the men he was supposed to be supporting die. "Fire!" he yelled.

"On the way. . . ."

The little girl buried her face in the protective nook between her mother's neck and shoulder as the first bursts of gunfire sounded. "Mother! Please, let us leave here!"

Fatima knew that the streets would be even more dangerous. She gripped her daughter tightly. "No, we are safe here. And your father will be with us soon."

The little girl's cries quieted. She pulled back and looked at her mother. "Please . . . can we go to Father? I want him now, Mother."

"Be patient, little one. . . ."

A loud explosion thundered above them and the entire mosque shook on its foundations. Bits of masonry and dust cascaded on the women and children gathered in the main room.

Hurry, Sayid, prayed Fatima Bakr. *Please hurry, my love.*

Sayid Bakr yelled into his radio again for the squad leader he'd sent to the mosque. "Send me a situation report, damn you!" he barked into the radio. Nothing. And then Bakr heard the distinctive boom of an Abrams 120mm main gun. "No. *No!*" he screamed, already running in the direction of the mosque as the tank's main gun barked again.

"Report, gunner!"

Sergeant Riley peered through the smoke that was slowly dissipating following his second round. As the scene cleared, his eyes widened. *"Oh my God,"* the gunner breathed, almost too low to be heard by the rest of the crew over the intercom. "Oh my *God.*"

Above him in the turret, the gunnery sergeant's PVS-7s were beginning to give him a detailed view. He saw several of the Iraqi commandos pick themselves up from the ground, and the lightly wounded began to give aid to their comrades. That was a good thing, so what the hell was Riley talking about? Adjusting the focus ring of his night-vision goggles, the NCO looked at the mosque again. Following the second HEAT round, the tower and roof of the mosque had collapsed into the ground floor. And the sound of what could only be secondary explosions began to pop. Apparently the local insurgents had quite a cache stashed there and the firefight had ignited it.

A huge fireball blossomed into the night sky above the house of worship. It was then that the NCO remembered the women and children they'd seen running into the mosque minutes earlier. Now he understood what his gunner meant . . . they'd seen no one leave the building yet. "No," he breathed. *"Please, no."*

Sayid Bakr burst through the door of the church into a firestorm. Jumping back, he barely averted a burning timber dropping from the building's ceiling. "Fatima! *Fatima*!"

Seeing a woman and child running toward him, Bakr's heart boomed in his chest. He grabbed the woman, pulling her and the child to him. "Fatima . . ."

When he looked into the woman's face, he saw only the frightened countenance of a stranger. Nor did he recognize the child. The woman shook her head and with a cry tore herself from the wild-eyed madman who had stopped her flight. Dragging the little girl behind her, the woman ran through the mosque's doorway and into the comparative safety of the courtyard beyond.

Bakr made his way through the rubble as he continued his search. He stiffened as he saw bodies lying sprawled in the center of the mosque. He pulled a flashlight from his utility belt to cut through the dust. He immediately recognized the mullah, the old man's large eyes staring sightlessly skyward through the shattered lenses of his glasses. And then Sayid Bakr's eyes drifted past the dead cleric. The commando stiffened, his heart lurching upward and into his throat. "Dear Allah, no. *Noooo!*"

The pickup halted in a cloud of dust at the makeshift allied headquarters on the edge of town. Sayid

Bakr moved efficiently, like an automaton. He grabbed his burdens from the rear of the truck and walked steadily and with purpose into the tent.

The Marine guard recognized the captain, but he also recognized that something out of the ordinary was going on. He stepped in front of the commando. "Captain Bakr, sir, I'm afraid—"

With his free hand Bakr shoved the Marine so hard that the man flew backward and hit the ground on his backside. "Out of my way," he growled.

Entering the tent, the first thing Bakr saw was Colonel al Hadi and his Marine counterpart. In front of them was a Marine captain—Sayid Bakr recognized him as the tank company commander who'd been in support of his team—and a Marine non-commissioned officer. The NCO was speaking.

"Colonel, I know the rules of engagement as well as anyone. But those commandos were being chopped to pieces in that courtyard. If we hadn't engaged, the whole bunch would have been massacred."

It was then that al Hadi saw Bakr approaching. The commando stepped around the Marine tank company commander and the man's NCO until he could see the faces of all four. He then gently laid the bodies of his wife and child on the ground between the men. He turned to the gunnery sergeant. "You did this?"

The NCO turned white. "We . . . we didn't mean to hurt any civilians. We were trying to protect your men."

Bakr turned and faced al Hadi, casting only a momentary sneer in the direction of the Marine colonel. "Colonel, will you continue to fight for these killers of women and children?"

The Iraqi colonel looked sadly from the bodies of Bakr's family to his younger protégé. "Sayid, it was an accident. If anyone is to blame, it was the insurgents who took over the mosque and made it a legitimate military target once they fired on your men."

"What?!" asked Bakr, incredulous. "Please do not tell me that you are going to continue following these, these . . . *swine.* You cannot, Colonel!"

The Marine captain stepped forward, his face reddening. "I sympathize with your loss, Captain, but *you* are the one who deviated from the plan. My men were only trying to aid—" The American captain, Sayid Bakr's knife now pressed to his throat, went silent.

The Marine colonel's voice broke the taut silence. "Step down, Captain Bakr," he said quietly.

Bakr's eyes flicked to the American, and then to his own commander. He sneered in disgust and spat on the ground at al Hadi's feet as he put the knife back into the sheath at his hip. "What happens now, be it on *all* of your heads," he said in a low voice. He looked down once at the bloodied pile of flesh and bones that had once been his world. Sayid Bakr bent and tenderly rubbed a hand along each of their cheeks. When he stood, he wiped the fresh blood from his family on the front of al Hadi's tunic. "You will see to their remains." It wasn't a question. With that the commando turned on his heel and left as quickly as he'd entered.

"Of course I will," said al Hadi sadly as he watched the man who had become as a son to him disappear into the night.

No one spoke for several long moments. Finally it was the Marine colonel who broke the silence. "Colonel? What exactly does Captain Bakr mean by *what happens now*?"

The Iraqi shook his head. "I do not know for certain, my friend. But I am most afraid that Sayid Bakr has replaced the Baathists with a new target for his rage."

"Who?"

Slowly al Hadi turned to his counterpart. "You. Me. America."

"What? That makes no sense. What happened to his family is horrible, but surely he can't hold—"

The Iraqi colonel held up a hand. "There is no need to explain to me, Colonel. I understand that in war, horrible things can occur when nothing but the best of intentions were meant." He paused and a sad look took hold of his countenance. "But I saw his eyes. They have the same look they held when he returned from the desert. And . . ." The colonel paused, considering his words. Slowly he shook his head, muttering to himself in Arabic.

"And?"

Al Hadi looked into the Marine's eyes. "And *this* time, there is no one to bring him back from the edge of the abyss."

It had been a long night for al Hadi. As if the incident with Sayid Bakr had not been enough, it had taken until two hours before dawn to subdue the remaining insurgent opposition in the town. But they were in control now, and al Hadi and his men would ensure the situation remained that way. The colonel had finally left the headquarters tent with directions for his assistant to wake him in an hour. Even a little sleep was better than none.

After years in uniform, the Iraqi officer snapped to immediately at the gentle touch on his shoulder. He sat up, at once aware that something was not quite right. He could tell by the quality of the darkness that it was earlier than he'd asked to be awakened. "What is wrong?" he asked the Marine who stood next to his cot, staring intently at him.

The young NCO was not sure how to respond. "Sir, I . . . I believe you should come with me."

After hastily pulling on his boots, al Hadi walked outside. The Marine had continued walking, but he now stopped twenty meters ahead, next to al Hadi's Hummer.

"What is it, Corporal?" asked the Iraqi officer, and then the young Marine turned on his flashlight. He recognized the gunnery sergeant from the headquarters tent, as well as the captain who had commanded the supporting tank company. Al Hadi could only assume the other three heads lining the hood of the Hummer belonged to the remaining members of the tank crew that had fired on the mosque. "And so it begins," murmured the colonel.

Chapter 2

_____

_____

_____

The Tommy

Somewhere in the Middle East
The Present

The boot connected with the prisoner's upper torso with a meaty thunk, the snapping sound indicating another broken rib. Patrick Dillon held back a scream. Lying naked and curled in a fetal position on the stone floor of his six-foot-by-six-foot cell, the American major struggled to his knees—a difficult task given that his hands were bound behind his back.

After a few moments Dillon swiveled his head tiredly toward a large Arab. Attached to the man's foot was the boot the American was becoming intimately familiar with. "Here's a thought," Dillon hissed through clenched teeth. "Muhammad liked little boys."

The jailer's boot moved in a straight line for Dillon's skull. The major's last coherent thought as he blacked out was that he'd been wrong. The asshole *did* speak English.

Fort Huachuca, Arizona
Two Days Earlier

Patrick Dillon gazed through an old-fashioned brass telescope at the harsh desert terrain to his front. Nothing moved save the heat waves dancing along the desert floor. At high noon in Arizona even the scorpions took refuge. But then in the distance, movement. . . .

"Look at that baby *go*," muttered the NCO standing next to Dillon. Master Sergeant Tom Crockett was the Army's premier master gunner. He knew the weapon systems of the M1A1 Abrams, the M1A2 Abrams, and the Stryker interim armored vehicle better than anyone alive. And now he was the Army's chief technical expert on the United States' latest armored vehicle. Named after General Tommy Franks, the U.S. Central Command commander who'd gained fame in the Middle Eastern desert during Operation Iraqi Freedom, the vehicle was designated the M4X1 Franks Combat System. But the team working the newest and most lethal armored vehicle the world had ever seen had its own name for the weapons system: the Tommy. The eighteen-ton vehicle was a quarter of the weight of a combat-loaded Abrams and yet packed twice the firepower and twice the survivability of its late-twentieth-century cousin.

As the soldiers watched, the Tommy took out the equivalent of a tank company in less than a minute. And the vehicle was being run remotely. If an actual three-man crew had been aboard, the times on target would have been better, much better. But the system was still in the early stages of final testing and the team had chosen to proceed with caution. The weapons systems integrated into the Tommy were so new that developers and testers were hesitant to put a human being in the cutting-edge vehicle without extensive unmanned testing. But it appeared to the men as though that would change after today. She—despite the masculine name, both soldiers standing on the hill thought of the system as a female—had performed magnificently.

Dillon dropped the telescope from his right eye—the left was covered by a leather eye patch thanks to injuries sustained during the Russo-Saudi war a year earlier—as the last target on the range fell, hit by the moving Tommy at a range of over six kilometers. The major telescoped the instrument into its stored configuration and stuffed it into his ever-present "fag bag"—the Army's nickname for an over-the-shoulder canvas satchel—and smiled. "Yeah, Sergeant Crockett, I have to concur. She is indeed one sweet bitch."

A grin split Crockett's face as he turned to look at his commanding officer. It had been infrequent enough that he'd seen Patrick Dillon smile. The major stood a couple of inches under six feet, but his broad shoulders and thick frame brought him in at close to two hundred pounds. The test group had heard the rumors surrounding Dillon: solid officer with an outstanding combat record; headed to high places because of his abilities, not through pedigree, before being "grounded" with a bad eye. Despite the fact that Dillon had been instrumental at the lowest tactical level—he'd personally planted an M1A1's main gun in the Russian ground forces commander's tent flap and offered the general a "surrender or else" ultimatum too good for the Russian to turn down—a military health board decided that a tank battalion S3, or Operations Officer, needed two good eyes.

According to popular gossip, the board's results were released fast on the heels of Dillon's wife deciding that she and the major needed a break in company. Dillon had shown up at Fort Huachuca, Arizona, duffel bags in hand, alone. His wife and four daughters remained in Colorado Springs, the family's last duty station. No one knew the exact nature of the separation, and once the personnel in Dillon's new unit took note of his perpetual, grim countenance, they didn't ask. Still, they observed that he continued wearing his wedding band. Again, the team didn't know for certain, but something had changed for Patrick Dillon in the past few weeks. When Dillon had first arrived, it was clear from snippets of phone conversations overheard by the troops that the major had been actively pursuing reconciliation with his estranged wife. Then the efforts suddenly stopped. At the same time the major's wedding band disappeared from his hand. Dillon's mood turned even darker for a month. But lately the commander seemed better, thought Crockett. Maybe it was that the project was proceeding so well, or maybe he'd come to terms with his demons. Whatever the reason, the NCO was glad to see the change. The guy definitely had a few breaks due him.

The Tommy pulled to a skidding stop two hundred meters forward of a group of dignitaries standing on a viewing platform that had been erected on the desert floor. The congressmen, senators, generals, and defense industry executives beat each other upon their backs. Good shit indeed. That was when all hell broke loose.

Patrick Dillon threw a thick and callused hand into the middle of Crockett's back and shoved the sergeant face-first into the hardscrabble desert floor, his own frame landing next to the NCO a fraction of a second later.

"What the fuck?" was all Crockett managed to say before the explosions rocked them, battering their bodies up and down roughly against the unforgiving terrain.

Looking down at the group of assembled dignitaries, Dillon saw nothing but a smoking pit. The cynical part of him smiled . . . *my God, so many turds gone in a single flush.* Then the professional military man in him assessed the situation: air-to-ground missiles—he'd known that a split second before impact when a flash in the sky alerted him to something out of the ordinary. But *how*? How the fucking *hell* in the middle of a classified U.S. government test area?

Prop wash blew over the two soldiers. Turning his head, Dillon saw a group of men in sand-colored camouflage rushing toward them from a tan Huey helicopter. Several thoughts went through his mind: not U.S. issue uniforms; a helicopter that hadn't been in government service in over two decades; and finally, far more Arab-looking individuals than he liked to see carrying automatic weapons.

Reaching to the old and battered leather holster beneath his left armpit, Dillon smoothly unbuckled the metal closure restraining his 9mm pistol and pulled the weapon free. In the field a soldier *always* carried a weapon. Normally the rifles, pistols, and crew-served weapons did nothing more than collect dust, just more pieces of equipment to clean on return to home station. He silently thanked God for the Tommy's top-secret project classification; it meant the team carried ammunition for their personal weapons.

Dillon extended the Beretta toward the advancing men. He silently cursed as he glanced at the pistol. On his tank he'd have had a .50 caliber machine gun that would have slowed these yahoos down fast, but as it was, he felt like he'd brought the proverbial knife to the proverbial gunfight.

"Do *not* move!" a voice screamed in halting English.

Dillon's first round took the speaker through his front teeth. One of the attacker's compatriots was directly behind him. The backwash of the projectile as it exited the dead man's brainpan splattered the eyes of the trailing Arab, blinding him. Dillon took advantage of the man's momentary helplessness to send him to Allah as well. And Allah *was* the appropriate deity, of that there was no doubt in Patrick Dillon's mind. The American officer had spent enough time in hell's sandbox to know a Middle Eastern accent when he heard one. Shit, he could practically smell the camel musk coming off of these guys.

"Go!" Dillon yelled to Crockett as he rolled to his left behind a large rock.

Tom Crockett had been in the Army too long to question an order given under fire. He rolled in the opposite direction that Dillon had taken, spun . . . and found himself staring into the gaping maw of an AK-

74 assault rifle. Although only 7.62mm in diameter, Crockett thought he'd never seen anything as deep and dark as the bore of the Kalashnikov.

"*Major,*" called an authoritative voice.

Dillon turned to see a swarthy man wearing a captain's insignia on his battle dress tunic. The officer had, bar none, the largest head Dillon had ever seen. Even under the current circumstances Dillon had to resist the urge to stare. He dropped to one knee and took a bead on the cranium of craniums. Used to firing at moving targets over two miles away from the rolling deck of an Abrams tank, he felt a little cheated as the head overwhelmed his Beretta's sight picture. A split second later two 9mm rounds impacted their target and the grand head lost much of its conversation value.

Mrs. Dillon's little boy hadn't always been the smartest kid in class, but he'd usually been one of the more mentally agile. The situation here was clear: if this group wanted him dead, he'd already be dead. Which meant they wanted—needed?—him alive for some unknown reason. Dillon smiled at the tactical flexibility the situation allowed him.

"*Major Dillon,*" called a calmer voice.

Dillon looked to his right. One of the attackers held a machine pistol to Crockett's head. Dillon's arm automatically extended in a ninety-degree angle that covered the new threat—a colonel in whatever military force these men served, according to his rank insignia.

The colonel smiled thinly. "Look around you, Major. You are surrounded."

Dillon took the opportunity to scan the immediate area. There were at least three choppers on the ground and over two dozen infiltrators with automatic weapons—all aimed at him.

Looking into the American's eye, the colonel spoke with confidence. "Yes, Major. You could kill me before I would be able to kill your subordinate. But if you do, my men will shoot you both. You have likely deduced we would prefer to take you alive." The man smiled. "If I were dead, the captain"—the officer motioned with the machine pistol at the steaming head—"might have been able to stop our men from acting hastily. But if both of us are dead . . . you see your dilemma. Now, put down the weapon, Major." The smile broadened.

Patrick Dillon flashed back over the last few months of his life. The Army had abandoned him to this shit duty assignment; an important job, yes, but shit nonetheless for an operator such as himself. Worse, his wife and best friend of over a decade had also abandoned him. Melissa's rationale had been simple: he hadn't been there for her when she'd needed him. *What the fuck was that supposed to mean*? reflected Dillon for the thousandth time. He glanced from the enemy colonel to Crockett, his good eye twinkling momentarily. Crockett knew what was coming. He shook his head imperceptibly. *You are insane,* the master sergeant's eyes screamed. *No, I just no longer give a fuck,* the major replied to Crockett's stare with his own working eye.

Dillon's first round struck the colonel holding Crockett a quarter inch above the right eye. As Crockett dropped to the ground, Dillon rolled and fired off the rest of the Beretta's magazine into the nearest group of invaders.

In his peripheral vision Dillon saw Tom Crockett, his captor down, free his own sidearm from a hip holster. As Dillon's Beretta's slide locked back after releasing its fifteenth—and final—round, a hammering pressure slammed into the back of his skull. One of the attackers had approached unseen from behind and put the butt of his rifle into the uncooperative American. Dillon's head slammed into the desert floor and for a few moments he lay there, stunned and unable to move. Putting his hands beneath his chest, he struggled to push himself from the ground. He felt the boot between his shoulder blades, and then the full weight of the man above pushed him back to the ground. And then an arm was reaching beneath him, a Russian bayonet in the owner's hand. Dillon felt the edge of the blade as it touched the left side of his throat, and his head was yanked backward by a hand placed to his forehead.

"*La!*" called a commanding voice from a few feet away. *No!*

From the way the soldier above him failed to move the bayonet from its place, it was clear that he was not happy with these new instructions.

A jabbering exchange in Arabic followed. The knife lowered ever so slightly, and then the man above him was bodily shoved off of Dillon to sprawl on the ground five feet away. The soldier stood and dusted himself off with one hand; the bayonet was still in the other. He glared angrily at the man behind Dillon who'd sent him sprawling. But his retaliation ended with the glare. Spitting into the dust, he walked away to join several of his fellow soldiers.

A shadow fell over Dillon and a moment later a figure was squatting next to him. "You are Major Patrick Dillon?" The man looked as much an Arab as the rest, but his English was flawless, no accent whatsoever.

"Fuck you."

Dillon's skull screamed from the impact of the fist that slammed into his cheek from above, pounding his head once more into the concretelike desert floor.

"I am well aware of your identify, Major," said the voice, calmly but with an underlying edge. "Understand that I am all that is keeping you alive, and I would personally prefer to see you dead. Do not push me."

For one of the few times in his life, Patrick Dillon decided to keep his mouth shut.

"Look at me, Major."

With an effort Dillon raised his head to look into the man's eyes.

"That is better," he said, a dark smile playing on his lips. "I am Sayid Bakr. I want you to know that on the off chance that you live to return to your Army one day. Now, just so that I am sure we understand one another . . ." Again a fist slammed into the back of Dillon's skull.

Dillon's head bounced twice and hit the ground facing the Tommy. His eyelids flickered as he saw the world's most state-of-the-art armored vehicle shimmering in the fading desert sky. A short distance away sat ten of the Tommy's sisters, the only other prototypes in existence. *Must be dreaming,* thought Dillon as he watched several large aircraft taxi across the desert floor in the direction of the vehicles. His eye flickered weakly as he realized what was happening. *Oh shit,* he thought. *The Tommies. They came for the fucking Tommies.* And darkness fell.

Chapter 3

Storm Clouds

Cielo Vista Ranch
Big Horn Mountain Range, Wyoming

"Get out of the way, Señor Luke! That devil is coming for you!" yelled the rangy foreman as he took a running leap over the corral's split-beam fence.

Luke Dodd, leaning against the fence and trying to catch his breath, turned toward the charging Morgan. Moments ago the horse had thrown Luke into the dust, for the fifth time in two hours, and tried to pound him into pulp with his hooves before bolting for the far side of the enclosed space, bellowing in defiance at his would-be rider.

Dodd was in his early thirties, six-two, and lean. And at the moment, pissed. Raised on his father's ranch near Jackson Hole, he knew horses. Which is why he felt stupid as he watched sixteen-plus hands and twelve hundred pounds of muscle and sinew bear down on him.

Until a few months earlier Luke Dodd had been one of the best field officers in the Central Intelligence Agency. A cover that had gained him access to the Russian president's inner sanctum—albeit as a gay chef—had been blown by a mole in the White House during the war with Russia and Saudi Arabia. Of course, he had returned to Moscow a few weeks later and kidnapped the Russian president, Konstantin Khartukov, and was still in the middle of a somewhat puzzling relationship with Khartukov's daughter, Natasha, so the Moscow time hadn't been a total loss. Dodd had abruptly dropped his quitting papers when his brother, Chris—the same Chris Dodd who ran the CIA—decided that his baby brother's butt had been on the line long enough and tagged him for an instructor position at the Agency's training facility in rural Virginia, commonly referred to as "the Farm." Within twenty-four hours Luke had packed up his old Jeep and headed west, stopping in his hometown of Alpine long enough to see his dad, get some advice on mountain properties to the north, and steal a few of his father's choice hands to work the ranch he intended to buy upstate.

Once he'd found Cielo Vista and settled in, Luke had gone looking for a good working horse. He'd always loved Morgans. The first American breed, the Morgan, while not as large as some of its cousins, was known to be hardworking, powerful, and loyal—and with a friendly disposition. At least Dodd had thought so until he met the one currently trying to kill him. Luke had seen the horse at an auction in Cody and fallen in love. The beast was huge, solid black, and spirited. Enrique, his foreman, had told him to pass almost immediately. "Have you wondered why the owner is selling such a magnificent specimen, Señor Luke? Look in his eyes. No man will ever own that animal." Luke, however, couldn't say no, even after finding out that his new mount's name was Malvado. Enrique had been beside himself on hearing this juicy morsel. "Do you know what malvado means, Señor Luke? It means *cruel*. I'm warning you. . . ." Luke was now at the point of wishing he'd listened to the grisly Mexican-American cowboy who'd had his father's ear for so many years. *No such thing as a mean Morgan*, he'd replied to Enrique. *Bullshit*, he now thought.

As the mountain of pure black horseflesh descended on him, Luke took a deep breath. Seeing the fire blazing in the animal's eyes, he realized *Cruel* was as apt a name as any. Easing onto the balls of his booted feet, Luke Dodd was a picture of relaxation as the ground trembled beneath him. The horse was so close that he could smell the musky scent of barn, grass, dust, and sweat. *Steady*, he thought.

Luke moved so quickly that it took Malvado a moment to realize the target of his wrath was no longer in front of him, but was grabbing the pommel and swinging low onto the hated saddle strapped to his back. The big horse reared. Keeping low, Luke waited until Malvado's front hooves struck the ground before leaning forward and whispering into the animal's ear, "You and I are going to come to an understanding, Mal." The horse reared again, front legs flailing.

Enrique climbed the side of the corral and took a seat on the top rail. Another of the ranch hands, hearing the commotion, joined him. "I see the boss is still in one piece," said the man as he struck a match and lit the cigarette dangling from the corner of his mouth. Reaching up, he tilted his hat back on his head and relaxed to enjoy the show.

Enrique crossed himself. "Only by the grace of God. That animal is evil, *mijo*."

The younger man, Benton, a local cowhand Luke had hired soon after taking over the Cielo Vista, looked to Enrique and frowned. "Enrique, I keep telling you, don't call me that. Just because your grandma used it on you ain't no reason to use the expression on me." He turned his head back toward the battle between man and horse, then added, "And the other boys don't like it neither."

Enrique's sun-weathered features creased into a good-natured grin. His leathery skin gave no indication of age, but all of the hands agreed the man was somewhere between forty and seventy, give or take a few years. "You are all my boys," he said. "My little *mijos*."

"Ain't right, talkin' 'bout grown men in such terms," grumbled Benton beneath his breath.

The two forgot the exchange quickly. For the next half hour they watched, mesmerized, as Luke Dodd and Malvado danced the dance seen less and less frequently over the past century as civilization crept from the east, the dance between man and horse that ultimately one of the battlers would lose.

Luke knew a fine line separated the breaking of a horse and the breaking of his spirit. Despite his newfound reluctant agreement with Enrique—the horse *did* have some issues—Luke still couldn't stand the thought of crushing the fire that burned in the animal's breast. The moment of truth came when Malvado, in desperation, threw himself onto his side in a last-ditch attempt to dislodge his stubborn rider. Holding tight to the pommel and not releasing the reins, Luke jumped free of the saddle just before his leg would have been crushed between the Morgan and the hard corral floor. The horse flew up, but Luke was on the animal's back again before Malvado had completely regained his feet. The effort and its fruitlessness took something out of the horse. He continued for a few more minutes with halfhearted attempts to dislodge the rider. Finally, the horse came to a standstill in the center of the corral, lathered in sweat and breathing through his nostrils in labored snorts.

Luke sat still for a full minute, giving his mount time to adjust to the change in the order of things. Then he reached down and gently patted the horse's neck and whispered, "It's a new day, boy. Now me and you, we'll get along just fine."

Dodd twitched his heels into the horse's flanks and broke him into a walk, then into a trot. After a few minutes he guided Malvado toward their audience. Dismounting, he looped the reins over the top rail. "Enrique, from here out, *you're* in charge of breaking the horses. This one's worn me out."

The foreman grinned. "*Sí*, Señor Luke. A magnificent ride."

Benton—no one knew if this was his first, last, or only name—smiled in agreement. "Not bad, boss. Not bad a'tall. But do you think you worked the mean outta him?"

Luke Dodd pulled off his old, sweat-soaked Stetson and wiped a sleeve across his forehead before nodding. "Yep. I know broke, and he's broke."

Behind Luke, Malvado seemed to catch the gist of the conversation. Something resembling a leer crossed his face as he leaned forward and opened his mouth to take a chunk of Dodd's shoulder between his large teeth. Before the black could make contact with flesh, Dodd wheeled and stepped forward. Malvado looked intently at the finger pushed squarely into his soft nose.

"Do we need to continue the lesson, Mal?" Dodd asked in a menacing undertone. "Is that it? I'm ready if you are."

Malvado stepped back and stood still, watching the man as he considered his options. Slowly he bent his head toward the ground and began nipping at nearby tufts of grass.

"Guess he still needs a little work," observed Dodd wryly.

"Evil," said Enrique. *"Muy malo."*

"He's not evil, 'Rique. Just spirited."

The Cielo Vista's foreman eyed the horse and made the sign of the cross once more. "*Sí*, Señor Luke. Whatever you say."

Luke laid his head back against the side of the hot tub and closed his eyes, letting his aching muscles relax in the water's rejuvenating heat. He opened them again after a few minutes, pulled his head erect long enough to take a pull from the Fat Tire ale in his hand, then laid it back again. He smiled a quiet smile as his eyes shifted from the view of the Bighorn

Range to his home. More of an alpine lodge than a house, the structure was exposed beam throughout. Its two stories and four thousand square feet with six bedrooms and three stone fireplaces at times seemed a little much to Luke, but it was the home he'd dreamed of all those years skulking behind enemy lines. Besides, he was young and there was plenty of time to fill the house with the family it was originally built to shelter.

The smile disappeared. Of course ultimately he'd need a wife. No, he checked himself. He didn't *need* a wife. But he would like someone with whom he could share his new life. Who knew, maybe even children. He'd thought a few months ago that Natasha Khartukov was that woman. Now he laughed at the thought.

Luke didn't blame Natasha for wanting her career. Her position at Russia's United Nations mission in New York City was one she'd earned and then fortified through her efforts to stop a possible global war her own father had begun. They'd enjoyed the time they had together, either her visiting the ranch, which she loved, or he visiting New York when the ranch schedule allowed, which wasn't often. But the relationship hadn't seemed to be progressing. They both knew that the relationship couldn't work the way it was, but both of them were too stubborn to change their career directions. The visits had slowed, as had the calls.

And then the bomb had dropped a month ago. One of Natasha's colleagues, a dashing Russian who was probably an Omar Sharif look-alike, had asked her to marry him. He knew this much from his last call, but no more. Natasha had been an emotional mess and in no condition to talk. So he'd given her time to herself, time to decide what direction she wanted her life to take, vowing to himself that he would wait until she contacted him with a decision. He hadn't heard a word since.

Luke took another sip of Fat Tire and mulled over

the situation. More and more lately he found himself turning into a muller. *Too much time on my hands*, he thought. *Mull, mull, mull.*

Enrique came through the French doors leading from the back of the main house. "Señor Luke, I have been looking everywhere for you. Your brother, he is on the phone." The foreman extended Luke's mobile phone to him. "Why you not keep it with you like your brother tell you?"

Luke frowned. "Because I'm not in the Company anymore, 'Rique. I don't need—or want—an electronic tether."

Enrique flashed a smile. "Señor Chris, he say you can never *really* leave the family business."

"Apparently some truth to that," mumbled Luke, extending his hand and taking the phone. "What the hell do you want, Chris? I know you well enough that you're not calling to give me the latest on how the Orioles are looking this season."

"I was just wondering if you might know what happened to the two cases of Fat Tire that were delivered to Dad's," replied his brother from his Langley office. "He said it was the funniest thing. They were there one day and gone the next."

Luke slid lower in the hot tub, took a pull of his ale, and smiled at Enrique. "No idea. Now what do you *really* want?"

There was a pause from the other end. "I need you on a plane, Luke. Now."

"And why would you need that, Chris?" asked Luke slowly. Chris Dodd might be his brother, but any son of a bitch they'd appoint to run the Central Intelligence Agency didn't merit trusting.

"I've got a job for you."

"I already told you no. I'm not cut out for wiping the noses of new recruits. Find someone else."

A noticeable pause preceded Chris Dodd's reply. "Luke . . . I can't get into this on a non-secure line. The job isn't for Luke Dodd, it's for Archangel."

Chris Dodd's use of his code name got Luke's full attention. Luke sat up and put his beer down on the hot tub's redwood deck. "I'm listening."

"Get to the airport, Luke. I'll have a jet meet you there in an hour. Once you're in the air, call me secure from the plane."

"I'm headed to D.C.?"

"No." Again, Chris Dodd paused. "A little farther east. I need someone capable that I trust to be my eyes and ears for a project."

Luke Dodd knew something big was up. "It's that important, isn't it?"

"Yeah, Luke. It's that important. And then some."

Chapter 4

Night of the Lupus

Office of the Inspector General
United States Central Command
MacDill Air Force Base, Florida

Colonel William Jebediah Jones glanced toward his office door as he exhaled smoke toward the battery-powered contraption his wife had purchased him for his forty-fourth birthday. It was the third cigarette Jones had chain-smoked with the intent of building his blood's nicotine content up to an acceptable level. The colonel mumbled to himself, "No smoking in government buildings, my ass. Bad enough I'm out of the real Army and stuck in this REMF job."

For the previous two years, Jones had commanded a heavy combat brigade in combat. But all good things someday come to an end and he'd had to move on. Jones considered himself many things, but a Rear Echelon Mother Fucker wasn't one of them. He thought about that, then laughed as he thought about his new job and title. "Inspector General, not commander. Maybe I am an REMF," he mused as the cigarettes' nicotine coursed pleasantly through his veins.

As he inhaled the last possible drag from the cigarette butt his door burst open. Jones heard his secretary's voice calling from behind the figure who entered the room and stopped in front of his desk. "Ma'am, you simply can *not* barge into the colonel's office without an appointment." The government civilian turned to Jones in apology. "I'm sorry, sir. She simply wouldn't take no for an answer."

Jones sat back in his chair and exhaled heavily. "It's all right, Mary. The lady and I go way back."

Smiling an apology at Jones, Mary transitioned the smile into a glare directed toward the visitor before leaving the room and shutting the door behind her.

"Is the Dragon Lady always so friendly to your guests, Bill?"

Jones smiled coldly. "Hello, Melissa. Long time no see."

Melissa Dillon, an attractive, auburn-haired woman in her mid-thirties, ignored the greeting. She leaned over Jones's oak desk, her palms flat against the wood. The fire in her eyes burned holes across the two feet of space separating her and the colonel. "Why won't you take my calls, Bill?"

Jones stared stonily at Melissa Dillon and didn't reply.

Melissa Dillon slammed a fist onto the desk. "Why!? He's my husband, dammit!"

"*Was* your husband, Melissa," Jones corrected. "Didn't the divorce that you force-fed on him go through a month ago?"

Some of the fire in the lady's eyes died. "That doesn't mean I don't love him." She shook her hands in the air, searching for the right words. "You don't understand, Bill," she finally said in a quiet voice. "You just don't understand."

"Wives don't abandon their husbands because they feel they have a duty to their country, Melissa." Jones turned to the paperwork cluttering his desk. "Not the kind of wives I call friend at any rate."

The fire was back in a flash. "Why, you cantankerous, judgmental son of a bitch," she began through clenched teeth.

Bill Jones cut her off. "I know Patrick Dillon. He is one of the finest officers—no, fuck that—one of the finest *men* it's been my privilege to call friend." Jones paused for effect. "And you shit all over him, little lady."

Just as it seemed Melissa Dillon would fly across the desk at the senior officer, attacking with teeth and nails, she collapsed into the chair next to her. She buried her face in her hands as the first tears started.

"Shit," muttered Jones. He moved around the desk and placed a comforting arm around the woman's shoulders. Melissa stood and put her head to his chest as the first deep racking sobs escaped her. Jones said nothing and let the pent-up grief run its course.

After a few minutes Melissa pulled back, dabbing at her eyes with the back of her ringless left finger. "Like I said, Bill, I still love him."

"You've got a damned funny way of showing it," said Jones.

Melissa ignored the remark. "I want him back."

"Back as in stateside in one piece, or back as in . . . ?"

Melissa shook her head. "It doesn't matter what I mean unless someone finds him and brings him home. Without that happening, it's a moot point."

Jones stood silent.

"And think of the girls, Bill. They need their father."

"You didn't seem to think they needed him very badly when you sent him off to Arizona alone."

"That's not fair, Bill," she said quietly. "And it's mean. And it's hurtful. *And it doesn't help.*"

The big colonel shook his head in helpless resignation. He knew Melissa Dillon was right, but *God* he couldn't help but twist the knife a little. Then he thought of Patrick Dillon's daughters. They did need their father. "I'll do what I can. But I can't tell you any specifics regarding the abduction. You've been around the block enough to understand that."

Melissa nodded. "I know. But the reason I flew half-way across the country was because you're the one man I trust to tell me the truth to this question: We *are* going after him, aren't we, Bill?"

Jones sat back on the edge of his desk, arms folded across his chest. "Melissa, you have to know the government's making every effort—"

"*Please* . . . ," she whispered in a soft voice. "Please get him back, Bill. Give me a chance to tell him how sorry I am."

Escobar Estate
North of Tucson, Arizona

Dr. Tomas Escobar looked south from his balcony. The distant lights of Tucson shimmered in the distance like a twilight mirage above the desert floor. From his vantage in the north Tucson foothills the city seemed to glow warmly with suffused light. Escobar gazed upward and took in the star-filled sky. The high-desert altitude combined with his distance from the city allowed for a view of the heavens seen by few. He closed his eyes, took a sip of his chilled tequila, and almost smiled as a cool desert wind touched his cheek. Escobar's thoughts turned to the weapons system whose R&D effort he'd poured so much of his life into. He couldn't believe all eleven of the M4s were gone. He had difficulty thinking of the machines—his creations to a large extent—as instruments of death. To him the Tommy project had begun as a challenge to his intellect. His undergrad work at Cal Poly and graduate work at MIT in mechanical engineering had been the start of his fascination with multi-ton vehicles that could speed along nonimproved surfaces at fifty miles an hour while reaching out and neutralizing— Tomas Escobar never used the word "destroy" when describing the results of one of his projects—a target over three miles away.

Escobar's dream of one day heading up a major research and development effort came true when he was offered the position of leading the M4 project based out of Fort Huachuca. It allowed him to return to his native Arizona with his wife, June, and their two sons, Ricardo and Juan, twin nine-year-olds. Not only to return, but to return as the conquering hero, the hometown boy who'd done well.

The doctor turned toward the hollow sound of a lady's shoes on tile. The sight of his wife, backlit as she was by the light glowing from their large Mediterranean dream home, finally *did* break a smile on Escobar's face. The M4s might be gone, but so long as he had his best research partner and the facilities to continue their work, they'd be back in business. The tragic events of yesterday's test would prove to be a stumbling block, not a death dirge.

Dr. June Escobar handed her husband a glass. "Thought you might be ready for another."

Escobar accepted the drink and kissed his wife on the cheek. "My thanks, *mi corazón*."

They turned to the view of the city below them, both momentarily lost in their own thoughts.

"Do you think they'll be able to exploit the Tommies, Tomas?" June asked finally, voicing the fear of both scientists. "To reverse engineer them and use the technology against us?" She shivered, though the night wasn't that cold. "The mere thought of it scares the hell out of me."

Tomas Escobar was silent for a few moments, his glass between his hands as he stared over the miles of rocky foothills toward Tucson. He took a sip of the drink his wife had brought him, his eyes shooting open momentarily when he realized it was a double. He looked to her and winked his thanks—after all these years, June knew what he needed and when better than he did.

"My dear, you know the system's safeguards as well as I do." Escobar laughed. "All right, likely much better, as you were part of the biometric development team." His smile disappeared. "But it is not the safeguards that will save our secrets, or failing to do so, reveal them to our enemies—whoever they are."

"The men," said June softly.

Her husband nodded. "Yes, Patrick Dillon and Tom Crockett. The security of the M4 project depends on how well Dillon and Crockett hold up under whatever pressure their captors mete out." He took another long drink and threw his glass over the balcony in frustration. Several seconds later he heard it shatter on the boulders at the base of their hilltop retreat. "We act as though we are demigods, June. Give us a large enough budget and the time, we can develop anything, can factor for any event, foreseeable or not. But we failed to realize the most fragile part of the M4—the men using them. And now," sighed Escobar, "those men are paying the price for our shortsightedness."

June put a comforting arm around her husband's shoulders, but remained silent.

From above, the faint sound of two black-clad bodies sliding down nylon ropes was lost to the two scientists, the noise covered by the sigh of the light desert wind blowing down the valley. The motion when both bodies slid to a stop, the men dangling over the chasm below the balcony, caught the Escobars' attention. Before the American scientists could do more than open their mouths in surprise, the intruders brought up their silenced 9mm automatic pistols. The big autos each coughed twice in the night. The Escobars fell forward, twin shadows on their foreheads marking the entry points of 9mm hollow-point projectiles. Without a word the two black-clad men, both ex–British Special Air Service members now operating as guns for hire to the highest bidder, swung onto the balcony and went toward the study. They didn't need to search for their target; they'd researched the villa's blueprints only an hour before takeoff. Their insertion helicopter's infrared scan of the villa before they rappelled to the rooftop had shown them that the only other persons resident were the Escobar twins, both tucked into bed for the evening, and the boys' nanny, Maria, currently watching a Mexican soap opera in her room adjacent to the children.

Five minutes after the American scientists died on their balcony, the mercenaries scaled a maintenance ladder mounted discreetly on the villa's east side. Once on the roof, the taller of the two pulled a white infrared chem light from his tactical vest's breast pocket and snapped it, breaking the glass vial inside the plastic tube. As the chemicals mixed the tube remained dark—to the human eye. The helcopter pilot hovering on station a mile away and wearing night-vision goggles, however, had no problem seeing the signal that indicated his passengers were ready for pickup. As the pilot moved in just above the villa's rooftop, the second intruder returned with the ropes they'd used to rappel to the balcony. The men hopped aboard and the helicopter banked north and headed into the night, running lights extinguished.

Two minutes later a series of explosions initiating from the Escobars' study—more specifically, from the areas of the office containing their computers, filing cabinets, and safe—ripped through the villa. What remained of the Escobar home slowly tilted on its foundation, finally sliding into the canyon below.

U.S. Highway 93
100 Miles Northwest of Phoenix

"Oh God," breathed Paul Glass. "*Jee*-zus." Glass pressed an index finger into his ear against the Nokia mobile phone's earpiece to hear over the wind's roar as the convertible tore through the night. His foot involuntarily relaxed off the Nissan 350Z's accelerator, the car slowing to match pace with its owner's spirits.

Glass shook his head in frustration. He'd been enjoying a good weekend in Las Vegas when he received the call alerting him that the project he'd been working on the past two years had suffered a major blow. Now it was one a.m., and he was in the middle of the godforsaken desert trying to get back to the lab to see what he and the rest of the Tommy team could do to pick up the pieces . . . and now the Escobars were dead. That made him the senior project lead.

"All right," the engineer yelled over the wind. "I'm still a few hours out. Continue attempting to contact the team members you haven't been able to get ahold of and tell them I want them on-site at the lab not later than seven o'clock tomorrow morning." Glass listened for a few moments and gritted his teeth in annoyance. "You know what I meant . . . *this* morning." He nodded as the speaker replied, realizing it would do no good to lose it in the middle of nowhere. "Okay. Talk to you soon." Glass hit the END key and ripped the earpiece out. Taking a deep breath, he leaned his head back and took a deep breath of the desert night. For a few moments he felt rejuvenated, despite the day's news. The smell of something— cactus?—always relaxed him. The first year he'd lived in Arizona he'd assumed that the smell so aromatic on the desert night air, particularly after a rain, was colitas. He'd always assumed colitas, a word made legend by the Eagles in the ballad "Hotel California," to be a desert flower. Then he'd found out the band had been referring to the tips of a marijuana branch, which were said to be more sappy and potent than the rest of the plant. Glass smiled. He didn't know if the story was true, but it made as much sense as the rest of the song.

A bright light on the side of the road caught Glass's attention. He slowed as he realized it was a roadside flare. A full-sized van was parked on the side of the road, the vehicle so black it blended with the night. As he got closer Glass saw a woman waving her arms over her head in an attempt to stop him. A Samaritan as trained by his Bible-thumping parents, the new Tommy lead braked to a stop on the road just short of the van.

"Thank God," said the woman, leaning over the 350's passenger door. "I've been out here for hours. I've only seen two cars the whole time and neither of them would stop."

Glass smiled tightly. Something didn't feel right. One didn't see many women driving Sammy Johns specials. She didn't look like a woman living anywhere within five hundred miles of this stretch of desolate highway. She was dressed in neck-to-toe form-fitting black spandex, and she was gorgeous, in a very goth way—dark hair, dark eyes, dark lipstick. He found it more than a little difficult to believe that any man passing this damsel would choose to keep driving. Maybe that, along with the other events of the night, was what made the alarm bells in his head override the other glandular sparks he was feeling. Still, he couldn't just leave her here in the middle of nowhere.

"Can I offer you my mobile? Or a ride to the next town?"

The woman smiled. "A ride would be wonderful. Just let me lock up and grab my purse."

"All righty then," said Glass under his breath as he watched her move to the van's rear doors. *Odd,* he reflected. *Who leaves a purse in the* back of a van? As he watched, the woman reached for the door handle. Glass just had time to note that the handle began turning before the woman touched it as the door swung open and a large figure burst forth.

Somewhere in Glass's subconscious his sense of self-preservation had been working overtime. He'd left the car in first gear. He slammed the accelerator to the floor, catching second in less than three seconds. He was moving southwest at eighty miles per hour and accelerating when the first rip of automatic fire cut through the night sky behind him. He ducked involuntarily. "Holy *shit*!"

Looking into his rearview mirror, Glass saw the van fishtail on the shoulder, finally stabilizing as it gained the highway's asphalt and took off in pursuit. Despite the circumstances, he had to smile. "Good luck with that," he said to the driver of the van. He didn't know who they were, but he did know one thing for certain—they weren't going to catch a 350Z on the open road in that machine. U.S. 93 ran roughly straight along this section—Glass had driven it several times over the past year—so he didn't hesitate to give the Nissan the juice. Glancing down at the speedometer, the engineer watched the needle nose past 100 mph. *Thanks, baby,* he thought. He rubbed the steering column in an attempt to let the Z know how much he appreciated her.

Three miles ahead, one hundred meters off the road, a dark speck rose into the sky. "Roger," spoke the pilot of the Puma helicopter. "Understand, target still on the move." He turned to his copilot. "So much for trying to be subtle," he said. "Arm the Hellfire."

Glass, with time to contemplate, had reinserted his mobile's earpiece and dialed the lab's security detachment. There was no way he could have noted the small red dot now painted on the Nissan's front grille. "It's Dr. Glass. Listen carefully, I don't think the Escobars' deaths were an accident. I—"

A split second later the AGM-114 Hellfire, riding on the beam of laser energy whose journey terminated on the Z's front end, roared home. The warhead's detonation drove the convertible's front end a foot into the asphalt. The rear end, its momentum checked but not stopped, somersaulted over, sending the car into a burning inferno that continued its crazy flipping pattern another fifty yards.

"Cease pursuit," radioed the Puma's pilot to the team in the van. "Target terminated."

Chapter 5

The Russian Who Came In from the Dead

The White House Situation Room
Washington, D.C.

"Tell it to me again," said the president. "And *this* time, concentrate on explaining to me how something like this can occur *on American soil*."

General Tom Werner, Chairman of the Joint Chiefs of Staff, cleared his throat. It was clear the U.S. military's highest ranking officer was at the moment uncomfortable. And when Werner was uncomfortable, he pulled few punches. "Well, *shit*, sir. What else can we tell you? A normal—admittedly ultra-important and ultra-secret training event—was compromised. We don't know how—yet."

"We'll worry about the security compromise at the test site later," said President Jonathan Drake. "For now, can someone tell me how all of those aircraft made it into—and more importantly, out of—the United States?"

"The helicopters and planes flew into the U.S. out of Mexican airspace, Mr. President," said Samantha Wright, the Secretary of the Department of Homeland Security. "They came in low under the radar and didn't have far to go once they crossed the border, only twenty or thirty miles at the most to the Fort Huachuca test site." The former Montana governor grimaced. "And it looks like they flew out the same way."

Jonathan Drake nodded his understanding. "All right, Sam, I can understand that. But surely once we were alerted by the attack we wouldn't lose them."

"Let me take it from there, sir."

Drake turned to Air Force General Nick "Blade" Lombardi. The four-star general, a former F-15E pilot, was the commander of U.S. Northern Command, the unified command based out of Peterson Air Force Base in Colorado Springs. The command was responsible for homeland defense and civil support for North America as far south as Central America, where U.S. Southern Command picked up the ball.

"Talk to me, Nick," said Drake. "What happened?"

The general kept his calm, despite the fact that he was clearly not pleased with what had happened within his area of responsibility. "Mr. President, I have to give you a little background, sir." Lombardi made an elliptical motion along the southwestern United States and Mexico on the large electronic map on the Situation Room's wall. "Sir, twenty minutes before the attack, we had high-speed entries at more than two dozen sites along the U.S.-Mexico border. Per our SOP, we sent our alert aircraft after them from across the region."

"What type of aircraft flew out of Mexico?" asked the president.

"You name it, sir," said Lombardi. "We had fixed-wing Cessnas, helos, hell—even a few World War Two–era fixed-wing fighter aircraft. It was all we could do to try to run them all down. It was a well-planned operation. They clearly knew our procedures and response time. They flew deep into U.S. territory and then turned once more for the border." The general paused and turned to his commander in chief. "And it was all one big red herring, Mr. President."

Drake stared at the screen, imagining the multitude of vectors crossing the United States across four states, and his Air Force attempting to track them all. He closed his eyes and shook his head. "So while we intercepted the border-crossing aircraft, the raid went in and out of Arizona."

Lombardi nodded. "Yes, sir, Mr. President."

"How long did it take to redirect assets after the C-130s carrying the M4X1s?"

"A half hour to forty-five minutes, Mr. President. The scene at the test site was chaotic at best. Most of the personnel were in the viewing stands and were either dead or in no condition to report in. Once we received word of the attack, it was clear what had happened."

"Have you located the aircraft?"

Blade Lombardi swallowed hard. "Yes, Mr. President. We located and intercepted them several hours later over the Pacific. Our fighters forced them to the nearest friendly landing fields."

"So we have the vehicles back?" asked the president, hope in his voice for the first time.

"No, sir," said Lombardi. "The aircraft were empty."

"So where are the M4s?" asked Drake. "They couldn't have just disappeared."

"In searching the C-130s, we found a lot of palletization materials, Mr. President," said the general. "The strapping and assorted hardware that would be necessary to sling-load equipment for air transport—or for said equipment to be air-dropped." Lombardi let that sink in for a few moments. "Sir, we believe that the Tommies were prepped—slung load onto pallets and parachutes installed—and then later dropped into Mexico somewhere before the aircraft went feet wet over the Pacific."

"They're light enough for that?" asked Drake.

Werner nodded. "Yes, sir. It was part of the mission needs statement for the system—to make the vehicle weigh less than thirty tons so that we could get them into hot theaters more quickly."

Silence fell over the room.

"At this point," continued Chairman Tom Werner, "they could be anywhere, Mr. President. Picked up by tractor trailers, moved to a port or an airfield to be loaded on other air transport. We're working with the Mexican government, but that's a big country and we lost a lot of time tracking the border crossings and chasing down the C-130s."

"What about the aircrews? Couldn't we get any information out of them?"

Werner shook his head, frustrated. "They appear to be of Middle Eastern persuasion, Mr. President, but they carried no identification, so we can't confirm that. And we won't be getting any information out of them, because they all killed themselves on landing before our security personnel could board the aircraft."

"My God," murmured Drake.

"Yes, sir. It appears they were keeping those ships in the air as long as they could to give their comrades on the ground with the Tommies as much time as possible to make their escape."

Drake had guided his nation through two wars in less than two years. He knew now that the feeling of contentment he'd felt following Russia's and Saudi Arabia's surrender a year earlier was for naught. "Okay. Let's start here: Who do we believe to be behind the operation?" The president's head swiveled slowly, taking in all present. "Anyone? Tom, you said the pilots appeared to be Middle Eastern, can't we get any closer than that?"

Werner's lips formed a tight line. He looked toward Christopher Dodd, the Director of Intelligence for the Central Intelligence Agency. Dodd in turn threw Werner a *thanks much, my brother* look before facing Drake and folding his hands in front of him. "Nothing concrete, Mr. President. Anything I tell you at this point is pure speculation on my part."

"Chrissss," hissed Jonathan Drake. "That's not the answer I want to hear."

"Sir," said Chris Dodd, holding his hands up in defense. "I didn't say we had no idea. I said we weren't certain. . . ."

Drake took a deep breath. "Your concerns are noted. Now . . . *who*?"

Dodd stared into his boss's eyes, unblinking. "Iran."

Silence fell over the room as the statement sank in. All knew that Iran, or more specifically the Iranian religious leader Ayatollah Mohammed Khalani, had been a major player in Iraq's decision to invade Kuwait two years earlier—a decision that ultimately backfired on the Iran-Iraq alliance, as it ultimately led to Iraq's current democratic state. Dodd, a field operative for most of his career, had been instrumental in obtaining candid photos of the ayatollah and a young dinner guest. The pictures had proven useful in convincing the Persian leader it was best if Iran quietly withdrew from the conflict before becoming a player in the actual fighting. Iraq, at this point on its own, had quickly succumbed as the United States and Kuwaiti forces shifted the mass of their efforts north, safe in the knowledge that the Iranian flank was secure.

"How certain are you?" asked Drake quietly.

Chris Dodd shook his head. "Based on evidence in hand, not very." He paused before continuing. "But . . ."

Drake lifted an eyebrow and steepled his fingers in front of his face, nodding for his chief spy to continue.

Dodd shook his head. How to explain bits and pieces of individually unrelated intelligence combined with field instincts honed over two decades. Tidbits of intel that when put together painted a picture to someone who knew how to make a picture of the puzzle pieces. "It's Iran, sir. I'll stake my job on it."

Before the CIA chief could proceed a State Department representative stood and banged a hand on the table. "Mr. Director, you cannot accuse a sovereign nation of a terrorist act without evidence!"

Jonathan Drake raised a hand to still the retort on Chris Dodd's lips. "Who are you, sir?"

"Harvey Kane, Mr. President. I'm here at the behest of Secretary—"

Drake raised his hand again. "Thank you for your input, Mr. Kane. Now please leave."

"But, Mr. President . . . ," began Kane.

"Harvey," said Jonathan Drake, "I'm sure you're a good man, but I do not *know* you. *That* man"—Drake pointed to Dodd—"has been with me through situations as bad as or worse than the one facing us now. And I will therefore give *him* the opportunity to say whatever he feels I need to hear. He's a known commodity, so to speak. What I will *not* allow is someone unknown to me to harangue him when I'm asking for his opinion."

Harvey Kane rose quickly, grabbing the papers in front of him into a loose bundle. "I didn't mean to offend you, Mr. President," the diplomat said.

Drake smiled and pointed toward the door. "Just leave, Harvey. Nice meeting you."

Once the door closed behind the State Department flunky Drake turned back to Dodd. "Go on, Chris."

"Sir, we know the ayatollah is still fuming over our little blackmail of him. I've got it on good authority that he took the matter rather personally."

Drake nodded.

"And we know he's a man to carry a grudge a long time."

Another nod.

Dodd paused for dramatic effect. "Did you know, Mr. President, that a certain Russian colonel, allegedly executed for war crimes following the Russo-Saudi war, has been seen in Iran?" A picture materialized on the sixty-inch plasma screen behind Dodd's shoulder: blond brush-cut hair, Russian army uniform with insignia identifying the man as a tank corps officer, and strong, clean facial features, except for a nose that clearly had problems.

"No," breathed the president.

Dodd continued, nodding. "Colonel Sergei Sedov,

heavy enforcer for Russia's Middle Eastern army during the last war. Caught on camera executing American service members clearly unarmed and attempting to surrender. Left . . ." Dodd paused, trying to think of the best way to describe Major Patrick Dillon declining to execute the colonel on the battlefield, and instead blasting 9mm slugs into the Russian's elbows and knees. ". . . *incapacitated* by our forces mopping up in Iraq at the end of the war."

"But he's supposed to be *dead*," said Drake, still in denial. "The man's a monster."

"Yes, sir." Chris Dodd nodded. "We only today learned that he's alive and well. Apparently the Iranian religious leader we've been discussing was impressed by the colonel's experience—and his tendency toward excess. The Iranians bribed Russian officials to execute a homeless man roughly Sedov's age, height, and weight. To say the least, the colonel feels somewhat in their debt. Plus he now has a nice Swiss bank account, courtesy of his new friends, that even love of Mother Russia can't compare with."

Drake leaned toward the plasma display. Forgetting decorum, he stared at Sedov's image. "What happened to his nose? I'd heard it was bad, but that is horrible."

Dodd nodded. "Yes, sir. If you'll recall, the First Cavalry commander's Jack Russell terrier used it as a chew toy after Sedov executed the general. One of Sedov's conditions for accepting employment with the ayatollah was that he receive reconstructive surgery on the nose." Dodd turned to the president with a grin. "Iran isn't exactly among the world's leaders in plastic surgery, but the Iranian leadership was afraid to send Sedov abroad for the procedure else he be recognized, his face—the nose in particular—having been the subject of global television news coverage during the war with Russia." Dodd pointed over his shoulder with the laser pointer and clicked it so that a red dot appeared on the Russian's new nose. "This is the result."

There were subdued snickers from around the room.

Drake raised a hand, commanding silence. "All right, Chris. How does this bear on the current situation with our missing personnel and vehicles?"

It was Dodd's chance now to turn to Werner.

"Technology leap, sir," said the general.

Drake shook his head. "Explain."

Werner looked at the president. "Mr. President, since the mid-1980s we've enjoyed owning the best series of tank in the world . . . fuck free world or Iron Block . . . the *entire* world."

"The Abrams," said the president.

"Yes, sir," replied Werner. "The Abrams tank." The general paused. "Mr. President, I'm telling you nothing new when I say the Abrams is getting a little long in the tooth. She's a sweet piece of kit, as my Limey friends would say, but she's old. That's why we've spent so much time and effort on the M4-series Franks Combat System. Instead of making slight improvements to the Abrams series, we wanted to leap into the future." The old warhorse paused. "And we did."

"And . . . ," led Drake.

"And now someone"—Werner looked to Dodd, who nodded silently—"likely the Iranians, have all of the M4 prototypes."

"Can they use them?"

Werner shrugged. "If you'd asked me six months ago, sir, I'd have said they couldn't do a nation like Iran much good. The Tommy's a great system, but eleven vehicles alone? They're not going to do you a great deal of good at the strategic level, to say the least." The general shook his head in semi-resignation. "But it's not six months ago, Mr. President. It's real-time. And they now have someone capable of helping them figure out how to do a great deal more with the Tommies than start their engines, someone knowledgeable in the art of tank design and testing, someone who can help them reverse engineer the Tommies. It's a whole new ball game, sir, and we're behind."

"Sedov is their armor expert." It was a statement, not a question.

Dodd nodded. "Yes, sir. He was one of the team leads in building the next generation of Russian tanks. Not close to the Tommy in capability, but—"

Drake finished the sentence. "But familiar enough with the process to fill in the blank spots." The president paused, mentally running through the ramifications of what his military adviser had said. "So, they have the Tommies. And if they are able, with Sedov's help, to reverse engineer the system, they can build more."

Werner nodded. "Exactly, sir, a lot more. Or, they can sell the specs to some other nation-state. And the odds of the buyer being a great fan of Uncle Sam are slim to none. So," Werner concluded, "if we don't find these systems and recover or destroy them, then the next ground conflict we're involved in could find us facing technology as good as our own."

"Maybe better."

All heads turned to Mark Sterling, Director of the Federal Bureau of Investigation. Sterling, a former Chi-Town police officer, had worked his way through night classes at Loyola University of Chicago's School of Law three decades earlier. Sterling's federal career began in the lower echelons of the Attorney General's office in Washington. His final posting before being tapped by Drake's predecessor as chief of the FBI was as United States Attorney in Denver. But at the moment Director Sterling had the look of the Chicago beat cop he'd once been, a cop who'd seen too much during his shift and wanted nothing more than to head to Marie's Riptide Lounge for a beer with the boys and then home to the wife, but who instead had to take a twenty-pound bag of the day's shit and drop it onto the brass's desk. And it was a leaky bag.

"Explain, Mark," said Jonathan Drake. "How could they build a system better than an M4 clone?"

Sterling rubbed the bridge of his nose between three fingers, then carefully placed his hands on the conference table. He turned slowly to face his boss. "Sir, I've received several messages in the past hour. All involved very suspicious 'accidents.' And these accidents all resulted in the deaths of research personnel at the top of the M4 project team." He paused. "People we would have a very hard time replacing."

"How many of the team's personnel?" asked Drake.

"Twenty thus far, all major players."

"My God," muttered Jonathan Drake. "It just keeps coming."

Sterling nodded. "Yes, sir. And whoever's behind it didn't stop there. They also hit the lead contractor's smart guys." A pained expression crossed the FBI chief's face, but he continued doggedly on, determined to finish his report. "And the research facilities at Huachuca were targeted; firebombs. The test data, schematics, engineering diagrams . . . gone."

Jonathan Drake turned to his military adviser. "Tom, can we recover from this? More precisely, can we recover from this before Iran or some other nation can begin fielding an army's worth of Tommies to throw at our forces deployed around the world?"

General Tom Werner stared at his big hands resting on the table in front of him. These questions and more had run through his mind as Sterling briefed. "In answer to your first question, yes, sir, we can recover. But in time, assuming we don't find the M4s and reclaim or destroy them?" The big Army officer shook his head. "Doubtful, Mr. President. Destroying the Huachuca facilities hurts us, but it's not a deathblow. Data storage is too cheap these days. It'll take a while, but we can recover ninety-plus percent of the information. But the scientists? Irreplaceable. We've got some smart sons of bitches spread across the country, but none who've been working on the M4 project. We can't recover the lessons learned by the team that developed the system, the dead trails they went down, why they decided on this particular subsystem versus an alternative subsystem that on paper looked better." Werner looked up. "With that said, we'll get back on the project today. We'll scour the universities and industry for team replacements, expedite their clearance processing. We'll pull government and military personnel from other projects if we think they can help. What we won't do is *quit*."

The commander in chief of the United States nodded in resignation. "Okay, Tom. If you run into any problems, let me know and I'll make them go away with a wave of the presidential wand."

Dodd stared at the ceiling, lost in thought. He dropped his gaze to Werner. "General, I'm assuming safeguards were built into the Tommies?"

Werner nodded. "Both biometric and code-protected. First, the Tommy requires retina recognition before the engine system can be enabled; same for the weapons system. Each of the three crew members' retinal signatures is contained in their Tommy's database."

Dodd had seen enough high-tech espionage films to understand the concept Werner was explaining. They used similar technology themselves at Langley. "And they're password protected?"

"Roger that. The vehicle commander has thirty seconds from engine ignition to input a ten-digit code into his onboard computer."

"And if he doesn't?" inquired the president.

"Total system meltdown, Mr. President," said the general. "Not in the physical sense, but electronically."

The president thought about what he'd just been told. Double fail-safes. "So, whose retinal signatures are input into the Tommies as of now? Whoever they are, I'm also going to assume that they know the codes? And that we've got them locked down someplace nice and safe?"

Werner looked like he'd eaten a bad burrito.

Jonathan Drake rolled his eyes. "Say it ain't so, Tom."

Tom Werner nodded resignedly. "Major Patrick Dillon and Master Sergeant Tom Crockett are the operators whose data is input into the prototypes' databases."

Drake sat silently for a long minute and then looked up. He turned to Chris Dodd. "I want those men and vehicles located, Chris. Soonest. I don't care what favors you call in, what cages you rattle, what feathers you ruffle, or who you offend. Am I clear?"

The Director of Central Intelligence nodded his understanding. "Yes, sir, Mr. President. Give me twenty-four hours."

The president nodded, knowing Chris Dodd would likely come through with the information in half that time.

Office of the Chairman of the Joint Chiefs of Staff
The Pentagon
Arlington, Virginia
One Hour Later

Tom Werner shook his leonine head as he spoke into the phone. "Dammit, Bill, you know I'd do anything for you. But this is an unusual request. And to be honest, if it weren't you asking, I'd have already hung up the phone."

Colonel Bill Jones hadn't been home in thirty-six hours. He was tired—mentally, emotionally, and spiritually. "Sir, I know I'm asking a lot. And I know the Bragg boys like to keep things in-house. I respect that. But, sir, this man will not detract from the mission. That I promise you."

Werner took a deep breath. He'd known Jones since

Wild Bill's days as a company commander in Werner's beloved 1st Cavalry Division at Fort Hood, and he respected the man. Hell, he even *liked* the son of a bitch—and Werner didn't like many people. He knew Jones was too close to this one. Way too close to make a rational call as to what was the best course of action. "Bill, I know you'd feel better sending a known quantity in should we locate our people and the Tommies. But—"

"Sir . . ." Jones was at a loss for words. He'd just interrupted the highest-ranking officer in the United States military and had no idea what he was going to say. How to explain to a four-star general that the man you're trying to send in with the big boys if a rescue effort takes place is the closest thing to a super soldier you've ever encountered. How the soldier in question, who would have excelled at Special Operations if he'd ever had any desire to leave the scouts, did not know the meaning of the word "failure." Jones shook his head. Hell, he wouldn't have listened to himself either. But he'd give it one last try. "Sir, I realize what I'm asking makes no sense, but please, trust me on this one. Neither you nor the Berets will regret it."

Nine hundred miles north of Tampa, Werner tapped his desk methodically, thinking. Why he was thinking what he was thinking he couldn't have explained. The bottom line was that Jones might be too close on the Dillon issue, but he was also one of the savviest soldiers the four-star knew. He trusted the man's instincts. The tapping stopped.

Jones, who'd been listening to the long-distance staccato, held his breath.

"I'm not making any promises, Bill. But I'll call Charlie to pave the way. It's his call."

Jones rolled his eyes in relief. "Understood, sir. But I'm going to get the ball rolling now."

"All right. Let me get back to you." Without further ado, Tom Werner flicked the telephone's flash hook and speed-dialed a number. The call was picked up after the second ring.

"Dodd."

Werner sat back in his leather chair. "Chris, Tom here. I need a favor. I know you've gotten things in motion, but assuming the call I'm about to place to Bragg goes well, you might have an extra player. How about letting me work this one?"

Two hours later, Jones was blowing a thick, hazy cloud of smoke into the whirring fan on his desk. He was nodding as he listened to the voice on the other end of the phone.

"What have I been telling you, Charlie? They won't be in the way. And I'll consider us even for the time I bailed you out of that Seoul cathouse one step in front of the MPs." Jones smiled. "Yeah, I thought you'd like that."

Charlie's voice turned serious. "All right, Bill. Despite my better judgment, I'm going to okay it. On two conditions."

Jones frowned at the handset before answering. "It's not like I'm in a position to bargain, is it, Charlie? Name them."

"Your guy and the spook stop by my place before moving into the target location. If they go in, I want to ensure they've got the right gear."

Jones smiled. This was good. No matter what type of kit the Agency Black Bag boys had put together for Luke Dodd and his own man, it wouldn't compare with what they'd get at Bragg. The Special Operations community issued their personnel only the best and latest in order for them to successfully carry out God's work. "Done. What's the other condition?"

"Bill, you and I have known each other a long time, but this one is nonnegotiable. If my team leader on the ground feels that the addition of these men will in any way jeopardize the op, they're out."

"I understand."

Jones could hear the smile in Charlie's voice. "All right then, we have a deal. And I don't want to ever hear about Mama Kwan's again, clear?"

Bill Jones laughed as he stubbed out the smoldering butt. "Who the hell is Mama Kwan?"

The two warhorses spoke for a few more minutes and signed off. Jones turned toward his open office door. "Mary!" he bellowed. "Could you get me Melissa Dillon's home number, please?"

"I put all of your contact information into your computer last week, Colonel," Mary called.

Bill Jones wasn't certain, but he thought he detected a challenging note in his assistant's voice.

"After you were here on Saturday and called me at home complaining you couldn't find the pizza delivery number?" she reminded him. There was an ever-so-slight pause before she continued. "Do you need help, sir?"

A man familiar with the latest innovations in any type of military hardware, Jones ironically continued to view computers with a jaundiced eye. They were like the bright soldiers who'd come through his door over the years: capable of accomplishing all sorts of missions if you knew which buttons to push. With men and women, Jones knew the buttons instinctively. His success rate with office automation, on the other hand, left something to be desired.

"No need," he called back, in a more subdued voice. "I got it.

"Let's see," he muttered, picking up his reading glasses and perching them on the tip of his nose. After a couple of mouse clicks he had the e-mail program open. Jones smiled. Two clicks later and the smile turned into a frown as he read the box in the center of his display. *Are you sure you want to permanently delete the selected item(s)?* Jones carefully moved the mouse over the block containing the word "No"— thinking in this case *Shit No* would be more appropriate, as he had no idea what the selected items under discussion were—and breathed a sigh of relief as the message disappeared, for all appearances taking none of the machine's data with it.

Jones stared at the screen for a few seconds, finally looking up and over the edge of his glasses as he heard the sound of footsteps entering the office. Mary moved behind him, deftly maneuvered the mouse a few times. Melissa Dillon's address, phone number, and e-mail address appeared on his screen. "Would you like me to place the call for you, sir?"

The burly colonel didn't meet her eyes, instead shaking his head and smiling tightly. "No, thank you, Mary. I've got it."

Mary returned the smile and left without another word, but Jones could tell she was enjoying herself. "Ingrate," he muttered as he picked up the phone and dialed the Colorado Springs number.

Chapter 6

_____

_____

_____

Midnight Express

Institute for Plant and Seed Modification Research
Third Subterranean Level
Karaj, Iran

Patrick Dillon took stock of his situation. It was a slight improvement over the accommodations he'd been occupying until two hours earlier, but not much. Whereas his previous lodging was dank, this was dry—fortunately for him, as his benefactors still hadn't deemed him worthy of clothing. Whereas his cell had contained no furniture or accoutrements of any type other than the eyebolt his chains had been secured to in the center of the floor, this room had an ancient chipped Formica-topped table with two rickety wooden chairs facing one another across the tabletop. He sat in one, his hands tied behind him. The cell had been dark; here a single high-wattage bulb dangled nakedly from the ceiling. The American had watched enough episodes of *NYPD Blue* to know an interrogation room when he saw one.

They'd softened him up with boots and fists to the point that he could barely move. His good eye was swollen so badly that he had only a sliver of vision. For some reason his masseur hadn't touched the bad eye. Dillon chuckled ruefully to himself as he stared at his miserable image in the mirrored wall facing him. The useless orb must not have appealed to the man's professional need to inflict pain and suffering. To add insult to injury, somewhere along the line his captors had taken his eyepatch. Dillon didn't wear the patch out of vanity—he could give a shit what he looked like. But while the eye couldn't focus on images, it still functioned well enough that it could sense light and shadow. When Dillon tried to use it in conjunction with his good eye, he tended to feel a bit pukey. He laughed again to himself. He had a feeling that nausea was going to be the least of his problems. *Luck of the Irish*, he thought bitterly. First the English occupation, then the potato famine, later the IRA lads. And now this. *Jesus.*

Iran's Supreme Leader, the Ayatollah Mohammed Khalani, shook his head in outraged disbelief as he watched Patrick Dillon through the one-way glass. "The infidel laughs? Clearly he is not broken, Colonel." The old man snarled. "A few more days with my more dedicated keepers will humble him."

Sergei Sedov raised a sardonic eyebrow. The odds were that he himself was the only true infidel in the building, being as he worshipped no god other than power, but the humor would be lost on this old goat. "You're joking."

The Iranian military guard standing at attention next to the bearded cleric, one of the elite cadre of zealots whose sole responsibility in life was to protect the Iranian leader, moved with speed. The hand that had been about to deliver a vicious cuff to the Russian was brought to a halt in mid-flight, only inches from the colonel's face.

The Russian officer had not moved his eyes from Khalani during the altercation. Now he did. He looked up into the straining face of the guard. "And what is this about?"

A drop of sweat rolled off of the man's nose as he strained against the Russian's grip. "You will address the Supreme Leader with the respect due him, if you address him at all, *dog.*"

A look of mock hurt crossed Sedov's face as he looked to the holy man. His hold on the guard's wrist tightened as he spoke, causing the soldier to grunt with pain. "I am sorry, Holiness. Please forgive this . . ." He paused to glance at the trembling guard. "What was it you called me?"

The Iranian soldier challenged Sedov with his eyes, refusing to speak. Sedov increased the pressure on the man's wrist, biting into a nerve bundle residing just below the skin's surface. He'd used it many times and knew the pain the man was going through to be excruciating. *"Dog,"* the soldier finally hissed through clenched teeth.

The Russian smiled and looked once more at the cleric seated opposite him. "Yes, that was it. Dog. Please forgive this *dog*, Your Holiness. I meant no offense, I assure you."

The ayatollah's head and eyes swiveled toward the Russian. It was a reptilian movement, reminding Sedov of a monitor lizard lazily eyeing his next meal. "Release him."

Sergei Sedov released the guard's wrist, at the same time giving the man a shove that sent him staggering backward. The soldier reached for his sidearm, but a subtle gesture from Khalani stopped him. "Leave us, Sergeant."

The guard was aghast as he looked from the old man to the Russian and back again. "Please, Father, allow me the honor of cutting out this foreign pig's heart."

Sergei Sedov grinned. "Oh dear. How *ghastly* a thought. But I thought I was a dog, not a pig." He smiled. "I like dogs. But a pig? Now I feel I'm being insulted." The Russian made as if to stand and the guard jumped back. One of the cleric's elite, he had now lost face twice in front of his leader. Knowing that the man would likely not see the new day's sunrise, Sedov barked a harsh laugh. "Go play with someone you can handle, idiot. Like a little girl."

Sputtering in his native tongue, the crimson-faced soldier drew his pistol from his belt and pointed it at Sedov's head from a distance of five feet. The man's arm shook, but not enough to make him miss.

Khalani stared at Colonel Sergei Sedov. Sedov, ignoring the pistol aimed at his head, returned the stare with a smile. Finally the Iranian leader glanced toward the guard, gave an almost imperceptible shake of his head, and gestured with a sweep of his fingers toward the door.

The soldier slowly lowered the pistol and returned it to its holster. Without further words he left the room, shutting the door quietly behind him.

Once they were alone, Khalani spoke quietly. The voice had the quality of fine-grained sandpaper rubbed over a sheet of papyrus. "Colonel, do not think yourself in a position of invulnerability. You lived at my whim." The cleric paused for a moment. "You can also die by my whim."

Sergei Sedov thought momentarily of pointing out to the old man facing him that he really could *not* in fact kill him. Not if he wanted the secrets of the American M4s unlocked. Then again, the Russian mused to himself, the peoples of the Middle East had proven time and again that sheer logic wasn't their strong suit. But Sedov was, if anything, a survivor. He nodded formally toward the ayatollah. "I am sorry, Holiness. I was merely trying to point out that the major"—he moved his head toward the one-way glass behind which Patrick Dillon sat stonily—"has enjoyed an admirable amount of attention from your hench . . . mmmm, *guards*. Much more and he will likely prove useless to me."

The cleric turned his obsidian gaze toward the American. "Then why does he smile?"

Sedov withdrew a pack of French cigarettes from the front pocket of his rankless tunic. He pulled one from the pack and began to put it in his mouth. Thinking better of it, he looked toward Khalani with an eyebrow raised in question. The cleric gave a brief nod and Sedov continued lighting the cigarette, taking in a deep pull. He exhaled slowly and then spoke to the Iranian through the smoke cloud separating them. "Why does he smile after everything he's been through?" The Russian shrugged. "Americans. I don't understand them. And unfortunately, most of the ones I meet, I kill before having ample opportunity to get to know them." The Russian laughed at his joke. The ayatollah remained stone-faced.

"Do not worry, Holiness," Sedov continued, wondering if he were confusing the term used to address a high-level Catholic priest with whatever term should be used toward the Iranian Holy of Holies without risk of getting a stinging blow across his cheek. He shrugged; who knew? "The American will be pliable."

"See that he is. Either he or the other American must talk. Without the codes, the stolen military hardware is useless to us."

Sergei Sedov smiled darkly. "Oh, Major Dillon will talk," the Russian said, rising from his chair. He moved stiffly toward the window, every step a painful reminder of the 9mm slugs the American in the next room had fired into his knees as he lay helpless in the middle of the Iraq desert. "Yes, Major Dillon will talk. Eventually. First he and I are going to have a little fun, though. A sort of homecoming if you will."

"And when does your time with the good major begin, Colonel Sedov?"

The Russian blew three perfect smoke rings toward the ceiling and smiled. "Oh, Holiness," he said, dropping the cigarette to the floor and crushing it beneath a boot. "Our time begins *now*."

Chapter 7

Angel and the Big Bad Wolf

CIA Bombardier Learjet 60
Somewhere Over Western Tennessee

Rolf Krieger felt as though an ax had split his skull. As he roused from sleep, he kept his eyes squeezed shut, afraid the pain inherent in opening them to the world of light would make matters worse than they were.

A soothing voice spoke near his ear. "I know you're awake, big guy. I've got something that'll make you feel better." The voice had a chuckle in it now. "That is, if you should choose to return to the land of the living. You've had yourself quite a time over the past twenty-four hours."

Krieger frowned, eyes remaining closed. Who was this? And where *the hell* was he?

"C'mon, Arnold, wake up," the voice coaxed.

Lieutenant Rolf Krieger's eyes snapped open to find the speaker so close that he could throttle him. The veteran soldier's uncanny resemblance to the famous actor was not something the ex–scout platoon sergeant liked to be teased about. While Krieger respected the governor, he had put himself through college as an Army enlisted man, gained respect as one of the best scouts in the history of his service, had received a battlefield commission in the recent war with Russia and Saudi Arabia, and held a Ph.D. in international relations. A garbled scream escaped his throat as light shot through his pupils and straight into his brain like a freight train from hell.

"Ouch," said the voice. "That looked painful." Rolf Krieger thought he heard real sympathy in the speaker, but couldn't be sure. "All right, close your eyes and drink this. *Slowly*."

Rolf Krieger wasn't used to following orders other than from those above him in his chain of command. On reflection, though, he thought it might not be a bad idea at the moment; the worst that could happen was that whatever the concoction was would kill him, and that didn't seem so bad compared to his current pain. Krieger leaned his head forward and felt a chilled glass touch his lips. He sipped at first and then began gulping greedily as the cold liquid spread energy through his depleted system.

"Easy, tiger."

Krieger leaned back against his seat's headrest, eyes closed. "Thank you," he muttered, a slight smile playing across his lips. "What was that? I feel better already."

The voice chuckled. "Forget Mama's home remedies. When it comes to hangovers, stick with the Company's recipe."

"The Company?"

The laugh was back in the speaker's voice. "Yep. You just received a megadose of B and C vitamins, along with a nice little sleep agent. When you go out again I'm going to hang a couple of electrolyte solutions to replenish your fluids. The sports drink companies wish they had patents on these babies. By the time you wake up in a couple of hours you'll feel a hundred percent better."

Luke Dodd reached into the jet's medical kit and withdrew a plastic, liquid-filled bag, a clear tube, and a needle. He smiled without looking at his guest as the man's first snores sounded.

Krieger's eyes snapped open as he felt a light tap on his shoulder. He recalled with perfect clarity the conversation with the unidentified male but was, if anything, more confused as to his current situation.

"Hey there," said the stranger, a smile on the corner of his mouth as he sat back, hooking a worn cowboy boot over his knee. "We need to talk before landing."

Krieger turned in his seat and looked toward the speaker. Same voice, but this was the first time he'd seen the man. Slightly over six feet; short, spiky hair that ran dark brown except for a few blond streaks, the result of a lot of time in the sun; rangy; jeans and boots along with a T-shirt sporting the University of Wyoming rugby team's logo. "Who are you?" the officer asked, frowning. He looked around him. "And why am I in an aircraft with you?"

The man leaned forward from the seat facing Krieger, hand extended. "Luke Dodd. Pleased to meet you—again—Lieutenant."

The large German American frowned, thinking. He took the extended hand reluctantly, at a complete loss as to where he'd met the stranger. "Exactly who do you work for, Mr. Dodd? And why am I here?"

Dodd grinned and sat back again. "I'm an operations officer for the Central Intelligence Agency. Normally I'd put you through all sorts of physical pain before admitting that, but you'd know soon enough at any rate as we will be working together."

The brashness of the man's statement forced Krieger to make a quick assessment of Dodd's ability to back up that statement.

Luke waited, understanding as only another alpha male could what was running through Krieger's mind. He smiled benignly as he gave Krieger his moment of contemplation. Coming from most men, Krieger would dismiss the words as brash and foolhardy. But with this man . . . Krieger looked into Dodd's eyes. Perhaps not. Luke Dodd struck him as a man who did not boast idly. He nodded at Dodd to continue.

"At the moment we're thirty minutes out of Fort

Bragg, where we have an appointment with someone who lives in one of those infamous back corners of the post."

Krieger nodded, accepting the reality of the man's words. "The purpose?"

Dodd frowned. "Do you remember anything of our meeting in Colorado Springs last night?"

The lieutenant frowned. "No, I do not. Perhaps you could refresh my memory, Mr. Dodd."

Luke Dodd hopped from the purloined military sedan he'd grabbed at the airfield and proceeded up the sidewalk to the address he'd been given. Nice older home on the west side of Colorado Springs. Luke guessed the Victorian bungalow to have been built in the early 1920s. Shake roof and a nice slate sidewalk leading up to the yellow structure. Not exactly where he'd have pictured a man of Rolf Krieger's reputation, especially considering the gingerbread trim and immaculately maintained flower beds surrounding the porch. Dodd arrived at the door and rapped three times. No answer. He switched from a light rap to a full-throttle bang. A thud sounded dimly from the other side of the closed door.

"What?!" bellowed a voice from inside the house. It had the pitch and timbre of a wounded bull elephant.

Luke took a half step back. Without thinking he reached for the SIG Sauer P226 9mm auto he'd taken to carrying for the past couple of months. His hand had just touched the large butt resting in a tactical shoulder holster beneath his denim jacket, but instead of drawing the weapon, he took a deep breath. Moving his hand back to his side, he called in a loud voice through the door's stained-glass window. "Lieutenant Krieger?" No reply. Luke raised his voice louder. "My name is Dodd, Lieutenant. We need to talk."

Luke Dodd heard footsteps thud on hardwood from the other side of the door. He braced himself as the door abruptly opened. A blond giant stood in front of him in paisley boxer shorts and an open bathrobe. Well over six feet tall and weighing in at over two hundred fifty pounds, the man was huge. Yet there wasn't an ounce of fat to be seen. Dodd now understood the nickname he'd heard hung on Krieger. And Rolf Krieger, first lieutenant, United States Army, didn't look happy. Worse, he reeked of bourbon.

"What do you want?" the big man asked, a vague slur to his words. Then a knowing smile crossed his angular face. "You're the one, aren't you?"

Dodd frowned and shook his head. "Lieutenant, I have no idea what you're talking about and I don't have a great deal of time. If you'll hear me out—"

Krieger smiled and nodded, interrupting. "Of course you do not know what I'm talking about." He stood back from the door and motioned with an arm toward the living room behind him. "Please, come in and sit down. I will explain everything to you."

Luke, a bit confused by the change in his host's temperament, walked across the threshold and past the officer. He sensed rather than heard Krieger as the large man reached for him. Dropping to a crouch and spinning on the heel of his left boot, the CIA officer extended his right leg and swept it beneath the back of the approaching giant's near ankle. Krieger flew backward, bouncing a couple of inches off the hardwood floor with a roar before beginning to sit up.

Luke Dodd kept his voice calm as he remained in a squatting position. "You really don't want to do this, Lieutenant."

Krieger didn't reply, but continued to rise.

Luke prepared for the man's next lunge, then heard a low growl from behind him. Keeping the drunken lieutenant in his peripheral vision, he turned his head slowly. A Jack Russell terrier stood on stiff legs, its hackles up, ears flat, small teeth bared.

Rolf Krieger belched loudly and then let out a

laugh. "You are in trouble now, whoever you are." The big man pointed at Luke Dodd. "Phantom, *attack*."

The dog moved in a white-and-brown blur. Dodd braced himself and prepared to ward off the animal— he didn't want to hurt it—when he realized the Jack had already run past him. Turning back to Rolf Krieger, he saw the soldier staring down at the dog as it pulled viciously on his bathrobe and growled, thrashing its head savagely side to side.

Luke Dodd grinned. "That's some dog you have there, Krieger."

The lieutenant looked stricken. "She has turned him against me," he muttered. With that, he passed out and hit the floor for the second time. Phantom—after quickly releasing his hold and sidestepping to avoid a fatal pin beneath his master's bulk—crawled onto Rolf Krieger's chest and lay down. Placing his head between his paws just below Krieger's chin, the dog eyed Dodd suspiciously, one side of his mouth curled up enough to expose a single canine fang to the stranger facing him.

"What the hell have you gotten me into, Chris?" Luke Dodd muttered, moving toward the supine pair. He reached for an arm to pull Krieger up. The terrier raised his head and growled, making clear that Luke would be his next victim. Gently putting the arm back down, Luke looked at the dog. "Fine, have it your way." Backing up, he grabbed each of the big man's feet and began sliding him through the entryway toward the living room.

Phantom turned his head over his shoulder and raised an inquisitive brown ear, but otherwise stayed prone on Krieger's chest. Luke shook his head as he struggled with the lieutenant's significant dead weight. He could swear the animal had some kind of doggy smile plastered on his face and was enjoying the ride. Phantom's stub of a tail began wagging back and forth furiously, lending credence to the observation.

"Can I help you?"

Luke dropped Krieger's feet and looked toward the open doorway as he straightened. The woman was tall with a mass of long, dark, curly hair. "Yes, ma'am, you can. This fella's a little on the heavy side. I was trying to put him . . ." At this point Luke scratched his head and smiled ruefully. "And the dog, I guess, on the couch."

Shelly Simitis didn't return the smile. "I'm giving you five seconds to start talking before I'm out of the door and screaming." She pointed at the unconscious Krieger. "And so help me, if you've hurt him . . ."

Luke Dodd's jaw dropped. "Me? Hurt *him*? I'm sent here on government business—and I was already in something of a hurry, by the way, when I was diverted to pick up this lug—and no sooner do I get here than I'm invited inside, at which point he jumps me."

The woman continued staring.

Luke held his hands up and reached into his jacket's breast pocket. "Hold on, I've got I.D." Withdrawing a slim leather wallet, he held it out and tossed it to the woman.

Simitis caught the billfold and opened it, not taking her eyes from the man facing her. She glanced at the photo, then to Luke, and then at the name on the credentials. "Luke Dodd, Central Intelligence Agency?"

Dodd put his hands down. "That's me. Now will you help me with him? Please?"

Shelly didn't move, instead folding her arms across her breasts and looking at Luke Dodd suspiciously. "What does the CIA want with Rolf?"

"Ma'am," Luke began, getting impatient, "I have no idea. All I can tell you is that my brother pulled me from the middle of a well-deserved break in my hot tub, had me on a plane to the East Coast, and then phones ten minutes after we're airborne and tells me to fly into Colorado Springs and to bring this guy with me. Believe me, right now I just want to get back to the airport—and to kick my brother's ass."

For the first time Shelly Simitis cracked a smile. Dodd's aggravation with his dilemma was genuine enough. She walked over and extended a hand. "Shelly Simitis," she said.

Luke relaxed and lifted his own hand. "Nice . . . *shit!*" The terrier had jumped from Krieger and latched on to the crotch of Dodd's Levi's. His fifteen pounds of furred muscle dangled back and forth like a pendulum.

"Easy, boy," Luke breathed. "There's a gooooood doggy." Phantom's lips curled back in the now-familiar snarl, but no sound issued.

"Ms. Simitis—Shelly—please . . ." Luke looked hopefully at the woman as a tooth broke through denim. He imagined he could feel cold enamel against his left testicle. At least he hoped he imagined it.

Shelly Simitis stepped forward. "Oh, Phantom," she said in exasperation. Putting her hands around the dog, she lifted the weight off of Dodd's groin. He exhaled a sigh of relief as the pressure eased, but the Jack was still clamped tight.

"Off, Phantom," Simitis commanded. *"Off."*

Phantom rounded his eyes toward Simitis questioningly, but didn't release his hold.

"Phantom," she hissed through clenched teeth.

The dog looked up and into Luke's eyes and wrinkled his muzzle twice, exerting a subtle but firm warning pressure that the man had better be on his best behavior. A moment later the jaws relaxed enough for Dodd to stumble backward onto the arm of the sofa.

Luke Dodd took a deep, cleansing breath. It shook in his chest. He saw that the canine now rested peacefully in the arms of Simitis.

"He can be somewhat overprotective," the woman explained with a hesitant smile.

Dodd nodded. "That's some dog," he said for the second time that night, now with an entirely different inflection to the words. "Thank God he's not a Rottweiler."

The woman scratched behind Phantom's ears. The dog closed his eyes and made a happy, mewling noise from deep in his chest. Simitis smiled, thinking of Phantom's encounter with the Russian colonel in Iraq. "You have no idea, Mr. Dodd." She eyed Krieger's body, where it lay on the floor, and shook her head.

A few minutes later she and Dodd managed to get Rolf Krieger onto the sofa.

Luke Dodd sat heavily in an overstuffed leather seat.

"Can I get you something to drink?" Simitis asked. "You look like you could use it."

Luke looked up hopefully as he realized he was in Colorado. "You wouldn't happen to have any Fat Tire ale, would you?"

"Coming up," the woman said, turning toward the kitchen and walking away.

Luke Dodd looked skyward and mouthed a silent "Thank you, Lord."

Returning to the room with two bottles of the amber ale brewed up the road in Boulder, Shelly handed one to Luke before taking up station at the end of the sofa, Krieger's size-thirteen feet cradled gently in her lap.

"So what's got the big boy so upset?" Dodd asked, taking a long pull from his beer.

"You say Rolf took a swing at you?" Simitis asked.

Dodd exhaled a quick snort. "Oh, yeah. You could say that. I don't think it was me *personally* he wanted to take out, just my head."

Simitis ignored the sarcasm. "And did he give you any indication why?"

Dodd nodded. "He said, 'You're the one, aren't you'—I probably don't have the accent right, sorry— just before he invited me inside."

Shelly, embarrassed, put a hand over her face. "Oh, my God," she muttered.

Luke raised an eyebrow but said nothing.

"It's a long story," Simitis began. "Rolf and I have been together for several months. He's from solid German stock and he's been indicating more and more lately that he'd like to make an honest woman of me."

"You mean get married?"

Shelly Simitis nodded.

"And you don't want that?"

It was Simitis's turn to raise an eyebrow. "Mr. Dodd, I'm a twenty-seven-year-old intelligence officer in the United States Army, a captain. I'm working on my master's. I do quite well on my own, thanks."

Luke smiled.

"So," she continued, "from his colloquial point of view, if I don't want to marry him, there must be another man involved." Shelly shrugged.

Luke's smile grew. "That's why he tried to kill me."

Simitis returned the smile. "Yes. That's why he tried to kill you. He wanted to discuss it again at lunch today. I'd been working on a paper for one of my graduate courses until four a.m. and went to work at Fort Carson on only two hours of sleep this morning. I didn't feel like getting into it. He got upset, so I left."

Dodd nodded thoughtfully. "And being a manly man, he buried his troubles in a bottle. Or tried to."

The woman shook her head. "Rolf doesn't drink much."

"Well, he made up for lost time today."

Simitis leaned forward. "I have no idea what this visit is about, Mr. Dodd, but I don't want Rolf's career to suffer because I was too tired to sit down and discuss this with him. It's *my* fault, understand?"

Luke Dodd sat back with a knowing look on his face. He tapped an index finger to the tip of his nose and winked. "So. You're a career woman. Don't need a man in your life to make you complete, despite how much you love him?"

"I'm a complete person without him, yes," said Shelly Simitis in a noncommittal voice.

"You don't *love him* enough to marry him."

A slow grin spread across Shelly's face. "You're having woman problems of your own, aren't you, Mr. Dodd?"

Dodd ignored the question, shifting uncomfortably. "Please, call me Luke."

"Fine," Simitis continued. "You're having woman problems of your own, aren't you, Luke?"

Dodd looked thoughtful. "In your own words, *Shelly*, no. I'm successful in my own right—professionally and financially. I live comfortably and have no trouble finding female companionship when I so choose." He looked into Shelly Simitis's eyes. "But I don't *need* anyone."

"So," coaxed Simitis, "who's the woman who broke your heart?"

Luke frowned. "Well . . ."

Two hours later Rolf Krieger cracked an aching eye to the world. He caught a glimpse of Shelly and an unknown man crying together. "What is going on?" he asked, confused by the scene before him and trying to sit up. "What is wrong?"

Shelly Simitis pushed him gently back onto the sofa and smiled through her tears. "Nothing to worry about, hon. You're going to Fort Bragg with this nice man."

Krieger looked toward Luke Dodd as the latter tried to wipe telltale tears from his face. "I am? Why would I do that?" He attempted to focus on Dodd through an alcohol-induced fog. "Who are you? Why are you crying?"

Dodd reached into a pocket. "I'm not crying, Lieutenant. And trust me," he said, bringing a syringe into view, "you'll thank me for this later."

Rolf Krieger frowned as the needle punctured the

muscle of his upper arm. Then a childlike smile crossed his lips and he closed his eyes.

"What was that?" asked Shelly.

Dodd smiled. "Mother's milk. Combination of vitamins and some other supplements that will make him feel better."

Shelly Simitis looked at Luke Dodd and nodded. After listening to the man bare his soul over the perceived loss of the love of his life for the past two hours, well . . . she trusted him. She took Luke Dodd's hand in her own. "I understand you can't tell me what this mission is about. But promise me one thing, Luke—that once he's briefed on what's happening, Rolf's participation will be his choice."

Luke nodded. "I promise. But if Bill Jones is asking him to do something, what do you think are the odds the young lieutenant here will say no?"

Simitis frowned. "Small to none."

Krieger looked at Luke Dodd thoughtfully as the CIA officer finished his tale. "I vaguely remember waking up on the couch at some point. Why were you crying, Mr. Dodd?"

Dodd, accustomed to operating behind enemy lines for months, even years, at a time, cringed. "I have no idea what you're talking about, Lieutenant Krieger." He leaned forward and stared hard into the big man's eyes. "And remember, you were pretty drunk."

A small smile crossed Rolf Krieger's face. "*Ja, ja. I* was drunk." He sat back, his smile broadening. "But *you* were crying."

Dodd plastered a professional mask on his face and turned away. "Let's talk about why we're here."

"Not why you were crying?"

"No."

"So you *were* crying?"

"*No!*" said Luke with exasperation. "I wasn't crying. What I meant was, *no,* let's talk about why we're going to Bragg instead of about your drunken hallucinations." A thoughtful look crossed his face. "But, if you really want to talk about women, stud, let's start with you. More to the point, why were you hitting the juice so hard yesterday?"

Krïeger grimaced, remembering bits and pieces of the previous day's events. "I overindulged. I do not do it often."

Dodd nodded. "So Shelly told me."

"What else did that woman tell you, eh, Mr. Dodd?" A suspicious note had worked its way into Krieger's voice. Shelly knew he detested discussing personal matters. The fact that she had apparently discussed their relationship with this man did not make him happy.

Luke interlaced his fingers and put them behind his neck. He slowly worked his neck to one side, then the other, stretching the muscles. "Man, all this flying sure gets you tight, doesn't it, Lieutenant?"

Krieger leaned forward, his patience gone. "What did she tell you, Dodd?"

The operations officer put his hands down and smiled slowly. "Relax, not much. Just that you had somehow worked it out in your head that because she didn't want to get married in the immediate future, you somehow translated that into she doesn't love you. And being the big, hunk-a-hunk of a guy that you are, you thought that meant another man was involved."

"She told you this?"

The smile disappeared. "When I'm told to pick up someone who may be participating in an operation with me, someone I might have to trust with my life, you can damned well bet I'm going to ensure he's emotionally stable." Dodd paused before leaning close again and continuing. "And yesterday, Lieutenant, you looked anything but stable to me. So yeah, you're damned right she told me."

Rolf Krieger sat stoically for a full minute, staring at his hands in his lap. "The man you met yesterday, that is not who I am."

Dodd said nothing.

Krieger continued. "I've never had the time nor the desire to have a real relationship with a woman, not until Shelly. I guess—well, I had been so sure she would want to marry. When she said no, I snapped. It appears my imagination took over." He looked into the other man's eyes. "I tell you these things because I assume that this mission is important. I want you to understand that normally I am quite—how did you put it?—emotionally stable."

Luke barked a laugh. "According to Bill Jones, if you were any more stable you would be inhuman."

A puzzled expression crossed Krieger's face. "When did you speak with the colonel?" Krieger knew many lieutenant colonels and colonels, but when he spoke of *the colonel,* it was always in reference to Jones.

"Last night. I was damnably close to walking away from that house without you. But I called my brother first. He gave me Jones's home number, told me that your participation in this op was a personal request of the colonel's. He asked that I call Jones before nixing you. Which I did." Dodd hesitated, uncomfortable. "He was a little surprised to hear of your condition."

Rolf Krieger's face turned a light shade of crimson. Most people's opinions mattered little to the man; he lived life the way he thought best and damn what others thought. Colonel Bill Jones was one of the few whose opinion mattered to him. "I'm sure he was," was all the big officer could manage.

"And," Luke Dodd continued, "he said if you were shit-faced, he was sure you had one helluva reason."

Krieger looked up, relieved. "I did have a good reason, even if I was wrong."

"Oh, I know. I met her, remember?"

The two sat in silence a few moments longer, then Dodd stood and walked to a small refrigerator in the aft end of the passenger cabin. He returned with a dark beer of Bavarian origin in hand. "Little hair of the dog what bit you?" He smiled.

Rolf Krieger cringed and shook his head.

"Didn't think so." Luke Dodd grinned and threw a bottle of orange juice into the lieutenant's lap with his other hand before sitting. "We won't be at Bragg but a few minutes—Pope Air Force Base, actually. People we can't discuss are going to drop off some gear that doesn't exist for us to take to our final destination, which for the moment is unknown."

Krieger drank half of the bottle of juice in two long pulls and shook his head. "And people wonder why the military does not like dealing with the Central Intelligence Agency."

Luke Dodd grinned. "Don't point fingers at us this time. These are *your* people."

Chapter 8

Hemp, Tantric Secrets & National Defense

The Oval Office
White House
Washington, D.C.

President Jonathan Drake looked over the documents in front of him. They were the background papers on personnel who would potentially lead the resurrection of the M4X1 project. He frowned and glared over the short reading glasses perched on the end of his nose. "You're kidding, right?"

Secretary of Defense Ronald Newman shook his silvery head. The former Air Force four-star, with more confirmed kills from his Phantom than any other fighter jock in Vietnam, knew he needed to tread lightly.

"No, Mr. President, we're not. You wanted to be kept informed of the decision on who would be heading up the Tommy research team because of the criticality of the effort. You say no, he's out. But both the Army and Department of Defense agree that Dr. Bernard is our best candidate—and we've looked at hundreds. Admittedly, he's had something of a checkered past. That's what has kept him from being approached for any defense projects before this." The SECDEF sighed. "Sir, we tried to think outside of the box on this one and come up with the best person for the job." He tapped a black-and-white photo of a man who appeared to be in his mid- to late forties. "This is him."

Drake looked back to the papers in his hand. "Clive Bernard. Born in Sausalito, California, October 1956. Attended Stanford on full scholarship, graduated summa cum laude with a BS in electrical engineering and a minor in mathematics, 1974." The president looked up. "Graduated 1974? But that would have made him . . ."

"Eighteen years old, Mr. President," replied the SECDEF. "He graduated high school at fifteen."

Drake went back to examining Bernard's life. "He then appears to have taken a year off to—what's this, *find himself*?"

Newman shifted uncomfortably. "It was the early seventies, sir. And this was a kid born and raised in the San Francisco Bay Area. I would imagine the pressure of being a teenage genius in that place and time could be quite profound."

The president continued. "Arrested 1975 in Santa Fe, New Mexico, for possession of marijuana."

"Less than an ounce, Mr. President," said the secretary, straight-faced.

Drake looked again over his reading glasses at Newman, his face stony. "Thanks. I feel much better about it now, Ron." He returned to the dossier. "What's this place he was staying in New Mexico? The Holistic Yoga Retreat?" He looked up and pulled off his glasses. "Dammit, Ron, I have never considered myself a stick-in-the-mud, but we're talking about someone who is potentially leading a highly sensitive, major defense project; more to the point, to *resurrect* a critical defense project from the grave with a team of newcomers. I'm not sure someone raised on a commune can pull that off, but maybe it's just me."

The SECDEF didn't miss the sarcasm. It was unlike

Jonathan Drake, but Newman understood the president was under significant pressure, as were they all. "Just keep reading, Mr. President. Please."

Jonathan Drake took a deep breath and bit off a sharp reply. "Returned to Stanford in 1977. Master's, again with honors, in materials science and engineering, 1978." Drake grimaced. "Two more arrests for possession of marijuana during this period, I see. And this time it looks as though Mr. Bernard did thirty days in county lockup as a graduation vacation for his efforts."

"Bear with me, Mr. President," said the SECDEF.

"Following his release from incarceration, it looks like your boy disappeared from the scope for a few years. Why?"

The secretary handed another sheet of paper to the president. "Here's a comprehensive list of Dr. Bernard's activities during those years, Mr. President. We didn't want it included in the official report until we'd confirmed the information."

The president took the proffered sheet. "And have you?"

"Yes, sir. Mark Sterling had his agents in the Hoover Building confirm it all. We wouldn't have made a final decision otherwise."

Drake nodded and continued. "Merchant marines?"

"That was because he didn't have enough money to travel overseas any other way, Mr. President."

"Two years in Australia living with Aboriginal tribesman? Three years in India?"

"He's actually a Yoga master of some sort now, sir."

"Four years in Tibet?"

Ron Newman closed his eyes. "Studying with a renowned monk, sir."

Jonathan Drake shook his head in disbelief but plunged on. "Looks like he returned to the States in 1991 on the death of—who is Nigel Bernard?"

"*Captain* Nigel Bernard was a mechanized infantry

company commander in the Twenty-fourth Infantry Division, sir—and Clive Bernard's younger brother. He was killed in action along the Euphrates River during the final days of Desert Storm." The SECDEF paused. "His brother's death hit Bernard hard. They were very close growing up. By the time Clive Bernard made it back to California, his brother had been long buried. And no one at home could tell him the circumstances of his brother's death. Bernard finally located a man who'd served with his brother's company during the war. He found out his brother's Bradley had been hit by tank cannon fire from a Republican Guard T-72. The fire that engulfed the Brad was so swift—all of the onboard 25mm ammunition and the TOW missiles went up—that none of the crew members escaped."

Drake thought of the horror of dying in such a manner, with flames so intense that a soldier didn't even have the two seconds it would take to exit a hatch. He handed the secretary the dossier, suddenly weary. "Give me the high points, Ron."

"Drake returned to school, the Massachusetts Institute of Technology this time, and pursued a Ph.D. in electrical engineering with a focus in metals and systems integration," said the SECDEF. He glanced down at the sheets in his hand, shuffling through them. "That would be late 1992. Since then he's applied for numerous jobs in the defense industry. Until now, he's been turned down."

"No great surprise there," said Drake. He leaned forward. "Ron, tell me this. Why did he want to suddenly go from a transcendentalist, or whatever the hell he was, to working with advanced weapons systems?"

"The FBI spoke with several of Bernard's colleagues from over the past decade and asked the same question. Bernard himself refused to discuss his reasons with them when the subject was raised." Newman raised a finger. "But, his ex-wife had some insights."

"Go on," said Drake. "It obviously has something

to do with the death of his brother, but if that means we've got someone who's obsessed with revenge and creating the tools with which to wreak it on those responsible, that frankly doesn't make me feel secure in having him head any kind of project, Ron—especially one this important."

"Just the opposite is the case, Mr. President," said the SECDEF. "According to Ms. . . . ." He pulled a report. "Adrian Foster. Ms. Foster said that Bernard had become obsessed with finding ways to keep others from experiencing the type of death suffered by his brother. Thus the focus in engineering and metals."

"I'll grant you the man sounds brilliant," said Jonathan Drake with a shake of his head. "But look at his history."

"It's been clean as a whistle for the past ten years, sir. And let's face it—it wasn't like he was a danger to society before that."

Drake held up his hands in surrender. "All right, all right. But think about this. His background may well suit the good doctor for working the survivability options for the Tommy—maybe even improving the work done by Dr. Escobar's team—but this is a *system*. We need someone who can competently oversee the project in its entirety."

"You're correct, but Dr. Bernard hasn't been sitting on his thumbs for the past decade, Mr. President. He's gotten plenty of systems integration exposure as the assistant team lead for the civilian spacecraft that was the first into space not too long ago."

"The ship's management team didn't have a problem with Bernard's background?"

The SECDEF shook his head. "Apparently not, sir. And if Paul Allen can cut through the bullshit and see the man, I think we should be able to as well. Additionally, from what I've read in interviews with those associated with the project, Bernard did a bang-up job." Newman frowned. "The only bit of unwanted publicity he received during that time was the Miss America scandal."

Jonathan Drake thought about what his chief civilian military adviser had just said; and then the light came on. "The Miss America who was defrocked for getting married during her one-year tenure?"

Newman grimaced. "Yes, Mr. President. That would be the aforementioned Ms. Foster."

Drake tried to recall the details. Six months or so into her year of representing all things good about America, the young lady in question—a lovely blonde from Idaho with legs that went on forever—had been out west and met . . . some sort of rocket scientist and fell head-over-heels in love. She couldn't even wait the few months it would have taken to pass on her crown before getting married, so she'd given it up. "*Bernard* is the rocket scientist? You're joking."

Ron Newman shook his silvery head. "No, sir. He's the one." A smile played at the corners of the SEC-DEF's mouth. "The gist is that our Miss America has a thing for the forty-pound-brain types to begin with. And she had also dabbled in meditation and holistic healing in the past."

"I've heard of it, but I have no idea what holistic healing is."

"Healing through nature, Mr. President. It's a whole mind-body-spirit process. . . ."

"Go on, I get the gist," said Drake. "Flake" was the word running through his mind.

"At any rate, as a gesture of goodwill, and because the Miss America pageant people knew it would be great publicity, our girl did the honors and handed over the big check after the third and final successful flight into space. She met Bernard formally at the reception that followed."

Drake glanced at his watch, knowing he had a full schedule. But this was getting interesting, God help him. He gave Newman a "more" gesture with his hand.

"They got to talking. She found that here was a man with the spiritual energy of an Eastern mystic combined with the brain of a top-tier scientist, and . . . well, the way the agent put it, her panties melted."

"But the age difference . . ."

"She was twenty-three. Bernard was in his mid-forties. But Bernard has been known to use the Eastern 'secrets' he learned in India to great advantage with the ladies."

"Are they still married?"

"No, sir. They've been divorced for thirteen months now."

"So she finally came to her senses."

Newman shook his head. "No, sir. The lady is still brokenhearted. It was Bernard who said he needed to move on to the next 'plane in this life,' as he put it. According to both of them, and their mutual acquaintances, they remain good friends."

A few silent moments passed before Drake nodded. "All right, Ron. I'll leave the final decision to you and the Army—I don't see any security implications from the relationship; no more than he already had going for him, anyway." The president reached for his coffee and took a swallow. "But I want some way of minimizing the chances of this happening again. The Iranians—whoever—must know that we're going to begin rebuilding the M4X1 program, and we can't afford the loss of future team members or facilities."

Newman shook his head. "Mr. President, there are no guarantees that we can keep the project safe." He paused. "But we've thought about this and agree—because whoever took the Tommies does not know at this point how long and/or how difficult reverse engineering them will be. They'll likely want to stay ahead of the game."

"So what's the plan?"

"Security into any of the M4X1 facilities was strict enough before. Now, someone's spouse will have a difficult time getting in the door from here on out unless they're part of the team. Next, we're going to provide security personnel to protect the team. Dr. Bernard and a few others will have twenty-four-seven protection."

Drake nodded.

"Let's address the facilities first. The new site is secluded, but that doesn't mean it's impenetrable. I've talked to a lot of my associates and come up with a security group headed by someone you're familiar with, sir." Newman opened a folder and slid it across the desk.

The president looked at the black-and-white photo staring at him. "Cobb."

The SECDEF nodded. "Yes, sir. Mr. Cobb will head the security team."

Drake slid the folder back to Ronald Newman. "That's good enough for me. God help the person or persons who decide to target the site."

The secretary smiled. "My thoughts exactly, Mr. President." He pushed the folder to the right and went on. "Now for Dr. Bernard's personal security team. As the coverage will be continuous, we selected two personnel. We wanted candidates for the job to have either a military police or Special Forces background. As we both know that our Green Berets have so many missions that they're being run ragged, we decided to go with the former group. Both selections are active-duty Army military police officers with the appropriate clearances in hand." Newman reached into the leather satchel he'd laid on the tabletop and withdrew two manila personnel folders, known as 201 files in the military. The 201 tells the service member's life story, from cadet through general.

Jonathan Drake leaned back in his leather chair. "Dazzle me, Ronald. Who did you find that could possibly deal with a left-wing, twenty-first-century Tommy Chong?"

Ronald Newman smiled. "I think you'll be pleased, Mr. President. Would you like to meet them . . . along with Dr. Bernard?"

The president consulted his watch. "I've got ten minutes, Ron. Bring them in."

Outside the Oval Office sat three people. Two of them wore the dark green Army Class-A uniform. On the lapels of their jackets were the crossed pistols insignia of the military police. The similarities ended there. The man was a major. He was tall, thick through the chest, and broad through the shoulders. Though it was difficult to tell from the tight military cut, his hair was red; his skin was pale, with the proper freckles to complement it. He sat tensely, his knees together. His black beret was folded neatly on top of his right knee; his hands were crossed in his lap. The woman, who wore the silver oak leaves of a lieutenant colonel on her shoulder epaulets, was fine-boned. Despite the fact that her uniform did its best to hide it, it was clear that she had the wispy figure of a ballerina, with a long, elegant neck. She was a couple of inches under six feet tall and her dark hair was cut short. Her lips were full, what some would call pouty, and her eyes, which had a slightly Asian cast to them, were a striking bronze color. Her nose was long and thin. Because of the nose, whenever she regarded someone seriously, they tended to feel like the scrapings from the bottom of a farmer's boot.

Clive Bernard sat facing the door of the Oval Office, across from the two officers. He made no pretense of hiding his examination of the woman. She really was *fetching*, he thought. He guessed her to be in her late thirties or early forties, but she carried the years well and could pass for much younger. And then the eyes turned on him and Bernard found himself being stared at down a lovely nose.

"Can I *help* you?" asked the woman quietly.

Bernard threw back his head and barked a quick laugh, his eyes twinkling with mischief.

The lieutenant colonel's head cocked at a slight angle and she frowned. "I'm sorry. Did I say something funny, Mr. . . . ?" She didn't know what to make of the man. For one thing, it was obvious they were all about to meet the leader of the free world. And he shows up wearing jeans, flip-flops, and a tie-dyed T-shirt containing so many colors that Joseph himself would be jealous? He reminded her of the actor Peter Horton, who'd played the college professor in the television series *thirtysomething* back in the mid-nineties. Tall, at least six-two, and thin, with long, curly blond hair that reached almost to his shoulders. And a sense of—what? Arrogance? Perhaps. Whatever it was, she didn't find it in the least attractive.

"Actually, it's *Doctor*." He stood and took the four steps necessary to close the distance between them and extended his hand. "Clive Bernard. And your name, Miss . . . ?"

The woman took the extended hand in hers, but she did not rise. "Actually, it's *Colonel*," she said coolly. "Lieutenant Colonel Sarah Hunter."

"Sarah. Such a lovely name." He bent the hand to his lips, the eyes again twinkling. "Or, more properly should I say, such a lovely name for such a lovely woman."

Sarah Hunter withdrew her hand and stood. "Dr. Bernard . . ."

Bernard smiled. "Please. Call me Clive."

"Dr. Bernard," she repeated, as though Bernard hadn't spoken, "I have no idea what could bring you, myself, and Major O'Sullivan together at the White House—"

"I know why *I* am here, it's the roles of you two that is a mystery to me."

"*Will* you quit interrupting me, Doctor?" Sarah Hunter, despite a height disadvantage of several inches, still somehow managed to look down her nose as she addressed him. "As I was saying, I know your type and I do not find you in the least charming, sophisticated, or worldly."

Clive Bernard threw his head back and laughed.

"Oh, my *dear*," he said, tears forming at the corners of his eyes. He held out a hand, trying to catch his breath. "You have me all wrong. I assure you, you are a bit too . . . *old* for my taste."

The color rose in Sarah Hunter's cheeks and she shook with outrage. "*Old?* Why, you . . . wait a second." A frown crossed her face as she bent forward and took a sniff of Bernard's T-shirt. "Is that *cannabis* I smell? You're about to meet with the president and you're smoking marijuana?"

Bernard stepped back and shook his head. "Okay, listen to me before you call in your DEA stormtroopers. When I was in Tibet, I took a nasty tumble on a mountain trail and twisted my back."

"Are you trying to tell me it's *medicinal*?" Hunter asked, a lock of her hair falling over one eye as she shook her head in disbelief.

For the first time Major O'Sullivan took an interest in the proceedings. While he didn't move his body, his eyes followed the verbal exchange and a slight smile materialized on his face.

"I'm not saying there's any validity to your claim, I am only saying that—"

"Do you realize that Major O'Sullivan and I are both military police officers?"

A frown creased Bernard's face as he pointed at the various hardware adorning Sarah Hunter's uniform jacket. "No, I haven't been around the military enough to understand what it is all of your bits and buttons signify, General."

"*Lieutenant Colonel,*" hissed Hunter between clenched teeth.

"Do you see what I mean?" Bernard smiled, glad to be off the topic of marijuana and police. "I'm out of my element, dear. Forgive me?" he asked, one eyebrow raised.

The next moment the Oval Office door opened and the Secretary of Defense stepped through it, stopping in confusion as he saw the confrontation taking place. "Is everything all right here?" he asked.

John O'Sullivan stood, and everyone's jaw dropped as he came fully erect. Because he'd arrived before Hunter, Bernard, and the SECDEF, no one realized the man stood six and a half feet tall. "Everything is fine, sir," rumbled O'Sullivan with a smile. "The colonel and the doctor were just getting to know one another."

Ron Newman smiled uneasily. "Well. Very good then. Shall we?" and he indicated the open doorway.

Chapter 9

Leverage

A woman's voice Jones didn't recognize answered the telephone. She sounded winded. Or frightened. "Dillon residence."

Jones eased his chair back. "Yes, ma'am, this is Colonel Bill Jones calling from United States Central Command in Tampa. Could I speak with Melissa, please?"

"I'm Alice Johnson, Colonel, Melissa's mother." A slight pause. "I'm afraid Melissa isn't . . . isn't here."

There was a definite note of anxiety in the woman's voice. "Mrs. Johnson, is something wrong?"

Jones could hear Alice Johnson take a deep breath before she replied. "Melissa phoned yesterday afternoon when she left your office, Colonel. She said she'd booked an early-evening return flight to Colorado Springs. But"—the woman paused, the worry in her voice more pronounced—"I haven't heard from her since, Colonel Jones."

Jones asked the obvious question. "Have you tried her mobile number?"

The fear was momentarily replaced with impatience as Alice Johnson raised her voice. "Of course I tried her mobile number. I'm old, Colonel, not senile."

Jones grimaced. He deserved that. "I apologize,

ma'am, I was just thinking out loud. Have you checked with the airline?"

"Yes. They said her flight landed in Colorado Springs at seven o'clock last night."

"And they confirmed she was on board?"

"Yes. And that she picked up her luggage on landing. And before you ask, yes, I phoned the police." The angry tone returned. "But they don't consider her missing since it hasn't been forty-eight hours. Where do they think she'd go, Colonel? *Where?*"

Bill Jones rubbed a weary hand across his face. "I don't know, ma'am. I don't know."

"She stirs," said the man in the van's passenger seat to his companion.

The driver took his eyes off the road for a few moments, just long enough to glance into the vehicle's rear cargo space. While he couldn't see their guest, he detected subtle movement from the van's floorboard. "Give her another injection." The driver looked over his shoulder to his accomplice as the man moved to obey. "But not too much. If she dies . . ."

The other man nodded. The sentence didn't need to be finished.

From her position in the rear of the van, Melissa Dillon slowly swam from the fog of unconsciousness. *Where am I?* she thought groggily, trying to sit up. Her head felt as though a pile of bricks weighted it down. She couldn't move her hands or feet—she couldn't even *feel* her hands or feet. Worst of all, she couldn't see. And then last night's events began coming back to her.

Melissa spotted her Ford Expedition across the airport parking garage and smiled weakly. She'd done all she could do regarding Patrick, and now she was almost home. From this point it was up to Jones and his cronies to help the man with whom she'd spent most of her adult life. She opened the big SUV's rear cargo door and deposited her overnight bag. She closed the hatch and moved toward the front of the truck. As her fingertips grazed the driver's door handle a voice spoke from behind her.

"Pardon me, miss."

Melissa turned, her thumb hovering over the keyless entry remote's panic button. The man spoke accented English—Middle Eastern? Though she flushed with guilt, Melissa Dillon couldn't help that since September 11th, her first reaction to people from that part of the world was fear. She forced a smile onto her face. He seemed nice enough; late twenties or early thirties, dark skin and hair, casually well dressed in khaki Dockers, a navy polo, and loafers. "Yes? Can I help you?"

The man smiled, embarrassed. "I am sorry. I did not mean to startle you, miss." He bent forward at the waist slightly in apology and greeting as he spoke. "Could you perhaps give me directions to the Ramada Inn?" He held up a small stack of papers for her to see. "I was told by the rental car representative that a map to the hotel would be placed in my paperwork, but there is nothing."

Melissa frowned, thinking. "Well, there's more than one Ramada in Colorado Springs." She felt a chill pass through her. If this man had a rental car, what was he doing in the airport's long-term parking garage asking for assistance? The rentals area was far removed from where he was now.

As the stranger saw the alarm in the woman's eyes, the smile disappeared from his face. His right hand moved in a blur, knocking the remote entry pad from Melissa's hand before her mind could will her thumb to depress it, then pulled her tightly in front of him, his arms securing her own to her sides. Stronger than he initially appeared, the man now held Melissa with only one arm. The other he wrapped around her mouth as her first scream was ready to be born. She screamed nonetheless, but little sound escaped. In terror she kicked and stomped at her attacker's feet and legs. Other than a pained grunt when her heel connected solidly with his instep, there was no change in the man's hold on Melissa.

A second man, also dark, also well dressed, moved into sight from behind the big Ford. He had a brown bottle in one hand and a white cloth in the other. This one smiled as he saw Melissa struggle. "A spirited wench, eh, Anwar?"

The first man spat a curse at his compatriot in his native tongue. "Hurry up, you *ass*. Someone will be along any minute."

The one with the bottle and cloth giggled as he dodged a kick directed at his crotch. "Very spirited, indeed," he said and laughed. Then his face turned serious. Stepping to one side, he brought the cloth around Melissa's right shoulder and pressed it against her mouth and nose. A medicinal smell washed over her. Her struggles increased for a few seconds, and then she slumped, unconscious.

Melissa was in a moving vehicle, that much she could tell. Lying immobile on her side, she heard road noises through the floorboards. The carpet was thin enough that she could feel the metal beneath. While her other awakening senses stood on end, she couldn't see. Blindfolded. Yet she sensed a presence.

"Be still, my little wildcat," said a calm voice from a few inches above her. "All is well."

Melissa felt a prick in her forearm. She wanted to scream but didn't have the energy. Once more she passed into darkness.

Institute for Plant and Seed Modification Research
Third Subterranean Level
Karaj, Iran

"Hello, Major," came a Russian-accented voice from the direction of the door. Patrick Dillon lifted his chin and squinted through his good eye. He knew that voice from somewhere. But all he could see was a large form walking—no, walking wasn't the word, more like lurching—toward him. Each step seemed to take the man a great deal of effort. His visitor settled into the chair facing Dillon and regarded him across the table.

"Oh, I am so sorry, Major," said the man. "You cannot see well through the swelling, can you?"

Dillon saw the man dig into a breast pocket and remove an object. "Now, Major, hold still. If you do not, you will have more than one damaged eye," he said, leaning across the table.

The American felt a cold tingling over his right eye as the object was placed against his eyelid, and then a flash of pain as the hand holding the object slid slowly across the swollen skin. Dillon willed himself not to move, knowing now that the man's hand held a razor blade or scalpel. He blinked his eye rapidly as he felt the pressure relieved. Blood and other fluids ran down his cheek.

"Let me help you," said the man soothingly.

He dabbed a coarse cloth gently at Dillon's eye and cheek and then held the cloth over the orbit for several seconds, exerting a steady pressure to staunch the flow of blood. When the hand withdrew, Patrick Dillon slowly opened the eye, blinking it rapidly several times to clear it. And then it fixed on the visitor. *"You,"* was the only word he said, but his body betrayed him, jerking involuntarily against the ropes securing his arms behind his chair as he instinctively wanted to go for the Russian's throat.

Sergei Sedov grinned at him from across the table. "Yes, Major Dillon. *Me.*"

Dillon didn't try to argue that Sedov was supposed to be dead. Clearly the Russian colonel was not. There wasn't even a chance that it was an identical twin facing him; with that nose, there was no doubt that this was indeed Colonel Sergei Sedov. Once again Dillon reflected that he should have put one more bullet into the Russian when he had the chance.

Sedov lit a cigarette and offered the pack to Patrick Dillon.

Dillon gestured with his head over his shoulder to his bound hands. "Untie me so I can enjoy it?"

The Russian laughed. "No, Major. For some reason I find that I do not trust you. I will, however, hold it for you." Sedov shook a cigarette loose so that the end protruded from the pack and extended it toward Dillon's mouth. The American noted the packaging was blue and artistic: Gitane Blondes. "No, thanks. I'm on a personal embargo of all things French." He smiled. "But if you've got any Cubans, I don't have a problem with that. I'm still not clear why that embargo's still in place."

Sedov exhaled and smiled. "Good, good. You are keeping your sense of humor."

The American leaned back in his chair and flexed his shoulders, relieving for a moment the strain on his aching muscles and joints. "Oh yeah, Ivan. I'm one funny son of a bitch. Ask anyone, they'll tell you." Dillon frowned as he stared at the Russian's wrist. "Nice watch."

Sergei Sedov smiled as he moved his arm in front of Dillon's face. "Ahhh, I forgot to thank you. I have always wanted a Zodiac—a fine Swiss timepiece is never out of style. And the Super SeaWolf, no less. You have excellent taste, Major."

"Glad you're happy with it, Ivan. I wouldn't get too used to it, though."

Sedov frowned and pulled again from the Gitane, palm toward mouth and fingers extended in the European fashion. "That is the second time you have called me Ivan. Why?"

Dillon shrugged. "It's a Cold War thing. All Soviets were Ivans to us."

The Russian smiled. "The Cold War," he mused, gazing toward the ceiling for a moment before looking back at the man he'd thought of so often over the past months. "Those were the days, were they not?"

Sedov continued, reflectively, forgetting for a moment everything that had transpired between him and the American bound to the chair across from him. "Everything was so *clear* in the eighties," he said, staring into space. "There was the Soviet Union and there was the United States. We had regiment upon regiment prepared to roll west, you had a smaller force and your vaunted technology." He sighed and took another pull from the Gitane, exhaling slowly. "I wonder what would have happened if the world had not gone insane, Major; if we'd actually gone into battle as everyone thought—no, as everyone *knew*—we ultimately would?"

Dillon snorted. "I suppose by 'gone insane' you refer to your European satellites throwing off the yoke of Communist rule?"

The Russian shrugged. "You say *tomato* . . ." He smiled.

Patrick Dillon returned the smile. "We'd have kicked your ass, Ivan, that's what would have happened."

Sedov ground the cigarette out in a battered tin ashtray. "Perhaps, Major. Perhaps." He stood stiffly and leaned against the table separating them. "But we have more contemporary issues to discuss, do we not?"

The American sat silently, watching the Russian.

"There is the matter of certain codes. Codes you know and that you will tell me."

"Fuck you."

Sergei Sedov smiled. "I'd forgotten how colorful your language could be, Major." The colonel gritted his teeth and stiffened as white-hot pain shot unexpectedly up his left knee. Grabbing the sides of the table, he took a few moments to control the pain, to will it down. Once more under control, the Russian looked up and into the smiling eye of the man responsible for his injuries.

"Like I said, fuck you," repeated Dillon. "Oh," he added, "and that looked *really* painful. What happened? Did you have some kind of accident while out dancing with the boys?"

For one of the few times in his life, Colonel Sergei Sedov lost his composure. With a howl he leaned across the table and backhanded the American's jaw with every ounce of strength he could summon, with the weight of the pain he'd felt over the past months. Pain due to *this* man, a man who, given the chance to put Sergei Sedov out of his misery following the American victory, couldn't even show the simple kindness of a bullet to the head, instead turning Sedov's bullet-riddled body over to his Russian keepers. The new Russian government had been looking long and hard for a face to attach the blame to for the ill-conceived war with the United States. And of course the free world had howled for his hide as well, aware of his atrocities via the twenty-four-hour news networks. Yes, Sergei Sedov, purveyor of battlefield atrocities, had fit the bill nicely. And now Patrick Dillon was his.

Dillon's head had snapped to one side and remained over his shoulder. He was already weak from prior beatings and lack of nourishment, and now the ropes were all that held the major in his chair. Not satisfied, Sergei Sedov delivered a vicious backhand that sent blood flying as Dillon's battered lips cracked open once more. The American's head whiplashed in the direction of the blow and then slumped forward on his chest. Sedov was about to repeat the cycle, but he regained some semblance of control over himself. With great deliberation he lowered the arm to his side and straightened, making a point not to use the chair to support his trembling legs.

Dillon, fresh blood mingling with the dried, brown-ish blood from his time with his Iranian jailers, summoned his remaining strength and slowly raised his head to stare into Sergei Sedov's eyes. "You hit like a girl, Ivan." Dillon grinned and blood leaked from the corner of his mouth. "Surprised your friends couldn't find you a cute little skirt, the kind your mother probably used to make you wear back in the good old days on the collective."

Sergei Sedov retook his seat and tapped out another Gitane. He smiled at Dillon. "While I have to admit that I achieved some small measure of pleasure—"

"And now you're rhyming. Guess you're a poet and don't know it."

Sedov shook his head in confusion, thinking not for the first time that perhaps Patrick Dillon was a little unstable, and then continued. "But my real pleasure will be in seeing you slowly break before you give me the information I want."

Dillon shook his head savagely. "It's not gonna happen. I officially no longer give a shit what happens to me, asshole."

The Russian exhaled, watching with a smile as the smoke coalesced into three concentric rings. He looked down at his guest. "Ah, do you speak of your current state, Major . . . or are you still depressed regarding your marital woes?"

Patrick Dillon remained silent.

"Yes, you'll never know how sorry I was to hear of your misfortunes in matters of the heart. The war hero returns home, but not to what you Americans like to call 'happily ever after.' You returned only to find you could not hold on to your woman." Sedov arched an eyebrow. "And such a lovely woman at that."

"Shut up."

Now the Russian was enjoying himself. "Major Dillon, it seems we've stumbled onto your Achilles' heel. But enough of that for now. We'll discuss your wife in more detail later."

Patrick Dillon didn't want to discuss Melissa at all. He especially didn't want to discuss her with *this* ass-hole. Besides, he was tired of bantering. Raising his head, he stared at the single bulb dangling from the ceiling and began speaking in a voice devoid of inflec-tion. "Dillon, Patrick M. . . ."

Sedov rolled his eyes. "Really, Major, there's no need . . ."

"Major, United States Army," continued Dillon, staring at the bulb above him. "Two-three-nine, three-eight, zero-zero . . ."

"Ah, your friend has joined us."

Dillon dropped his head and turned it toward the door. Three of the more vicious guards were escorting a handcuffed Master Sergeant Tom Crockett through the doorway. The big NCO wore a blindfold and the orange coveralls that every group of terrorists in the Middle East seemed to have a never-ending supply of. Dillon noted how painful each step was for Crockett; the sergeant was getting as bad or worse treatment than he was. Dillon screamed inside. But he didn't let the Russian—and whoever was behind the one-way glass—see how much his man's condition bothered him. That's what they wanted. With deliberation Pat-rick Dillon turned his head once more toward Sergei Sedov. The Russian, elbow on table, chin cupped in his hand, stared at him expectantly through a haze of smoke.

"No jokes, Major?" the Russian asked with a smile.

Dillon's own lips turned up. He looked down at his nakedness and back to Sedov. "No. But I would like one of those orange jumpsuits. They're groovy."

Sedov's smile disappeared. He turned toward the guards and nodded. Looking again to Dillon, he stood. "Be it on your head, Major." He nodded to the other side of the room. The guards were chaining Tom Crockett's hands to an eyebolt in the low ceiling. Once finished, they secured each of his feet to separate eyebolts in the concrete floor. The Russian bent close to Patrick Dillon's ear and whispered, *"Let the games begin."*

And with that the Iranians laid into Crockett. The burly NCO grunted, refusing to scream as the three took turns snapping punches to his face, ribs, and kidneys.

Dillon snarled. "You mother*fucker*."

Sedov sat on the edge of the table and took a slow pull from the Gitane as he watched the proceedings. "You are what you are, Major. I am but what I am. One of God's creatures, made in his likeness."

Patrick Dillon brought himself under control with an effort. "Turn him loose, Sedov. You don't need him."

"Really, Major? So do I take that to mean you will cooperate, give me the information I require?"

Dillon clamped his lips tight. Somehow the Russian and his new friends knew about the Tommy codes that only he and Crockett could provide. If he were back at the Armor School at Fort Knox, the class would likely agree with his assessment that his current position was untenable.

One of the guards looked toward Sedov inquiringly, for a moment halting the beating. The Russian gave him a small nod. The guard grasped his two hands together and delivered a vicious blow to the American's ribs. The sound of bone snapping was heard clearly across the room at the table where Patrick Dillon sat. Before Crockett had braced his legs, keeping his weight off of his wrists. Now he hung loosely, grunting with each blow, slowly turning in the direction momentum carried him as his assailants took turns.

"Stop them, Sedov," said Dillon in a low voice.

"It is not up to *me*, Major."

Dillon remained silent, teeth gritted. He made himself look at Crockett. *By God,* he thought, *that's the least I can do. Not ignore the man's pain.*

"Have you seen what the Iranians can do with knives, Major?"

Iranians. At least now he knew who was behind the theft of the Tommies. Then the Russian's words struck him. "What?"

"Knives," repeated Sedov, almost purring the word. "Edged instruments. I hear the techniques developed by their Persian brothers centuries ago have been refined to an art form."

"Don't . . ."

The Russian laughed. "Not yet, Major Dillon, not yet." He leaned conspiratorially toward Dillon. "They are actually quite fastidious buggers. They do not like to soil themselves any more than they must."

Patrick Dillon looked away from Crockett and stared at Sedov. "What are you talking about?"

Sedov nodded toward the lead guard again, a large fellow with a thick, black beard. Despite his bulk, there was a femininity about the man.

Dillon jerked on his bonds as he realized what was about to happen. *"No."*

The Iranian stepped back and started working the buttons on his fly as his fellow guards roughly pulled Tom Crockett's jumpsuit to his knees. Crockett thrashed weakly in his chains, realizing on some level, despite his physical condition, what was about to happen.

Now Sedov's smile was genuine. "You can stop this any time, Major. Your sergeant's fate is in your hands."

Dillon tore his gaze from Crockett when the big guard gave a satisfied grunt, but he said nothing. And then Tom Crockett screamed for the first time. It wouldn't be the last, not for a long time yet.

Chapter 10

Magic Carpet Ride

**Market Square
Karaj, Iran
Twilight**

The Iranian man took a nervous pull from his cigarette and nervously glanced once more toward the walls of the plant and seed research facility two blocks to the north. The facility's lights had winked to life five minutes ago as the sun faded into the Karaj River a kilometer to the west. Glancing at his watch, a battered Timex from the days of the Shah, he threw the cigarette to the sidewalk and turned to step into the street. Before his foot could touch the asphalt a horn blared just inches away. The pedestrian quickly backpedaled a few feet until he was once more safe on the sidewalk. The car, a late-model Citröen, flashed past, water skis secured to the roof of the sparkling red vehicle. The man caught a glimpse of a couple in Western clothes, en route for a weekend of water sports at the Amir Kabir Dam. Despite the hammering in his chest, the man smiled privately. Slowly the free world was creeping into his country—today, water skiing, tomorrow . . . who knew? But it could only get better.

The voice at his shoulder set his heart hammering again. *"Ava soma be Landan miravid?"* a tall stranger asked. *Are you going to London?*

The young man looked over the new arrival, for all

appearances just another local—dark skin, dark hair, dark eyes. *"Man anja miravam,"* he replied. *Yes, I am going there.* And then he added under his breath, "Once my country is free to once more make its own laws rather than being forced to bow down to old men who know nothing but their books and prayers."

The stranger's mouth didn't move, but his eyes smiled. "Your English is excellent," he said quietly.

The Iranian's gaze swept over the shops in the vicinity, at the people on the sidewalk. The crowds were dying as the sun faded. It was the way of Iran these days.

"It's all right," said the stranger, watching the young Iranian. "We've been watching the location for hours. It's safe."

His companion shook his head. "None of us are safe."

The stranger shrugged. Having spent the better part of a year undercover in Iran, he couldn't really argue the point. He motioned toward a coffeehouse a half-block away. Several tables littered the sidewalk, but all of the patrons were inside. They took a seat. When the waiter came out, the tall man ordered each of them a cup of tea. Most of the local population was drinking teas these days, as coffee prices were prohibitive.

Once the waiter departed, the local man looked to his new acquaintance and smiled, a little more relaxed now that a squad of the Ayatollah's secret police hadn't jerked him from the street and marched him to a prison cell. "Your Persian is excellent, Mr. . . . ?"

The tall stranger smiled. "Call me Ali."

"And I am Monsoor," replied the Iranian.

The one called Ali smiled. "Protected by God? Let us hope so."

"My mother's idea," said the Iranian with a shrug.

Ali nodded and looked his companion over as the young man sat silently. A CIA operations officer for over a decade, he was automatically suspicious of anyone who would betray his country. But the American was under pressure from the top to find two missing military men and/or several pieces of high-tech hardware, and to find them quickly. He'd received word at his Tehran flat that this man, Monsoor, might have a lead. Normally he would have taken all the time necessary to check out the source's background, his motivations, his weaknesses; his motivation, or motivations, for turning his back on his government. To ascertain if the potential source could in actuality be secret police in a sting operation to draw out foreign espionage agents. But Ali hadn't had time for his normal procedures, and that scared the hell out of him. He'd quickly gotten the man's basic background—father a colonel in the Shah's regime in the 1970s; father, for all appearances a patriot, unceremoniously executed immediately after the fundamentalists took over Iran in 1979; lived with his mother and younger sister since that time; graduate degree in chemistry from the Iran University of Science and Technology two years earlier; employed since then by the Institute for Plant and Seed Modification Research here in Karaj. And that was it. No run-ins with the fundamentalists, no links to dissident groups found.

"You are curious as to why I risk my life, my position . . . correct?" asked Monsoor, not unaware of the man's attention.

Ali nodded. "Yes, but for the moment, at least, your motivation is not important. I was told you had information regarding two men. I was not told what you wanted in return for the information."

Monsoor looked up as two veiled women passed by them on the sidewalk, paper bags from the market bazaar in hand, headed home to their families. The women cast furtive glances at the two men, quickly averted their eyes, and increased their pace. Once they were out of earshot, Monsoor looked once more at the man sitting across the table from him. "For myself, nothing."

Oh shit, thought the American. Greed, he could appreciate. But this could be his worst nightmare—an idealist. Idealists had a tendency to get too caught up in their dreams of change. And to get captured. And to talk. And to get American operatives killed.

Monsoor smiled, reading his companion's expression. "All right, that is not completely true."

"What is it that you *do* want, Monsoor? Assuming your information is of any value to me?"

"I want my mother and my sister out of Iran," he said, the smile disappearing. He nodded at the pair of women retreating down the sidewalk. "I do not want them to any longer have to hide behind veils, to have no voice. They are intelligent, caring women who deserve better than the austere lives that have been forced upon them." He shook his head, scowling. "At least I can remember, as a child, what a real life was like. Perhaps that is my problem. I remember my father, I remember going to see Western films on Saturdays, eating ice cream, seeing adults free to argue politics and religion. My sister"—he paused, and then continued deliberately—"she was so young when the government fell. This"—he gestured at the city around him, and at the same time to much more than merely the city—"this is all she knows. I have hoped for years that change would come, that as people like myself grew older, that our voices would become louder and louder until the mullahs in their mosques had no choice but to listen. That our president, who so much sounded like he would make a difference for Iran, would help us." Monsoor shook his head in resignation. "But none of this has come to pass. If we will be free, it will not be soon. So, I want my family out of Iran. To the United States, to Canada, I don't really care; but somewhere where they can be *free*."

Ali remained silent for a few moments. "Let us assume that that can be arranged. I would assume that you would want to leave as well?"

Monsoor nodded. "I'd have no reason to remain in Iran."

The American nodded. "I understand, but I am not

authorized to agree to terms. I will forward your request to my superiors . . . again, assuming your information is as advertised."

The young Iranian smiled. "If we were playing poker, this would be where you're asking to see my cards, correct?"

"Correct," said Ali. "And if you're bluffing . . ."

Monsoor shook his head quickly. "No, I have what you want."

"We don't have a great deal of time, Monsoor. I suggest you tell me what you know. The sooner you do, the sooner I can try to help you."

Monsoor nodded. "Yes, of course." He lowered his voice a few octaves. "You are seeking two Americans, correct?"

Ali nodded. Monsoor began his tale. "A few days ago I needed to retrieve some lab equipment from one of the lower levels of the institute," he said, nodding toward the building looming in the distance, now fully illuminated, the dominating feature for blocks around. "As I was leaving the storage room, I was practically run over by a squad of soldiers." He leaned forward. "There were two men with the soldiers, surrounded by them, really. I couldn't see much through the press of bodies, but I had a long enough look to see the men's hands were lashed with plastic bindings. And that they were blindfolded," he added quietly.

The American stared into the man's eyes. He knew there was always the chance that this Iranian was leading him down a false trail for any of a host of reasons. But "Ali" had no small amount of experience in judging sources—and potential sources. His gut and his years of experience told him this was the real deal. "Monsoor," he said quietly. "Listen to me and listen well. I need to know *everything* you can tell me about the two men, where they were being led—"

The Iranian interrupted. "I could not tell you that. It was clear the guards were not expecting to encounter anyone. As quickly as my feet hit the hallway, I was shoved roughly back into the storage room." He looked down, thinking that he'd failed—not the American, but his mother and sister. "I am sorry," he said. "I have nothing further that could be of use to you."

"You don't know what you know yet, Monsoor. You've been at the Institute for a significant amount of time, correct?"

A nod.

"You know the layout. What you don't know, you can find out."

The young man shook his head, but it was clear he was thinking. "The security in the building, it is quite stringent."

The American said nothing. He knew Monsoor was weighing his chances of success against the opportunity to help his family. Sometimes saying less said more, so the American remained silent.

"I know someone who may be able to find out more," Monsoor said finally. "But I will not put his life at risk."

"I recommend you bring no one into this that doesn't absolutely have to be brought in. Every additional person who knows what you're doing exponentially increases the chances of you failing."

But the Iranian was shaking his head. "It is the only way if you want to know your people's location. The *only* way."

Ali reluctantly nodded. "When can you get back with me?"

"I will be here again tomorrow at the same time. If I am not, I will not be returning."

The American nodded grimly.

**U.S. Special Forces Command Post
Vicinity Baghdad International Airport (BIAP)
Baghdad, Iraq**

"Say *again*," the lieutenant colonel practically yelled into the phone. A Cisco Systems voice-over-IP telephone, the system was plugged directly into a top-secret computer network that spanned the globe. At the moment it was connected to the officer's higher headquarters at Fort Bragg.

"Listen, Stan," said the speaker. "I understand your concerns, but I know Bill Jones. . . ."

"With all due respect, sir," said the light colonel, "I do *not* know Colonel Jones. Nor do I really give a shit whether I ever meet him or not. What I *do* care about, in order of priority, is getting my men back in one piece and the success of this mission. And a last-minute change to the team's composition threatens both. This group has been together, trained together, for months. For Christ's sake, they're one organism at this point. You should know what a change to that dynamic could mean at the eleventh hour. *Sir.*"

Charlie took a deep breath and went to his window, which was open. He let the sound of the wind sighing through the pines soothe him for a few moments before he spoke. "Stan, you will let the captain in charge of the team make the call. If he says it's a no-go after meeting the inbounds, I'm behind you. But you'll let him meet them and come to his own conclusion. Am I clear?"

Lieutenant Colonel Stanley Wloczewski took a deep breath and remembered who was on the other end of the secure line. A man he knew well and respected. "All right, sir," he said finally. "When are they due in?"

"Last I heard they were en route. Just left Al Udeid airbase in Qatar."

"Roger that," the lieutenant colonel sighed into the phone. "We'll ensure they get a warm welcome."

"All right, Stan. Let me know what's going on quickest. My understanding is you'll have a final location for the targets within the next twenty-four hours." The man called Charlie had been on the phone with Chris Dodd not ten minutes earlier. He thought now of all the things that could go wrong in Iran and then shook the negative thoughts away.

Melissa awoke with a start. Without a blindfold for the first time in days, the sudden brightness forced her to close her eyes. She opened them again, but slowly, and only enough to see what was happening. She felt a weight and bulk move against her right side. In waking she'd jerked, and apparently her escort had noted this fact.

"Welcome back to the world of the living, Mrs. Dillon," said a familiar male voice.

Melissa cringed. It hadn't been a nightmare after all. The man speaking was the same one who'd been with her in the rear of the moving van. Now she found herself once more in a moving vehicle, this time an automobile. She was in the backseat. But she could see—not well, but she could see. It was as though she were looking through a Halloween mask, a slitted view of the world. She saw the man who'd approached her in the parking garage seated behind the wheel driving, but now he was dressed in some type of robe and wore a headdress she'd heard Patrick refer to as a towel. So they were Middle Eastern. And apparently she was in the Middle East. In the post-9/11 free world, someone who didn't want to attract attention wouldn't drive around in such garb.

"You have nothing to say after almost two days of slumber?"

Melissa turned and looked at the man next to her. He also was dressed in Middle Eastern robes and headdress. "Where am I? Why have you taken me?"

The man laughed. "In time, my beauty. In time."

Melissa Dillon tried to move her hands, but they were bound together in her lap. Looking down, she saw that she was wearing some type of black garment that was more or less a loose-fitting robe. Her bound hands could not be seen within the robe's folds. She suddenly realized why her sight was hindered—she must be wearing the headdress commonly worn among Arab women. It would conceal her auburn hair such that, from a glance, no one would realize she was a Westerner.

"Should you decide to voice an outcry," said the driver, his eyes meeting hers in the rearview mirror, "I assure you that my associate will cuff you into unconsciousness. And no one will think twice seeing an Arab man disciplining his wife."

So Melissa Dillon sat back and waited. And finally she saw that they were entering a walled compound.

Chapter 11

In Country

Baghdad International Airport (BIAP)
Secured Military Entry Area
Baghdad, Iraq

Luke Dodd and Rolf Krieger stepped off of the C-130 aircraft's rear ramp and into fading sunlight, both wearing desert utility uniforms with no name tapes, unit patches, or other identifying insignia. They knew they were in Baghdad only because the flight crew they'd met on the ground at Al Udeid had deigned to tell them that was their destination. They still hadn't been briefed on the details of the upcoming mission.

Krieger stared at the barren landscape, a few scrub palms the only vegetation. "The more time I spend in this part of the world, the more I love it," murmured the big German-American officer, hands on hips.

Luke looked around. "I've spent most of my career in other . . . parts of the world. You really *like* the Middle East?"

Krieger shook his head. "No, not really. It sucks. So, when do we find out why we're here?"

Dodd looked down the airstrip. A white Toyota Land Cruiser with its spare tire mounted to the hood was moving toward them. "I think right about now."

The SUV pulled to a stop at the back of the ramp. Two men exited the vehicle. Both wore denim jeans, desert boots, and black fleece pullovers. They walked to the Air Force NCO who was the aircraft's loadmas-

ter and took possession of the equipment bags Dodd
and Krieger had picked up at Fort Bragg, as well as
their personal gear contained in two duffel bags. The
passenger left the loading to the driver. He approached and stopped in front of the two new arrivals.
He did not offer his hand, but he did take off his
mirrored Oakley wraparounds and nod.

"I'm Captain Jack Kelly." Although not quite as
large, Kelly could have been Krieger's brother, except
with longer hair. Tall, blond, broad shoulders, thick
arms, narrow waist. He had a no-nonsense air about
him that was pure operator. The captain nodded at his
companion, a bald, black giant carrying the equipment
bags, each weighing in excess of two hundred pounds,
as though they were filled with goose down. "That's
Chief Warrant Officer Three Jon Dell."

Dell threw the baggage into the rear of the Land
Cruiser, slammed the hatch shut, and slowly turned.
He took a good look at Krieger, ignoring Luke Dodd.
Then he walked over and stood in front of the lieuten-
ant, hands on hips, their faces mere inches apart. Not
many men could look Krieger in the eye, nor present
him with a challenge when it came to sheer muscle.
Dell did.

With no warning the big warrant officer threw himself at Rolf Krieger, grabbing his head in a headlock
with a massive arm. A split second later Dell was on
the ground, Krieger kneeling on his chest, a black
knife at the warrant officer's throat.

"Still carrying that Carson M-16, I see, Wolf," Dell
rasped through clenched teeth. "Now could you get
off of me, please? You haven't gotten any lighter over
the years, man. In fact, I think you put on a few
pounds."

Krieger flicked the Carson closed as he stood. He
grinned—a first in Luke Dodd's experience with the
man—and reached down a hand to haul Dell from
the ground.

"I take it this is the same Krieger you knew?" said Kelly dryly.

Dell rubbed his neck with the back of a hand and winced. "Oh yeah. This is the Wolf, all right."

"The Wolf?"

Dell laughed from deep in his chest. "Yeah. We used to call him Arno—well, something else. He didn't like it much, so we went with the Wolf, 'cause he was one sneaky and deadly motherfucker in the field."

Krieger nodded at Dodd. "This is Luke Dodd. He works for one of those 'Other Government Agencies.' Luke, this is Chief Dell. We taught at the Scout Platoon Leader Course at Fort Knox together a few years back. That was before Dell sold out the Cav and decided he wanted to be Rambo."

Dell held out a massive paw to Dodd. "Oh, we've been briefed on *you*, Mr. Dodd."

"Good to meet you, Chief," said Luke, extending his hand. He winced. "And that's my shooting hand, so take it easy, okay?" He smiled. "I'm a lover, not a fighter."

The warrant officer laughed again, dropping Dodd's hand. "That's not what I hear, Mr. Dodd. Word about Russia made its way to us. That was some fine work, my friend."

Luke Dodd's face reddened. "It sounds to me as though someone's mouth got away from them." Operational security was what kept field officers alive. Thus, when someone in the rear with the gear flaps their mouth to show how in the know they are, it angered men like Luke Dodd. He didn't want to end up a star on the wall at Langley.

The smile disappeared from Dell's face. "Take it easy, Spooky. It was a pull from our end."

"I don't give a shit how—"

"And it came from your brother."

"My brother?" Luke shook his head in disbelief. "He wouldn't—"

Kelly cut in. "Yeah. He would. Look, we had to see your bona fides, so to speak, before we'd even consider taking you with us on an op. We're a tight team and last-minute changes make us nervous. Comprende, amigo?"

Luke Dodd nodded reluctantly. "Yeah, I suppose I do." He pointed at one of his hosts, then the other. "But quit calling me Spooky."

"So you called by anything else, Secret Squirrel Man?" asked Dell.

Luke thought of telling them his real code name, Archangel, but changed his mind. First, the fewer people who associated it with him, the better. Second, the testosterone-laden trio facing him would manage to put an unmanly spin on it. So he shook his head. "No."

"Well, it's our team's custom that everybody gets a name, and Chief Dell does the naming . . . so you're Spooky."

Dell smiled.

Kelly looked Luke Dodd over carefully and finally nodded. "Yep. Spooky works." He moved around the Toyota and climbed into the passenger seat. "Let's move. I want to be back at the CJSOTF headquarters before dark." Pronounced "see-jay-so-tuf," the acronym stood for Combined Joint Special Operations Headquarters, which indicated these men were American Special Forces troops, otherwise known as Green Berets, snake eaters, the quiet professionals, warrior diplomats, and, last but not least . . . sneaky petes.

The men piled into the vehicle, Dell behind the wheel.

"Hey, Bull," Krieger said from the backseat. "You went SF? I thought you were trying to get on with that *other* group when you left Knox for Fort Bragg." The unit Krieger referred to was the Army's 1st Special Forces Operational Detachment—D, better known as Delta Force. Though few details were known regarding the organization other than within a few close military and government circles, far *too* much was known about them and their methods as far as Delta was concerned. A couple of books written by former Delta members who should have known better—to include Delta's founding officer, Colonel Charles Beckwith—made the publicity even less palatable.

Another deep laugh rumbled from Dell. "I did. Thought I'd kicked ass, too. I outmarched, outshot, outfought, and outnavigated every man in the Assessment and Selection Course." The warrant officer looked into the rear seat toward Krieger. "And I'm a smart son of a bitch, too. You *know* that's the truth, Wolf."

Krieger smiled. "Yes. And modest as well. So what happened?"

A string of curses erupted from Dell as he slammed his hamlike fists into the steering wheel.

Kelly turned, a smile on his face for the first time. "He failed the psychological evaluation."

"Psychological evaluation, my *ass*. It was *bullshit*, man, that's what it was!" yelled the big warrant officer, reentering the fray. "What kind of test asks a man if he played with dolls *more often than other kids his age* when he was young? Huh? Let's assume for the sake of argument that some dude, a stone-cold-stud kinda dude, grew up in a houseful of sisters. What the hell was I supposed to do, man? Huh!? And I'll tell you something else. I seen studies—*scientific studies*— that have proven that men who were exposed to that kind of thing as children are better adapted than all them boys playing cowboys and Indians. It's a global village, ya know, Wolf . . . a *global fuckin' village*. We don't need all that aggression being trained at such a young age. Bound to fuck them boys up."

"Dolls. That explains a great deal," said Krieger, nodding and managing to keep a straight face. "A very great deal."

Dell slammed on the brakes, skidding the big SUV

to a halt in a cloud of dust. He closed his eyes and spoke softly between clenched teeth. "Don't make me pull you out this truck and whup your big ass, Wolf. Swear to God I'll do it, man. I like you, but I'll do it."

"Move out, Chief," said Kelly quietly, but with steel behind the words. As the Toyota picked up speed the captain stared through the front window. "So, are we talking standard Barbies, or those ugly Cabbage Patch things?"

Dell's black fingers paled as he clenched the steering wheel in an iron grip. "Don't push me, Sonny," he said in a controlled voice, shaking his head. "That was just *wrong*, man."

The other three men burst out laughing. After a few moments of colorful swearing, CW3 Dell joined in.

Kelly turned to look at Krieger. "The committee actually liked the big brute quite a bit. They wanted him, but their hands were tied. They called my boss down at Third Group, thought maybe we had a place for a big, smart bag of hot air. So we put him to work at Bragg until our next assessment course came around. Bull passed it with flying colors and went on to graduate the prelim training and the Q-Course near the top of his group," he added, referring to the initial phases of Special Forces training taught at the John F. Kennedy Special Warfare Center and School.

The assessment phase involves hellish land navigation courses up to fifty kilometers in length, timed, of course. The candidates carry their weapon and a ruck that gets heavier and heavier as the course goes on. Once past assessment, the students move to Phase I training that teaches skills in such areas as patrolling, small-unit tactics, cross-country navigation, and special operations techniques—the basics. Then they go on to learn their career management field (CMF) 18 specialties in Phase II. The students are assigned and qualified as an 18B (weapons sergeant), 18C (engineer sergeant), 18D (medical sergeant), or 18E (communications sergeant). At a later date they cross-train to learn another specialty so their team has redundancy. The officers go through 18A trainer, teaching them the skills necessary to become a detachment commander. Then comes the final phase, the Special Forces Qualification Course, or Q-Course, as it's popularly known. The field training exercise integrates and reinforces both the specialty and common skills training the candidates learned in the prior phases. Organized into operating detachments, the soldiers practice all the training previously received in a realistic environment. They are forced to deal with simulated guerrillas, as they would in a real operational situation. They are hunted by "enemy" forces and attack targets manned by live defenders. Upon finishing the field exercise, the students are ready for the operations they will conduct after graduation as members of one of the Special Forces groups. And only then are they issued their green berets.

"I thought Third Group was responsible for Africa?" Krieger remarked.

The captain nodded. "Yeah, but with all the activity in Iraq and Afghanistan, we had to let all the groups share the pie." He laughed dryly. "There's plenty to go around."

A thought struck Krieger and he turned to Jack Kelly, recognition dawning. "You're Sergeant Major Jack Kelly's son, aren't you, Captain?"

That perked Luke's interest. "The same Captain Kelly that captured the Iraqi president a couple of years ago?" The photo of the blond Airborne trooper had been spread across the cover of *USA Today*, full color. Few had missed it. Or the irony that Jack Kelly, Sr., sergeant major, U.S. Army, had been the war's first American casualty.

The SF officer nodded. "Yeah, that was a long time ago. I was a company commander in the Three-twenty-fifth then." He sat silently for a few moments before continuing. "It was hard after Dad died. When I first found out—I mean, hell, we were in the middle of a shooting war. And then I came home." Again, silence. "After that I needed a change, but I couldn't see leaving the military. So . . . I decided to go SF."

No one said anything for a few minutes. It was Rolf Krieger who broke the silence. "Captain?"

Kelly turned. "Yes?"

"I knew your father well, sir. He was a good man." It was enough.

Kelly nodded. "Thanks." He turned back to stare out the front window.

Rolf Krieger nodded, and thinking it was time to change the subject, said, "So how are you liking the new line of work, Bull? You were a hell of a scout—not as good as me, but good. I hated to see you go."

"Yeah, I dug the scout thing, man," Dell said and laughed. "But I was ready to move on and try something different, you know, man?"

"Not really," replied Krieger seriously. He couldn't imagine doing anything in the Army other than scouting. It had occupied most of his adult life, and he was so very good at it. A general watching Krieger's platoon in action at Fort Irwin's National Training Center had once remarked that few people were fortunate enough to have a natural gift—like Albert Einstein's mind, Babe Ruth's bat, or Ernest Hemingway's pen. But Rolf Krieger leading a team of scouts in a tactical environment, it was a beautiful thing to behold.

"You wait, man, until you meet the rest of the team," Dell said. "You might just change your mind. And hey, when did you pin on that bar, man?"

"During the war. My lieutenant was promoted to company commander before the final offensive. They decided to give me the platoon, and the bar to go with it."

Dell nodded. "Yeah, that was some shit," he said quietly, referring to the war in Iraq against the Russians and Saudis.

"You were there?"

Dell nodded again. "Yeah, me and Jack here, along

with the other boys, were sent to Saudi. We flew in just as the first Russian armor was crossing the Saudi border into Iraq—High Altitude–High Opening night jump. Man, seemed like we was gliding forever, couldn't hear nothin' but the wind. Won't shit for a moon, either. Anyway, we set up on a few rooftops around Riyadh and hunkered down over our satellite radios and lasers." He laughed. "Can't get precision munitions on them Saudi palaces without somebody on the ground to guide the big boys in." The operator shook his head. "Shit was a trip, my man. A fuckin' *trip.*"

Luke Dodd had listened to the talk silently, taking it in, getting a feel for the two men in the front of the vehicle, and for Rolf Krieger. If Krieger was known to men such as these, he *was* good. Luke leaned forward from the rear seat. "So, when do we find out what the hell it is that we're about to do?"

Kelly half turned. "First, let me be perfectly frank, gentlemen. The decision for you to go in has not been made."

"You know, Duke . . . ," began Luke Dodd.

"It's Jack, or Captain Kelly," corrected the captain.

"You don't have a handle like everyone else?"

Kelly shook his head. "Jack works for me."

Dell snuffled. "Of course we have a name for old Jack. Otherwise he wouldn't feel the love."

Kelly rankled. "Bull . . ."

Dell was smiling ear to ear. "We call him Sonny Boy."

"Dammit, Chief . . ."

" 'Cause every NCO in the Army knew his daddy."

Kelly sat in the passenger seat, eyes once more roving the road ahead of them. "Just Sonny is fine," he said through clenched teeth. "And, Chief, you might spend a little more time keeping your eyes open for IEDs and a little less flapping your gums," he added.

"He don't like it much," Bull Dell added with a straight face. He then took a quick scan of the shoulder of the road because Kelly had a point. Improvised Explosive Devices, or IEDs, were the biggest threat allied troops and the Iraqi soldiers and police faced these days. It only took one asshole with a stash of old howitzer rounds, mortars, or other ordnance to make a nice little surprise for passing vehicles or foot patrols. In the first days of the war with Iraq the goobers had placed the devices beneath piles of rocks. A decent technique, but one that U.S. troops caught on to quickly. Then the local zealots had gotten creative. Dead animals were nothing out of the ordinary on Iraq's roads—not surprising considering most of Baghdad's citizenry drove with a vigor that would do the Dukes of Hazard proud. So stuff a dog's or goat's body with ten pounds of boom-boom and wait for the nasty Americans to drive by. There were variations, of course, once soldiers caught on to the change in modus operandi, so the deviations continued. Dell shook his head. If the indigenous terrorists put half the time into getting their country back on its feet that they took in trying to tear it apart from the inside, Iraq would be the jewel of the Middle East.

"So," said Krieger, "when do we find out what this mission's about?"

Kelly looked in the direction of his second in command.

"Tell 'em," said Dell, not taking his eyes from the road.

For the next five minutes Kelly did just that.

"So we don't even know where Dillon and Crockett are? Or the Tommies?" asked Krieger.

"Mr. Dodd's brother had a pretty good idea we were dealing with the Iranians," said Kelly. "So he focused a lot of national assets in that region. One of his men, guy who goes by the handle Ali, thinks he's found our boys. But no sign of the vehicles yet."

Luke Dodd thought about the name . . . Ali. Yes, that was it. George Greenfield. Thirty-two years old, graduate of Dartmouth. Had a chance to play pro football. He'd been an All-American tight end his final two years, catching passes from none other than ex-Dolphin Jay Fiedler—but had blown out his knee at the North-South game in Alabama. So George had taken his Ivy League degree and gone to the Central Intelligence Agency. He and Luke had gone through the Farm at the same time and had become friends. Though they'd lost contact as the years passed, Luke had kept up with George through his brother and knew he'd been working Tehran for the past year. A tough assignment for anyone, particularly tough for a Jew who knew what would happen to him if he were captured. Bottom line, George was a first-class ops officer.

"If it's coming from Ali, it's good intel," said Luke.

"You know him?"

Luke nodded.

"Well, your boy should be meeting with his source"—Kelly glanced at his watch, a huge black Suunto monstrosity roughly the size of a saucer that was the favorite of operators, as it was free. It had altimeter and navigational features, plus it was tough as hell—"right about now. Hopefully he will then be able to confirm the location of our targets."

"Assuming that's the case, when do we go in?" asked Krieger.

"*Whether or not* you go in is my call, Lieutenant," said Kelly quietly, not so subtly reminding Krieger of the rank structure and where he stood in it.

The big scout was silent for a few moments before replying. "Captain, you seem to be a good man. And I respected your father a great deal. But I know Major Dillon. I have met his daughters." He leaned forward. "And I *will* be with whatever team goes in after him. With you or without you."

Kelly sneered. "That's *my* A-Team, mister. Why the hell wouldn't I be with them?"

"It is difficult to participate in an operation from the infirmary ward," said Krieger without the slightest hint of a threat in his voice.

Kelly stared intently at the brash junior officer in the backseat. And then he burst out laughing. "*Jesus*, Bull. You weren't kidding about this cowboy, were you?"

"Tried to tell you he had more piss 'n' vinegar in him than a horny bobcat, Sonny," drawled the big warrant officer. He shook his head. "Fuckin' Wolf. Some things never change, man."

"You were joking?" asked Krieger, surprise evident on his face . . . and a little anger.

"Sure," Kelly said. He looked back at Krieger. "Weren't you?"

Krieger said nothing, instead staring stonily at the Special Operations officer.

"All right, the bottom line is that you're a go for the mission," said Kelly. "But understand, gentlemen, this is our op. If I didn't think the two of you added to the mission's chance of success, I'd have your asses on a plane back to Qatar faster than a Bragg Boulevard hooker can snatch a PFC's end-of-month paycheck."

"And that's pretty damn quick," muttered Bull Dell knowingly.

"I'm in charge, I give the orders," continued Kelly. He swiveled his head to look between the two men. "Can you deal with that?"

Krieger and Dodd nodded in unison, though it was clear that neither liked the idea of being shackled to the orders of someone they hadn't worked with.

"All right then," said Kelly with a nod. "Let's find out where these fuckers have stashed our boys."

Bull Dell nodded, his eyes never leaving the road, his voice holding the note of true conviction. "And then we're going to bring their asses *out*."

Chapter 12

Family Ties

Institute for Plant and Seed Modification Research
Employee Prayer Room
Karaj, Iran
Maghrib (Sunset Prayer Hour)

"So, old man, what did you find out?" Monsoor's words sounded disrespectful, but they were delivered with warmth and a twinkle in the eyes.

The old man—he could have been any age between fifty and seventy—leaned back on his heels, an intricate prayer rug beneath him. He did not take his eyes from the distance in front of him. Still, he smiled.

He and Monsoor had remained behind at the end of the *Maghrib* prayers, the fourth set they'd offered this day. They would say the fifth and final prayers, the *Isha*, or evening prayers, before retiring for the night, taking time to remember Allah's presence, guidance, mercy, and forgiveness. Then again, like many Iranians, they might not be as consistent in saying the prayers at home as they were when being observed by those in power. When the *Adhan*, the Islamic call to prayer, sounded at the institute, it was wise for one to heed its siren song. The institute's employees were state workers and the state had made its wishes clear.

As the last of the workers filed from the room, the old man spoke. "Monsoor, that a good boy would speak in such a way to his elders." He tsked quietly. "It is shameful."

"I am curious. Did my father act as shamefully, wise one?" asked Monsoor.

"You acknowledge the intelligence my years on this earth have endowed upon me." He sighed. "Perhaps there is hope for you." Again the shade of a smile crossed the old man's lips. "Doubtful, but perhaps. Allah is good, Allah is all, His will be done."

"And my father? Your brother's son?"

"You have heard many times the stories of your father's youth as told from these same lips." The old man paused and looked skyward, shaking his head at the heavens in apparent misery. "Your father—it is a miracle that he survived to sire children."

Monsoor smiled. "But he did."

The old man looked to his young companion. "And before my eyes is the result of that miracle of Allah. And to think our bloodline might end with you. What a shame that would be. An event too terrible to think upon."

They sat in companionable silence for a few more moments. Both knew to stay too long would raise suspicions. Then the old man nodded to himself, his decision made. "I have the information you seek, Monsoor," the uncle said quietly. "But I must ask, what is its importance to *you*?"

Monsoor looked toward the floor and closed his eyes. Finally he spoke in subdued tones. "I would rather not say, Uncle. It is better that way."

The old man's name was Kaspar. He nodded once. "I know that life has not treated our family kindly, Monsoor. We are taught from infancy that the ways of Allah are not always clear. Even so, the loss of your father . . ." The old man broke off. "Your father was the son I never had. When my brother died, I tried to become a father to him."

Monsoor's eyes moistened. "He loved you, Uncle. You know that. No son could love a father more than he loved you."

Kaspar nodded, a sad smile playing across his lips.

"I admit that I am at a loss to understand how taking such a good man from this world, from his family, so early . . . well, how it can be part of God's plan. And I look around us now, at the crimes taking place in Iran in the name of religion." The old man's hands clenched into fists. "It angers me so, and I confess I fail to see His will in this as well." Kaspar's voice choked off for a moment before continuing. "But I must believe His will is being done. I *must*."

"Why do you not leave this place, Uncle?" whispered Monsoor, opening his eyes and glancing sideways to ensure himself no one was attempting to overhear their conversation. "There are ways."

Kaspar shook his head. "Those ways are difficult on one as old as I," he said. "Besides, things are changing, even as we speak."

"I tire, Uncle, of hearing how things will change," said the nephew in an angry hiss. "The president and other reformers win more and more seats in the Parliament, but the church has already disqualified over *seven hundred* winners—all reformers. Those who would see change somehow *still* manage to win more seats at every vote, but they do nothing once in office because they fear the consequences. The ayatollah and his mullahs are the power, Uncle; that never changes. What the clerics want—no matter how different from the desires of their people—is what will be. They talk condescendingly of businessmen in the West, those with money and power taken at their people's expense, and I tell you, Uncle, *they are no better*. The ayatollah and his mullahs isolate themselves from the people . . . and they isolate Iran from the world." Monsoor shook his head. "And now they play games with the United Nations regarding nuclear capabilities. It seems it is not enough to have us under their heel, they are determined to see us dead."

Kaspar stood and slowly rolled his prayer rug, securing it closed with a thin strip of leather. "I see that you have your father's sense of justice. That is admirable,

Nephew. It also got your father killed. All because he would not leave Iran when he could. Because he wanted to stay to help his country out of a crisis."

Monsoor rose. "And I learned a lesson from my father, Uncle. Not to assume that our religious leaders are to be trusted, nor that they speak for God. They speak for themselves."

The old man nodded and turned, at the same time slipping a rolled set of light blue sheets of paper from his sleeve into the end of Monsoor's rug. "I have marked the location of the interrogation room where the American major is being held."

The younger man's jaw dropped. He had told his uncle nothing other than that he needed to know if two prisoners were being held in the institute and if so, where. "How did you know . . . ?"

"I am an old man, but I have worked within these walls for many years." He chuckled softly. "Even during the days when *seed research* was still the primary work being conducted here."

Monsoor shook his head. "Uncle, I am afraid that you have delved too deeply into this matter. Should those in charge find out you've taken blueprints—"

"Monsoor," Kaspar softly interrupted. "Again, I am an old man. My dear sister-in-law and my beloved niece and nephew are all I care about now. I have lived a long life, and if I died tomorrow, I would die happy knowing their futures were secure. For I know that this is the only reason you would ask for such information." His brown eyes twinkled in the room's subdued light. "Besides, I took some care. I am not stupid, Nephew—with years comes caution."

Before Monsoor could say more, Kaspar continued. "As I said, the room in which the major is being held is marked with an x. There is a makeshift infirmary two doors further down the hallway from this room. They have been moving additional medical equipment and supplies into that room all day. The other American is whispered to be in poor physical condition." He frowned, knowing the character of the guards assigned to the lowest level of the institute. "I can only imagine why. Still, he may be in the infirmary. It is marked with a double x."

"Have you heard whispers of military equipment, Uncle?"

The old man shook his head. "I have heard that some type of shipment is en route, but no more. I do not believe it has arrived."

Monsoor nodded. "Very well." He reached out and silently took the old man's hand, grasping it hard. "Thank you, Uncle."

Kaspar shook his head and gripped the younger man's hand with a strength that belied his years. "There is more, Nephew."

"More?"

Kaspar nodded in distaste. "They are holding a woman as well."

"A woman? But I have heard nothing of this from—"

The old man pulled his hand away from his nephew's and held it up. "No. I do not want to know to whom you are delivering this information. Though I could guess." He smiled. "But yes, I am certain regarding this. A woman is being held on the third level along with the other two captives. A Western woman."

Two hours later Monsoor sat at the same table he and the man known to him as Ali had previously shared. He sipped his tea nervously and watched as passersby entered and exited the illumination of nearby streetlamps. He kept an eye on the few who loitered, for all appearances browsing at the market stalls still open after sunset. And he watched two sets of people as well—one a couple, the other two old men—who had stopped to chat in the pleasantly cool early-evening air. He glanced at his watch. Ali was fifteen minutes late—the maximum time he was to wait. He was told if this occurred to go with the fall-back plan—they would meet at a rug merchant's store two blocks to the north tomorrow at the same time. He nodded to himself, his decision to leave made. He took a final sip of his tea as he stood to leave. A hand touched his shoulder and hot liquid scalded Monsoor's lower jaw and chest as he jumped.

"By the *prophet's beard*!" he said, spinning around and seeing who was there. "I am certain I look suspicious enough as it is! Do not do that again."

George Greenfield, a.k.a. Ali, smiled and withdrew his hand. "I did not mean to startle you, Monsoor. I assure you the area is clear."

The young man scowled, still irked. "Perhaps I should begin meeting you after the assigned time, as it seems you are always late."

Greenfield turned serious. "Nothing personal. But I do not know you, Monsoor. And I wasn't late—I had this area under surveillance two hours before you arrived."

Monsoor shook his head in disgust. He was not cut out for these cat-and-mouse spy games. "Very well, let us walk toward the river, two old friends chatting."

George Greenfield nodded at the rolled rug Monsoor had picked up from the table and placed beneath his arm. "Off to the mosque after our meeting?"

The Iranian smiled. "Why no. As a matter of fact, it is a gift for *you*, my new friend. Consider it an introduction to the true religion of Islam."

His companion nodded understanding. "My thanks in advance. So—what were you able to discover? Time may be critical."

It took but a few minutes to relay what Monsoor had learned from his uncle and to explain the marked blueprints nestled within the prayer rug. And then the Iranian passed on the final piece of information his uncle had imparted.

Greenfield shook his head in bewilderment. "A woman? You're certain?"

Monsoor nodded. "Yes. My source is reliable."

A thoughtful look passed over the Agency officer's face. If he'd had doubts about Monsoor before, they were evaporating. If the Iranians were setting him up, they'd keep it simple. Pass on the information—or at least part of it—that they knew he wanted, but no more. They wouldn't complicate the scenario with something like this.

"What of my mother and sister?" continued Monsoor. "When do they leave Iran—and how?"

The American shook his head. "These things take time, Monsoor. You've got to understand that."

The Iranian stopped walking in mid-stride. He stood on the sidewalk, staring at the American's back until Greenfield stopped and turned. Once he had the American's attention, he spoke slowly and deliberately. "I am a man of my word. I trust that you are as well, Ali."

The agent walked back and put his arm through the younger man's in the manner of the region. They continued their stroll, arms linked. Greenfield leaned over and spoke quietly into the younger man's ear. "You will have the details within twenty-four hours."

A doubtful look crossed the Iranian's face.

This time it was the American who stopped. Withdrawing his arm, he held out his hand. "You have my word. You don't know me, but in the circles of people who do, my promise is not taken lightly."

Monsoor took the outstretched hand and gripped it firmly. "I am trusting in you, my friend. With the things I love most in this world, I am trusting you."

George Greenfield nodded grimly. One more responsibility placed on his shoulders. As if he didn't have enough to worry about in getting an A-Team into Iran, rescuing *three* hostages, as it now stood, trying to locate the prototype American vehicles, and getting the team and the hostages out. All in a country in which 90 percent of the population would like to see him flayed because he occasionally wore a yarmulke. He shook his head. He would much rather be standing in the pocket under a collapsing offensive line with a 280-pound defensive end thundering down on him.

Institute for Plant and Seed Modification Research
Employee Prayer Room
Karaj, Iran

Three blocks distant a phone rang in the institute's subterranean depths. "Yes?" said Sergei Sedov, sipping from a very difficult to obtain bottle of Stolichnaya. It was almost as difficult to keep the vodka properly chilled as it was to obtain it in this pestilent land. To say the Iranian power grids were unreliable was being kind.

Sedov spun his chair to one side as he listened to the caller, a smile playing across his face. "When?"

"I should think two days," replied a male voice. "Three at the most."

The smile broadened. "Excellent. Keep me informed of progress."

Depressing the phone's hook flash, the Russian dialed an internal number. "I just received a call from Captain Rowhani regarding our recent equipment acquisition. The *Sword of Arabia* is through the Strait of Hormuz and will dock in Bushehr tomorrow evening. It will take a few hours to move the vehicles off the ship and onto their transport trucks, but they should be here within the next three days."

"Very good news, Colonel," replied the Ayatollah Khalani. A pause. "I also have news, but it is not so good as your own."

Sergei Sedov shrugged off the minor effects of the vodka. He knew the Iranian leader well enough by now to detect in his voice that something unplanned had occurred. "What is it?"

"It appears the Americans are assembling a team to reinitiate their M4 program sooner than we expected."

Sedov let the words sink in, thinking about what they meant. He'd personally planned the targets in the United States following the hijacking of the Tommies to ensure that it would be at least several months before the Americans could begin to get the program back on track. Still . . .

"I do not think it is anything to worry about," said the Russian finally. "But, as the Americans themselves say, better safe than sorry."

"I agree," came the Iranian's rasping reply.

Sedov shuddered inwardly. The man reminded him of a lizard in human form.

The ayatollah continued. "Our friend Bakr has returned from his sabbatical in the desert. I am going to put him on the problem. He should be able to buy us a few additional months by identifying and neutralizing the key player or players now in charge of the project."

Sedov poured and shot back another ounce of the Stolichnaya, wincing as the ice-cold alcohol rushed to his brain. Yes, the Iraqi was like a guided missile. How fortunate for them that they'd been able to convince him that the best way to strike at the Americans was to strike at the weapons system the United States military apparatus was placing so much stock in. The man had gone so far as to refuse payment for other than his expenses. Sedov grunted a laugh. Heaven—should such a place exist—save them from idealists. "A grand idea if you can locate the project's new base of operations. I am assuming it is no longer in Arizona."

Khalani smiled thinly, his papyrus-like skin stretching to the point that it looked as though it would tear. "Yes, it took some effort and the burning of a few long-emplaced assets in the United States, but we were able to ascertain the location."

"Then it should be a simple matter," replied the

Russian. "I am convinced the Iraqi is semi-insane, but you cannot argue with his results. If we had not sent him to Arizona with the hit team, both Dillon and Crockett would be dead."

"It is so," said Khalani, his tone indicating that the conversation was over and that he had made the decision to send Sayid Bakr *before* informing Sedov. "Now I believe it is time for you to report to the infirmary, is it not?"

Sedov threw back another shot of vodka and grimaced. "Yes, it is, Majesty. I was just preparing for the appointment when the call came in from our shipmaster."

"The best of fortunes," said Khalani, irritation in his voice as he ended the call. *What an insolent toad this Russian is*, thought the cleric. *But one day I will need him no longer.*

Sergei Sedov slowly refilled his glass, the bottle still cold to the touch. He looked around at the office's phone, bulky and antiquated automation equipment, and other furnishings, all circa 1960. He grimaced. "In this backward ass-wart of a country, I will need all the good fortune I can get." He laughed to himself. "I'm almost tempted to pray."

Combined Joint Special Operations Task Force (CJSOTF) Headquarters
Baghdad, Iraq

An athletic-looking Special Forces operator dressed in black fleece pullover, civilian trousers, and tan boots— apparently the standard uniform for Green Berets in theater—called out to Luke Dodd. "Mr. Dodd? You have a call, sir." He pointed to the secure Cisco IP phone in the corner of the operations center. "You can take it there."

The man's face and hands were sun- and wind-chapped, testament to the amount of time he'd spent in the field over the past months in-country. Luke had a hard time telling who held what rank at the CJSOTF, as no one wore any. The operators, officers and NCOs alike considered one another to be on equal footing.

"Thanks," Luke replied. Picking up his coffee, he walked to the phone and picked up the handset. "Go."

"Luke?" came a voice that was crystal clear despite the thousands of miles separating the callers. "It's Chris."

Luke Dodd smiled. "Well, now that I know what's going on, I guess I should send flowers or a thank-you ham to Langley," he said, the sarcasm heavy in his voice. "This is way more fun than frolicking on the ranch. *Way* more."

"I told you it was important, didn't I?" returned his brother.

Luke turned serious. "Yeah. Yeah, you did. And yes it is. All we're waiting for now is to find out if the location of Dillon and Crockett has been confirmed."

"That's why I'm calling. The CJSOTF staff is getting the word now, but I wanted to talk to you myself and let you know the situation has become more complicated."

The younger Dodd brother sighed. "I should know better than to ask, but how in the hell could it become any more complicated?"

"When our man in Iran sent us his report—by the way, you know it's George, right?"

"Yeah. I figured that much out. That's good news, at any rate. He's a first-class act in the field."

Dodd continued. "Yeah. Sometimes we manage, either by God's grace or through blind luck, to have the right guy in the right place when we need him. At any rate, George just informed us that there's a Western woman being held captive as well. Same facility, same area."

"A woman?" replied Luke in disbelief. "That makes no sense, Chris. Dillon and Crockett . . . yeah, I get that; whoever's working the Tommies needs the knowledge locked away in their heads. But why would they kidnap someone else? That complicates things, and that ain't smart in our business."

"I just got off the horn with Bill Jones to let him know that you and his boy would be going in with the snake eaters," replied Dodd. "He passed on a seeming nonrelated piece of information that actually shed light on our mystery hostage."

"I'm listening."

"We're pretty sure—hell, ninety-nine-point-nine percent sure—that Sergei Sedov is hip-deep with the Iranians on this one."

"Sedov? But I thought—"

"He was dead," interrupted Chris Dodd. "Yeah, a once popular theory." The CIA chief took a couple of minutes to bring Luke Dodd up to speed.

"All right, I got it. But what does Sedov have to do with our female hostage?" asked Luke.

"I don't know if you're aware of the shared history between Patrick Dillon and Sergei Sedov," Chris Dodd said. "During the war, it was Dillon who took Sedov down. Took him down *very* hard."

"I still don't see the connection," said Luke, confusion evident in his tired voice.

"Sedov needs leverage to get the Tommy codes from either Dillon or Crockett."

"Right. But what does that have to do with—"

"Luke," the CIA director interrupted, "listen to me. Melissa Dillon, Patrick Dillon's ex-wife, is missing."

A moment of silence filled the line connecting the brothers, finally broken by Luke. "Does Sedov know they're divorced?"

"Unknown, but does it matter?" replied Chris Dodd. "If a mad dog like Sedov thought he could get the codes and at the same time make Dillon suffer, he'd do it."

"Shit," breathed Luke, rubbing a hand across his beard-stubbled chin.

"Concur, baby brother. Concur."

Chapter 13

_____

_____

_____

Surgery Takes Many Forms

Institute for Plant and Seed Modification Research
Third Subterranean Level, Infirmary
Karaj, Iran

"Are you ready, Herr Colonel?" asked the doctor from behind Sedov's shoulder.

Sergei Sedov stared into the mirror intently. He looked at the macabre image that had replaced a visage he had once been so proud to show the world. Looking to the right he saw the reflection of the German doctor's anxious face over his shoulder. He looked back to his battered visage. Once upon a time he had been vain about his looks, his body. But that damned dog and Patrick Dillon had remedied that—the dog had mangled his face, Dillon his body. Once he fell from the wall, none of the Iranian-provided surgeons had yet managed to put him back together again. Perhaps the German could. Perhaps. It was clear he was delighted with the idea of beginning the surgery. This was a great adventure for the fat turd, otherwise he wouldn't look so absurdly happy.

"You see, Colonel," the surgeon pandered, "you presented me with quite a dilemma. Never in my thirty years of experience—short of a patient who had rampant cancer in the nasal region—have I seen such tissue loss."

"It was more than 'tissue loss,' Doctor," muttered Sedov, his voice slurred from his earlier self-medication. "My nose, for all intents and purposes, is *fucking gone!*"

"Exactly," said the doctor, taking a half step back. "Not only is the majority of the original tissue missing, but it was removed in such a traumatic fashion that it left the site . . . *difficult* to work with at best. Practically unviable."

The Russian thought back to that fateful day in Iraq's western desert, what should have been—what *had been* until *that dog* showed up—his moment of greatest glory. The T-90 main battle tanks of his regiment, the most modern pieces of ground hardware in Mother Russia's inventories, had blown through the battered vehicles of America's famed 1st Cavalry Division. The American cavalry had manned what was said to be the most high-tech military systems in the world. Those systems had rained hell on the first echelons of Russian units moving into Iraq. By the time Sedov's regiment came into their range, the Americans were out of both ammunition and fuel. Then, when the cavalrymen were surrendering, like a Great White scenting blood in the water and seeing weak prey, Sedov and his unit went into a feeding frenzy, killing everything and everyone in sight.

And then that damnable dog—Sedov could still feel the white-hot pain of the animal's teeth locked onto his nose, its neck thrashing back and forth in an effort to detach it from his face. He could feel the hard desert scrabble beneath his shoulders as he flailed on his back and attempted to dislodge the beast as his world simultaneously sped into super-quick motion and a series of still shots.

The Russian shook his head. At least the hound from hell was dead. His gunner had machine-gunned the terrier in the day's last dying light as it fled east.

For the first time Sergei Sedov wondered about that. His gunner had raked their tank's 7.62mm coaxial machine gun back and forth across the desert floor, zigzagging the turret as the Russian sergeant had followed the dog's erratic escape route. In retrospect, it seemed a coincidence of some proportion that the gunner's claim that he had hit the animal corresponded so nicely with his machine gun running out of ammunition. Sedov forgave himself for not thinking of it at the time . . . he was in significant pain, was trying to bandage his face, and, most important, he had more Americans to kill.

The surgeon brought him back to the moment. "Another problem with this procedure were those— how do the Americans say it?—*quacks* that your benefactors brought in to clean up the mess. They did quite a job on you, Colonel." This last was delivered with deadpan sarcasm.

"What?" asked Sedov in surprise.

The German folded his pudgy fingers together in front of him over his belly and his voice took on a lecturing tone. "Patients presenting for nasal reconstruction vary widely, Colonel," he began. "On one end of the spectrum are the patients with insignificant defects; in such cases the surgeon may elect to recommend a nonsurgical treatment. Small defects of the *medial canthus* are often successfully treated with second-intention healing." The doctor paused before moving on to the more important point he was trying to make. "On the opposite end of the spectrum are patients who present following subtotal nasectomy, where a majority of the cutaneous surface of the lower nose is missing, along with a variable amount of underlying support. These patients generally require a multiple-stage procedure over many months. Most patients fall between these extremes. You, Colonel Sedov," he concluded, "fall into the latter category. And as I have stated, your case—because of prior medical blunders—is made all the more difficult."

Medical blunders? Sedov made a mental note to come back to that remark, but he had more immediate concerns. "Was it not explained that I do not have *months*, Doctor? I was told that you could take care of my—problem—in a single surgery with only minor follow-up."

The German's belly shook slightly as he laughed. "That is exactly why I was called, Colonel. I have been pioneering new surgical techniques. Through my work with cadavers. . . ."

"Cadavers?" said Sedov in revulsion. "Do not even think that I will allow you to taint my body in such a manner, Doctor."

The German surgeon heard the threat in his patient's voice. "No, no, Colonel. I assure you that this will not be the case. What I was trying to explain is that I used them extensively in my surgical research for the technique we will be using."

Sedov stared at the man behind his shoulder. "So long as we understand one another, Doctor. Now, about these surgical blunders . . . I was assured the best plastic surgeons in Europe were brought in to perform the surgeries."

The German laughed. "*Scheisse*. The *best*? The best available perhaps. I understand that one of the conditions in accepting your position at the institute was an agreement on the part of the Iranians that they would take care of the operations before you began performing your, ah, *duties and services* here—whatever they may be." It was clear that the German did not know, nor did he care, what it was that Sergei Sedov did for the Iranians. So long as he was paid.

The Russian bent over the porcelain sink beneath the mirror. His knuckles turned white as he quietly seethed at this news. *"Nyet,"* he breathed. One more strike against his Iranian handlers.

Seeing how distressed his patient was becoming, the doctor backed off another half step. Like the rest of the world, he had seen the videos of Sedov's atrocities during the past war and had heard the term "mad dog" used more than once to describe the Russian. "No, no, Colonel," the surgeon mewled, "I am not being totally serious. You could say my words were more a matter of professional jealousy that I was not consulted to begin with. You understand what I mean, *ja*?"

Sedov reached down to a stainless steel tray and removed a shiny scalpel. Holding it at eye level, he slowly turned it so the ceiling's light caught on the blade. He held it thus for the better part of a minute before speaking to his companion. "And you, *Herr Doctor*, had better hope that they selected the right man for the job this time . . . *da*?"

The German paled visibly, his Adam's apple bobbed several times, and a light sheen of sweat broke out on his forehead before he managed to wheeze a single word. "*Ja*. . . . Uh, I mean *da*."

"Now for the other part of the operation," Sedov said, for all appearances once more in total control of himself. "You were briefed that I needed certain functionalities following the surgeries . . . how long?"

Dabbing himself with a handkerchief, the surgeon stuttered, "Th-that is one of the concerns I wanted to speak to you about before we began the procedure, Colonel. You must understand that carrying out a second surgery—especially another so specialized—at the same time as we work on your nose, it presents certain *hazards*." He smiled painfully at the Russian officer. "I was hoping to convince you to postpone the operation on your nose until later, perhaps in another month?"

"*Nyet!*" screamed Sedov, banging a fist into the mirror so hard that the glass shattered into a spiderweb pattern. "You will execute both surgeries, Doctor. *Today*." He held up the scalpel again. "Now answer my question."

"You should have the required functionality within twenty-four hours, though you may not have one hundred percent use of the organ for a few days," croaked the surgeon.

Sergei Sedov smiled. "Excellent. Now understand me, Herr Doctor. If you fail—on either surgery—you had better ensure that I die on the operating table."

Despite trying to hide it, a ray of hope, and perhaps calculation, crept into the fat German's eyes.

The Russian's smile broadened. "And, Doctor, if I die, I know exactly which guards the Holy One will turn you over to for some leisure time before your head is removed from your shoulders."

The light disappeared from the surgeon's eyes. It was all that he could do to manage a nod.

Civilian Personnel Office
Fort Bragg, North Carolina

Sayid Bakr rolled up his window with one hand as he interrupted a rivulet of sweat running down his forehead with the other. He then started the engine of the rental car and turned on the air conditioning. Despite the calendar saying that it was autumn, he'd quickly found upon landing that calendars didn't mean much in the American Southland. Yesterday had been a beautiful day with temperatures in the high sixties; today it was almost eighty degrees and humid.

A man of approximately forty years of age, dark-haired and dark-skinned, exited the front of the building Bakr had been surveilling. The Iraqi did not need to double-check the photo on the passenger seat to confirm that this was the man he'd been waiting for, but he was nothing if not thorough. Yes, that was his man. He watched as his target of interest moved toward the green Chevrolet Malibu the man had arrived in earlier. For the hundredth time since parking, Bakr glanced around the parking lot to ensure himself that he had not attracted undue attention . . . nothing. As the Malibu moved toward the parking lot's exit point, Sayid Bakr eased his own vehicle's transmission into gear and followed.

*   *   *

Twenty minutes later the green sedan pulled into a parking space at an apartment complex in Fayetteville, five miles outside of Fort Bragg's main gate. The man picked up a satchel and walked to the door of a first-floor unit, moments later letting himself in and closing the door.

Bakr gave the man ten minutes to settle down and then moved toward the apartment. He knocked lightly. No response. The Iraqi knocked a little harder, taking a quick glance to ensure no neighbors were watching.

The door opened and the man whose face looked so much like his own—at least to Westerners, who tended to think all dark-skinned people of Middle Eastern descent looked pretty much the same—smiled hesitantly. "Yes? Can I help you?"

Bakr grinned. *"Salaam,"* he said, extending his hand. "Peace."

The man returned the smile hesitantly as he took in his visitor. *"Salaam.* Can I help you in some way?"

Sayid Bakr's smile grew. "If I can have but a few moments of your time, yes, I believe you can help me greatly, my friend."

At a loss but not wanting to offend, the man stepped back into his apartment and gestured the stranger inside.

Bakr moved toward the door a half hour later. As he was about to open it, he stopped. Turning around, he moved the thermostat on the wall outside of the master bedroom. He turned it to its lowest setting. He did not want the corpse of his host ripening too soon and drawing attention if there were other scorching days to follow.

Letting himself out, the Iraqi once more looked about the apartment complex. Other than a mail truck servicing a multibox station fifty yards away at the other end of the grounds, no one was apparent. He opened the rental's door and slid into what he was beginning to think of as "the sweat box." *At least in Iraq it was a dry heat,* he mused. His years in New York had not prepared him for this. Bakr started the engine and drove to the rental agency he'd picked the car up from a week earlier. Going inside, he returned the inane smile of the female attendant behind the service counter.

"Good afternoon and thank you for choosing Thrifty! What can I do for you today?" the middle-aged blond woman asked and grinned.

Bakr took in the thick accent common in this region of the United States, the red eyeglasses the size of dinner plates, and the woman's fake nails, which appeared to be far overdue for maintenance. It took all of his considerable self-control to return what passed for a genuine smile. He slid his rental agreement across the counter. "I would like to exchange vehicles, please."

The woman looked alarm, her mouth dropping open and a forlorn expression crossing her face. "Oh my goodness! I hope there's not a problem with your car?"

"No, no, not at all. It is only that it is not, how do you say it . . . me?"

The woman's smile returned, large enough now that the nicotine stains on her teeth seemed to jump out at her customer. Bakr winced.

"Why, we can take care of that," she said, throwing a wink. "What did you have in mind?"

"I think I would like to try one of your four-wheel-drive vehicles. Preferably something in a dark color?"

Another wink. "You're going to fit in just fine down here, darlin'. Nothing like an SUV to make you look like a local."

"My thoughts exactly." Sayid Bakr grinned, with sincerity this time.

Combined Joint Special Operations Task Force (CJSOTF)
Headquarters
Team Ready Room
Baghdad, Iraq

"All right, gentlemen . . . ," began Jack Kelly.

"*Gentlemen*. He must be talkin' to the two new boys," interjected a soldier with brown hair, sideburns, and a semi-handlebar mustache. Like everyone else in the room he was dressed head to toe in a black one-piece, fire-resistant jumpsuit. The remark prompted snickers and catcalls from the team's other members.

"At ease, Catfish," Kelly directed the stocky operator, one of his two comms NCOs. He turned back to the room at large. "As I was about to say, we're on a shortened timeline. We've confirmed the location of the two hostages."

"Fuckin' ay," said a slight, mustachioed Hispanic soldier in a low tone. "Time to buy the baby some new chews, 'ey *'mano*?" he added, turning to his partner, a tall, bearded Anglo.

The bearded man turned to the speaker. "Vega, why don't you quit it with the barrio-speak? You've got a fucking degree in English lit, for Christ's sake." He shook his head in disgust. "Don't understand why you can't just be comfortable in your own skin."

"Listen, Lurch," replied Vega, reaching up to point a stiff index finger in the big man's lower sternum. "Don't tell me how and when I can fall back on my ancestry. Clear, *'mano*?"

The bearded soldier waved the hand away with a light swat. "Sure, sure, Hefe. Whatever you say, *mi wee amigo*."

"And don't patronize me, asshole."

"Ladies?" said Kelly. "If I may proceed? Not that I want to interrupt anything important."

Silence.

"All right, before we go over the plan, I want to

introduce you to the gentlemen who will be accompanying us on the mission.''

A man with a cleanly shaven head stepped forward. He was lean and dark-skinned, with a long, sharp nose that dominated his face. "I don't like this, Sonny," he said in a quiet voice. Despite the low tone, it was clear in the way that all heads turned to listen that the man's opinion carried a lot of weight with the team.

"We might as well start the introductions now," said Kelly. He hooked a thumb at the bald man. "This is Master Sergeant Neil 'Hawk' Davies. Hawk's our Team Sergeant, sometimes referred to as the Team Daddy. Hawk's the guy that really runs this team, but he's good enough to let Bull and me feel as though we're in charge when we're around."

Davies shook his head. "I'm not kidding, Cap. This is bullshit and you know it. Changing the team composition at the last minute is a recipe for the fuckup follies to begin." The dark-skinned man paused for effect before going on. "And fuckups mean body bags."

It struck Rolf Krieger as he listened to the master sergeant that what he'd heard about the SOF teams was true—the team members looked on one another as equals. In the regular Army, if an NCO, even a senior NCO, had stood up and spoken to his commander like Davies just had in front of that commander's troops, he'd have his balls handed to him on a platter.

"I hear what you're saying, Hawk," said Kelly. "Mr. Dodd here is a member of the Agency. Our point man on the ground is from the same organization and Dodd knows him."

Several of the men in the room nodded agreement. That turn of events was a definite plus.

"What about him?" asked Davies, pointing a finger at Krieger.

"I'll vouch for the Wolf," said Chief Dell. Normally

the big man's voice held a note of humor just below the surface. It was nowhere in evidence now.

The team's senior NCO stared at Dell for several long, silent seconds. Finally he nodded. "Okay." No resentment or anger in the master sergeant's voice. Dell knew the deal. If he said Krieger was good to go, Davies accepted him at his word.

A tall soldier with the build of a swimmer stepped forward and shook both Krieger's and Dodd's hand. "Jim Corbett," he said. "I'm the intelligence sergeant. I also help out Hawk here when he needs a hand."

"Gentleman Jim is also our best Arabic speaker," added Kelly. "We've all had some training, but Jim can speak several dialects like a local."

Corbett smiled. "It's a gift."

The Hispanic soldier and his bearded partner stepped forward. "Luis Vega," he said. "Friends call me Hefe. Me and Lurch—that's the tall ugly fucker here who's officially Staff Sergeant Will Purdue—are the weapons guys."

Even Krieger had to look up to see Purdue. The tall NCO grinned down at the newcomers. "If you have any equipment with the capability of being raised in anger, we're your men," he said in a baritone.

"Only reason I put up with the asshole is because he's good for carrying the heavy machine guns, mortars and such," added Vega, but it was clear that he and Purdue were tight.

The rest of the team filed forward.

"Crapper Taylor," said a bookish-looking operator. "Engineer. Me and Sergeant First Class Eastbrook are your builders and blowers."

Krieger and Dodd shook the demo men's hands. Krieger noted that between them there were sixteen fingers and four thumbs—a good sign that they took care when engaging in their trade. "Crapper?" asked Luke Dodd.

Taylor grinned ruefully. "Long story, boss."

"Rick Hill," said a tall and solid NCO whose sandy hair was beginning to look a little lean. "Senior medic."

"Let me guess," said Dodd. "They call you Doc, right?"

Hill's ears turned red. "Uhhh, no."

The other medic relieved Hill of the need for further clarification. "Steve Tice, Assistant Medical Sergeant," he said, shaking hands. "Rick's a little embarrassed about his handle. See, he's also got his nursing license. We call him Betty."

Hill grinned. "And Steve here is better known as Bedpan."

Bull Dell stepped forward. "Keep in mind, gentlemen, that not only can our docs save your ass on the battlefield, they're also trained to lead and train up to a company of indigenous troops in the field." He turned to the final two men who'd stepped up. "Same with our communicators," he said, nodding at the solid figure of the operator previously identified as Catfish and a red-haired and freckled man sporting a wispy beard.

The redhead stuck out his hand. "Mickey O'Riley," he said. "Call me Mick."

The other communication sergeant walked up. "Catfish Clayton," he said, pulling a dark plug of chewing tobacco from a pocket flap. He cut a chunk off with a very sharp-looking knife. Bringing the blade to his lips, the NCO dropped the chew into his mouth and began working it with relish. "You boys wanna try some of this? Black Maria. It's some good shit and hard to find in these parts; luckily I got a brother in Alabama that sends it to me by the case."

Krieger and Dodd shook their heads no.

"All right then," said Clayton, pointing the knife at them. "But I'll tell ya, if ya start to doze off at night in the field, just a little trickle of juice down the back of your throat—shit, man, you're good for another two hours."

Mick O'Riley rolled his eyes. "Don't listen to him. I tried that little trick of Clayton's in Afghanistan when I'd been on the go through the mountains for two days and didn't think I could keep my eyes open." He shook his head. "All I can say is puking your guts out in the dark is not the most tactically advisable course of action." He pointed at a scar on his forehead. "One of them fucking cave-dwelling pussies we had on the run took a shot at me based off of the racket I was making. Good thing for me I just caught some rock fragments." He glared at Catfish Clayton.

"Shit, Mick," drawled the operator. "Said I was fuckin' sorry. You gotta let it go, brother."

As the Special Forces troops worked their way back to their seats, Dell walked over and handed the two visitors cups of black coffee. "Remember," he said, "these guys are trained inside and out for their specialties—whether that be weapons, comms, or whatever. But all of them have language training and all have cross-trained in other areas. Add to that additional skills—SCUBA, free fall, sniper, and so on."

Rolf Krieger nodded thoughtfully. These seemed like good men—fit, intelligent, resourceful. He was beginning to feel at home.

Chapter 14

The Compound

Tommy Compound
Fort Bragg, North Carolina

"Dr. Bernard," said the white-coated researcher, leaning over and rapping on the conference table with his knuckles. "Did you hear what I said, sir?"

Clive Bernard's gaze drifted from the window. He'd found himself once again staring at the unrelenting pine trees in the distance. Lots of pines. More pines than he'd ever seen in his life. In the past two days he'd begun to understand the horror stories of those who'd been snowed in for long periods. The first flurries were pretty; the white, crystalline blanket that covered the countryside was wondrous; and then after a few days the poor bastards were ready to blow their brains out from staring at a pure white world. His world was the same now, but it was an unbroken green. *So much green.*

Clive Bernard had never been to North Carolina. When the powers that be decided that the only way to ensure the project's security and that of the researchers involved was to move it to a remote and secure facility—and quickly—he'd been pleasantly surprised to hear the choice; he'd been afraid it would be somewhere more Siberian in nature. Crisp cool autumn weather, hardwoods in full autumn colors, and the people seemed genuinely pleasant.

So he'd arrived at Fort Bragg, North Carolina, with

a smile on his face; it was the home of the 82nd Airborne Division, the Green Berets, and other military units whose existence was only rumored. In the words of the garrison commander at his team's initial base in-brief, this wasn't tank country. But the colonel had had no idea where to set up his new guests until one of his staff officers had reminded him of a large site located in the southwestern corner of the two-hundred-fifty-square-mile installation. One of the shadowy Special Operations organizations had occupied it, but they'd built a new facility two years earlier. And now Bernard and his hastily assembled group of the nation's top civilian and military researchers had a home.

Clive had been pleased when he'd seen the modern structures scattered throughout the base—no wonder it had won the military installation of the year award the past two years. But when they hit the last part of "civilization" on the southern end of Fort Bragg, his little convoy had kept going, passing weapons ranges and training areas, then passing various jump zones and lakes. They'd continued driving over the pothole-ridden two-lane blacktop. The only sign that they were still on a military base was the occasional C-130 aircraft droning in low to drop paratroopers for their monthly training; first one small speck would detach itself from a low-flying aircraft, then another, and another. A few seconds later the first jumper's static line would pull his chute into the sky and he'd begin drifting slowly toward the ground. It didn't take long for the sky to fill with the OD-green parachutes. For the final miles of the trip all Bernard saw was pine trees lining either side as the convoy twisted along the winding roadway. Finally they began to turn off the road and he had done a double take; it looked as if they were driving straight into the forest. Then he saw the dirt track. Within a quarter mile they passed through a chain-link fence and the road surface turned to well-maintained gravel. Though they didn't see anyone, the

gate opened as the convoy arrived at the fence and
closed immediately behind them. They quickly passed
through two more tall walls of concertina-wire-topped
fencing before bursting through into bright sunshine.
The team was awed.

Within this forest, in the middle of nowhere, was a
huge clearing of at least ten acres. Multiple buildings
dotted the grounds. A helipad was close to the center
and an Olympic-size pool could be seen in the distance. A running track and basketball court occupied
another corner. The convoy pulled in front of what
appeared to be a one-story administrative building
and stopped.

"Welcome home," said the major from Bragg who'd
escorted them. "I'm going to leave you in Mr. Cobb's
capable hands and then I'll be off."

"Who is Mr. Cobb?" asked Bernard.

The major smiled. "Doctor, this facility is yours. I'm
going to send out a few people tomorrow to help you
with the admin stuff, but the rest is up to you. However," he went on, "one of the conditions placed on
us by General Werner was to ensure the security of
this site—and of your team. We have . . . people . . .
on Fort Bragg with extensive experience in such
things—guarding ambassadors and securing embassies,
among other things."

Clive Bernard cocked his head and a corner of his
mouth lifted in a half smile. "So Mr. Cobb works for
these . . . people?"

"He used to," answered the major. "Mr. Cobb is
retired now. Still, we maintain him on the federal pay-
roll as a GS employee." The major paused before continuing, as if in explanation to a question that hadn't
been asked. "When you need someone with his gifts,
it's nice knowing that person is close at hand."

"Gentlemen, Colonel," called a voice from behind
them. Bernard and the rest turned toward the front
of the administrative building and saw a completely
unspectacular-appearing man exiting the front door.

Just under six feet tall; not really thin, but neither was he overly muscular; thinning, sandy hair and blue eyes lined in the corners from years in the sun. In short, he was Mr. Ordinary, someone who would never stand out in a crowd. Then Bernard understood and smiled—not standing out in a crowd would be of true benefit to an organization that shunned publicity. He reminded Bernard of someone, but he couldn't quite place it . . . then he had it. The actor Ed Harris. A completely unremarkable man at a glance, until he turned those laser-blue eyes on you, pinning you to your seat.

"I'm Cobb."

"It's a pleasure to meet you. . . ."

"Let me begin with this," continued Cobb, as though Clive Bernard hadn't spoken. "No one leaves this compound without my permission. No one from outside of the team who is not already cleared for access to the compound comes in without my authorization—and I'll need a minimum of forty-eight hours in order to properly clear them. We will operate on an internal computer network. If you need outside access—whether it is normal Internet, the secret-level Sipper net, or the top-secret JWICS network run through the DIA—we've got workstations designated for it. All activity, to include e-mail traffic, will be screened by our network administrators. Conspiracy theorists among you, listen to that last statement carefully so that you fully understand—I didn't say your Internet activity *could* be screened, I said it *would be.* Any questions thus far?"

"You know, Major," said Bernard, taking a lead from Cobb's penchant for interruption and turning to his military escort, "I could have sworn that you said I was in charge here." He shook his head and laughed. "I've got to be honest with you, old sod—it doesn't seem that way to me."

Cobb may have seemed an everyman before, but the air surrounding him now seemed charged, despite the fact that he hadn't spoken or moved a muscle other than to swing his gaze toward Clive Bernard and lock on. "Dr. Bernard . . ."

"No," said Bernard, the smile disappearing. "*You* hold on, G-man." He turned to the garrison representative again. "Major, you bring us out here . . ." The doctor paused and waved his hands helplessly at the unbroken ranks of Carolina pines surrounding the clearing. "Bring us here to the middle of nowhere. And now *this* guy," he continued, hooking a thumb over his shoulder toward Cobb. "*This* guy starts some *fascist* line of *bullshit* before we've even had an opportunity to take a much-needed piss break. I don't goosestep for anybody, Major. Got it?"

Despite herself, Lieutenant Colonel Sarah Hunter snorted a quick laugh. By the time the group glanced at her she'd recovered and gave no indication that she'd found any humor in the situation.

"You find this funny, Sarah?" asked Clive Bernard, incredulous and angry at the same time.

"*Colonel Hunter,*" corrected the military police officer. "And no, I do not find this situation funny, Doctor. I do, however, find *you* unbelievable to the point of hilarity."

Bernard drew himself up to his full height and tried to look authoritative. "I've asked you to call me Clive, Sarah."

"Shut up, *Clive,*" Hunter replied hotly. "Yes, you're in charge of this project. But in case you've forgotten, a whole lot of people, people who were performing the same job you and the rest of your team will be performing, are dead. That's *dead, Clive.* And the M4X FCS project is in a shambles. Mr. Cobb's job, *Clive,* is to keep you alive while you're at Fort Bragg and to ensure whatever progress your team makes isn't lost."

Bernard couldn't help but smile. She'd finally called him Clive, despite the implied sarcasm. "I thought it was the job of you and Major O'Sullivan to keep me alive?" he said innocently.

Sarah Hunter balled her shapely hands into fists to the point that her nails were almost drawing blood from her palms. "Major O'Sullivan and myself, if we never slept, could not possibly keep a secluded place like this secure." She pointed to the outlying pine forest. "How difficult do you think it would be, without Mr. Cobb's help, to guarantee you that someone with designs on your life couldn't climb one of those trees and bring a high-power rifle to bear on you?"

Bernard looked down at his Havaianas and nudged some gravel around with the edge of one of the flip-flops. "I see your point."

Silence reigned for several seconds. A woodpecker's efforts to bore a thousandth hole into the bole of a nearby tree permeated the air.

"Thank you, Colonel Hunter," said Cobb quietly, breaking the silence.

Hunter wheeled toward the team's security lead. "And *you*—I know your type as well, Cobb. You should have worked with enough State Department types by now to know that you can't treat a group of civilians as though they're a platoon of soldiers reporting for basic training and expect them to dress-right-dress."

For the first time a slight smile creased Cobb's face. "Noted, ma'am," he said. He turned to Bernard. "Doctor," he began, wincing with the effort required to be civil, "I will attempt to ensure that you and your people are allowed to work and live in as unfettered a manner as possible while you're in this camp. In fact, you'll find the living conditions here aren't bad at all. But," he added, wagging a finger, "security is king, and in that arena I will allow no half measures. Do we understand one another?"

Bernard nodded. "All right, Mr. Cobb. Agreed." He looked around the compound, squinting at the various structures. "You know, this all looks pretty cool. But I'm something of an amateur gardener. You wouldn't have, like, a greenhouse on the grounds?"

"Doctor?"

"Yeah?"

Though he smiled, all charm was gone from Cobb's gaze. "Don't even think about it."

And here they were, two days later.

The speaker repeated himself. "Dr. Bernard? Sir, did you . . ."

Bernard dragged his gaze reluctantly from the mesmerizing green of the forest. He had to shake himself from the miasma he'd found himself in since taking on this project. It wasn't just the never-ending ranks of pines. The dream had come back last night. It had been years, but he remembered it well. His brother smiling . . . and then his brother disappearing in a ball of flame. The only change this time was that instead of waking up screaming alone or with a beautiful woman with whom he'd shared carnal bliss screaming along with him, there'd been a silent and serious-faced Sarah Hunter. His almost-constant companion had come into the room with a raised 9mm, and in the end had gently brought him back to wakefulness.

"Doctor?"

Bernard looked up and smiled. "Yeah. Yeah, I heard you."

The researcher was pure academic. A project assistant lead on multiple military programs, his lab coat was starched, his wingtips highly shined, his glasses polished. He smiled, somewhat smugly, at Bernard. Visions of parlaying his work on the Tommy program into a higher position for his next project—preferably in a scenic location with cheap real estate—floated through his mind behind his designer glasses frames. "Then you agree that the best way to focus our efforts is to concentrate on getting the M4X . . ."

Bernard blinked. *A little Mary Jane would go a long*

way in bringing this guy down to a near-human level, he thought. Despite what his current associates thought—and he had to admit he'd done nothing to dissuade them from the idea—he'd rarely smoked since his brother's death. Only a handful of times over the past decade. What the lovely lieutenant colonel had smelled on his shirt outside the Oval Office was merely a by-product of his hobby. He'd been burning hemp for a new line of jewelry he'd thought he might need to depend upon if he didn't get the Tommy job. He smiled, knowing he could probably make more money if he'd stuck with the hemp jewelry line. But on the few occasions he *had* smoked, he'd always been in his cups and/or his host had run out of alcohol. But *this* guy. The Tommy lead shook his head. *What this dude could use was a good colon cleansing.* It would do him a world of good.

"What's your name?" Bernard finally asked. Instead of waiting for a reply, he focused on the name embroidered on his lab coat's left side. "Butler?"

Butler straightened. "Yes. Dr. Peter Butler."

Bernard smiled. "You're looking at this all wrong, Butler."

"*Doctor* Butler," sniffed the researcher. *Who did this middle-aged hippy think he was?* The only saving grace was that at this rate Bernard would receive the boot soon. Once that happened, *he* would be the natural man to take over the project.

"I'm not going to quibble about names—just ask Sarah," continued Bernard tiredly, taking the time to throw a weary smile at Hunter where she sat in a corner facing the conference room door. "Shit, call me Clive. What's in a name? My point is this—you're looking at this from a purely M4X standpoint."

Butler was dumbfounded. "Jesus, man. That's the sole reason we were gathered together as a team."

Clive Bernard steepled his fingers in front of his face, closed his eyes, and took a deep, cleansing breath. "I disagree."

"You disagree? You *disagree*?! Who are you to disagree, *Clive*? You're an overeducated seventies reject with no clue how to run—"

Bernard opened his eyes. "Who is your assistant, Dr. Butler?"

Butler sputtered, confused at the change in tack. "Sue Kwan. . . ."

Bernard turned to his right, toward an attractive woman of Asian ancestry who'd begun to raise her hand. "Would that be Dr. Kwan, Butler?" He kept his eyes on the assistant as he delivered the question.

"Yes."

"Dr. Kwan?"

The woman straightened, clearly uncomfortable.

"Dr. Kwan, do you know your job well?"

She straightened. "Yes."

"How do you feel about Butler?"

"Dr. Butler is a fine researcher and—"

Bernard sighed. "No, *really*. How do you *feel* about him?"

Sue Kwan looked toward Butler. He was glaring at her and she knew her job was riding on the reply. Looking to Clive Bernard, she shrugged. "He's the biggest pain in the ass I've ever worked with. A real prima donna prick more than willing to use his people as stepping-stones to a higher position."

Butler's face flamed red. "Sue—"

"Dr. Kwan," the woman corrected.

"But, Sue . . . Doctor . . ."

Bernard held up a hand and silence descended. "Dr. Kwan . . ."

Kwan smiled. There was something about Bernard that set her soul at peace. "Call me Sue."

Clive Bernard beamed. "And please, call me Clive. Sue, would you be willing to assume Dr. Butler's duties?"

"Now see *here*!" Butler boomed, slamming a fist on the table in front of him. "You . . . you . . . hippy freak! You do not have the authority . . ."

Bernard turned to the corner where his security chief had begun hanging out when not doing whatever else it was security chiefs did. "Mr. Cobb?"

Cobb looked up with sleepy eyes. "Yes, Doctor?"

"If I asked you to have Dr. Butler escorted from the compound, would you do so?"

Cobb shifted his gaze, the motion of his neck turning reminding Butler of a machine gun smoothly rotating on a pedestal he'd designed a few years earlier. He shuddered.

Cobb considered the request. He wasn't overly fond of Bernard thus far, but he was the boss, and something about the toad in question bothered him. From the little experience he'd had with these people, the guy was definitely an asshole. No matter how smart Butler was, this team needed to be tight if it was to be successful. Pricks had a way of nibbling away at an organization's unity, particularly when the prick or pricks in question were in positions of authority. He turned to Bernard. "You bet, Doc."

"This is outrageous!"

Cobb looked to Bernard. Bernard nodded. Cobb in turn nodded to a tall, lean security guard sitting in the corner opposite him. The man wore lightweight battle dress uniform, devoid of insignia, and had ex-operator written all over him. Without a word the guard stood, walked to the screaming Butler, took him by an elbow—placing just enough thumb on a pressure point there to make the good doctor's knees weaken—and escorted him from the room.

No one said a word or moved for several seconds. Bernard turned to Cobb and nodded silent thanks. In response Cobb raised an inquisitive eyebrow, as if asking, *So now what are you going to do, Doc?*

Sue Kwan cleared her throat. "Dr. Bern . . . Clive?"

Bernard turned from Cobb and looked at his new number two. Concern was etched in the lines across her forehead. "Let me guess, you're a little worried about what you've gotten yourself into? You're thinking Butler was an asshole, but he was a very intelligent asshole. And you're thinking is there any possible way that a—what did Butler call me?—a seventies reject with a ponytail and flip-flops could be right if his thinking of the correct direction for the Tommy project is radically different from Butler's? Is that a decent summation of your concerns, Sue?"

Kwan nodded. The rest of the team watched.

Clive Bernard nodded thoughtfully. He hoped he was right about this. He was likely exceeding his authority—which was one reason Butler had to go. Bernard knew that he needed some time to convince his team that the course of action it had taken him a sleepless night to construct was the right path. And Butler would have been screaming *the sky is falling* too quickly for Bernard to have had that time.

"We're going to split our team. One half will continue to work the Tommy—"

A chorus of voices rang out, cutting off Bernard. He shook his head in frustration. If he couldn't win his own team over . . .

"I think I see what the doc's getting at," said a gruff voice from the rear of the room.

All eyes turned to the speaker, who stared back at the assembled scientists. "Why is everyone looking at me like I just farted in church? Give the man a chance to explain himself."

"And who are you?" asked one of the team.

The man grinned. "Jones. Colonel Bill Jones."

Institute for Plant and Seed Modification Research
Third Subterranean Level, Infirmary
Karaj, Iran

"It has been twenty-four hours, Herr Colonel. Are you ready for me to remove the bandages?"

"Speak quietly, damn you!" yelled Sergei Sedov from his bed. He held his hands to his head and took deep breaths, the sound of his breathing muffled by the gauze covering his face.

The doctor's fear of Sedov both rooted him in place and made him wish to flee. In the end he remained standing by the door and hoped for the best. The surgeon had known this moment would not go well. Sedov, in a twelve-hour period, had undergone surgical procedures that normally would have been undertaken over a period of months, if not years.

The doctor spoke in a whisper. "Colonel, I realize you are in significant pain, but we must take a look beneath the bandages in order to ensure no postoperative complications have arisen. You understand, *ja*?"

Sergei Sedov did not move. His head lay like an overripe melon on his pillow. "I am so very tempted to kill you, you fat German toad. . . ."

Despite the fact that there was an entire room between them and that Sedov did not have the energy to beat his way out of a wet paper bag, the German hesitated. "Ve . . . very well, Colonel. Perhaps I should return later."

"No, damn you," Sedov said weakly. "Let us get this over with." The single functioning eye beneath the bandages pinned the doctor in place. "And God help you if the results are less than expected."

"I will call one of the guards to help you sit up."

"No!" grunted the Russian.

The German surgeon could not help but marvel at his patient's iron will. The Russian had insisted that he did not have time to delay his duties for more than twenty-four hours. Nor had he wanted more than a token amount of painkillers. *I think the bastard is actually enjoying the pain*, the doctor thought as he watched Sergei Sedov grasp the hospital bed's rails. The only indication that the former Russian officer was in agonizing pain was in the way his limbs shook, as if he were in the throes of a grand mal seizure as he slowly, inch by inch, levered himself into a sitting position. Sedov's breath wheezed through the slit in his bandages and his shoulders shook as he attained his goal. After two minutes, the bandaged head swiveled toward the German. "Take them off."

The doctor moved hesitantly toward the bed. A tray of sterilized medical instruments had been brought in earlier and the surgeon reached to it now, picking up a pair of scissors. "If I may . . . ?"

"Just *do* it, damn you!"

Being as gentle as possible, the portly surgeon snipped the bandages and began unrolling them. Slowly the bandages came off, layer by layer, until all that remained were white gauze pads taped lightly in place over Sedov's nose and one of his eyes.

"You will feel a light pressure as I remove the tape."

"If I tell you one more time to get on with it, Doctor, it will be the last words you hear. That I promise you. And it will *not* be a light pressure."

The surgeon bit off further comment and continued with the job at hand. As the first piece of tape holding the gauze pad to his nose was removed, the Russian shook with pain. Once all of the tape was removed, the doctor gently pulled the sterile pad free.

Sergei Sedov watched the German's face as he laid eyes on his handiwork for the first time since the surgery was complete. He knew the procedure had been successful before the surgeon said a word, the beaming smile saying everything that needed to be said. "Oh, yes. This is good. *Ja, very* good."

"Get on with it," grumbled Sedov. Despite his tone, the Russian was elated. He'd been vain about his golden-boy looks before the war. Now, at long last, he would return to some semblance of his former beauty.

"Colonel," began the surgeon, "as I've told you, it is not a good idea to remove the bandages covering your eye so early. Give it a few more days. As of now, the eye will be so sensitive . . ."

Sedov's functioning eye spoke volumes.

"Very well, very well," muttered the doctor. He was not happy to have his professional recommendations overridden, but he was terrified of the Russian. He removed the remaining gauze with quick, efficient motions. Sedov cried out as laserlike pain flashed into his skull.

"I am sorry, Colonel," the German groveled. "As I said, you should have allowed the eye more time to heal."

Sedov's chest heaved up and down like that of a wounded animal. "You . . . can cover it again when we're finished here. For now, I need to know that it will function."

The German hesitated.

"Doctor, you try my patience."

The surgeon shook his head in frustration. "Colonel, you think you have felt pain to this point? The only way of checking your eye is to—"

"Do what you have to do, damn you!"

Reaching into the breast pocket of his lab coat, the doctor removed a penlight. As gently as possible he held open the lids of the Russian's right eye. A grunt of muffled pain was Sedov's only reaction. Without turning the light on, the surgeon moved the penlight side to side. "Follow my hand. . . ."

The eye moved back and forth, tracking the movements of the doctor's hand from side to side. Now the surgeon moved his hand up and down. "Continue to follow my hand." Sedov's eye moved in time with the doctor's hand once more. "Good," said the doctor. He clicked on the penlight. "Now . . ."

Sergei Sedov's scream could be heard throughout the institute's lower level. A prisoner brought in for questioning down the hall, despite the fact that he had no knowledge of the crimes he was accused of committing, chose that moment to give a full confession. The prisoner had held out against almost continuous beatings for forty-eight hours, but Sedov's scream of pure torment sent him over the edge. Any punishment was better than experiencing whatever had caused such agony in a human being.

The German surgeon jumped backward. "I . . . I tried to warn you, Colonel Sedov."

The Russian had gone silent, but his body still shook. "Finish it," he croaked.

Having learned not to argue, the doctor moved the light in the direction of Sedov's face. Without shining the beam directly into Sedov's eye, he observed the reaction of his patient's pupils.

The light clicked off. "Never a doubt in my mind. The operation was a complete success."

"You are certain?"

The surgeon folded his pudgy hands across his paunch and rocked back and forth on his heels, a smile on his face for the first time in several minutes. "Oh yes. Completely."

Sergei Sedov did not so much nod as let gravity take hold of his head. When he looked up again, he stared into the surgeon's face. "And my nose? You are certain that it will be . . . normal."

The doctor shrugged, a touch of his old arrogance finding its way back into his voice. "I believe so, yes. But I tell you this, Colonel . . . if it is not, there is nothing that I or any other surgeon can do."

"A poor choice of words on your part, Doctor," said Sedov weakly.

The surgeon blinked, confused. "What do you mean?"

With a speed the surgeon would not have thought possible for a man in his condition, Sergei Sedov snatched a scalpel from the tray of instruments and rammed it deeply into the portly doctor's right eye.

The German went down without a sound, collapsing to the floor in a puddle of spreading blood.

The Russian looked at the twitching body for a moment, and then he lay back on his pillow. "I have wanted to do that for soooo long," he whispered to himself as he closed his eyes.

Market District
Karaj, Iran

Monsoor sat in the courtyard of a friend's family villa, a friend on extended loan to the University of Tehran. He closed his eyes as he listened to the gentle bubbling of the water pipe, or *qalyoun*, as he pulled the cool smoke into his lungs.

"Mind if I have a go?" asked George "Ali" Greenfield, settling down on a cushion next to the young Iranian. He accepted the stem of the pipe with a smile and let the smoke roll into his lungs. "I see that, this time, you do not jump as if you have seen a wraith," he said, handing the stem back to Monsoor.

The Iranian smiled. "That is because I no longer try to predict your comings and goings, Ali. But I do hope you bring me good news." The smile disappeared as he uttered the latter part of his statement.

Greenfield nodded. "Have you spoken with your mother and sister? Are they prepared to pick up and leave at a moment's notice?"

Monsoor nodded. "They do not know any details—let's be honest, nor do I—but yes, they know that transportation is being arranged."

"It is imperative that, until the time they move to the rendezvous, they keep up the appearance of their normal daily activities."

The Iranian nodded. "I have ensured they understand this."

"Very well. Tomorrow night, tell them to be here," Greenfield said, pointing at a location on his map. "Tell them not to be there before midnight, else they might rouse suspicion."

"That is it? Tell them to show up at a location with

no further instructions?" Monsoor was irate. "These are my family!"

"Monsoor, *I* will be there. *I* will ensure they are safe. I assume that you will be there as well?"

The younger man shook his head. "I have decided to remain."

"But *why*, for God's sake?" asked Greenfield. "There are sure to be questions when they disappear so close on the heels of a strike at the institute. You must leave with them, Monsoor. You *must*."

For the first time since they'd known one another, the Iranian smiled a true smile with no doubts. "You have just moved up several notches in trust, my friend."

George Greenfield shook his head. "Why?"

"Because, if all you cared about was the success of your intelligence efforts in Iran, you would beg me to stay in place," Monsoor said with a note of sadness.

"But why stay? What can you hope to accomplish?"

Monsoor thought of his uncle. "It is not always about the greater good of the people. Sometimes, it is about loyalty . . . about family."

Greenfield looked to his watch. "I have no more time. But I will ask you—do not answer now—to reconsider. There will be a place for you."

Inhaling on the *qalyoun* stem, Monsoor nodded and smiled.

Chapter 15

The Reluctant Free-Faller

Combined Joint Special Operations Task Force (CJSOTF) Headquarters
Team Ready Room
Baghdad, Iraq

"All right, seats," said Jack Kelly. He pointed to an area northeast of Tehran on the wall map. "We'll be going in high altitude, high opening—HAHO—jumping from thirty thousand feet. That should keep our boys in blue above radar coverage. When we hit the jet stream, we'll be about twenty miles from our LZ." Kelly nodded toward Davies. "Hawk, you'll lead the jump and we'll stack on you."

The master sergeant nodded. It was a heavy responsibility, but with fifty-plus high-altitude jumps under his belt, he was up for it. When the team exited the rear of their transport aircraft in the dead of night carrying over a hundred pounds each of weapons and equipment, oxygen masks in place because of the thin air in the upper atmosphere, Davies would get the team oriented on their landing zone, using way points to keep them on track. They'd deploy their chutes after fifteen seconds of free fall, at roughly twenty-seven thousand feet, and glide toward their objective, a clearing in the desert ten miles outside of Karaj, with enough surrounding terrain to give them some privacy.

"We got anybody on the ground, Sonny?" asked Master Sergeant Davies.

Kelly nodded. "Mr. Dodd's associate, code name Ali. He'll have the LZ marked with infrared lights. We'll pick them up easy enough with our NODs," the captain added, referring to their night-vision devices.

Davies nodded, and then a thought crossed his mind. He turned to Dodd and Krieger. "You two ever HAHO'd?" he asked.

Both men nodded, Dodd a second before Krieger. Hawk Davies eyed Rolf Krieger but said nothing. Finally, Davies nodded, eyes still on the scout lieutenant.

Kelly continued. "Once on the ground Ali will have transportation waiting to move us into town closer to the object. He'll also give us any last-minute intel updates we might need." Kelly turned to CW3 Dell. "Have you got the Urban Recon info input and ready to go, Bull?"

"Roger, Sonny, she's ready to go." The big warrant moved toward a corner of the room where a large black table stood. To one side was a laptop computer. The team gathered around the table as Dell began manipulating the laptop's keyboard. He paused for a moment and stole a glance at Krieger. "You're gonna dig this shit, Wolf. If you're with the boys, you get the good toys." He hit the ENTER key.

A green city exploded from the table. Individual buildings and streets, trees, the river, it was all there to scale in a ten-foot-by-seven-foot glowing hologram that stretched two feet above the table's surface. "Gentlemen, let me introduce you to Karaj, Iran."

Rolf Krieger's jaw dropped. Krieger thought of the hours he and his scout platoon had spent, when time allowed, making detailed three-dimensional models of areas in which they'd be operating in order to better plan their reconnaissance and security missions. When time was short they'd simply had to rely on map recons. "We can do this? It is accurate?"

Dell laughed. "Hell yeah, it's accurate. Best tool around for mission planning."

"This is the new LIDAR system I've heard about?" asked Dodd.

Dell nodded. "Yeah. We flew a stealth platform over the city yesterday to pull the collection mission. Just got the finished product back a few hours ago." The warrant officer grinned as he looked over the city. "Man, this shit is *sweet*. Beats the hell out of map or photo recons."

Krieger pointed to an object on one of the side streets. "Is that a dog?"

"Shit, man," Dell said and laughed. "I said the shit was good, not fuckin' magic. That's a bush."

Kelly took control of the briefing again. "Bull," he said, pointing to a walled compound, "could you navigate to the block surrounding the institute?" The hologram shimmered, seemed to disappear and reshape, now only the area surrounding the institute visible. "Good. Enlarge."

Dell executed a few keystrokes. "And . . . we're there."

"All right, let's get busy." Kelly pointed to a structure outside of the walled complex. "This is an air vent located outside the compound walls. Now I'm sure that the Iranian powers that be would prefer that this shaft—and others dotting the terrain outside the institute's walls—were a little more secure. But they're trying to play down the fact that anything more than agricultural research is taking place in Karaj." He jabbed a finger at the building under discussion. "But the designers screwed the pooch on this one. When they began excavating the ground for the lower levels, they didn't calculate that they'd need vent shafts to keep a pure airflow—and they do. So they built them after the fact. And the lower levels expand out farther than the aboveground facility, so now they got a problem. Fortunately for them, the local population, for the most part, really believe the institute is as advertised, an agency full of good-intentioned scientists trying to figure out how to get more bushels of product from the average date bush."

"Actually, the date comes from a *tree*, Sonny," said Catfish Clayton, working his chew of tobacco from one side of his mouth to the other as he spoke. "A date palm, to be specific."

Jack Kelly stared at his comms sergeant. "I stand corrected," he deadpanned. "But again, the locals don't realize the extent of what they've got beneath the streets of their city. So the Iranian government decided to go with a passive defense. They broke surface ground for the vents at night and threw up corrugated tin 'maintenance shacks' over the openings. Nobody from the town has any idea what the shacks are covering, nor do they really care." Now Kelly pointed out a dozen guard towers spaced at regular intervals along the institute's walls. "But the soldiers manning these positions know exactly what the shacks are disguising. And one of their primary functions is to ensure that nobody goes poking into them." He pointed out a guard tower, then another. "Specifically, these two towers have eyes on *our* shaft."

"How are the shafts secured, Sonny?" asked the engineer sergeant, Eastbrook.

The captain turned to his senior engineer. "No worries, Boom. They're corrugated tin with wood frames, secured by a length of chain and a padlock. The inner shaft cover is steel rebar, also secured by a padlock."

"Type of locks?"

"Figure them as series-200 equivalent," said Kelly.

Eastbrook and Taylor exchanged smiles. Use the bolt cutters now, save their C4 for a bigger boom somewhere else.

"I'm told that the inner wall of the vent has ladder handholds running the length of the shaft to allow maintenance teams access, so we'll have no trouble on egress." If the handholds hadn't been in place, the team could have rappelled to the third level, but getting out—that would have taken some imagination.

The captain turned to his weapons men. "Purdue, Vega, I want your sniper rifles set up well before we go in. On my signal, I need those guards to go down quick."

The two weapons NCOs nodded, Vega pulling a thin cigar out and lighting it. He walked up and looked at the map, then at the blueprints, then back to the map. He puffed on the cigar a few seconds and then turned to Kelly. "Give us twenty minutes to get in position, Sonny."

"Where do you see yourself locating?" asked the captain.

Hefe Vega pointed his cigar at a building two hundred meters from the walls. "This looks like it should work. Map legend says it's a library, shouldn't be anyone nosing around it at night." He looked to Dell. "Chief, can you bring up line of sight from that perch?"

"You got it." Dell manipulated the keyboard. Green lines, indicating clear line of sight, began a few meters past the library, extending out to cover the majority of the institute's grounds where the team would be going in. The only red lines, indicating the shooter would have no visual in that area, was directly below Vega's selected spot in the lee of his own building.

"Out-fucking-standing," said Vega, taking a large pull on his cigar. He pointed to another building one hundred meters to the north of the library. "School; that'll be my alternate if the library's a no-go. Bring it up, Bull?" Vega smiled at the lines of sight. "My work here is done."

Lurch Purdue ambled up and studied the compound and the surrounding neighborhood. He pointed to a mosque that overlooked the area surrounding the shack. "Could you let me see the lines from the minaret, Chief," he said, pointing at the upper portion of the tower outside the mosque. He looked over the lines, noting he had coverage in the few dead spots in Vega's coverage. He nodded after making a sniper's mental calculations. "Good to go," said Purdue. "And it gives me a little separation from Poncho Villa here."

Vega shook his head. "That's bad juju, Lurch, man. Using a church."

Purdue pulled a cigar from the pouch protruding from Vega's front pocket. "But I'm going to be doing God's work, brother," he said as he lit the cheroot and grinned through his bushy beard.

Kelly nodded. "All right. You two will be first in, last out. Once we're clear, hightail it to the linkup point. As one or more of our rescuees may not be ambulatory, you'll probably be moving a lot faster than us. Give us one minute, then bug out, clear?"

Both weapons men nodded.

"Next, power." Kelly turned to his second in command. "Bull, I want you and Taylor moving as soon as the guards are taken down. Once the shack and vent are open, you two have to get down there and take us to lights out. I'll point out the master power shutoff in a minute."

Dell and Taylor nodded.

Jack Kelly reached for a roll of blueprints. "Unfortunately we don't have the assets in place to map the building's interior, so we're going to have to old school it." Extracting a set of plans, he posted it on a bulletin board. "Here's where our shaft terminates on Level Three. Ali's source says that it's a standard wood door and that it's unsecured—only cleared personnel have access to the lower levels, so it makes the maintenance crew's job easier."

The men looked over the blueprints. The access closet the team would be exiting was at the far end of the central corridor. Kelly pointed to the first room to the left of the closet they'd be piling through. "This is the generator room. Bull, you and Crapper need to get in there as soon as you hit ground. The master power control is on the wall to your left. I'm told you can't miss it."

Dell had had enough of such assurances in the past to roll his eyes.

Kelly ignored his second in command's doubts and continued. "If the switch is somewhere else in the room—and it's *gotta* be in the room—find it. Cut the power and then take care of the backup generators, conveniently located in the same room."

"How many?" asked Crapper Taylor.

"Five," said Kelly. "And I don't know which ones power what portion of the institute, so you will have to take them all down."

Taylor did the mental arithmetic of how much C4 he'd need per generator, looked at Dell, and nodded.

"We got it," said the big warrant.

"We'll be stackin' at the top of the pipe when you go down, waiting for lights out," said Kelly.

"Good to go, my man," said the big operator with a smile. "*Good* to *fuckin'* go."

Kelly ran his finger down the length of the hallway. "You'll note four rooms are marked. The first is Dillon's last known location, the second is Crockett's, and finally, the third is what passes for an interrogation cell." Kelly tapped for emphasis on a fourth room. "This is the guard room. So far as we can tell, the Iranian military pulling securities are pure blue-collar types. Feed the prisoners, watch them, play poker—or whatever the fucking Arab equivalent of poker is."

A loud splash preceded Catfish Clayton's interruption as he let fly with a stream of Black Maria. *"Ghahveh,"* he drawled. "They play *ghahveh.*"

Kelly stared at him.

The soldier grinned, exposing tobacco-stained teeth. "It's kind of like their version of spades—very popular."

"Thanks, Catfish. You're a plethora of information."

The sarcasm was lost on the Alabaman. "You're welcome, Sonny. Glad I could help."

"At any rate," Kelly continued, "it doesn't appear they have any type of night-vision goggles. I've posted pictures of the friendlies. Memorize them, but be prepared for them to look worse. You see anyone else in the corridor, take them out."

"Where's Melissa Dillon?" asked Rolf Krieger.

The captain shook his head. "Unknown. Our best guess," he said, indicating two rooms adjacent to Patrick Dillon's, "is in one of these."

A moan went up from a couple of the SF troops. The best course of action would be to hit all three spaces at the same time—use surprise and shock, simultaneously breaching the doors of each room and popping any bad guys present. But now they had an unknown and that wouldn't be possible.

"Hawk, you and Mick take the guard room."

Davies and the senior comms man nodded silently.

"Catfish, you and Boom take Crockett's room."

"Roger that," said Clayton, sending a long stream of black spittle into a coffee can filled with sand positioned on the floor between his feet. Boom Eastbrook stared at the blueprints a few more moments, looking for questions but coming up blank for the moment. "Not a problem," he said finally.

"Betty, you and Crapper go for the major. Bull, myself, and the rest of the team will hit the interrogation room."

After answering a few questions, Kelly turned to them. "You two," he said, pointing at them, "once you reach the bottom, take up a position outside of the shaft entrance and secure it."

A few moments of silence. "In other words, stay out of the way," said Krieger.

Kelly smiled. "Exactly."

Krieger and Dodd nodded acknowledgment, but the team could tell both men took it a little personally that they were being looked at as potential liabilities. But they were professional enough to understand, even though it rankled.

Bull Dell grinned. "Nothing personal, boys. I'm sure you're both up for the game, but this is a well-oiled machine. And you know the best way to keep a well-oiled machine runnin' . . . ya don't fuck with it."

Kelly pointed to a warehouse on the map two blocks outside the institute walls. "We'll link up with Ali here. Again, he'll have transportation waiting to take us to our pickup location, where we'll link up with our Nightstalker ride out."

Nightstalkers was what the men of the 160th Special Operations Aviation Regiment—or SOAR—called themselves. They were the most skilled helo drivers in the world and their sole mission in life was to support U.S. Special Operations forces. And they dearly loved the night.

Kelly pointed to a location one mile from the institute. "If everything goes to hell in a handbasket and you become separated, work your way here. It's a safe house Ali has set up, and we'll work an alternate pickup for you at a later time." The captain glanced at his Suunto. "Take a smoke break if you need one and grab a cup of coffee. For the next twenty minutes, I want each of you to take turns on the LIDAR display running through our routes from the infil point to the target, and back along the primary and alternate exfil routes."

The briefing broke up into back-and-forth questions and fine-tuning for another fifteen minutes. Finally, Kelly turned to his men. "Any questions? No? All right, get your shit together," he concluded. "We'll meet at the aircraft in"—he consulted his Suunto wrist computer once more—"one hour."

While the men gathered their gear, Krieger stood, looking dumbly at his jump helmet, oxygen bottle, parachute, and other equipment.

"Problem?" asked Luke Dodd.

"Well, at least I recognize the M4A1 rifle and the knife," he said, shaking his head.

"What?"

Krieger looked up. "I have never jumped out of an airplane," he said in a low voice.

Luke Dodd's jaw dropped. "But you said . . ."

"Keep your voice down," hissed Krieger. "I *know* what I said. But nothing is going to keep me from this mission, Luke. Do you understand? *Nothing.*" He frowned as he picked up his chute and examined it. "After all, how hard can it be?"

"Oh, good Lord," muttered Luke Dodd, shaking his head in exasperation. Between his years in the Marine Corps' elite Force Recon and his infiltrations into various hotspots around the globe, he'd done anything and everything with a parachute that was in the Special Operations community's kit bag. He knew the clusterfuck that Krieger'd worked himself into. And he had no idea what to do about it. "This is insane, Rolf," he said. "You're not even Airborne qualified—and that's the easy stuff: stand up, hook up, shuffle to the door. That way all you have to worry about is not breaking a leg on landing." He shook his head again for emphasis. "HAHO is an entirely different animal, man."

Krieger reached out a massive hand and grabbed Dodd by his black coveralls, almost lifting the field officer's feet from the floor. Fire burned in his eyes. "Keep your voice *down.*"

Luke Dodd went very still. "Put me down, Rolf."

The lieutenant continued to stare into Luke Dodd's eyes.

"Now."

Rolf Krieger released Dodd, and then seemed to deflate. "I am a *scout*, for God's sake. I operate in armored units. Have you ever seen an Abrams or Bradley dropped with a parachute? I can tell you when they have tried it, it wasn't pretty."

"Hey . . ."

Krieger shook his head. "I should have known better than to think I could bluff my way through this. But I thought we'd go in by helicopter."

Luke Dodd looked around slowly. Master Sergeant Hawk Davies was making his way over to them. "Oh shit," Luke said beneath his breath.

"Problem?" asked the NCO when he arrived.

Luke Dodd held his tongue, but he cast a furtive glance at Krieger.

Now it was Davies's turn to surveil the ready room before turning back to the pair. "Krieger?"

Rolf Krieger looked into the master sergeant's eyes. "Yes, Sergeant?"

"Hawk. Call me Hawk."

Krieger nodded.

"I know I gave you two a hard time, but it's my job to make sure I bring these guys out with their collective hides intact. Got it?"

Rolf Krieger nodded.

"I've heard of you," Davies continued, looking once more at Krieger. He actually laughed—*laughed*. "I tell ya, though, the stories don't do you justice."

Krieger looked at the team sergeant in confusion. "What do you mean?"

"I'd heard you had balls of stone, but never having jumped from a plane and now you're willing to do a HAHO into enemy territory? At night? Jesus. I don't know *anybody* that would do that."

The big lieutenant began gathering his gear. "I will let Captain Kelly know that I won't be—"

Davies grabbed Krieger's shoulder. "Listen, kid. It's your lucky day. There's only one guy who can get you ready to do what you're gonna have to do in the time available—that is, if you're smart, listen well, and have a bit of luck in you." He dropped his arm and stared at the big scout. "So, you in or you out? It's your call. No one's gonna judge you for it if you hang here."

Krieger smiled. "I am in, Hawk."

Hawk Davies rubbed a hand across his eyes. "Shit, I was afraid you were gonna say that. Okay, we better get started."

Tommy Compound
Fort Bragg, North Carolina

So this is Bill Jones, thought Clive Bernard; the project's new subject matter expert, or SME. In his jeans and Hawaiian shirt—a very loud, floral Hawaiian shirt in bright blues, whites, and reds—the man didn't look like much of an armor expert. But Bernard had insisted that he needed someone senior with years of experience in tank warfare and the machines that waged it if they were going to come up with the right answers to complex issues and problems in the shortest time possible. And what they'd sent him was a rather tall and solid man in his mid-forties with just the beginnings of a paunch. But the SME didn't look soft; on the contrary, he looked—and now Bernard knew the man also *sounded*—as though he were carved from a block of granite. But Jones didn't look hard in a mean way, just . . . weathered. There was no doubt the SME either had been or still was an active-duty soldier; the bearing told him that much. Whoever he was, he was throwing Bernard a life preserver at the moment. And for that the doctor was grateful.

Bernard walked to the back of the room, the slap of his flip-flops echoing off linoleum the only sound in the room. He held out a hand. "We haven't met. I'm Clive Bernard."

The man stood and took Bernard's hand, looking into the Tommy lead's face as if searching for something. He finally nodded. "Jones. William Jebediah Jones. Colonel, United States Army." The craggy face split into a smile. "And I wanted to say thanks for dragging me from a desk job that was killing me." The smile died. "You don't mind if I smoke in the building, do you?"

Clive Bernard hesitated, taking the question wrong.

Cobb intervened. "Cigarettes, Doc. *Tobacco* cigarettes."

"Oh . . . no, man. That's cool."

Jones's smile threatened to break his face as he pulled a pack of smokes from his front pocket. "Knew you'd be all right, Doc. Your brother spoke highly of you."

Bernard's breath caught at the unexpected mention of his sibling.

Cobb took a sensing and turned to the rest of the team. "Let's take a ten-minute break so Dr. Bernard can bring Colonel Jones up to speed on what's going on. Let's say"—he glanced at his watch—"top of the hour."

Clive Bernard looked at Cobb and nodded thanks. As time moved on Cobb was proving to be more than just a security expert.

Cobb nodded a silent acknowledgment as he filed into the hallway and toward the coffee bar with the rest of the project personnel. Only Sarah Hunter remained with Bernard and Jones.

"You don't have to stay by my side twenty-four hours a day, Sarah," Bernard said, somewhat embarrassed by his constant shadows. If it wasn't Hunter, it was the big lug O'Sullivan.

"To the contrary, Doctor. But it doesn't matter, I'm growing to love your company so much that I'd do it anyway."

Her smile gave no hint of irony, but Clive Bernard knew Sarah Hunter well enough by now to know it was there as surely as there was a Great Wall in China. He smiled predatorily, for the entire world taking the remark at face value. "I knew you'd come around, dear. It was just a matter of time."

Hunter rolled her eyes. "Colonel, can you keep an eye on my charge for a few minutes? I think I could use a cup of coffee after all."

Jones nodded and smiled through a cloud of smoke, happy as a pig in shit to be legally smoking once again in a government facility. "Not a problem." He watched Sarah Hunter exit the room before turning to Bernard. "Let's have a seat, Doc."

Bernard sat in a seat at the end of the conference table. Jones pulled up a chair to sit a few feet away and began looking through the cups on the table until he found one suitably empty. Dropping the cigarette he'd smoked to just above the filter into a half inch of cold coffee, he pulled another from his pack and lit it with a battered Zippo lighter.

Bernard couldn't help but smile. "Good, huh?"

Jones nodded. "You have no idea what I've been through these past months, my friend. Pure hell."

"Of course I do. You've been working in government buildings where the individual's rights are sacrificed for the greater good."

A laugh ripped from Jones. "You can turn it off, Doc. Nigel told me about you. Think his words were something to the effect that you loved to come off as the radical type, but it wasn't really in you."

Bernard sobered. "So . . . you knew my brother."

Jones nodded, squinting through the haze of smoke enveloping his head and shoulders. "Yep. And he was a good man, Doc. A good fucking man."

"But where . . . how did you know him?"

"We served together in the Second Brigade of the Twenty-fourth Mech. I was a tank battalion S3 at the time; your brother was a company commander in one of the brigade's mech infantry battalions. When we deployed for Desert Storm, he was task organized over to us."

"So . . ."

"So I did the planning and wrote the operations orders for our task force during the war," Jones said slowly. "And I was out front with the task force commander when we executed those orders."

"Including the last one?" asked Bernard quietly.

Bill Jones dropped the half-smoked cigarette into the coffee next to its dead mate. It sizzled as it splashed into the black morass. He closed his eyes and drifted back over a decade in time, smelling the diesel fumes heavy in the air, hearing the cries of orders and updates over the radios, seeing the burning Republican Guard armored vehicles as the 24th cut off the elite Iraqi units trying to escape north. . . .

Major Bill Jones grunted as the driver of his M1A1 tank slammed on the brakes, throwing Jones into his .50 caliber machine gun as his body's momentum carried him forward in the tank's cupola. His unlit cigarette went flying from his mouth. Jones flipped his CVC switch to the intercom position. "Shit, Murph. Could you give somebody a fucking heads-up the next time? I've only got so many smokes left."

The driver's reply had nothing to do with his breaking ability or the number of cigarettes available in the Kuwait theater of operations. "We got a T-72, sir! Eleven o'clock and about five hundred meters out."

Jones felt sweat break out all over his body despite the morning's cool temperature. He and his turret were facing in more of a two o'clock position, searching for a Republican Guard tank they'd seen disappear behind a berm a few minutes earlier. Simultaneously Jones reached into the turret, grabbing the tank commander's override, swinging the turret left and swiveling his head counterclockwise in the direction of the reported threat. He saw the Russian-made tank's gunner make a final adjustment, bringing the large, dark 125mm cannon's mouth to rest aiming straight at the American tank. Despite the M1A1's ability to take a licking and keep on ticking, the extreme close range ensured that significant damage—or destruction—was imminent. No time to let the gunner get sorted out and take a better shot. "Fuck! From my position, *on the way!*" Squatting in his commander's cupola as the turret spun so that only his head was outside of the turret, Jones squeezed the trigger on his commander's control handle as soon as the tank's big 120mm gun tube was pointed in the general direction of the Republican Guard tank. The Abrams rocked backward and a cloud of smoke enveloped the M1A1.

Jones knew that unless he was very lucky—*and let's face it,* he thought, *if I was really lucky that son of a bitch wouldn't have been able to pop out of nowhere five hundred meters to our front*—he'd missed with his shot. But killing the tank hadn't been what he'd had in mind. As the Iraqi gunner was squeezing the trigger, Jones had wanted to give him something to think about, something that could take away his concentration just enough to throw his shot off the mark.

"Give me another sabot, loader!" Jones yelled into his boom mike.

"Working it, boss!" came the strained reply as the loader activated the knee switch at the rear of the crew compartment and withdrew another sabot round, flipping it expertly in midair and jamming it into the gaping maw of the 120mm breech. "Up!"

The Abrams rocked as a sabot from the T-72 struck it. The American major felt the tank list to port as the suspension system designed to carry the sixty-eight-ton Abrams's weight collapsed. But their turret and fire control systems were alive.

"Gunner . . . !"

"Give me a fucking second, boss," the gunner almost whispered as he brought his sight picture to the desired location, overlaying the T-72. He lazed. "I'm on!"

"Fire!"

The Abrams rocked backward again, unhinging itself more from the damaged left track.

Jones stared in the direction of the Iraqi tank. He could see nothing because of the smoke emitted from the big 120mm gun tube following the M1A1's last shot. Within seconds it dissipated enough for the major to make out a burning hulk. "Target!" And then he saw the Iraqi tank's wingman pop around the berm they'd been watching earlier—oriented on them. "Oh, Christ. . . ."

And then heaven decided to throw Jones and his crew a favor. As if in slow motion, a missile came into his sight headed for the second T-72. It looked as though it had overshot, as second-generation TOW missiles tend to do, but at the last second it made a final downward plunge into the enemy's thin top armor. Jones squinted as the spall from the explosion blew outward in the cool desert air. He scanned the surrounding area, praying there were no more surprises as he and his crew sat in place like sitting ducks. It looked clear. In the distance he could see other companies and teams from his task force moving forward across the smoking battlefield with no opposition.

The radio squawked through his CVC helmet's integrated speakers. *"Wildcat Three, Dragon Six. I think you and your crew owe me and my crew a case of the beverage of our choice, over."*

Jones grinned as he wiped the perspiration from his eyes with the back of a grimy hand. Even if he hadn't heard Dragon 6's call sign, he'd have known the distinct, laid-back California voice of his attached mech company commander, Nigel Bernard. He turned from his position in the cupola to see Bernard's Bradley three hundred meters to his rear right. The blond captain waved in Jones's direction, the man's ever-present Ray-Bans visible above his smile.

"You got it, Dragon," said Jones. *"But I'll make Mrs. Jones pay for the booze . . . she's the one that would be suffering if anything happened to me."*

Bernard's laugh rang clear over the radio. *"I hear you. . . ."*

The white noise hit Jones at the same time that the hidden Iraqi tank's sabot round tore into Bernard's infantry fighting vehicle. Jones barely noticed as an Air Force A-10 Warthog, just arrived on the scene, peppered the T-72 with 30mm depleted uranium cannon rounds, exploding the enemy tank into the desert sky.

The two men sat quietly, not speaking. Each stared at the wall opposite him.

"Mind if I have one of those smokes?" asked Bernard finally.

Jones raised an eyebrow. "Didn't think you smoked this . . . brand."

A chuckle escaped Clive Bernard's throat. "It's an easy transition."

Again, neither man spoke for several minutes. The only break in the shared silence was when one of the team members attempted to enter the room. Apparently Cobb was just outside the door; as fast as the man's head and shoulders appeared, he was lifted bodily from behind and pulled out of sight, the door quietly closing upon his disappearance.

Bernard leaned against the table, staring into space. "He saved your life."

Jones exhaled smoke deeply. He too stared into space. "Yeah," he said, nodding, "that he did."

Bernard nodded. "How . . . how fast . . ."

Bill Jones's head swung toward Bernard. "Doc. Look at me, Doc."

Slowly Bernard's head turned and he focused on Jones.

The colonel stared into Bernard's eyes and spoke slowly. "I was there. I saw it. He didn't feel a thing."

"You're certain?"

Jones nodded, the image of the Bradley exploding as fresh in his mind now as it had been in 1991. "Yeah. I am."

"The thoughts of him . . . burning. It was what pushed me in the direction of military research. Figured maybe, just maybe, I could do something to . . . to . . ."

"Help someone else's brother from going through the same pain you've felt for over a decade?"

A half smile crossed Bernard's lips as he dropped the remains of his cigarette into the coffee cup. It went under, bobbed to the surface once, disappeared momentarily, and then rose slowly, settling into position next to the logjam of butts created by Jones. "Something like that."

The door cracked open and Cobb looked questioningly at the two men.

"Bring them in, Mr. Cobb," said Bernard. "I believe a family meeting is in order."

As Cobb disappeared, the doctor shook his head. "Sometimes it's not easy being a genius with vision. They're not going to like this."

Jones held up his cigarette. "Doc, you've given me reason to continue living. You can count on my full support."

"But you don't even know what I have in mind."

The colonel grinned. "Sure I do. You're going to work on upgrading the Abrams and completing the work on the Tommy in parallel."

Bernard's jaw dropped. "How did you know?"

Jones exhaled three concentric smoke rings. As they floated to earth, he smiled. "You don't have a monopoly on brains, Doc. That's exactly what I'd do."

Five minutes later the heated arguments had begun to die down.

"In summary," said Bernard, "we have to look at our mission as not only rebuilding the Tommy project. We have to regard safeguarding the research already accomplished as being just as critical, if not more so. That means if the Tommies spirited away aren't recovered, they have to be destroyed."

Sue Kwan raised a hand.

"Sue," said Bernard. "You're not in grad school anymore. Just state your case."

Kwan blushed. "Clive, I'm not a military person. I'm a scientist, an engineer. But . . ." At this point she looked toward Cobb. She wasn't sure what the man had done in his previous life, but she assumed it was relevant to her next statement. "Don't we have . . . *people* . . . who can find the vehicles and destroy them? Why go to the effort of upgrading the Abrams tanks if it isn't necessary? The time, the manpower . . ."

Bernard looked at Cobb. Cobb smirked. Bernard turned to Jones, who took a long draw off of his cigarette and gave an encouraging nod. Bernard turned back to Kwan. "Sue, in the best of all worlds, we'll recover the Tommies. If we do not, they must need be destroyed. We cannot allow a belligerent foreign power access to the technology."

Nods from around the room.

"So if they have to be destroyed," continued Bernard, "what if a Special Operations unit *cannot* get to them? What if the M4Xs are reverse engineered before we can come up with a vehicle that is at least the equal of the Tommies in the enemy's hands?"

Everyone stared at Clive Bernard. His shoulders sagged as he looked around the table. "You just . . . don't . . . get it."

Dead silence. Until Colonel Bill Jones stood, opening a fresh pack of cigarettes. "Anyone mind if I smoke?" The light in his eye as he asked the question indicated that he really didn't care if there were objections.

"What Doc is trying to say, people, is that the best mechanism for taking out an armored vehicle, no matter how technologically advanced, is another armored vehicle."

Jones waited to see if there was any disagreement. There was none.

"And if we have to take out the Tommies in enemy hands, the quickest way to do it is with our own vehicles."

Sue Kwan began to raise a hand but lowered it quickly. "Colonel Jones, none of our current combat systems can come close to defeating the M4X in combat."

Jones exhaled a cloud of smoke and smiled. "You're right, darlin'. You're damned well right. Which is why the doc here is trying to say that half of our first order of business is to make the Abrams-series tank a match, or near match, against the Tommy. If we can't recover them, we have to kill 'em. *Comprende*?"

At first there was no reaction from the audience, then slowly heads began to nod. Jones looked to Bernard and threw in a nod of his own. The ball was back in the doctor's court.

"All right, then," began Bernard. "I believe the first order of business is to split into two teams . . . the Tommy team and an Abrams team." He turned to Sue Kwan. "Sue, I've examined your credentials. They're exemplary. You will head the Tommy team's efforts."

Bernard paused as Kwan opened and closed her mouth like a land-washed fish. After fifteen seconds, when no real speech had escaped her, he leaned over the conference table and stared into her eyes. "You know what needs to be done, Sue. Are you up to the task?"

Sue Kwan composed herself. Slowly she looked around the room. Finally she turned to Bernard and nodded. "Yes, sir. I'm ready."

Clive Bernard smiled. "Excellent!" He stood back from the table and clasped his hands behind his back. "For my part, I will take over the effort of upgrading the Abrams armor and ammunition in order for it to meet the M4X. No easy task, but it's a fine tank, and with recent breakthroughs in technology, I think we can do it."

At this point the doctor nodded to a young assistant sitting expectantly behind a laptop. "Bring up the modified organizational chart, Brent."

Two seconds later a hierarchy was displayed on the screen at the far end of the room. "You'll see here that I'd foreseen Dr. Butler's farewell from our team."

A few titters from the audience.

"My psychic abilities notwithstanding, here's what I came up with last night. You'll see your names divided between my and Dr. Kwan's teams. Make no mistake . . . neither half of the project is more important than the other. We must regain the technology lost when the M4Xs were stolen and our research destroyed. This is imperative for us to maintain our position as the possessor of the best armored platform in the world."

The nods from around the room came more quickly now. They were starting to believe, thank God.

"At the same time," he continued, "we must give our vintage Abrams the ability to meet the Tommy on the battlefield with some hope of success."

Rather than nods, heads were lowered. The team knew that if the Iranians gained access to the M4Xs combat systems too soon—if the M4Xs were made capable of rolling onto a battlefield—the other side would almost certainly lose, despite the team's best efforts.

"May I, Doc?" asked Bill Jones quietly, sensing the mood of the group.

Bernard, frustrated, nodded.

Jones, pro forma, lit another cigarette. For nearly a minute he looked around at the men and women responsible for fixing the mess that the U.S. military community found itself in. In the end, again pro forma, he grinned and exhaled. "Ladies, gentlemen . . . I don't have Doc Bernard's education. I'm a simple military man who has had the privilege of leading great soldiers on the field of battle."

No one moved or spoke, the only sound the ever present and persistent woodpecker from the compound's treeline.

"And what you're missing from Doc's speech goes back to exactly that . . . we have—bar none—the greatest soldiers this world has ever seen. Sparta? Rome? *Pussies*."

A few subdued laughs from around the table.

"So when the good doc here talks about the possibility of building up Abrams tanks to go against Tommies, keep that in mind. The Tommies—God forbid they're made operational by our enemies—will be manned by people who haven't won a war against a real by-God enemy since before the birth of Jesus Christ." Jones brought the cigarette back to his lips and inhaled. "We, on the other hand, would be manning the most up-to-date combat system in the world—short of the M4X—with a group of soldiers who come from the same stock that beat back the British—twice—saved Europe—twice, though there are times I'd give it all back to see the French where they deserve to be—and who have never lost a war tactically. And this action, should it come to pass, will be based on just that . . . tactics. And battlefield savvy. And the *men*."

Jones dropped the smoldering butt that had begun to burn his fingers into the cup of coffee in front of him. It bounced weekly off its forebears and then stayed still. "God help the sons of bitches who oppose them."

A tentative female voice sounded from the rear of the room. "Colonel Jones? Assuming we can make these upgrades, who will organize this group of men?"

Jones pulled the pack of cigarettes from the front pocket of his shirt. He looked to Clive Bernard and smiled as he tapped out a fresh one. "I'm glad you asked, darlin'. That would be me. And I've got a few friends who should be here anytime to help with the effort." The Zippo appeared from nowhere, flicked open, drew flame, and then disappeared. The pigpenlike cloud of smoke the team would soon come to associate with Bill Jones appeared around his head. "They will be a few of the men I was speaking of earlier."

The hiss of air brakes sounded clearly from outside the building. "And I think that would be them."

Sayid Bakr smiled from his position in the driver's seat of the bus as he watched the large gate slide open on its wheeled track. He shook his head in reluctant admiration. While no security was perfect, as demonstrated by his current position, he had to admit whoever had set up this compound's defenses had been very thorough.

Within seconds of pulling off of the main road he'd been forced to stop at an inner ring of fencing. Three guards wearing unmarked battle dress uniforms and carrying M4 carbines quickly stepped from the surrounding woods and motioned for Bakr to open the bus's passenger door. One of them stepped aboard, another stationed himself in front of the bus in a position to provide outside security, and the final guard picked up a telescopic piece of equipment from a box next to the gate and began running it beneath the vehicle—Bakr was certain that the instrument would pick up even the slightest amounts of explosive ordnance or chemicals.

The Iraqi smiled at the guard who'd stepped aboard the bus and stopped next to him.

"Identification, please," said the guard, watching Bakr from behind his sunglasses with a face that showed no laugh lines.

"Of course," Bakr replied, continuing to smile. He reached to the sun visor above his head and withdrew the identification card he'd acquired only yesterday from the unfortunate Mr. Faisal Hamarinah, a recent U.S. immigrant from Jordan. Bakr ignored the itch caused by the prosthetic nose he'd added earlier in the morning to bring his appearance in line with Mr. Hamarinah's visage. He reminded himself that he would have to phone his new employers at Fort Bragg and inform them that, most unfortunately, he would need to quit his job due to the fact that his mother had fallen quite ill.

Satisfied, the guard handed the identification back to Sayid Bakr with a nod and moved toward the rear of the bus. Bakr relaxed as he watched the guard check the passengers' IDs. Glancing beneath the dash, he confirmed that the cigarette-pack-sized black box he'd magnetically attached was not visible to anyone standing inside the bus.

Bakr had activated the piece of German electronics upon turning off the main road. Designed by a dwarfish madman in a Munich cellar for the German government's *Bundesnachrichtendienst*, or Federal Intelligence Service, the device was an amazing piece of electronic hardware. Known in very few circles, the piece of hardware was simply known as the box. Once activated, it passively collected numerous types of sensor systems, seismic, acoustic, and infrared among them. The type and GPS coordinates of each individual sensor was then stored in the box for later download and analysis. Bakr's smile was quite real when he waved good-bye to the guard as the man exited the bus and opened the first gate into the Tommy compound.

Chapter 16

Reunion in Hell

**Institute for Plant and Seed Modification Research
Employee Prayer Room
Karaj, Iran**

Silence, thought Patrick Dillon as he lay on the floor of his cell. *Finally . . . golden, blessed, fucking silence.*

Sedov had made him sit through the repeated abuse of Tom Crockett in the interrogation room two days earlier; at least he estimated it to have been two days ago. He really had no way of knowing for certain.

Once Crockett's screams had stopped, the whimpers had begun. Finally, the NCO had passed out. But even in unconsciousness the man found no peace, his body rebelling with grunts of protest as Sedov's Iranian henchmen continued their twisted work. After what seemed an eternity, Crockett had been dragged away and Dillon was once more alone with the Russian. Sedov hadn't said a word. He'd only stared at Patrick Dillon across the table, smoking his cigarettes, for nearly an hour. Dillon, his mind numb, had also sat in silence, staring at a spot on the table he'd identified earlier and made his own. Finally, his ashtray overflowing, Sergei Sedov had risen. As he limped around the table and drew abreast of his prisoner, the Russian had paused and leaned close to Dillon's ear. "Your pain has only begun, Major. You and I . . . we still have much catching up to do."

Once the Russian departed, two of the guards had

come for him. Dillon had fallen face-first onto the concrete floor when the restraints binding his hands were released. He couldn't feel his arms or shoulders; they'd passed through the numb and burning pain stages much earlier. His legs had been asleep, numb; if only his mind had been. They'd jerked him upright and helped him finally put on one of the much-sought-after orange jumpsuits. Then they'd dragged him back to his cell.

For a few hours he'd lain as though in a coma. But then he'd heard the cell next door—Tom Crockett's cell—being opened. He heard Crockett's voice, though it wasn't the voice Crockett used to possess . . . *No, no more*, the stranger's voice had said. *Please*. And the process had started once more. And Dillon had put his hands to his ears.

Patrick Dillon smiled in the darkness of his cell. He'd never realized what a joyous thing silence could be. Somewhere, a part of him wondered if Tom Crockett were dead. Another part hoped that the sergeant was, because he knew his friend would never again be whole.

As to Sedov's promise of the pain in store for him, Dillon had thus far seen nothing. Perhaps the Russian was giving him time to reflect on Crockett's ordeal, time to wonder if and when the same fate would befall him in the hope that he would break beneath the strain.

Fuck him! Dillon screamed within his own head, letting the hate fill him, needing *something* to hold on to. He screwed his eyes tightly closed and focused on the hate, embracing it like a lover. *Fuck that Russian son of a bitch!*

The sound of keys jangling in his cell door brought Patrick Dillon back to the moment. A narrow gap appeared in the darkness, heralded by the screech of rusty hinges. For a moment all Dillon could see was a line of blinding white light. Grunting, he forced himself to sit upright, holding a hand in front of his face to ward off the brightness. As his eye adjusted, Dillon slowly lowered the hand to his side. The smiling profile of a face moved into the light. Dillon squinted. It was Sedov, grinning from ear to ear like the madman he was. But something was different about the Russian. It wasn't the patch that now covered one eye. It was . . .

Then Patrick Dillon giggled. Even to him the sound contained a note of insanity. The giggle turned into a snicker, and the snicker grew into a laugh that echoed off the stone walls.

Sergei Sedov remained weak from his surgeries, but he smiled nonetheless. "You know, Dillon, I despise you more than any creature on the face of the earth, yet I cannot help but admire your ability to face adversity with a smile."

Dillon attempted to speak, but instead doubled up with racking laughter once more.

The Russian's smile faltered. "What *is it* you find so amusing, Major?"

The American officer clamped his lips shut and held up a hand, signaling for Sedov to give him a moment to compose himself. Finally he gave up and lowered his hand, roaring louder than ever, his open palm striking the cell floor over and over like a living exclamation point highlighting the laughter.

Despite himself, Sedov became caught up in Dillon's euphoria and allowed himself a small laugh.

This helped sober Dillon enough to catch his breath. He wiped his eyes. "What are *you* laughing at, Ivan?"

Sedov shrugged. "Whatever it is that *you* find so humorous, I suppose."

Dillon almost lost it again, but he managed to contain himself. "That's showing character, Ivan. They say it takes a big man to laugh at himself."

All trace of humor left Sedov. "What do you mean?"

Patrick Dillon pointed at the Russian's face.

"Please . . . *please* tell me you didn't *pay* for that nose job." And the laughter rolled again.

Sergei Sedov limped the three painful steps separating him from Patrick Dillon's side. With all of his strength the Russian lashed out with a booted foot, Dillon's grunt of pain more than making up for the pain that shot up his semi-crippled leg . . . but it didn't stop the American's laughter. "You're mad!" screamed the Russian, lashing out with his boot again and again, each time emphasizing the strike of leather on midsection by saying, *"You are mad! You are mad!"*

When the American finally lay silent, Sedov limped backward to the cell's doorway and motioned for the two Iranian guards posted in the hallway. "Take him to the interrogation room."

Dillon awoke with a start, gasping at the fresh pain. How many broken ribs could one man endure without his chest caving in? the major wondered.

Dillon felt the familiar caress of rough rope on his wrists, bonds lashing his hands behind the back of the chair once more, bonds so tight that he felt his shoulders were about to pop from their sockets. Yes, he knew this seat well enough. He squinted at the light emanating from the single bulb above the table. He turned to look over his shoulder at the sound of the door opening and closing. The American couldn't see who'd entered, but he recognized the limping cadence of the visitor's step. "Time for round two, Ivan?" he asked. He attempted to sound nonchalant, but the words were cut short by the pain ripping through his chest with each breath. "Sure you're . . . up for it? You're walking a little slowly. Really . . . you have to learn to . . . pace yourself, Ivan."

Sergei Sedov didn't reply as he made his way to the opposite side of the table. Pulling back the chair opposite Dillon's, the Russian sat. He withdrew his Gitanes from a breast pocket and lit one, smiling as he exhaled smoke in Dillon's direction. "So, how have you been, Major?" he asked, as though he'd forgotten he'd been playing kickball with Dillon's torso not ten minutes earlier.

Patrick Dillon closed his eyes and shook his head in resignation. He was so very *tired* of the Russian's games.

"You no longer wish to speak with me, Major?"

It was time to go away. Dillon searched the table a moment, finally finding the marred blemish of wood that he had decided was *his*. The longer he stared at it, the small yet infinite spot of wood on a battered table in a Middle Eastern hellhole, the further Sedov receded from his reality. It was a marvelous abberation on an otherwise plain surface and Patrick Dillon had decided that he would take as long as he needed to ponder its complexities. How long had it been there? How had it *come* to be there? Who was the offending party? The possibilities were endless, as were the mental byways resulting from each.

Sedov leaned across the table and slapped the side of Dillon's face viciously. "Can you hear me now, Major?" he asked in a voice suitable to a piano teacher, or a poet, a voice soft and melodic.

Lifting his head, Dillon tore his gaze from the table and stared at the Russian. It was an odd sensation, as both of them had only one functioning eye, each on the right side of his face. The major's lips twitched in a quick half smile. "*Fuck* you, Ivan." Then his head dropped, his gaze returned to his spot, marveling once again in its many and varied nuances.

"I see you once more fall back on your extensive vocabulary," sighed the Russian.

Dillon forced himself to look into Sergei Sedov's face. "I'd have preferred to simply flash you the bird, but unfortunately . . ." At this point he shrugged and looked over his shoulder at his bound hands.

"Yes," agreed the Russian. "That would have been *much* less gauche." But Sedov saw that his words were lost on his captive. The American was staring at the table again. He extinguished his cigarette in the ashtray and shrugged. "Very well. If you will not speak with me, perhaps you will have more to say to another of my guests."

Somewhere in Dillon's mind the statement caused surprise—he had believed Tom Crockett dead by this point, as he'd heard nothing from the NCO's cell in hours—days? He didn't know, but was not surprised enough to tear himself away from his mental musings. The door to the interrogation chamber opened and closed with a clang, but Patrick Dillon was too far into his mental journey to hear it. *Fascinating*, he thought, staring at a particular swirl within his blemish. *I wonder if that's natural or if it happened when . . .*

"Pa-Patrick?" called a quavering voice.

Dillon continued staring at the table, but a frown crossed his face. That voice . . . he knew that voice.

"Patrick?" A note of urgency now. "Can you hear me? Please, Patrick . . . *please*."

Patrick Dillon's head shot up and he strained at his bonds, grunting as the rope's rough fibers dug into his freshly injured ribs. And in front of him . . .

"Melissa?" This could not be real. Good God in heaven above, this could *not* be real. He shook his head savagely and returned his gaze to the table, willing the apparition of his former wife to be gone, to be anywhere in space and time except for this hellish place. "No," he said firmly, but in a quiet voice, again shaking his head. "You're not here. Not *here*."

Sergei Sedov leaned across the table, the smile on his face almost audible in his whispered words. "Oh, I assure you, she *is* here, Major. Did I not tell you that your pain had only just begun?"

With every ounce of strength left in his body Patrick Dillon surged against his restraints in an attempt to sink his teeth into the jugular of the animal in human form across the table from him. The soldier's chair lifted free of the floor as his body lunged at the Russian. Sedov, his smile of moments before now replaced by a desperate look of sheer terror, threw himself backward, spilling from his chair onto the floor. Dillon, still bound to his own chair, now lay sideways on the table, his face flat against its cold finish. He panted like a wounded animal, his sides heaving as he stared deep into the black core of Sergei Sedov. "Whatever happens, Sedov," he grunted through his pain, "I promise . . . you will die."

An Iranian guard grabbed the chair with Dillon attached and threw it from the table with a great heave as the Russian struggled to a standing position. Somewhere in his mind, Dillon heard Melissa scream as he flew through the air. His world exploded into a thousand starbursts as he hit the concrete floor, his body and head bouncing twice before finally coming to a rest in a corner of the room. The familiar limping gait approached. The Russian's boots stopped inches from Dillon's face, and then the Russian leaned down and grabbed Dillon by the hair, jerking his head upward to look into his face. "You were saying, Major?"

Patrick Dillon struggled to maintain consciousness, his vision going in and out as he focused on Sedov's mad visage. "By . . . my hand, Sedov. You will die . . . by . . . *my* hand." And all was darkness once again.

Chapter 17

The Boys Are Back in Town

Tommy Compound
Fort Bragg, North Carolina

Cobb stood in the gravel outside the compound's administrative building. He waited two feet outside of the entrance next to a foldout table that he'd erected a few minutes earlier. On it was a laptop computer wirelessly linked to a secure biometrics server in northern Virginia.

Bill Jones stepped out of the building and strode over to Cobb. "Is this really necessary, Cobb? And I've been meaning to ask you, do you have a name other than Cobb?"

Cobb grunted a laugh. "I've had lots of names, Colonel. Cobb will do." He ran a hand over the equipment on top of the table and nodded. "And yes, this is necessary."

"Even if I can personally vouch for the men's identities?"

Cobb didn't answer for a few moments. He finally turned to Jones. "Colonel, would it surprise you to learn that, given three days' notice, I could have your twin—down to the floral shirt and Zippo—walk off that bus and greet you? Only those closest to you would notice any difference, and it would still take them a lot of one-on-one time to figure it out."

Jones tapped a cigarette out and lit it. "You're shitting me."

Cobb shook his head. "I don't shit, Colonel."

Jones raised an eyebrow at the remark. Cobb just smiled. *You know, I think I believe him,* thought Bill Jones. *It would explain a lot.* "You're a scary fucker, Cobb."

"So I've been told," Cobb said quietly as he placed some peripheral equipment on the table next to the laptop and hooked it all together via USB ports.

Sayid Bakr braked the bus to a stop and took a quick visual reconnaissance of the compound's grounds. Not a great deal of security was apparent to the uneducated observer, but the Iraqi knew that looks could be deceiving. He conducted a slow scan of the surrounding woodline and noted quick flashes of light from two locations—guards with either binoculars or scopes. Satisfied that he had all of the information he needed, Bakr turned his attention to the administrative building in front of him. He froze—immediately he recognized the biometric software kit sitting on the table outside the building. His identification card had been enough to get him this far, but he knew his iris and fingerprint data were resident in the United States' global database in Washington from his time with the SWAT commandos. He cursed himself for being shortsighted, but quickly moved on; there was nothing to be done about it now. Either he would be called off the bus or he would not. Tempting though it was to call on Allah, Bakr did not. His god had abandoned him long ago. He was many things, Sayid Bakr told himself, but he was no hypocrite. What happened in the next few minutes was in the hands of Fate, as was all else that had happened in his life.

The passengers behind him began filing from the bus. Still anxious due to the computer setup a short distance away, Bakr started involuntarily when the first soldier tapped him on the shoulder before exiting. The man had merely expressed a very Western "thanks for the ride" to the driver, but seeing Bakr's reaction, the soldier paused.

"You better take it easy, my friend. Stress kills. Everything all right?"

Bakr felt the first beads of perspiration break on his forehead as he looked into the mustachioed man's face. Was that suspicion he saw behind the passenger's glasses, or merely concern? The Iraqi forced a quick smile. "I am fine, thank you. It is only that I just noticed the time," he said, tapping his watch. "I had not counted on it taking so long to get here."

The soldier's gaze appeared to soften. "You have some medicine to take?"

"No, worse . . . I have a nagging wife who is expecting me home within the hour," Bakr returned with a grin.

"Well, I'll not be holding you up," the man said with a laugh. "Thanks again."

"You are most welcome," called Bakr to the man's back, relaxing once more. And then his brain kicked into gear. This was a close call as it was; there was no need to take chances. He "accidentally" dropped his sunglasses to the floor. As he retrieved them, he reached beneath the dash and flipped off the box.

The first man off the bus, who proudly wore what could only be called a handlebar mustache, neatly waxed at the tips, took a single step from the vehicle's open double doors and stopped. Hands on hips, he took a deep breath of the pine-scented autumn air and turned in a slow circle. "My God but this is *bracing*." He wore thin glasses in Armani frames, khaki twill trousers, and a button-down white cotton shirt—stiffly starched, of course. A tweed jacket topped off the ensemble, along with the pièce de résistance, a yellow cavalry ascot tucked neatly into the open collar of his shirt.

"Dave Barnett," growled Jones. "When the hell are you going to get rid of that throw rug?"

Barnett spun to his old commander's voice and gave each point of his mustache a tweak. "Colonel, by *God* but it's good to see you, sir." He stepped forward and the two men embraced awkwardly, giving each other a few manly thumps on the back before parting.

Cobb gave Jones an eyebrow.

"Fuck off, Mr. Cobb," said the colonel in a low voice. "Don't tell me you've never been so happy to see an old comrade that you man-hugged him."

Cobb smiled and gave a cryptic *to each his own* shrug. Then he paused, looking at his laptop's screen.

"What is it?" asked Jones, noting the change in the security man's demeanor.

Cobb tapped a command into the computer's keyboard before replying. "I don't know . . . ," he said, eyes glued to the machine's display. "I've got a few of the compound's security systems messaging this box if they receive unusual hits. For a minute there . . ." He stopped talking as he typed more commands, a look of frustration crossing his normally placid features.

"For a minute there . . . ," prompted Jones.

Cobb shook his head. "It looked like one of our electronic sensors located atop the admin building picked up some kind of energy source that hadn't shown up on the compound previously." A few more pecks of the keyboard, then a frown. "Whatever it was, it's gone now."

"What do you think it was?"

"No idea," replied Cobb. "Whatever it was, I've got its signature. Could have been a mobile phone or wirelessly connected Blackberry device belonging to one of the guys on the bus. Some of our gear is pretty sensitive, so it could have been anything. Still, I'll run through it again tonight, call in some people if need be."

"I have the utmost confidence you'll get to the bottom of the mystery, Mr. Cobb," Jones said with a straight face. "You strike me as a dog who doesn't let go of a bone until he's reached that rich marrow center."

Despite himself, Cobb smiled. He picked up a digital camera that was wired into the laptop. "Enough on that topic, let's get to the business at hand. Say cheese, Colonel Barnett." With that he snapped a photo. Quickly transitioning, the security chief picked up another piece of hardware. It featured a rounded, slotted space running along its top edge. "Index finger, please, Colonel." Barnett held out his right hand and placed his index finger into the slot until a yellow light winked on and off. "Thank you, sir," said Cobb, putting down the fingerprint device and picking up what looked like a small plastic sighting mechanism. "Please look into the aperture . . . don't blink . . . good, thanks. That does it."

"Now what?" asked Jones.

"Stand by," said Cobb distractedly. He typed a few instructions into the laptop and hit the ENTER button. Within seconds a reply returned from Virginia. He read it over, speaking out loud. "Confirmed, Lieutenant Colonel David Llewellen Barnett, U.S. Army." He looked up from the screen. "Welcome, Colonel. Glad to have you aboard."

Jones looked down at the screen. "It says that the fingerprint and iris scan positively match to Barnett, but that the facial recognition was a miss."

Cobb grunted. "The facial recognition software is still in developmental infancy. Hit and miss at best; we're working on it."

Others continued to climb from the bus. Shortly, a small crowd gathered around the table. A man with blondish red hair, just above average height and with that lean yet muscular look common to white guys who played shooting guard in northeastern universities, stepped forward. "How goes it, Colonel?"

"Mike!" said Jones, stepping forward and grasping

the newcomer's outstretched hand. "Damned good to
see you, son. Sorry to hear you had to withdraw from
Leavenworth so soon into the start of your class."

Mike Stuart shrugged. "Command and General
Staff College can wait, Colonel," he said. "Sometimes
in life, you have to prioritize."

Jones flipped the Zippo open and closed so quickly
that no one saw him light the cigarette dangling from
his lip. He withdrew it and pointed the glowing tip
toward his former subordinate. "Truer fucking words
have rarely been spoken, son, and that's no shit."

Stuart nodded solemnly. Normally an easygoing
man who was quick to smile, Dillon's abduction had
hit the young major hard. He and Dillon had been
company commanders together in the Iron Tigers of
2-77 Armor at Fort Carson. They'd fought two wars
together. And they'd been best friends. Their last few
conversations had dealt with plans for a bachelor
Thanksgiving in Arizona—sketchy discussions at best,
primarily dealing with details about Mexican steak and
beans along with lots of Negra Modelo beer. They'd
agreed that if they were to be thankful, there was
better fare than turkey and dressing to feast upon.

It had been good to hear his friend slowly coming
back to his old self following the divorce. Mike Stuart,
like most of Dillon's friends, had been angry with Melissa Dillon. And like most of Dillon's single friends,
seeing what they'd thought the perfect marriage—
something they could look at and aspire to for themselves one day—end for no apparent reason, they'd
felt betrayed almost as much as Dillon himself. But
Stuart knew now that Melissa was missing. He also
knew she'd gone to see Bill Jones in Tampa in an
attempt to get Jones to get the big Army wheels moving to find his friend and her former husband. Stuart
was having a hard time maintaining his resentment for
Melissa now. He was at the point where he just
wanted it all to go away. As that wasn't going to happen, he did the next best thing . . . he'd hung up on

Bill Jones five minutes after Jones had phoned him at Fort Leavenworth, Kansas, and sped to the airport, taking only a few minutes at his place to throw together his personal kit bag of field gear.

"So let me see," said Jones, stepping forward. "Who else've we got?"

A beefy mountain of a man separated himself from the group. Because of his height, width, and ever-present five o'clock shadow, the man was known by only one name in armor circles. "Bluto!" exclaimed Jones. "How are you, man? And that's a damned fine-looking shirt."

Bluto Wyatt, a newly promoted captain who'd been packing his bags for Fort Knox and the Armor Officer Advanced Course in preparation for a company command position, twirled to display a shirt that could have been the twin of Jones's own. The big man grinned and turned a slow circle, arms extended from his sides, to better display the amalgamation of swirling floral patterns. "Thanks, sir. Fucking Doc has been bitching for hours that it was so loud his ears were starting to hurt."

"That's because it's the most hideous piece of apparel I've ever seen," said a tall, thin officer as he stepped forward, hand outstretched. "Good to see you, Colonel. Only sorry about the circumstances."

Jones reflected how much Doc Hancock had grown and matured from the newly commissioned second lieutenant who'd served under him during the defense of Kuwait two years earlier. "Doc, glad you could make it, son."

"Wouldn't miss it for the world, sir. Major Dillon did enough for me. It's time to return the favor," said the tall, thin first lieutenant. Like Bluto Wyatt, Hancock had served under Patrick Dillon's command in C Company, 2-77 Armor, the unit better known to the world—thanks to embedded reporting during the Russo-Saudi war—as Cold Steel.

"What the hell happened to your trademark glasses,

Doc? Something just doesn't look right seeing you without them."

Hancock grinned. "Took the LASIK plunge last year. Army's dime."

Jones nodded. "And how does Sam like the new look?"

"She likes it just fine," called a feminine voice from the back of the crowd. The men parted and a woman with shoulder-length auburn hair, creamy white skin, and green eyes stepped forward to wrap Jones in a hug.

"Easy, darlin'," said Jones, gently pushing Sam Mathison-Hancock back for a better look. "You know my old ticker can't take but so much excitement." The old warhorse's eyes twinkled merrily. "You're looking good, Sam. Motherhood agrees with you."

"Shut up, Bill," said Sam, giving Jones a small shove for emphasis. "You're still in your forties and fit as a fiddle, but you make it sound for the world as if you're ready for the Old Soldiers Home. Why, if I hadn't allowed Doc to tie me up so early in life, I think I could have had a little fling with you." She wiggled her eyebrows. "Maybe more."

"You'd have been the death of me, darlin', and that's the truth." A frown crossed Jones's face as he began to speak again.

Sam cut him off. "Dammit, Colonel, I know what you're about to say. *There's no place here for an attack helo pilot* or *a woman, so what are you doing here? Am I right?*"

Jones nodded, the smile in his eyes gone. "That pretty well sums it up, Sammy."

"Well, that's too damned bad, sir, because I owe Patrick Dillon my life." The Kiowa Warrior driver looked taller than her five and a half feet as she placed her fists on her hips and stared up at Jones. "You try to keep me off this team, Colonel, I swear to God you'll regret it to your dying day."

Jones, married for over two decades and with a

houseful of daughters of his own, didn't take the threat lightly. "But what can you do, Sam? I need tankers, not aviators. And what about your baby?"

Sam flushed. "I note you didn't have a problem with Doc making the trip. You didn't ask *him* who was watching his child."

"Whoaaaaa, Nelly," began Jones, hands thrust protectively in front of him. "I didn't mean . . ."

Sam's finger was in the senior officer's face. "The hell you didn't!"

Jones looked toward Doc Hancock. The lieutenant shook his head in sympathy but said nothing. It was clear Jones was on his own. The colonel turned his head, hoping possibly Cobb would come to his aid. The operator just grinned. He finally looked back to Sam Hancock, the girl who'd over the years become like another of his daughters. "What can I tell you, Sam? You're right. It was an asshole thing to say. But you've got to throw me a bone here—I'm trying to get used to this new Army, but it's tough at times for an old man—"

Sam Hancock began to interrupt, but Jones threw up a hand. "For a *soldier* such as myself with *years of experience*. In the old days women didn't go to war, at least not to the front lines." He looked toward the ground. "Besides, I kind of like Little Bill, I worry about him." The colonel paused a moment. "*And* I worry about his mother." Jones looked up, a small amount of defiance now in his eyes. "Is that all right with you?"

Sam Hancock's stern look slowly melted. She couldn't stay angry long with the man she thought so much of that she and Doc had decided to name their firstborn child after him. "Listen, you old dinosaur, I'll pull my weight. You're going to need some help around here. I've got staff and operational experience, so I'll find a way to contribute. All right?"

Jones nodded, knowing when to fold his cards. "Good enough, darlin'. Good enough."

He turned and surveiled the remaining members of the group. He recognized a few of the other officers and NCOs from 3rd Brigade and the 24th ID. The ones he didn't recognize he knew to be the personnel that old friends from around the community had recommended. They'd all volunteered with little knowledge of exactly what it was they were volunteering for other than that the request came from the legend, Wild Bill Jones. That had been good enough for these men. And thanks to Tom Werner, they'd all been released on temporary duty for as long as he needed them.

Jones crushed his cigarette beneath his shoe and looked up with a smile. "Gentlemen—and lady—I want to thank you all for leaving your duties on such short notice, with little idea of what exactly it was you were volunteering for. We're going to fix that now. Once you've heard what I've got to say, you all still have the option of opting out. Clear?"

No one replied. If anything, the group appeared a little insulted by the final remark.

"Colonel?"

Jones turned to Cobb and raised an eyebrow in question.

"We need to finish the screening first, sir. I don't think you want to give out too much detail until we get inside. You never know who's listening."

Jones scoffed. "Shit, Cobb, the woods are cleared for over a hundred meters in every direction. Assuming there was anyone nearby, how the hell could they hear anything said?"

Instead of replying to Jones, Cobb spoke into the thin boom mike attached to the wireless headset he wore. "Sector Two, report."

A sage-and-brown speck that had moments ago seemed a part of the forest took a step into the clearing. Cobb set the radio on his belt to speaker.

"Two, sector clear, continuing to monitor," came a disembodied voice from the radio. "And you tell the colonel if he thinks he can train a SOF operator to handle those steel beasts of his, he can sign me up now."

Cobb smiled.

Jones grimaced. "All right, folks. As soon as Mr. Cobb gives you the green light, meet me inside."

Fresh sweat trickled down the back of Sayid Bakr's shirt despite the bus's air conditioning system being set to its most frigid temperature. Only three men remained to be screened by the biometrics system, and then . . .

The Iraqi noticed one of the compound guards break away from the group remaining outside the admin building and move his way. Before the man had a chance to knock on the door, Bakr opened it. The guard stepped into the bus and pulled his sunglasses free of his face. Pulling a handkerchief from his rear pocket, the guard wiped his brow.

"You hanging around for any particular reason?" asked the guard, replacing the handkerchief.

Sayid Bakr inwardly sighed. "I did not know if anyone needed to return to the main post," he said.

The guard twirled an index finger in the air above his head. "Nope. You can move out." He then keyed the radio on his hip and spoke into his headset as he stepped from the bus. "Open the gate, bus is clear."

Chapter 18

Unto the Breach

South of Karaj, Iran

Rolf Krieger lifted himself from the ground and gingerly reached a hand around to ensure his sore backside was still in one piece. Yes; painful, but there. The MC-4 parachutes used by the team, designed specifically for high-altitude combat jumps, had seemed to ensure the rest of the team landed as lightly on their feet as ballerinas. Krieger had managed more of a sack-of-potatoes thud into the desert floor, but he wasn't complaining. He knew he was lucky to be alive—and that he wouldn't be if it hadn't been for Hawk Davies's intense tutoring.

He was still removing his harness when Jack Kelly approached. "You all right? That was about the ugliest landing I've ever seen. And I was in the Eighty-second Airborne Division, so that's no small statement."

Krieger nodded, noting that Kelly had already bagged and stashed his own jump gear and was ready to move out. "Yes, sir. I'm fine. I caught a . . . slip wind . . . just before I landed." Krieger hoped that "catching a slip wind" made some manner of sense, but as a "nasty leg" he was over his head when it came to Airborne slang.

Kelly frowned and was about to say more when Davies and Luke Dodd joined them. The rest of the ODA had already spread out to provide local security of the LZ. "Come on, Lieutenant, we gotta get movin'," said the master sergeant, helping Krieger with his gear. "I got him, Sonny. You can get back to work."

Kelly nodded and walked away to link up with George Greenfield, who'd acknowledged a firm visual on the team by radio a minute earlier.

Hawk Davies began laughing under his breath once Kelly was a few feet away. "That was fucking beautiful, Krieger."

"Beautiful? Did you not see me smash into the desert and get pulled along by my parachute for fifty meters?"

"Yeah," said Davies, cutting the laugh short but still smiling. "But you should be dead, mister. I didn't give you a snowball's chance in hell."

"Then why did you let me jump?"

The smile disappeared from the Green Beret's face. "Good question." He shook his head. "Can't say for sure. First, I knew it would take an act of God to stop you. Second, you were no real danger to anyone but yourself. Finally . . ." The NCO shrugged. "I just had a feelin', that's all."

"Thank you, Hawk," said Krieger seriously. "I am in your debt."

Hawk straightened and stared into Krieger's earnest face, embarrassed by the sincerity in the scout's tone. He looked away for a moment before turning to Krieger and nodding in the direction Kelly'd moved. "Move the fuck out, Lieutenant. I ain't babysittin' ya anymore."

Krieger finished adjusting his gear, grabbed his M4, and moved out with a nod. Davies watched the scout as he moved away silently, blending with the night. Davies smiled. The kid might be an accident waiting to happen in the air, but he was smooth as silk on the ground.

"You did good work there, Hawk," said Luke Dodd.

Davies jumped. He'd forgotten the CIA officer was behind him. He finished stashing Krieger's jump kit beneath a pile of rocks before straightening and wiping his hands on his pants. He shrugged as he turned back to Dodd. "That's my job, Mr. Dodd."

Dodd shook his head. "Don't bullshit me. I've got almost as many high-altitude jumps under my belt as you. What you did for Krieger was above and beyond. If it had been anyone else but that big lug I think they'd still be floating up there, probably landing atop one of the Ayatollah's palaces in Tehran sometime next spring. Assuming they lived."

Davies said nothing, so Dodd continued. "But you took care of him, and he's so smart that he was able to absorb enough to get him down in one piece." Luke Dodd shook his head, looking at the curtain of darkness into which Rolf Krieger had disappeared. "I haven't known him much longer than you, but . . ." Dodd paused, seeking the right words. "The man has more heart than anyone I've ever known." He shook his head again. "I dunno, it's difficult to explain. But somehow, with your help, I knew he'd be all right."

The Special Forces NCO nodded. "Yeah, the kid does have potential, doesn't he? I might make a SOF soldier of him yet."

Vicinity: Institute for Plant and Seed Modification Research
Karaj, Iran

An hour later George Greenfield, replete in the local robes of a good Iranian citizen, clapped a hand to Jack "Sonny" Kelly's shoulder. "All right, Captain. I'll see you on the high ground when you finish up."

Kelly, his facial features hidden beneath dark camouflage paint, shook his head. "God knows it must be bad when Agency spooks start talking in Army-speak."

Another thump on the shoulder. "Don't worry,

Captain, I've got faith in you guys. Get in, grab our people, and get out of there. Remember from the time you call 'go' to me, it'll take fifteen minutes for the Nightstalkers to have the Black Hawks in position at the linkup point for a pickup."

Both men knew that the birds hauling them out weren't your garden-variety MH-60 Black Hawks. Designed with much input from the 160th SOAR's pilots, the MH-60K was the Army's premier Special Operations Aircraft (SOA) medium helicopter. Featuring a fully integrated night-vision-goggle-compatible glass cockpit, it could carry twelve men over seven hundred fifty miles without refueling. With its forward-looking infrared (FLIR) system, electronic sensors and countermeasures suites, digital map generator, and terrain avoidance–terrain following multimode radar, the 60K was designed to get operators into and out of hostile territory in pitch-black conditions and adverse weather. With two General Electric T700 turboshaft engines, the birds weren't slow in carrying out the missions. The ability of the aircraft to mount two .50 caliber heavy machine guns or two rapid-firing 7.62mm "mini-guns" also gave the 160th pilots a certain warm and fuzzy feeling when things got hairy and their beloved Little Bird aircraft weren't available for covering fire.

Jack Kelly gave George "Ali" Greenfield a nod. "Sure you won't be coming with us?"

Greenfield shook his head as he jogged away. "Are you kidding?" he called over his shoulder. "Things are just starting to get interesting in this country. Think I'll hang around to see what happens."

Kelly turned to the job at hand. Raising his night-vision goggles, he looked at the maintenance shack through which he and his men would enter the ventilation shaft and gain access to the institute's lower level. He spoke into a thin boom mike. "Hefe . . . you in position?"

"Roger," Vega whispered from his vantage. "I got eyes on target, 'mano."

The captain looked toward the mosque where Will Purdue was to set up. "Lurch?"

"In a minute," came back Purdue. "An overzealous mullah spotted me accessing my position, so I got sidetracked for a minute telling him a bedtime story and putting him to sleep. I'll be set in one mike."

Vega's voice could barely be heard over the comm sets. "Told you it was bad juju . . . *el stupido*." To Purdue's credit, he didn't reply to the jibe.

"Give me an up when you're in, Lurch," said Kelly. "And cut the chatter over my net."

Two minutes later Purdue came over the team comms link. "I'm set."

"Roger, execute."

Kelly barely had time to picture his two snipers peering through the night optics mounted to their M24 sniper rifles when two soft hisses sounded so close together that they could have been one sound.

"Tower one down," said Vega as he watched his Iranian target silently tumble forty feet to the ground, a 7.62mm round having made a small hole between his eyes. The sniper knew the exit wound would be considerably larger and uglier.

"Tower two down," said Purdue. "You're clear, Sonny. We've got your back."

"Go, Crapper," called Kelly over the team comms link.

"Give me ten seconds, Sonny," called the young engineer, Taylor, as he sprinted for the shack. Kelly watched through his night-vision goggles as Taylor arrived at the shack, pulled a pair of small, specially designed bolt cutters, and entered the shack, all within moments. "I'm in, Sonny. Hitting the vent. Move."

"Move out," said Kelly. He didn't wait for the rest of the team; he knew they'd be with him. The Berets made little noise as they sprinted toward the shack. They were the select of the select, and noise discipline—ensuring no equipment clanked from metal on metal contact, for example—was second nature.

They'd trained and operated for so many hours wearing NVGs mounted to their faces that they could live the rest of their lives in a green world and not notice much difference. As the team reached the shack entrance, Bull Dell was in the lead. He hit the vent—already open, with a grinning Crapper Taylor extending an inviting hand downward—and kept moving, the senior team engineer, Boom Eastbrook, on his tail. The remaining members of the team, minus the snipers, spread out within the shack and waited for lights out.

Jack Kelly stood over the shaft entrance peering down. He saw a light source from the bottom. It was briefly interrupted as Bull Dell and Boom Eastbrook opened the access door on the third level and moved into the hallway. Kelly didn't bother transmitting, but hissed in a harsh whisper that the men in the shack could clearly hear. "All right, they're in. Stand by." Without realizing it, the ten men standing in the darkness leaned toward the dark shaft pit, listening for gunfire that would tell them their teammates had been spotted and were in need of assistance. But the sound of gunfire didn't come.

Patrick Dillon again found himself bound in front of the interrogation room's single piece of furniture other than the two chairs. But now he wasn't thinking of the intricacies of his table's blemish. Now he faced his former wife. Melissa Dillon was tied much as he was, facing him across the expanse of wood. She looked as though she hadn't been groomed in a couple of days, but otherwise appeared unharmed.

"Patrick, I'm so sorry," she said quietly.

Dillon cocked his head in consternation. "Sorry? What do you have to be sorry for?"

Melissa hung her head for a few seconds before looking up and replying with tears in her eyes. "For *everything*," she whispered.

Dillon didn't speak. Instead he raised his eyes above his former wife's head and glared at the grinning visage of Sergei Sedov, who stood just behind her. "I'll give you the codes. Just leave her alone."

The Russian laughed as he lit a Gitane. "*Now* you want to give me the codes?" he asked through a pall of blue smoke. "Bravo, Major." The smile disappeared. "I have had your codes for the past twenty-four hours. I will say this for your man Crockett—he held out longer than I could have." It was difficult to say whether the shudder than ran through Sergei Sedov before he continued was real or contrived. "Omar, his guard—you remember, the big fellow who took such a liking to Master Sergeant Crockett? Apparently his attentions became too much. And, as was inevitable, the codes came spilling out."

"Then *why*?" Dillon screamed, lurching against his bonds. He threw his head in Melissa's direction. "You don't need her. Hell, you don't even need me any longer."

Sedov grinned. "I will get much more from you than codes, Major." He glanced down at Melissa Dillon and the smile widened. *"Much more."*

It took every bit of the American officer's discipline not to do a mental and emotional breakdown. He looked steadily at the man he hated like no other in the world, the man he hated with a hate he had not known himself capable of feeling. "You've got the codes. Let her go."

"Let her go? The woman you love?"

Patrick Dillon laughed and shook his head. "You're so proud of yourself, you piece of shit *prick*. But you didn't do your homework. We're divorced."

For the first time since the session had begun, Sergei Sedov was at a loss for words. He searched Patrick Dillon's face. "Divorced?"

"Yeah, *divorced*, you nimrod," replied Dillon, smiling. "As in no longer married. As in she was seeing another man. *Why in the hell would I give a shit what you do to her?!*"

The shock on Melissa's face was all too real. "You . . . knew?"

Dillon looked from Sedov to his former wife, the mother of his children, his countenance softening, a small smile forming along his mouth. "I'm a tanker, sweetheart, but I'm not stupid."

"This is all very touching," Sedov interrupted, "but—"

"Shut the fuck up and stay out of this," snapped Dillon.

Sergei Sedov sneered and reached a hand over Melissa Dillon's shoulder and grasped her right breast in a fierce grip, forcing a scream of pain from her. "Then you will not care if I entertain myself, Major? Right here in front of you? After all, you don't care what happens to her, do you?" He smiled knowingly. "Or . . . do you?"

Dillon stared at the man across from him. "Just remember what I told you. By *my* hand. And now it's going to be painful."

Sedov moved around the table until he stood at Dillon's side. "Do you think that I do not know what you're thinking, Major? That despite the fact that I have the codes in hand, you can still somehow find a way to delay aiding us in our efforts?" The Russian barked a harsh laugh. "I *have* done my homework, Major Dillon. I know that, even with an authorized individual such as yourself or Sergeant Crockett, that through a minute movement of your eye during the iris scanning process you can force a negative response from the system, thus making it impossible for us to gain access to the machines' inner workings." And now a real smile crossed his face. "But that is no longer a concern."

The Russian reached to his face and tore away the bandage covering his left eye. The first thought to strike Dillon was that the Russian's eye was the same striking, deep green as Tom Crockett's. He stiffened against his seat in horror. "You fucking *monster!*"

Sergei Sedov threw back his head and howled in maniacal glee. "*Monster?* Perhaps I am, Major. But part of the monstrosity I have become is thanks to what you did to me on that battlefield in Iraq, for leaving me a living, breathing cripple who would later be thrown to his former masters!" He backhanded Dillon across the face. Melissa screamed.

Sedov turned to the American woman and smiled. "Oh, I am so sorry. I'd almost forgotten you, my dear." Melissa shrank away as the Russian limped toward her, a smile lighting his face.

"Sedovvvvvv," growled Patrick Dillon in a low voice.

The Russian ripped Melissa Dillon's blouse from her. "I tried to tell you, Major. Your pain has only begun." He caressed the upper contours of Melissa's breast. "And *your* pleasure is about to begin," he whispered to Melissa.

Melissa Dillon's scream reached its crescendo as the room went dark.

Tommy Compound
Fort Bragg, North Carolina

Clive Bernard, Bill Jones, and Dave Barnett sat in Bernard's office. The reason for the meeting: a brainstorming session to get the M1 piece of their work jump-started.

"We've got to look at this problem in reverse, Clive," said Jones. "You want an M1-series tank to survive in the field against a Tommy, so what do you do? You look at what the Tommy can dish out and what the Abrams can take. As your subject matter expert, I know the Abrams's capabilities intimately. But the M4X1 project has been so secret, I know next to nothing from that side of the equation." Two seconds later a halo of smoke engulfed his head as he lit up. His face appeared as he bent forward, staring at the project lead. "So where do we stand, Clive?"

Clive Bernard was an expert in metals and systems technology. He had pored over every scrap of data available on the M4X1 Franks Combat System. Although Sue Kwan would be handling the Tommy project on a daily basis as Bernard himself worked the Abrams upgrade piece, the scientist knew that he'd have to be intimately familiar with the Tommies. He exhaled with a defeated shrug and stared at Jones. "Picture an M1A2-SEP Abrams," he said, referring to the most advanced version of the Abrams, "going toe-to-toe with Herbie the Love Bug. That's the best analogy I can give you, Bill."

"And our Abrams is *Herbie*?" deadpanned Jones. "The fucking hell you say!"

Dave Barnett took a gentle pull from his briar-bowl pipe, eyes closed, enjoying his latest blend—Smoked Cavendish. He pulled the pipe from between his teeth and bent his head conspiratorially toward Jones. "Sir, I take it, as we all volunteered for this mission, that we're free to pull out at any time?"

"Fuck you, Dave," said Jones, never taking his eyes from Bernard. "You're in this with the rest of us."

Barnett nodded thoughtfully as he returned the pipe to his mouth. "Well, it was a question that begged asking, sir." He turned away from Jones. "But no one said anything about this being a *suicide* mission," he muttered in an aside.

Jones ignored his 2IC. Despite his blustering, it would take both hell and high water to keep Barnett from the mission. "But if we took Herbie and girded him sufficiently to survive an Abrams's go-to-war depleted-uranium munitions and put a gun on him *geared toward* defeating the Tommy's armor . . . the Love Bug would have a chance?" he ventured, knowing from the look on Clive Bernard's face as he said the words that he was grasping at straws.

Instead of answering, Bernard turned his head and watched one of the project assistants, a leggy blonde of twenty-two, walk past his office door. He smiled appreciatively and a vacant expression momentarily washed over his face as he allowed himself a minor diversion from the project's stresses.

"Doc!" yelled Jones, standing and slamming the door shut.

"All right, all right," said Bernard, shaking his head. "Listen, it's not that simple, Colonel. And the Abrams gun system isn't our biggest challenge." The scientist turned and paced, gesturing in the air as he attempted to explain. "Here's the problem. You continue thinking in terms of the Abrams because that's all you've known for the past two decades—and rightly so, as it's been the finest tank in the world. But you see, the Tommy's gun system is *plasma*-based. Its ammunition can more closely be compared to a super HEAT round," continued the scientist, referring to the high-explosive antitank rounds that were in actuality not used against other tanks, but only against lightly armored vehicles or trucks. "It's the only ammunition the Tommy's main gun fires and it can burn its way through any armored system currently fielded in less than a second." He paused and raised a finger. "Oh, it also fields a four-pack of the latest-generation Stinger antiair missiles on the right side of the turret and a two-pack antitank missile that's accurate to almost ten klicks on its left. And a .50 caliber machine gun for lightly armored vehicles that can be fired remotely, thus not exposing the two crewmen in the turret."

Jones stared silently for a few seconds. "Is that it?"

Bernard stopped pacing and turned to Jones and Barnett. He shook his head. "The M4X1 features a sighting system like nothing ever seen on a ground combat vehicle. There's no gunner with his face to a sight. The tank commander and gunner each have optics imbedded into the face shield of their combat vehicle crewman helmet that gives them a panoramic view of what the system's external sight is viewing—very similar to the heads-up display, or HUD, you've seen on the latest generation of American fighter aircraft. Once they have a target in view, the commander or gunner merely has to say 'lock on' and 'fire' to engage. On the 'lock on' command, the firing system will automatically calculate range, environmental conditions, vehicle cant, and so on, and be ready to fire in less than a second." Bernard paused, a serious expression on his face. "But I digress. The bottom line, you see, our major hurdle to crack, is making the Abrams survivable against the Tommy. If we can't do that . . ."

Silence ensued for several seconds following Bernard's words.

"Fuck me," muttered Jones finally.

"Fuck you?" said Barnett. "Fuck *us*. Royally."

Bernard was nodding in agreement with the lieutenant colonel's assessment. "That's right, we're a team."

Jones and Barnett stared at the scientist. It was Jones who asked the question. "So, Dr. Bernard, you're planning on accompanying us if this venture goes down?"

Shock etched its way across Clive Bernard's features. "Well . . . no."

Barnett knocked his pipe against the bottom of one of his Doc Martens and pocketed it. "Then *you're* not royally fucked, Doc."

Bernard grimaced. "I see what you mean."

"All right, Doc, let's get down to it," said Jones. "What can we do? Let's start with surviving long enough to hit the Tommies. They've got AT missiles and a plasma cannon, along with some other shit."

"Quite a synopsis," said Bernard. " 'Plasma cannon along with some other shit.' But yes, in a nutshell, that's the gist of it."

"I do have a way with words, you gotta give me that," said Jones without breaking stride. "What mods can we make to an Abrams that will help it survive an engagement against a Tommy?" He didn't add "quickly," as it went without saying that there was no time for an R&D effort.

"It's not as hopeless as it looks, Colonel," said Bernard. "Contrary to popular belief, not everyone connected with cutting-edge military ground research was taken out by the strikes against the first Tommy team. We've got some of the brightest minds from the American defense industry with us here at Fort Bragg, as well as other groups from around the country remotely helping us with our efforts. The answer to the missile problem is the simplest fix. A team at General Dynamics' Land System Division has been working that problem for a few years and have a killer system developed—well, almost developed—that can allegedly confuse the hell out of any AT missile on the market." Bernard leaned forward, excited to be imparting some good news for a change. "Are you familiar with the Russian Shtora-1 antitank missile countermeasures system used on Russia's latest tanks?"

"I know I am," said Barnett. "I got a good look at several of the Shtora systems as I cruised by burning Russian T-90 tanks hit by American AT missiles during the war last year. Mind-boggling how well the system worked for them."

"I was going to say, the technology is similar, but that the Russian system wasn't ready for prime time," said Bernard. "General Dynamics' system, which they're calling Shield . . ."

"What does Shield stand for?" asked Jones.

Bernard frowned. "It doesn't stand for anything. It's so named because of the concept, a shield protecting the tanks from—"

"It's not an acronym for something like Shoving Hardware Into Electronic Light Devices?"

"No," said Bernard, shaking his head in exasperation. "May I continue now?"

Jones turned to Barnett. "I *hate* fucking acronyms."

Barnett nodded sympathetically. "I concur, sir. At a certain point the brain goes into a-b-c overload."

"It's not an acronym! Can I go on?"

"Jeez, Doc . . . yeah, go ahead," said Jones.

"All right. The Shield system is about a fifteen-minute install—later versions will be more hard-mounted, but for now the system is designed for rapid installation and removal for the testing phase. It has three key components: an electro-optical interface station that includes a jammer, modulator, and control panel; a laser warning system; and a control system comprised of a control panel, microprocessor, and a manual screen-laying panel. The control system processes the information from the external sensors and activates the onboard smoke dispensers as necessary to provide a smoke screen. Infrared lights—one on either side of the main gun—continuously emit coded, pulsed infrared jamming when an incoming ATGM has been detected."

"Field of view?" asked Barnett.

"Three hundred sixty degrees horizontally and negative five to twenty-five degrees in elevation," replied Bernard. "As I said, other than integrating the suite with the onboard smoke dispensers already mounted on the Abrams—the Russians have a separate aerosol set of dispensers that's worthless—we're talking the same technologies. Only ours has actually *worked* in testing to date."

But Bill Jones was shaking his head. "Clive, if I had a dime for every new system I heard that was going to be the best thing since the laser rangefinder—and I noted that even you used the terms 'allegedly' and 'almost developed' . . ." Jones left the rest unsaid, but it was clear that he was unimpressed.

Clive Bernard's mouth tightened and his ears began taking on color. "Colonel, I know a lot of people think my life has been something of a waste. And maybe they're right. But I'll tell you this," he continued, building momentum. "I'm a *smart* dude. And I've kept my finger on the pulse of the defense industry for the past decade. I've seen the data—the GD team *is* close. And I lit a fire under their collective asses a week ago. They're bringing some systems here for testing tomorrow, and you and your war dogs *will* install them on the Abrams we trucked in from Knox and you *will* test them. Am I clear?"

Bill Jones's face broke out in a grin that lit his craggy features from ear to ear. "You know, Doc, that's the first time I've seen some fire in your eyes." The old tanker nodded. "Yeah, I'm clear, boss." He turned to Barnett. "'War dogs,'" he said. "That's kinda catchy, don't you think, Dave?"

Barnett nodded. "Very sexy, sir."

Jones turned back to Bernard. "All right, Clive. Me and my war dogs will give the Shield systems a thorough shakedown . . . but when the M1A2s arrive from Fort Hood, we'll need to redo the tests."

Bernard nodded. "Of course. But for now, we'll at least find out if the systems work. If the effort goes well on the A1s, they should work on the A2-SEPs . . . just a matter of integration at that point."

"Exactly," said Jones. "Assuming the Shield testing pans out, what about this Star-Wars-plasma-cannon bullshit?"

Instead of answering, Bernard reached for a Motorola communication device on his hip. Bringing it to his lips, he pressed the transmit button. "Mordechai?"

Two seconds later a heavily accented voiced answered. "Yes, Clive?"

"Could you come to my office, please? And bring your samples."

A moment's hesitation. "All . . . all right. On my way."

Jones looked at Bernard curiously as the doctor pocketed his radio. "What was that about?"

Bernard shifted uncomfortably. "Mordechai is a recent immigrant to America, Colonel. He's still not entirely comfortable in his new surroundings."

Barnett repacked his pipe, an agitation in his movements not normally present making his ritual look jerky. "A *recent immigrant*? And you've got him working a top-secret project that's already been struck at once?"

"Listen," flared Bernard, "the next time you're handed a critical mission that's falling apart at the seams, with little to no data to fall back on, and you're told to pick the best people available to help you get the *fucking* job done, you let me know how *you'd* go about it. All right, Colonel?"

Dave Barnett smiled over the top of his pipe as he struck a match and inhaled. "Your explanation is noted, Doctor. I'll withhold judgment until we meet . . . what was his name?"

"Mordechai. Dr. Mordechai Levy."

"Israeli?" asked Jones.

Bernard nodded. "Yes."

"So why is an Israeli scientist working the project?" asked Barnett. "It doesn't make any sense, Doc."

"Mordechai Levy was a member of Israel's military defense research and development community for the past two decades." The doctor shifted uncomfortably. "His duties included frequent trips to the U.S. to visit defense industry contractor facilities and academic institutions to discuss projects in which we and Israel shared common interests."

"He was a fucking spy, wasn't he?" stated Jones flatly.

"And got caught with his hand in the cookie jar?" ventured Barnett.

"Quite," said Bernard with a pained smile. "He made the mistake of attempting to bribe what he thought was a university assistant professor to gain access to cutting-edge satellite radio technology. Instead he found himself being handcuffed by what turned out to be an undercover FBI agent."

"So why is he here rather than in a federal prison or being exchanged with the Israelis?" asked Jones.

"As it turns out, Israel had great plans for Mordechai. They were going to move him to the U.S. in the hopes that he could unearth even more technology for them—he had quite a track record, you know. What they didn't realize was that the FBI had been onto Levy for months and had been feeding him his recent 'acquisitions'—harmless stuff that the government didn't really care about—to gain enough evidence to seal the case airtight. By the time he was apprehended in Boston three months ago, Dr. Levy had already relocated his wife—who grew up in New York's Brighton Beach—and their two youngest children to Massachusetts. Needless to say, Mrs. Levy wasn't thrilled to find her husband, the father of her children, had been spying on the land of her birth for years."

"And . . . ," prompted Barnett.

"Levy decided to relocate, giving the U.S. government access to any and all knowledge that he'd gained for Israel over the years."

Jones smiled. "His wife made him turn, didn't she? Grabbed him by the short hairs and gave 'em a twist?"

"Let us just say that Dr. Levy felt it prudent to fully explore his options with the United States government and eventually decided to ask for asylum," said Bernard. "Now the good news. One of Israel's brightest coups over the past decade was Levy's theft of our plasma-cannon technology two years ago, well before we were onto his clandestine activities. The good news is that for the past two years Levy himself has led an Israeli effort to come up with an answer to the cannon on the off chance one of their neighbors gained the technology and they had to one day counter it."

"Oh yes," said Barnett, "all for self-defense. I'm sure they don't have plasma cannons of their own ready to mount to their next generation of Merkava main battle tanks."

"It wouldn't surprise me," admitted Bernard. "What would you do in their place?"

Barnett ignored the question. "Doc, I'm really uncomfortable with a former spy helping us develop answers to life-and-death questions at this particular juncture of my life," said Barnett.

"You be the judge," said Bernard. "As you pointed out yourself, if we end up sending the SEPs in after the Tommies, it'll be *your* collective asses on the line, not mine." Bernard smiled. "If it makes you feel any better, we have a group of American scientists who've been working around the clock on an answer to the plasma-cannon issue, and they've come up with some sample products for you to take a look at. So you two listen to what Mordechai Levy has to say and check out what he's brought to show you, along with some samples of the American team's current product, and you be the judge. Your call completely." Bernard ended with a large grin spreading across his face.

"Why are you smiling like that?" asked Jones, suspicion thick in his voice.

Before Bernard could answer, a light knock sounded on the door. "Come in, Mordechai," called the doctor, standing from his position behind his desk.

The door opened and a middle-aged man entered the office, a large and apparently heavy case grasped in his two hands.

"No wonder he was such an effective spy," said Barnett, taking in the man's rumpled suit and Albert Einstein–ish crazy salt-and-pepper hair. "He looks like my old rabbi, not someone out to steal state secrets."

"You're Jewish?" asked Jones, trying to keep the note of incredulity from his voice and failing.

Barnett shrugged. "I dabbled in Judaism for a time."

The colonel knew Barnett well enough not to be surprised. He asked no further questions, because he was sure he would find out a lot more than he really wanted to know.

"Spying is such a harsh term," said the doctor in a quiet voice. He lowered the case to the floor with a ground-shaking thud and reached out to shake the American officers' hands. "I am Mordechai Levy. *Shalom.*"

"*L'chayim,*" replied Barnett.

Levy laughed, something he apparently did often,

judging by the lines surrounding his eyes. "To life, indeed, Lieutenant Colonel Barnett. That is my hope," he said, glancing down at the case. "That we can save some lives."

Jones rolled his eyes as he listened to Barnett speaking Yiddish as though he'd grown up in the shadow of the Wailing Wall. He'd never figure the man out. He took Levy's hand as the scientist extended it. "Bill Jones, Doc. If you've got something that'll give us a chance, we're more than willing to look at it." His expression sharpened before he spoke again. "But I have to tell you, Dr. Levy, I'm not thrilled at working with someone who has stolen U.S. military technology secrets."

Mordechai Levy nodded sadly. "I understand, Colonel. You should have heard my wife when she learned the truth . . . *oy vay*," he added, looking to the ceiling and slapping the side of his face with an open palm. "But the truth is, Colonel Jones, that you have the luxury of being a military man. Things are so . . . so . . . *black and white* in your world. Do you suspect though that perhaps, even at this moment, your country has agents attempting to gain whatever secrets they think might be useful from Israel and other of your 'allies'?"

Bill Jones chose not to reply.

"I can assure you, Colonel—you do." Levy paused, looking Jones directly in the eyes. "I am not ashamed of what I did for my country, Colonel. But I promise you, it was not an attempt to harm America, but a matter of protecting the state of Israel in whatever small way I could." And now a smile lit his face and he wagged a finger at Jones. "And in the case of your plasma-cannon, I think you will be happy that I purloined that technology. If not . . . well, you would not now find yourself with a possible answer to your problem of how to defend an Abrams tank against the M4X1's main gun. It took my team and I almost two years, but we think we found a viable solution that we can have working in a matter of days."

Levy stood, grinning and silent, staring at the American officers expectantly. Jones and Barnett glanced at each other, finally turning back to Levy. "Well?" said Barnett. "Where is it?"

"Go ahead and show them, Mordechai," said Bernard.

"Yes, yes, of course." The scientist reached down and picked up the case he'd brought in. "May I?" he asked Bernard, gesturing with his head at a worktable in the office's corner.

"Surely," said Bernard, coming around his desk and walking toward the table himself. "Gentlemen? Join us."

As the three Americans gathered round, Levy dropped the case with a thump and laid it on its side. He opened it in such a way that Jones and Barnett couldn't see the case's contents. Mordechai Levy was smiling in anticipation over the top of the case's open lid.

"Dr. Levy, *please* . . . ," said Jones.

"Very well, very well," said Levy, his annoyed gestures making it clear he didn't like having his moment of glory rushed. "First, let me explain. You are familiar with the concept of appliqué armor?"

Both of the tank officers nodded, Barnett taking the lead. "Bolt-on 'bricks,' usually of some composite material designed to mount on an armored vehicle, thus adding to the vehicle's survivability."

"I've gotta tell you, Dr. Levy," said Jones with a worried shake of his head, "an Abrams M1A2-SEP already weighs in at sixty-nine and a half tons, and the additional weight necessary to protect only the most critical portions of the tank's exterior will likely make this a no-go from the start."

Levy grinned again as he reached into the case. Before withdrawing whatever he held, he explained,

"The system I want to mount to your Abrams will not have that problem, I assure you, Colonel. It's a two-part solution." He withdrew a small pane, roughly four inches by six inches and less than a quarter inch thick. "This mounts directly to the surface of your tank."

"You're kidding, right?" asked Barnett. He turned to Clive Bernard. "Clive? Please tell me he's kidding."

"Let him finish," said Bernard with a smile.

"But it's a fucking piece of *mirror*, for Christ's sake!" yelled the normally unflappable Barnett. "Assuming that mirror-based appliqué will work against a plasma round, the enemy would see us coming from fifty miles away!"

"This is not an ordinary mirror, I assure you, Colonel Barnett," said Levy, still smiling. "It is as strong as steel and will absorb only the smallest amount of the plasma round's force before deflecting the round's energy away from your tanks."

"For how long?" asked Jones. "Even the starship *Enterprise*'s shields couldn't hold up against repeated photon torpedo hits."

"A very *logical* question," countered Levy, his eyes twinkling. He turned to Bernard. "I do so love Spock—what a mind on that one. But I digress. We do not know yet how much punishment an individual brick can take and still provide protection. But we estimate that an individual section of our armor should be able to take at least two or three hits, possibly more. We have not had an opportunity to fully test it. But," he added, "it has performed well in the lab testing."

"And do you have an answer to the problem of us looking like rolling disco balls?"

"Disco ball . . . you are a funny man, Colonel Barnett." He handed Barnett the section of armored mirror and withdrew another object from the case. Holding it up, it was obvious that the object's width and length matched that of the mirror, but it was slightly thicker, closer to a half inch. He tossed it to Jones.

"Lightweight," said Jones, rolling the brick over in his hands. It was a dark brown color and slightly translucent. "Plexiglas?"

Levy shrugged. "A close enough comparison. But much stronger and more pliable." The Israeli turned on a high-intensity lamp that sat on the table. "Hold the brick directly beneath the light, please, Colonel."

Jones did so. "No reflection," he observed.

"Exactly," said Bernard. "Not only does the outer laminate not reflect sunlight, but it's been designed to absorb energy that strikes it . . . as in targeting lasers."

"No shit?" asked Jones, pulling the block out and looking it over with a newfound respect.

"Not one hundred percent, but in combination with your Shield systems . . ."

Jones took the mirrored section from Barnett and mated it to the brown piece of laminate armor. "What do you think, Dave?"

Barnett shrugged. "It briefs well, I'll say that. And our Abrams won't be able to feel a difference in weight." He turned to Bernard. "But I'd feel better seeing what the American team came up with to counter the plasma cannon." He glanced at Levy. "No offense, Dr. Levy."

"None taken," said Mordechai Levy, still smiling.

Bernard nodded. "Go ahead and show it to them, Mordechai."

Levy reached into the case with both hands and grunted as he withdrew a block of what appeared to be steel, roughly the same size as Levy's appliqué armor blocks when mated. He dropped it on the table, gouging the wood surface deeply.

"How much does that thing weigh?" asked Jones, taking a step back.

"Roughly twenty-five pounds," said Bernard. "The good news is we're pretty sure that it will hold up against at least one direct hit from a plasma round."

Jones and Barnett each did the calculations, estimating the number of armored blocks necessary to protect an Abrams and how much additional weight this would add to the nearly seventy-ton monster. They looked at each other and nodded.

Jones held out his hand. "Dr. Levy, I'm looking forward to working with you, sir." He glanced at the block partially embedded in the tabletop. "And please, I'm sure someone needs a doorstop, so can you get that thing out of my sight?"

"I tell *you*, Colonel," said Levy as he shook Jones's hand with vigor, a large smile plastered to his face as his head bobbed up and down. "I am overjoyed to hear that I do not have to carry that monstrosity in my briefcase any longer. For security reasons I could not explain to Mrs. Levy the decline in my stamina over the past week." His eyes twinkled. "But now? A stallion, I tell you! Once more, I will be a *stallion*."

"That's way too much information, Dr. Levy," said Barnett, a note of seriousness in his voice that could not be faked. "But thanks for sharing."

Jones grimaced. "Yeah. Thanks." The big colonel closed his eyes and began thinking of dead puppies in an attempt to clear his mental buffers.

Of the three Americans, only Clive Bernard smiled. "Dude, you should have come to see me before it got to be a problem. I could have turned you on to some Tantric techniques that would've knocked your old lady's socks off, no matter how 'under the weather' you were feeling."

"Really?" said Mordechai Levy, intrigued. "Please tell me more, Clive."

Jones interrupted. "Gentlemen, can we just get to work? We've got plenty to keep us busy."

"Second," agreed Barnett. "*Please.*"

Chapter 19

De Opresso Liber

**Institute for Plant and Seed Modification Research
Karaj, Iran**

Jack Kelly dropped into the airshaft without a word as he saw the light at the bottom disappear, the rest of his team fast on his heels.

Luke Dodd was used to operating solo in the field, thus he was amazed that ten men, without a sound, could simply disappear so quickly. One second the shack was full, the next he and Krieger stood looking at each other. "I think that was our cue," he said meekly.

"I concur," said Krieger, climbing into the shaft and clambering to catch up with the Green Berets below.

Momentarily alone, Dodd saw the shack's door was partially open. He stepped over to close it, afraid a curious passerby might question why a maintenance shed normally secured would be open in the middle of the night. As he grasped the handle he was struck by the number of stars shining down from above, bright diamonds on a black canvas. And suddenly Luke Dodd felt very small in the larger scheme of things. And he thought of Natasha Khartukov, wherever she was. *Damn you, Natasha*, he thought, *not now*. Falling back on a Catholic upbringing that he hadn't done much with over the past couple of decades, the CIA officer made the sign of the cross and stared at the heavens shimmering down on him from above. "Please, God . . . don't let us fuck this up."

Two minutes earlier Bull Dell and Crapper Taylor had eased open the door leading from the maintenance access closet to Level Three.

"Whatdya see?" asked Taylor.

"Hold on a second," answered Dell in a harsh whisper. "I don't see nothin' yet, but let's give it a few seconds."

Ten seconds was all Taylor could take. "Bulllll . . ."

Dell rolled his eyes and turned around. "Man, don't be tellin' me you gotta take a dump."

Taylor gave the warrant officer a tight-lipped grin and nodded. "They don't call me Crapper for nothin', now do they, Chief?"

"I don't know how you made it through the assessment process, man," he said in disgust. "I never in my life met *anybody* that gets a case of the shits like you."

"I'm all right as long as I'm *doin'* something, dammit!" hissed Taylor.

Bull Dell eased the door open and took another look into the hallway. Nothing. "All right, all right. We goin'."

Dell eased into the hallway and saw the generator room's door a few feet away. He moved for it, Taylor at his back and turned facing the opposite direction. As Dell opened the door he immediately saw the master power switch against the left wall as advertised . . . and an Iranian with a clipboard turning to stare at him. The local's jaw dropped when he saw the black-clad giant carrying an M4A1 rifle with attached SOP-MOD (Special Operations Peculiar Modification) kit that included a silencer, an M203 40mm grenade launcher, and night-vision device. Dell grinned as the man began to yell. "I'm real sorry about this," he said as he swung the carbine's buttstock into the man's chin. The Iranian hit the floor, unconscious. Dell turned to Taylor and raised an inquisitive eyebrow.

"Our rear is clear," said the engineer.

Dell continued looking at him. "I know *mine* is, but . . ."

"I'm *all right*," said Taylor in indignation. "As long as I'm *doin'* something, I'm fine."

"Okay, then," rumbled Dell. "Let's start with the generators instead of wastin' the light. Once we're down to the final one, you cut it and I'll hit the switch and take us to lights out."

"You got it, Chief," said Taylor, pulling his rubber-handled bolt cutters from the kit bag hanging at his side.

One minute later they were down to the last cable. Taylor stood poised beside it looking at Dell. "Ready?"

Dell nodded. "Go."

The two Special Forces operators paused as they heard a scream down the hallway. Crapper Taylor cocked his head. "That was a woman."

Chief Warrant Officer Three Bull Dell almost always had a smile on his face. When he didn't, the man's countenance was frightful to behold—as it was now. "Time for a FRAGO," said Dell, giving the shortened name for a fragmentary order, a "change of plans" type of deviation from an original order.

"Fuckin' ay," said Taylor. "Gotta be the interrogation room."

Dell nodded. "Cut it," he said shortly.

In the span of two seconds the generators backing up the institute were out of commission and the master power off, casting the entire facility into darkness. The two operators dropped their night-vision goggles into place and headed for the door.

Dell spoke into his comm link's boom mike as he opened the door to the hallway. "Change of plans, Sonny," he said in a low voice. "Me and Taylor are headed for the interrogation room. Sounds like there's a lady down here who ain't exactly havin' a good time . . . and I only know of one woman on this floor."

Kelly was halfway down the shaft. "Roger that," he said. "I'll link up with you there."

A guard stepped into the hallway as the two Berets were halfway to the interrogation center. Dell didn't break stride, sending a three-round burst of silenced 5.56mm centermass of the man's chest as he continued moving. The guard dropped with a grunt and the hallway immediately filled with the smell of cordite mixed with freshly released bowels.

"What the hell's he been *eatin'*?" whispered a disgusted Dell as he reached the door to their target room.

Taylor ignored the query. "On three?"

Dell nodded. "I'll hit the door and toss a flash-bang. Once it goes, I'll take the left side of the room, you come in behind me and take the right."

"You got it, Chief," the NCO replied.

"All right. One, two . . ." Dell kicked the door open with a massive boot, tossed the cylindrical flash-bang grenade into the room, and stepped back into the hallway, squeezing his eyes tightly shut.

A muffled explosion sounded and both operators went sprinting in. "American Special Forces!" they yelled in unison, identifying themselves to the hostages.

Flash-bang grenades are beautiful things. While nonlethal, to those in the target room it is as if their world has come to an end. Harsh white light makes the room's occupants feel as though the sun itself has exploded, followed within a microsecond by an explosion that rattles every filling in their teeth. The operators entering on the heels of the detonation inevitably find a group of very disoriented individuals. Dell and Taylor immediately identified Melissa Dillon bound at the table in the room's center, along with another bound figure in a jumpsuit sitting opposite her with his back to them.

"I'm Dillon!" the man with his back to them yelled over his shoulder. "The lady and I are the only friendlies in the room. Somewhere there's a bag-of-shit Russian . . . find him, but he's mine!"

"You got it, Major," said Dell as he scanned the room. He looked through the smoke cloud created by the flash-bang and saw a figure cowering in one of the room's back corners. "I got him! Crapper, take care of the major and the lady."

Taylor released Melissa Dillon as Dell stalked to the back of the room. Melissa was on her feet and moving to her ex-husband's side. "Please step back, ma'am," said Taylor in a businesslike, yet not unkind voice. Within seconds Dillon's bonds dropped and he was falling out of his chair.

"Patrick!"

"I got him, ma'am, I got him," said Taylor as he pulled one of Patrick Dillon's arms around his neck and put one of his own arms around the major's waist, lifting him to a standing position. "Now get behind me, lady. When we move, we'll be movin' fast."

"What we got here?" asked Dell as he stood over Sergei Sedov.

In the darkness, Sedov couldn't see as much as sense the hulking presence looming over him. Though he should have known better, Sedov slowly reached for the pistol holstered at his side. He heard a *tsk-tsk* sound from the American.

"I wouldn't be doin' that shit," said Dell in a low, rumbling voice. He reached down and pulled the weapon from its holster, ejected the magazine and jacked the slide back, releasing the round in the chamber. Finally he tossed the 9mm into the corner opposite the Russian. "Piece of Chinese shit anyway. You'd be lucky if it didn't blow up in your face."

Breaking away from Taylor, Dillon moved across the room on wobbly legs in the direction of the voices. "He's *mine*," the major hissed as he reached Dell's shoulder. "Give me a fucking knife."

"Sir," said Dell as Kelly entered the room, "while I respect your enthusiasm, I'm gonna have to say no."

Sedov, sensing an opening, attempted to grab Dell's M4. The big warrant, though speaking to Dillon and holding the burly officer back with one arm, had never taken his eyes from the Russian. He sent the same boot that had splintered a two-inch-thick door into the side of the Russian's head with equal force. "Dumbass," he observed with a sad shake of his head.

"What do we have, Bull?" asked Jack Kelly.

"Power's out, generator's down for the count," reported Dell. "We got the major and Mrs. Dillon in hand. Both look a little worse for wear, but Mrs. Dillon appears to be ambulatory, the major so-so."

"Who's this?" asked the SF captain, nodding down.

"Sergei Sedov," said Dillon, standing on rubbery legs at Bull Dell's shoulder, his initial burst of adrenaline gone and now leaning on the big operator for support.

Dell stiffened at Dillon's words. His hand moved in the darkness and the raspy whisper of steel being withdrawn from nylon sounded as Dell pulled his twelve-and-a-half-inch U.S. Special Forces–only issue Yarborough knife from its sheath. He shoved it into Patrick Dillon's hand.

"Bull?" said Kelly, an uneasy note in his voice. "What are you doing, man?"

"The major asked for a knife," said Dell, images of this Russian and his forces slaughtering unarmed American troops running through his mind. "Now that I know who we got here, I understand the request . . . and I agree. We'd be doin' the human race a favor." He pulled a small penlight from his vest and gave that to Dillon as well.

Patrick Dillon removed his hand from Dell's shoulder and took a step forward, the penlight illuminating Sedov, the Yarborough's seven-inch blacked blade dully reflecting the light.

A low growl escaped his throat as Jack Kelly placed a restraining hand on his arm. "Major . . . no."

"What the *fuck*?" exclaimed Dillon, turning on rubbery legs. "Do you *know* who this son of a bitch is? What he's done? What he was *about* to do?"

"Yes, sir," said Kelly. "I know." He turned to his second in command. "Get Mr. Dodd, Bull."

"Roger," said Dell, turning to do as his commander ordered. "But I don't fuckin' like it." And he was gone.

Kelly spoke into his boom mike as he stared at the unconscious Russian, a distasteful look on his face. "SITREP."

The remaining members of the ODA quickly checked in. The guardroom was secured—that the guards were all dead did not need to be stated. No further contact. And then Catfish Clayton checked in, the sound of a long spit of Black Maria heralding his transmission. "Checking Crockett's cell now . . . oh, shit. I'll get back with you, Sonny."

"Sonny, Hefe," called Vega from his perch outside.

"Go," said Kelly.

"Looks like you're going to have some company pretty quickly," said the sniper, watching what looked like a platoon of Iranian infantry swarming from a barracks building and heading for one of the institute's side doors.

"Can you buy us some time?" asked Kelly, glancing at his Suunto. They'd been underground two minutes and the clock was ticking.

It was Will Purdue's rumbling voice that answered. "You got it, boss." As Purdue's transmission trailed off in his earpiece, Kelly heard the bark of the big NCO's M24 7.62mm sniper rifle.

"Shag ass, Sonny," said Vega. "We can give you a few minutes. . . ." The transmission paused long enough for the operator to squeeze off a round, dropping the second Iranian who'd reached the door atop Purdue's target like a rag doll. The rest of the platoon had stopped and began scanning the area surrounding the grounds. "But these boys are excited."

"Understand," said Kelly. "We'll be out ASAP. Do what you can, don't get tied down."

Vega ducked as a burst of 7.62mm rounds spattered masonry around his head. "Not a problem. But hurry your ass up, *hombre*."

As Kelly finished digesting the latest intel from outside, Dell and Luke Dodd entered. "What do you have?" asked Dodd.

Kelly's response was short. "Sedov. Is he worth taking back? Otherwise, we have a plan for him." He glanced down at the Russian. "I'm hoping you say no."

The night-vision goggles mounted to Luke Dodd's face looked like a long proboscis sniffing the ground as he bent his neck to stare at the Russian. He hesitated, finally saying, "Yeah. He's got a lot of info on the Iranians' activities." He shook his head. "As much as I'd like to smoke his ass, we better retrieve him."

Kelly nodded at Dell and pointed at the unconscious Russian. "Take him, Bull. I'll help the major." He turned his head in the darkness. "Mrs. Dillon? If you'd grab on to the back of my tactical vest?"

Melissa felt the nylon beneath her questing fingers. "All right," she said. "I'm ready."

Kelly nodded and spoke into his boom mike. "Let's move, people. Catfish . . . what do you have?"

Clayton transmitted from Tom Crockett's cell. "We've got a fuckin' mess here, Sonny," he reported in a voice clearly under strain. "I've got Master Sergeant Crockett, but he ain't lookin' good. We're hittin' the hall now, heading for the ventilator shaft."

"Roger. You copy, Vega? Purdue?"

"Lurch is a little . . ." Vega squeezed off a round, dropping another enemy troop on the steps. ". . . busy. But yeah, we read you. Be advised, the local boys got tired of trying to take us out and at least ten of them have made it into the building." Kelly could almost hear the smile in the Latin sergeant's voice as he spoke his next words. "But I tell you, Sonny . . . the dozen left in the courtyard, they won't be an issue."

"And our exit route?" asked Kelly, grabbing Dillon

around his waist as they all headed for the door that would take them back to the surface.

"It's clear," replied Purdue in a controlled voice. "Hold on a second. Damn but that boy is—" The sound of a round being fired. "*Was* fast. Move it, Sonny."

"We're gone," called Kelly as they hit the hallway. He could see the rest of the team collapsing toward the closet housing their way out, carbines bristling in all directions as they covered one another. At the entrance Rolf Krieger stood waiting, stolid and unmoving, overwatching the approach of the rest of the team and feeling a little useless.

As the first of the team members moved past the big scout and up the shaft to secure the exterior opening, three Iranians wearing night-vision goggles strapped to their faces poured into the corridor from an access door thirty feet away. The lead man quickly brought his AK-47 to bear on the trailing member of the Special Forces team, Hawk Davies.

Three operators trained their weapons toward the Iranian, but before any of them could squeeze a trigger, Krieger's right hand was at his waist and flashing in the direction of the new threat.

"Sum *bitch*," said Clayton in a subdued voice from Krieger's side, his jaw hanging in disbelief as he stared at the Carson M16 knife buried in the lead Iranian's left eye as the local collapsed onto his face.

Krieger shook his head as the two remaining infantrymen were cut down before firing a round. "I was aiming for the right eye," he said in disgust.

Clayton grunted a laugh. "You're a weird dude, Wolf," he said. "But I like ya." And then the big Alabaman was moving up the shaft rung by rung, Crockett's heavy body secured to his back by several quick-release nylon straps. Beneath him, Boom Eastbrook tried to help by taking some of the big master gunner's weight on his shoulders as he climbed.

"I owe you, kid," Davies said in a quiet voice. He

slapped Krieger on the shoulder. "Now let's get the hell out of here."

As they moved into the closet, they saw Bull Dell with a still-unconscious Sergei Sedov, the Russian's hands bound behind him with disposable quick-zip strips, thrown nonchalantly over one massive shoulder. "You having fun, Wolf?" He grinned.

"Move it, Chief! We ain't got time to be fuckin' around!" said Davies.

The grin never left the big warrant's face. "After you," he said, gesturing at the darkness that was the access shaft. "Wouldn't want this fuckstick slobberin' down on your heads."

After Davies and Krieger had begun the climb, Bull Dell gave Sedov a quick shift, settling the Russian's bulk into a more comfortable position, and began the climb.

Fifteen feet up the shaft, Sergei Sedov slowly opened his eyes. He was staring down the American's back and legs at the maintenance closet below, though he could not see much in the darkness. His lips slowly formed a smile, and then he threw his weight backward.

The unexpected weight shift startled Dell and he paused, hanging on to the rungs to catch his balance. Then the Russian's grinning countenance was in front of him. The Russian clung to the big operator as if in a lover's embrace. "Hello, monkey," whispered Sedov.

"Monkey?" said Dell, incensed and forgetting for a moment how dangerous the animal in front of him was. "Who you callin' a fuckin' *monkey*?"

And then the Russian's right knee crashed into the operator's testicles with a sickening thud.

Dell grimaced. "That shit's just *wrong*, man," he squeaked, holding on for dear life as pain racked his abdominal area and he watched Sergei Sedov drop and disappear into the darkness below. The big man exhaled deeply several times, trying to will the pain away enough for him to move. Tears filled his eyes.

He considered going after the Russian, but he knew that it was pointless; Sedov would be long gone by the time he reached the third level. Maybe, Dell thought, the son of a bitch had broken his neck. He looked down, the bottom of the shaft shining greenly through his night-vision goggles. Nothing; the Russian was gone. He painfully began working his way up after Davies and Krieger. As he'd neared the top, Rolf Krieger reached a hand down and grasped the big operator by his tactical vest, pulling him upward the remaining distance into the shack.

Krieger stared in disbelief. "Where is Sedov?"

Davies was next to Krieger. "Chief? What the hell's going on?"

Dell hung his head in dejection. *"He . . ."* The word came out high-pitched and ended in a hiss of pain.

"He *what*?" asked Davies.

Bull Dell shook his head in frustration, beads of sweat dripping from his chin. "Nut . . . shot."

"Nut shot?" asked Krieger, not understanding. "What is this *nut shot*?"

Davies shook his head in disgust and spit onto the dirt floor. "He got kicked in the balls. And the Russian got away."

Dell looked to his longtime friend, squinting in pain and nodding.

"Can you walk?" asked Krieger.

"Ye . . . yeah," answered Dell. "I'm feeling a little better."

"That's good," said Davies. "Because we need to shag ass."

As the team's final three members stepped from the shack, the courtyard was awash in haphazardly strewn bodies. The A-Team members not supporting hostages, along with Luke Dodd, had formed a protective perimeter outside and looked relieved as the trio appeared. An M24 sniper rifle barked and another Iranian fell, what appeared to be the last of them.

"Vamanos!" said Vega via the team's comms link. "Move it, people. You're clear, but I don't know how long it will stay that way."

The detachment had begun melting into the shadows in the direction of the pickup point when two troop transport trucks roared from around a blind corner of the institute in a splash of headlights and gravel.

Will Purdue spat a curse and rapid-fired three rounds of match-grade 7.62 through the driver's-side windshield. The truck careened wildly to the right without slowing and hit the side of the other transport. The second truck kept moving after the initial collision, brushing away with a squeal of metal on metal. Its mate teetered slowly to the right as if in a yawn, finally falling to the ground on its side in a cloud of dust when the supporting bulk of the other truck moved away.

"You made that shit happen, Hefe!" said Purdue into his boom mike. *"But I don't know for how long,"* he mimicked. "Bad luck, man, that's what you called down on us!"

Vega ignored his partner, a skill he'd learned long ago in order to keep his sanity. "Sonny, we can give you a couple more minutes, that's about it. Then we're going to have to beat boots outta here, my man."

"Roger, understand," replied Kelly as Krieger moved beside him to help support Patrick Dillon. "Do what you can, we can cover our asses as we move if we have to."

A third truck thundered into the courtyard. The team, as well as Vega and Purdue, knew that they'd never make it back to the pickup point with two injured personnel and this many Iranians on their asses.

Vega fired again and called to Purdue. "How you doin', Lurch?"

The tall, bearded operator did the math as he watched his teammates and the former hostages slowly exfil the area. Twenty-plus infantry poured from the lead truck, stopped just fifty meters short of the maintenance shack. The third truck would be there in moments as well. Purdue shook his head fatalistically, but his voice was calm, almost jovial. "Shit, *Hefe*," he said. "I'm having so much fun, think I might just stay a while."

"That's what I thought, *'mano*," replied Vega quietly. He squeezed off another round, dropping an Iranian with an RPG-7 rocket-propelled grenade launcher. Had to take out the high-value targets first.

"Nice one," said Purdue, bringing down two more infantrymen within a second of one another. He did a mental check on his remaining ammunition as he glanced down at the empty brass cartridges surrounding his position. He swallowed hard and put his check back to his rifle's stock, sighting through the scope into the courtyard.

"Hey," called Vega, "you want some company?"

"Wouldn't have it any other way, *hermano*," said Purdue, squeezing off a round.

Kelly's voice was strained. "Wait a damned minute, you two. . . ."

"Sonny," said Vega, "you're a leader . . . so lead. You know we're right."

Tom Crockett had awakened halfway up the shaft and had Clayton release him once they were topside. He was unsteady and looked like hell, with a filthy bandage wrapped around his head, covering one eye. But with a little assistance from Clayton, he could walk. The NCO paused next to Kelly as he overheard the A-Team leader talking to his snipers. And he got the gist of the conversation.

"Give me your weapon, Captain," Crockett said in a hushed tone, interrupting the exchange.

"Sergeant Crockett, I don't have time . . . ," began Kelly.

"No, sir. You don't," said Crockett. In his battered condition and filthy jumpsuit, he looked like anything but a professional soldier. Yet somehow as he straightened his back and stared into the captain's eyes, that was *exactly* what he looked like. "I'm not sure whether or not you can understand this, Captain . . . but I really can't go back."

Dillon tore himself loose from Kelly and Krieger. He staggered drunkenly toward Crockett and grabbed him by his collar, shaking him savagely. "Tom, cut the bullshit. We're getting out of here. Me and you. *Together*."

The big NCO looked back to where the two snipers were holding off a small army and shook his head before turning once more to Jack Kelly. "Give me your weapon, sir. Please."

For the first time Kelly saw the haunted look in Crockett's eyes. And he realized what the NCO had gone through. He silently extended his SOPMOD M4A1 and four spare clips of ammunition. "Good luck, Sergeant," he said simply. "And thank you."

"No!" cried Dillon, grasping the back of Crockett's coveralls as his NCO moved away.

Tom Crockett slowed and turned. It surprised Dillon that the smile on his face was genuine. "Sir," he said quietly, "I want to do this." He stared deeply at Dillon. "Sir . . . Pat . . . if anyone should understand, it's *you*. You were there."

"Fuck that, Tom! I'm not going to let you—"

And then Rolf Krieger's fist slammed into the side of Patrick Dillon's head and the burly major dropped to the ground.

Crockett looked down at his boss.

"You didn't have to do that!" cried Melissa Dillon. "After all he's already been through . . . you didn't have to do that!"

"Yes, I did," said Krieger. "Or in less than a minute he would have been going back with Sergeant Crockett. Is that what you want?"

Melissa shook her head as she bent over the unconscious man who'd been so large a part of her life. "You didn't have to . . . do . . . *that*."

"He will be fine," said Krieger, handing all of his

spare 5.56mm ammunition magazines to Crockett. "I know him, he has a head like a rock."

The NCO nodded. "Yeah, he'll be fine. He's a good man." He smiled. "I'm going to miss his sunny disposition." And then Crockett's face turned serious. "Now get out of here."

Krieger handed his carbine to Kelly, who was busy getting the rest of the team moving. He then threw Dillon's two hundred pounds over a shoulder with the smallest of grunts and held out a hand. "It has been an honor, Sergeant," said Krieger, shaking Crockett's hand. Then the scout spun and was off after the rest of the team, Melissa Dillon behind him.

Kelly, the last remaining operator on the scene, spoke into his headset. "Vega, Purdue, listen up. Master Sergeant Crockett is returning to the shack to secure the rear—no questions on this one. I want you to take out every long gun or RPG you can identify and cover him until he gets there. Then drop everything you've got and head for the pickup point on the run. Clear?"

"Clear," said Vega, not understanding but knowing Kelly well enough not to question his commander.

"Roger that, boss," said Purdue, his M24 opening up again. "Tell Crockett to make it snappy. We'll get him there."

Before Jack Kelly could say a word, Tom Crockett was running, Vega and Purdue pouring a protective rain of lead hell on the Iranians in the courtyard.

George Greenfield checked his chronometer. Based on his call when he left the institute, Kelly should have been here by now. And based on what sounded like a small war from the direction of the institute, the CIA officer knew that the exfiltration hadn't gone unnoticed by the locals.

"Where are the Americans?" asked Monsoor. He looked worriedly to where his mother and sister huddled in the corner of the dark building, one small suit-

case between them. Ali had been as good as his word;
his mother and sister were leaving the country with
the rescue team. But something told the young Iranian
that time was running out.

"They'll be here, they'll be here," said Greenfield,
refusing to call Kelly when he knew the Special Forces
captain had enough on his plate. But he was beginning
to feel the weight of the clock as well. He looked once
more at the young man whom he'd learned to trust
over the past few days. He hated the thought of anything happening to him in the fallout of tonight's operation. "Are you sure you won't go with them,
Monsoor? There's plenty of room."

Monsoor shook his head. "Change must begin from
within, my friend. My place is here. Just make sure
my family is taken care of, all right, Ali?"

Greenfield nodded. "And it's George."

"You do not strike me as a George," Monsoor said
with a smile. "I think I shall continue to call you Ali."

"Monsoor?"

The young man, along with Greenfield, turned to
find the Iranian's sister at his shoulder. She shivered
in the chilly night air. Monsoor, forcing a smile,
reached out to tighten the collar of his sister's robe.
"It will not be much longer, Dorri. Do not worry. Go
sit with Mother."

The young woman shook her head, dark curls
bouncing along her shoulders. "No, you do not understand, Monsoor." She held out her hand. In it was a
slip of folded paper. "Uncle gave this to me this afternoon. I didn't know why, because we did not know
what was planned. He said, 'You will know when to
give this to your brother, but do not let it be too
soon.' "

Monsoor took the paper, glancing at Greenfield.
"Do you have a light?"

The American reached into a vest pocket. "Keep
the light close to the paper." The operative looked

around, glancing once more at his wrist. "But make it quick."

Monsoor unfolded the sheet before turning on the small flashlight. He recognized the familiar flowing script of his uncle. . . .

> *Monsoor, there is little left to say. And nothing you can do to change what I am about to tell you. As you read this, I have already written my confession to the institute's director. I did it tonight, sending it to his personal e-mail account. You know as well as I that if you stay, you will be arrested for nothing more than being a member of my family . . . especially considering who your father was. I am an old man, Nephew. This is the last thing I can do to honor my brother, your father; to see that all of his family makes it out of this country and to a better life. Do not grieve for me. My heart soars as I know I will soon be in Paradise. I am ready for it, my son. And that is what you have become to me, Monsoor, as a son. Take care of your mother and sister. Until we meet in Heaven . . .*

Monsoor shook his head. "No. Noooooo!"

"What is it?" asked Greenfield.

No reply. He took the note and light. In his rapid reading of the Arabic script, the American knew he'd missed some of the message's nuances, but he understood the gist. Greenfield looked up. "That does it. You're going out with them. No arguments, unless you're dead set on suicide."

Monsoor said nothing.

"Uncle also asked me to give you this," said Dorri, extending a small package wrapped neatly in brown paper and twine.

With numbed fingers the young man untied the twine, the sound of fighting drawing nearer unnoticed. Pulling loose the brown paper, he saw his beloved uncle's ancient Koran. Its leather cover was soft and worn, its pages tissue-thin from constant use over many decades. His tears began to flow, silent racking sobs shaking him as he held the book to his chest.

Then the world exploded around them as a cyclone-like wind whipped through the courtyard next to the abandoned building in which they'd waited. As if from nowhere, first one, then two more dark shapes settled to the ground, rotors spooling down but not stopping.

Greenfield ran toward the lead aircraft's open cargo door. A dark figure removed his helmet and shouted, *"Where the hell is everybody?!"*

The CIA man grimaced and motioned behind him with his light. Monsoor, his mother, and his sister appeared at his shoulder.

"Who are they?"

"Three extra bodies," yelled Greenfield. "You have the space."

"Not part of the plan," yelled the crew chief. "The old man ain't gonna like it." The NCO disappeared into the aircraft. Thirty seconds later another flight-suit-clad figure jumped from the cargo door.

"I'm Bertetto, John. Captain, United States fucking Army."

"Greenfield . . ."

"I'm not fucking finished, sizzle-chest," said the captain. "Hell man, I'm just getting fucking *started*. You fucking understand me, Greenwald?"

"Green*field*," said the officer, beginning to get annoyed.

"What-the-fuck-ever," retorted the stocky figure next to him. "You see these fucking birds?" he asked, gesturing with a thumb over his shoulder at the huge MH-60K Black Hawks behind him. "You know how much these fucking babies cost? And Uncle Sam, Mom and Pop, the entire fucking American populace expects me to get them back in one fucking piece. That's a lot of your fucking tax dollars at work, Mr. Greenspan."

"Captain . . ."

"I still ain't fucking finished," said the captain. "You see these fucking men manning machine guns, covering your fucking ass? The other pilots sittin' here packing their fucking collective *puds*?! Don't even fucking try to put a price tag on their asses—you couldn't fucking afford it. Am I starting to fucking get through to you, Greenwald?"

"Yes . . ."

"Out-fucking-standing," said Bertetto. "Now before I ask who the *fuck* these people are, where are *my* operators?"

"En route."

"En route?" asked the pilot, noting the sounds of battle moving closer. "En-the-*fuck* route?" A note of concern entered his voice for the first time. "You got an ETA?"

Greenfield shook his head.

"Shit," breathed Bertetto, and then he remembered the other people standing outside the aircraft. "So who the fuck are they?"

"If it wasn't for this man," said Greenfield, clapping a hand to Monsoor's shoulder, "those hostages would have been sitting in Iran permanently." He gestured at the women. "This is his mother and sister. I promised I would get them out."

"You promised? Key fucking word is *you*, buddy," spat Bertetto. "They weren't mentioned anywhere in my fucking briefing."

Dorri moved forward and gently grasped the aviator's hand in her own. A tear trickled down her cheek. "Please, Captain," she said quietly. *"Help us."*

Bertetto looked over his shoulder at his crew chief. The senior NCO was staring at him with a knowing smile plastered across his face. "What the fuck you lookin' at?"

"Nothin', sir," the NCO said. "Should I let the other birds know we got extra passengers?"

John Bertetto looked into the Iranian girl's eyes and felt his insides begin to melt. He turned to Greenfield with an angry glare. He bent so that he could speak directly into the CIA officer's ear without being overheard. "You fucking do this on purpose? Pull a local fucking hottie just to get them on board?"

Greenfield stared at him. "You're kidding, right?"

"Please, Captain," said Dorri, the tears beginning to stream. "We have nowhere else to turn."

The captain looked up and made a self-disgusted sound before turning to his crew chief. "Find space for 'em. They'll be on this bird. Let the rest of the flight know."

Dorri stepped forward quickly and wrapped herself around Bertetto in a hug. "Thank you. Thank you so much."

After prolonging the embrace a few seconds longer than necessary, the captain pulled back. "That's all right, ma'am. Please climb aboard the aircraft."

"Very well," said Dorri, taking the crew chief's hand. But then she turned back once more. "But you really should stop cursing so much. A man as attractive and intelligent as yourself, it is beneath you."

Bertetto blushed in the darkness. "Yes, ma'am," he replied meekly.

Monsoor helped his mother aboard. Before climbing in himself, he turned to Greenfield. "Thank you, my friend. I will not forget you."

Greenfield felt his throat tighten. He nodded. "Good luck," he said simply. "Now go."

And then it was just him and Bertetto. The aviator shook his head. "I'm gettin' a little worried here, Chief. We came in low and quiet, but that don't mean no one fucking pinged us with radar at some point during the trip in. And if they did, and they hear what's goin' down at the institute . . ."

"Do we have any air cover?"

"Would I look this fucking worried if I had fucking air cover?" asked the captain, straight-faced.

And then the A-Team led by Jack Kelly burst into

the courtyard with the sound of gunfire close behind them.

Bertetto hopped into the aircraft. He turned back and held out his hand. "Good meeting you, Greenstein." He smiled. "Maybe we can do it again sometime. It's been a fucking hoot."

"Green*field*," said the officer tiredly.

Bertetto winked. "I fucking know that, Chief. I'm just yanking your chain."

Greenfield turned toward the approaching A-Team as Bertetto disappeared into the depths of the modified Black Hawk. "This everybody?" he asked Kelly. "Where's the third hostage?"

"Master Sergeant Crockett didn't make it," Kelly said simply. He turned to Davies. "Hawk, get everyone split between the birds."

"You have three in this one already," said Greenfield. He'd briefed Kelly on the Iranians before the team had moved on the institute, so it came as no surprise.

"Roger, got it," said Davies, turning and moving away to oversee the loading of his team.

"I've still got two men out there," said Kelly. A mortar landed on one of the buildings on the side of the courtyard from which the team had entered. "*Shit.* And it looks like they're attracting a little attention."

From behind them the staccato sound of machine-gun fire erupted as an Iranian attack helicopter burst onto the scene. Both men ducked. A dozen MH-4s and the crew-served weapons of all three helicopters reacted instantly, sending multiple streams of tracers in the direction of the Iranian aircraft, a modified Cobra gunship, causing the pilot to veer away and his cannon rounds to pass harmlessly between the trail MH-60Ks sitting on the ground.

"Come on," said Kelly to himself, urging on Vega and Purdue. Slowly it began to dawn on him that the two operators might not be making it back.

Davies appeared at his shoulder, and both men alternately looked east toward the spot their snipers would appear from, and then around them in search of the attack helicopter that would be making a more informed pass very soon. "Everybody's loaded up, Sonny," the NCO said. "Me, you, and our slow-footed snipers will be on this bird."

Luke Dodd trotted over from the next aircraft in line. He held out his hand to Greenfield. "George, good to see you again . . . sorry about the circumstances."

Greenfield looked toward the sky in search of the Iranian gunship. "Yeah, they could be better."

"You did good work here, George," said Dodd seriously. "Really good work."

George Greenfield nodded and smiled humbly, then the smile turned into a grin. "Tell your brother I want a step-promotion when you get back."

"You got it," said Luke.

Kelly looked at Davies, but didn't say what was on his mind. The sergeant already knew and the look in his eyes said to his captain, "Don't fucking say it." Kelly looked east, knowing that as the seconds ticked off, it became more and more certain that they'd lost two of their own. And then the helo was back. The modified Cobra had just opened up its chain gun when, without warning, it dropped into the western edge of the courtyard in a ball of fire.

"What the . . . ," said Kelly, speaking for everyone present.

Simultaneously Dodd and Greenfield reached into pockets to retrieve their Company-issue miniature radios. As each saw this, they looked at one another, baffled. They should be the only people within two hundred miles who had the state-of-the-art communication devices—and they hadn't called one another. Greenfield repocketed his own handset as he saw Dodd click his unit's speaker button.

"Dodd," Luke said. "Who the hell is this?"

A familiar voice echoed from the radio's speaker. "Well, isn't that just gratitude for you?"

Luke looked at the radio incredulously. *"Moran?"*

Greenfield looked at Luke. "Ted Moran? Your pilot buddy?"

"That's me, baby." Moran laughed. "And you're welcome."

Luke shook his head. "Where the hell are you?"

"Well, if you'll look at your nine o'clock . . ."

The four men turned in the direction indicated, at first not seeing or hearing anything.

"Let me give it a little waggle for you," said Moran. A spot darker than the rest of the night, hovering forty feet off the ground, just above a line of buildings, shifted slightly side to side, then began to move. A sleek black helicopter, bristling with missiles, guns, and antennas, moved without seeming to make a sound until the men could see it in the light of the burning Iranian aircraft.

"What *is* that thing?" Luke asked into the radio.

They could hear Moran's laugh before the former Marine aviator and current Company pilot extraordinaire transmitted. "You ever hear those stories from out west? The UFO freaks talking about black aircraft hovering in the night?"

Dodd stared dumbly. It was like looking twenty years into the future of avionics. "Yeah," he said simply.

"Well, let me just say those cattle-mutilation stories are highly exaggerated," Moran said. The pilot's voice turned serious. "Captain Kelly with you, Luke?"

"Affirmative."

"Captain, I got eyes on your boys. They're hotfooting it like Daniel Boone and Mingo with a pack of Shawnee on their asses. Be ready to lift off in one minute."

Before anyone could reply, Moran shifted the dark

bird silently in the direction of the approaching operators. "Now if you'll excuse me, I'm going to give them
a little covering fire. Later, Luke."

The helo, if that's what it was, had disappeared once
more in the surrounding darkness. But the darkness
was short-lived. As Vega and Purdue burst into the
clearing, the night exploded with the sound of 25mm
chain guns and the ripples of air-to-ground missiles
hissing off of weapons pylons. Night turned to day
behind the two operators and, not knowing whom the
fire was directed toward, if anything they increased
their already record-breaking pace to the pickup point.

Kelly motioned for Vega and Purdue to enter the
Black Hawk behind him. Both men almost dropped
from exhaustion as they reached the craft. Kelly and
Davies bodily lifted them from the ground and threw
them into the waiting arms of the 60K's crew.

"What the *fuck* . . . is . . . that . . . *thing*?" asked
Vega as he disappeared into the Black Hawk's
interior.

"A guardian angel, brother," murmured Kelly. As
the captain climbed aboard, Moran's aircraft continued slamming the approaching Iranians. Kelly motioned from the door for Luke Dodd to mount his
aircraft, then went to the nearest empty seat and
strapped himself in.

Dodd nodded. "George, see you in the big city," he
said simply.

Greenfield held up a thumb and melted into the
night as the three Nightstalker helos lifted from the
ground in a cloud of dust and headed toward Iraqi
airspace at low altitude, lights out.

Moran ceased engaging the ground targets and
turned his aircraft in the direction of the departing
Black Hawks. Within seconds he was above the formation, though they didn't know it. He snickered. With
all of the sensors at his disposal, it hadn't been difficult
monitoring what had been happening on the ground.
"No air cover, *my ass!* Whoooooo-hooooo!" He

rubbed the ship's control stick gently. "Have I told you lately, Bertha my darlin', just how much I love you?"

Shortly after takeoff the toll taken on Patrick Dillon had caught up with him and he'd passed out. A medic had quickly checked his vitals and ensured Melissa Dillon that he was in no danger. They'd injected an IV to bring up his fluid levels and left him to sleep. He awoke with a start somewhere over Iraqi airspace. He felt a hand on his own and lifted his head to look. It was Melissa, sleeping in her cargo seat next to him, her head against the Black Hawk's fuselage. As he watched her, she opened her eyes and smiled at him sleepily. She leaned to his ear. "We need to talk, Patrick."

Dillon dropped his head and closed his eyes a few moments. When he opened them he tried to sit up, but stopped, grimacing, as his broken ribs sent a stab of pain through his chest. Melissa leaned down. "What is it?" she asked.

Patrick Dillon shook his head and thought of the past year, not meeting her gaze. "I'm glad you're safe, Melissa, but I can't deal with this now." He shut his eyes again. "I simply can't," he repeated, and was asleep again.

An hour later they, along with the A-Team, Krieger, and Dodd, were aboard a high-speed transport bound for the United States.

Chapter 20

Sandhill Nights

Dugan's Pub
Village of Pinehurst, North Carolina

Clive Bernard hefted a pint of Bass ale and angled the rim at the man across the table from him. "You know, Cobb, you continue to surprise me. Sometimes you actually seem, what's the word I'm looking for . . . human."

Cobb smiled faintly over his own beer. "There's a difference between observing the proper security protocols and having a stick up your ass, Doctor. Besides, you guys need a night out before you hit it hot and heavy tomorrow."

"Fucking 'ay right," said Jones from his ethereal shroud, happy to once more be in a state where public smoking was allowed. He thought of the M1A1s they'd be putting through their paces with their new appliqué armor and missile-defense systems. He shook his head, telling himself he would simply enjoy tonight, the first he and the rest of the team's senior leadership had enjoyed since arriving at the compound. "This place is great. And the band's not bad either. Not exactly what I'd expect in a golf town though."

Cobb smiled faintly as the trio of musicians made their way back to the stage for their second set. The bass player, a thin man in his early twenties with dark, spiky hair, sideburns, a goatee, and a tie-dyed T-shirt sporting a grinning Elmer Fudd in the center ("I'm a Weal Wascal" read the legend beneath), patted the ex-operator's shoulder as he made his way to his guitar. "Don't worry, Cobb, we haven't forgotten you, bro."

The security man smiled acknowledgment and tipped his beer in the bass player's direction. "You boys are yet to disappoint, Danny."

"You know these guys?" asked Jones.

Cobb shrugged. "Bad Monkey. Best little band in North Carolina. They come through once a month or so. Hang around long enough, you get to know most people around here." He nodded in Danny's direction. "Take Danny there. His dad's a retired chief warrant officer from one of the Groups," Cobb said, referring to the Army Special Forces Groups stationed at Fort Bragg.

At this point another of the band members stopped by.

"Bill, this is Brian," said Cobb.

As the two began to exchange greetings, a dapperly dressed man, a little on the short side, with red hair and wire-framed glasses, stepped up to the table. "Brian, you guys turn down the bass or you'll never play here again, that I promise you."

Silence at the table as the drummer nodded.

Cobb frowned and then stood. "Pardon me," he said, and then turned to the other man. "A moment of your time, Allen?"

"Who's that guy?" asked Jones.

"The owner," the drummer said. "Sometimes he gets a little wired."

Jones grunted. "Sometimes it seems he can be a little bit of a *prick*."

"Yeah, that, too."

They watched as Cobb and the owner stopped in a corner and briefly conversed, the owner gesturing.

Cobb leaned over and whispered something into the man's ear. That was it, and then they were back at the table.

"You guys are fine," said the owner. "Don't worry about it."

The drummer nodded. As the owner walked away, Brian pulled a pair of Vic Firth drumsticks from the back pocket of his jeans and twirled them briefly between his fingers. "You fucking rock, Cobb," he said with a laugh, then walked with a grin to the stage.

A few minutes later the sound of the lead and bass guitarists warming up and Brian limbering his wrists with a few sharp tattoos cut off further conversation. The lead singer, Chris, approached the microphone. He wore his shoulder-length brown hair pulled back into a Japanese-style ponytail and knew how to make magic with a guitar. He pointed at Cobb. "All right. We got what you want, Brother Cobb." He grinned. "Hope the bass ain't too loud for you folks, but we have to go where our muse takes us. *It's a music thang.*" The opening licks of "Interstate Love Song" sounded to the enthusiastic applause of the crowd. Cobb's lips momentarily curled into a smile, and then he took another sip of beer as he nodded his head to the rhythm of the tune.

Clive Bernard leaned across the table, raising his voice to be heard above the music. "I wouldn't have figured you for a Stone Temple Pilots man, Cobb. Merle Haggard, maybe, but definitely not STP."

"Don't try to pigeonhole me, Dr. Bernard," said Cobb, straight-faced. "It will only drive you insane."

Dugan's Pub occupied a piece of corner real estate in the heart of Pinehurst. Upstairs was a bar with a few tables for those wishing a quick drink or meal. There was also a formal dining room for patrons wishing a little more intimacy. Antique pictures and golfing advertisements dating back to the turn of the twentieth century adorned the walls, along with leather golf bags and wooden clubs belonging to a bygone era. Walking into the establishment made one feel the magic of what had pulled golfers from around the world for decades to the small village nestled in the North Carolina sandhills.

But the team had taken a left when they entered the pub, heading down a set of dimly lit steps to the cellar. It wasn't clear which hit them first, the smoky haze that immediately made Jones feel at home or the wave of music.

Occupying the center of the room was a large, four-sided bar. Unfinished brick arches supported a low wooden ceiling. The walls were green, with two televisions at either end of the room tuned to sports stations, the sound turned off. The large-screen set at the end closest to the stairs featured the University of North Carolina versus Duke basketball game being played up the road in Chapel Hill, and on the other the Carolina Panthers, who were on a five-game winning streak, were playing the New Orleans Saints in Louisiana's Superdome. Most patrons paying attention watched the basketball game—this might be golf country, but it was still Tobacco Road. Three dartboards—real bristle boards, not the electronic type overtaking most drinking establishments—completed the room. But at the moment they were off-limits, as they were adjacent to the stage . . . and the Monkeys had a strict "no darts in the band area" when they were in the house.

"So how did you stumble on this place, Cobb?" asked Jones as he pulled his cigarettes from a breast pocket, preparing to make his contribution to the cellar's ambience.

Cobb frowned as he thought over the question. His life was a mystery to these people, he knew that. Hell, he kind of *liked* that. Then again, it was a mystery to almost everyone except the men who'd served with him in the military over the past two-plus decades. He and a few others among his peers had decided long ago that Fayetteville's growing population and bright lights weren't for them. Their after-duty world, when they were fortunate enough to be home, had nothing to do with Fort Bragg or the military city surrounding it like a cocoon to its north. When they left Bragg, these men went out the back gate. Pinehurst was thirty miles removed from anything military. Its claim to fame was its championship-caliber golf courses, so most of the people in town at any given time were tourists, golfers from around the world who wished to say they'd played the same links as Jones, Hogan, Palmer, Woods, and so many of the other greats from the past hundred years.

Cobb and his associates chose Pinehurst, Southern Pines, or one of the other surrounding hamlets for reasons other than the quality of their fairways. When they left Operator World, they wore jeans, T-shirts, and maybe a fleece pullover or Windbreaker if there was a chill in the air, not khakis and polo shirts with the obligatory Bass slip-ons. When they walked in the door at Dugan's, the people behind the bar didn't ask what these men wanted to drink—they knew. Their beverages of choice, which ranged from ice water to hot green tea to a chilled Absolut starter along with a pint of Newcastle—Cobb's personal choice—were set before them.

Cobb had broken his own rule; he'd brought strangers into his house. His frown deepened. Why in the hell had he done *that*? He rolled the question around in his mind. For most of his military career, Cobb had operated behind the scenes. He'd been officially removed from the Army's rolls as a staff sergeant almost two decades earlier. Despite this, he'd continued to pick up paychecks—well-earned paychecks—for years afterward. And continued to do so now in his "retirement."

But he'd brought a few of the team personnel he'd instinctively known would play key roles over the days to come—Bernard, Hunter, Jones, the new kid Stuart, and of course the dandy, Barnett—to his sanctuary, the place he'd found years earlier when he needed a night of peace.

Cobb's wife, Ruth, and their young son had moved from Fort Lewis to Fort Bragg in the early eighties at the start of his new Army career. Initially Ruth had loved the small-town feel and was the happiest Cobb could remember seeing her. No more commissary lines, no more doing all the Christmas shopping at the Post Exchange. But then the months of late-hour days during his initial assessment and selection, followed by long months of advanced training in the skills of his new trade, began to wear on her. During this period, Ruth's despair manifested itself in periodic bouts of depression. Later, she sought refuge in a bottle.

The situation worsened when Cobb's team became operational. With no notice and no idea where he was going, Cobb and his men disappeared for months at a time. Once in a while, when the team returned, there would be a missing face or two. The families would inevitably be told there was a "training accident." Within this small and elite world, Cobb's reputation grew. Despite his relative youth, the sergeant's intelligence, nerve, combat skills, and leadership ability put him on the fast track in a world of fast-trackers.

In the early days Cobb enjoyed the reunions with his family, as they tended to pull Ruth from the dark morass she lived in the rest of the time, at least for a little while. Cobb would enjoy his family for whatever time he could, using them to reclaim his center, his soul. But the drinking had begun to consume Ruth as she saw less and less of her husband. Neighbors had begun to help out with their son, Ethan.

Cobb shook his head, knowing that as well as he'd learned to handle himself in the field, he'd never managed to break his own family's code. He hadn't known what to do to help Ruth. She refused to seek help, insisting instead that Cobb leave the military, that if he'd only find a civilian job with the attendant nine-to-five hours, things would get better. He'd refused, calling her selfish and weak. That was when the new, and last, phase had begun: the screaming. And so Cobb had found Dugan's, his Fortress of Solitude from a home that made him feel as though it were filled with energy-sapping Kryptonite. He would sit for a few hours, long enough for Ruth to pass out, and listen to the tourists compare the strengths and weaknesses of each of the local courses, the quaintness of the village, and the relative merits of one German automobile make versus another, the latest consensus being that Mercedes had overtaken BMW in popularity. A few of his team members, hearing through the grapevine of Cobb's marital problems, had begun joining him. The primary reason was that he was their friend and they wanted to help. The other reason— someone with personal problems could get people killed in their line of work. So they monitored the situation.

One night Cobb looked at his watch and judged it safe to return home. But instead of his small front yard being illuminated by the porch light as it normally was, it was illuminated by red and blue flashing strobes. As he climbed from his truck, an ambulance crew wheeled a gurney through the front door, a sheet completely covering the body resting on it. Running alongside the gurney crying for his mother was Ethan. Cobb grabbed his son into his arms, at the same time explaining who he was to the paramedics.

Ruth, it seemed, had graduated from booze to prescription drugs without her husband being any the wiser, in this case, tranquilizers. That night she'd mixed a dangerous cocktail that had been too much for her. His son screamed at him, asking him why he hadn't been at home, why he was *never* at home, telling him it was his fault that Mommy was dead.

Following the funeral, Cobb had taken off enough time to move his son to his mother's home in Tennessee and get him settled. The ex-operator shook his head. He realized now what a mistake that had been. He should have pulled Ethan to him and held on no matter what it meant to his career. But he hadn't. He'd been young and stupid, but it was too late to take it back now, no matter how much he wished he could. Instead he'd returned to work, determined to use the job as a means of scrubbing his soul clean. The problem was, he found it was like using charcoal to wash mud from your hands; the mud disappeared, but the darkness remained with you.

So Cobb had slowly clicked off all emotions. He listened, sad on a deep level, as he learned that his son never fully recovered from the events of that night years ago. Ethan had begun a long series of appearances in the juvenile court system. But one day the boy, because of a line running through a calendar, had found himself not in kiddie court but before a real judge and a real prosecutor.

But Dugan's had always been there for him. Cobb looked around the table. Had he found the place? Or had it found him?

Sayid Bakr had breached the compound's outer security easily enough earlier in the day, thanks to the priceless data from his German black box. The site's security might be state of the art, but no security was impervious to exploitation and intrusion in this day and age. With the technical piece out of the way, his primary concern when planning the earlier mission had been ensuring that the numerous guards on the grounds—some of whom patrolled on foot, the rest manning hide positions that overwatched likely approach routes—did not spot him. From the way they performed their duties, Bakr knew the guards were well trained. And all ex-military, if he didn't miss his guess.

He had conducted a reconnaissance of the camp just after sunset. Despite knowing the location and types of sensors installed by the compound's security team, and despite having the technology in his small rucksack that would render him all but invisible to the sensors, it had still taken the former commando over three hours to make his way to the inner fence line. Several times he had been forced to go to ground to avoid patrols. Other times he'd had to don a gilley suit—a throw-over poncho composed of numerous twigs and rags made popular by snipers around the world—and low crawl, sometimes able to move only an inch or two every several minutes, through areas he knew to be under observation.

By the time he'd returned to his vehicle, Sayid Bakr had all of the information he needed regarding the compound's security setup. It would have been good to actually recon the grounds of the camp proper, but unfortunately there was no part of the open ground not under constant observation by at least one of several sentries scattered about the woodline surrounding the encampment. He would have had to take direct action against one or more of the manned posts, and that would have drawn a great deal of attention, something he did not want; not yet at any rate. So Bakr satisfied himself with ensuring he could make a rapid approach onto the grounds. He also identified three possible egress routes, the one he'd take depending on what the situation was when he exfiltrated the area after his mission was completed.

It was all Bakr could do to stifle a laugh when he finally reached the inner fence and had seen the man that the Iranians so dearly wanted killed. To listen to his current masters, Clive Bernard was the most dangerous threat to the Arab world since George Walker Bush. Bakr shook his head as he took in the boyishly dressed man with the long hair of a woman. Bernard had been bouncing some kind of leather sack up and down with his foot during a break from his work in the lab, laughing like a child. The Iraqi shrugged. So long as Bernard's death hurt the Americans, it was enough for him. And he'd been assured that it *would* hurt them.

Bakr looked about the compound to see what else he could do to slow down the team's progress in rebuilding their program. Adjusting the monocular lens of his night-vision goggles, the Iraqi saw a medium-sized concrete structure fifty meters removed from the main building. He'd have thought it a storage building except for several air-conditioning units running continuously outside. Numerous cables were strung between the building and a set of generators. That did not tell him much, but the several fiber-optic cables hastily run along the ground from the building to the administrative building did. Sayid Bakr smiled. That would be the team's computer server farm.

Gaining entry into the admin building where the team proper worked would be dangerous, too dangerous. Sayid Bakr was willing to take risks, but he was no martyr. He wanted to hurt the United States and keep on hurting her. Thus, taking out a great number of the scientists themselves or their computer systems, if it entailed going into the admin facility, was not an option. But, just as critical as the systems utilized by the scientists on a daily basis were the servers that fed the workstations the data they so desperately needed to accomplish their mission. If he'd arrived a few days later, the fiber-optic lines would have been run through protective conduit pipes and buried. But Allah had smiled on Sayid Bakr, leaving him a breadcrumb trail.

When he'd arrived at his SUV following his reconnaissance mission, Bakr had stored his electronic gear in the false bottom of a beer cooler and replaced the insert containing crushed ice and Budweiser, along with a turkey-and-cheese sandwich in a Ziploc bag. The remainder of the cargo space was taken up by what the Wal-Mart associate in nearby Aberdeen had assured Bakr was all the gear a deer hunter needed—doe-in-heat musk, spare socks and boots and an assortment of orange and camouflaged gear, along with numerous canisters of Slim Jim sausages. A bolt-action .30-.30 Winchester rounded out his kit, along with a completely legitimate hunting license in the late Mr. Hamarinah's name. *Who would have guessed the man enjoyed deer hunting?* mused Bakr. He'd taken the license along with his victim's other identification after dispatching him. His momentary smile at the thought of a deer-hunting Arab dressed in camouflage and orange and smelling of deer urine disappeared when he heard several vehicles leaving the hidden trail to the compound.

What are they doing? Bakr jumped behind the wheel of his four-wheel-drive rental, which had been hidden amongst the pines on the far side of the road. This went against the team's established pattern, and Sayid Bakr did not like changes to patterns. They inevitably introduced the element of chance into the equation, and chance had nothing to do with planning and skill.

He fell in behind the convoy. Glancing in his rear-view mirror, the Iraqi noted cars approaching from the rear at a high rate of speed. At first alarmed, he quickly deduced these were personnel from Fort Bragg living in the smaller towns south and west of the main post. They were apparently in a rush to get home. Bakr allowed two vehicles to pass him before accelerating to keep the three Chevrolet Tahoes in sight. They'd turned right after a few miles and moved into a town called Southern Pines, and then continued on for a few more miles along winding narrow roads through a tunnel of overhanging pine boughs, large horse farms occasionally popping up on each side of the road. And then Bakr saw a new sign: VILLAGE OF PINEHURST, HOME OF THE 2005 U.S. OPEN.

Sayid Bakr watched the three vehicles park. The passengers exited the SUVs and entered a restaurant in the heart of the small town. He began to follow, but hesitated. He looked down the length of his body at his one-piece black jumpsuit. The attire might not blend so well in this hamlet. Looking across the street, he saw a solution. He quickly crossed the small road and entered a men's clothier, a small brass bell over the door heralding his arrival. His jaw dropped as he noted the assortment of bright colors.

"Oh *my*," said a dapperly dressed gentleman, one arm across his chest, the other held to his face in a look of surprise. "Aren't we looking just a bit *goth* for a golfing vacation?"

Bakr looked at the man and blinked. Like the mannequins in the window, the man's wardrobe was like nothing the Iraqi had seen previously, not even in New York during medical school. Checkered twill slacks and a lime golf shirt with white shoes. "Pardon me?"

"I take it you're looking for some golfing togs?" He smiled. "And who can blame you?"

Bakr smiled. "Yes. Golf togs are exactly what I am in search of."

The man clapped his hands twice and a smile lit his face. "Sir, I think I can help you. Oh, indeed yes."

The smile on the Iraqi's face disappeared, replaced by a grimace of dread as he looked again at the store's racks and shelves. "How delightful," he managed.

Cobb leaned back in his chair. How had he found this place? "Stay around here long enough, Colonel, you pretty much know everyone and everything."

"Including how to play Number Two . . . *gratis*?" asked Jones with a wink.

Cobb's face remained serious. "When all this is over, we'll see. I know a few people."

Jones's jaw dropped. Last he'd heard, it cost around five hundred dollars to play a round on the crown jewel course designed by Donald Ross.

"You understand that Number Two is Stewart's course?" Cobb continued.

Jones nodded, still sobered at the religious experience potentially awaiting him.

"Stewart's course?" asked Sarah Hunter.

Bill Jones, who loved golf but could normally afford only municipal and military courses because of the expense inherent in raising a houseful of women, explained. "In 1999 Payne Stewart won the U.S. Open on Number Two after what's often called the best round of golf ever played. Won it by draining a twenty-foot putt on the seventy-second hole. Four months later, the Learjet he was aboard, en route from Orlando to the Tour Championship in Houston, lost radio contact shortly after takeoff." Jones paused. "A few hours later it left a ten-foot crater in the ground somewhere near Mino, South Dakota, everyone aboard dead."

Hunter shook her head, doing the mental geography. "How'd they end up in South Dakota flying from Florida to Texas?"

Cobb took over. "No one really knows. The speculation is that there was a loss of cabin pressure shortly after they went wheels up and everyone aboard passed out. The jet was on autopilot, so it just kept flying. Air Force birds shadowed it, trying to get someone to answer a radio. Finally, out of fuel, the Lear went down."

"Oh my God," Hunter whispered. "That's horrible."

Jones's eyes twinkled. "Yeah, but Stewart was having a great year, with the 1999 Open being his crowning glory." The soldier thought of the handsome, grinning Scot in his colorful knickers and smiled. "Although I'm sure he'd have hung around longer if he could, still . . . I think he'd have kind of liked ending on a high note, forever young, forever the champion."

"Colonel?"

Jones focused on Cobb. "Yeah?"

"As I said, Number Two is Stewart's course. If I get you on, you have to wear the pants."

Bill Jones, in the middle of drying his suddenly parched throat with a swig of ale, sputtered. "Cobb . . . no."

The operator shrugged. "Your call." He smiled. "But if I get you on, I make the rules."

"You evil son of a bitch," muttered Jones, picturing himself in loud knickers.

"And the argyle knee-highs and cap."

Jones said nothing more. Sometimes you really did have to dance with the devil to get the things you wanted in life.

"It looks like your protégé is having a productive evening, Bill," observed Clive Bernard.

A few feet away, Mike Stuart sat on the end of a leather bar stool sipping a pint of Guinness. Serving it was an attractive brunette who, while not hanging on the captain's every word, was definitely enjoying the attention.

Cobb turned in his chair. Catching Stuart's eye, he motioned the younger man over to the table. He noted that the captain left his beer in place to hold his seat when he moved from his stool.

"What's up?" asked Stuart.

"That young lady," said Cobb, pointing at the bartender.

"Nicole?" asked Stuart.

Cobb nodded. "Nicole."

"What about her?" Stuart shook his head in confusion. "I'm missing something here, Mr. Cobb."

"Quite possibly," said Cobb. "What has she told you about herself?"

"That she's single," Stuart said and smiled.

"Did she tell you she had a son?"

Mike Stuart's face turned serious and he nodded. "You know, *Mister* Cobb, or whatever the fuck rank you are or were, she did happen to mention it. He sounds like a great kid. Oh, one more thing . . . it's none of your fucking business what we discussed. And now, I'm finished playing Twenty Questions with you." He looked at the others at the table. "If you'll excuse me?"

As Stuart began to turn, Cobb's tone as much as

his words stopped the officer. "Captain, did she tell you about her ex-husband?"

Mike Stuart turned to Cobb again, hesitant now. "No."

Cobb nodded. "No, she probably wouldn't want to tell you about it. That's because he was a no-good bag of shit."

"You knew him?"

Cobb shook his head, a thoughtful half smile playing across his face. "Not well. He was a sergeant in the Eighty-second Airborne. When she finally figured out that not only she but also her son were better off alone, Nicole left him. She's putting herself through college now, accounting. She'll graduate in a couple of months at the top of her class."

"You certainly seem to know a lot about her," said Stuart. He looked to the pretty bartender, then returned his gaze to the stoic Cobb. Although he could barely conceive the notion as possible, he nonetheless asked the question. "You know, if you two have some sort of—"

Cobb barked a laugh. "No, Captain Stuart. She's a friend. A good friend." All humor left the operator. "And I wouldn't want to see her hurt because of a one-night stand with another G.I."

Stuart's face always appeared to have a slight reddish tint, as though he'd spent a few minutes too long in the hot sun. Now it burned crimson as blood rushed to it. "Look, for the record, I'm not big on one-night stands myself. She's an intelligent, beautiful woman and I'm likely headed into the shit real soon—again. Can you blame me if a few hours of conversation with her is the way I choose to spend tonight?"

Cobb smiled and—it happened so fast, no one could be quite sure—it looked as though he winked at Stuart. "Can't say that I'd blame you a bit, son." The smile remained, but the note of promise that crept into Cobb's voice was anything but friendly. "So long as we understand one another."

Stuart walked away, shaking his head. "Unbelievable," he muttered.

"That was interesting," said Bernard, looking at Cobb and waiting for some sort of explanation.

Cobb ignored the remark and threw a menu in the doctor's direction as he looked off into a distant corner. "If you're hungry, I highly recommend the beef tenderloin sandwich. The goat cheese sets it up nicely." But as he spoke, his mind appeared to be elsewhere as he stared across the room.

Sarah Hunter followed his gaze and then looked back to the security specialist. "What is it, Cobb?"

The ex-operator shook his head as he looked to Hunter, the question surprising him. "What do you mean?"

"Something caught your attention," she said. "I can tell. What was it?"

Bernard hoisted his beer. "Ahhh, a boogeyman behind every curtain, is it? Don't you people ever *relax*?"

Cobb remained silent, staring.

Hunter ignored Bernard as well. "Cobb . . . *what*?"

Cobb shook his head as he turned to look at the lieutenant colonel. "Nothing. I thought I saw someone paying a little too much attention to our table, but he was just watching the game."

"More likely he was ogling dear Sarah," Bernard said with a smile. "She's looking quite tasty tonight." He waggled his eyebrows and made a growling sound from deep inside his throat as he looked over her thin, spaghetti-strapped blouse that showed just the right amount of cleavage.

"Shut up, Clive," said Hunter distractedly, staring across the room herself now. She'd begun to respect Cobb's hunches. And Clive Bernard could be such a *pig*.

Bakr had stationed himself in a dark corner of the pub and settled down to see what he could find out about the team members. He knew this might be his only opportunity to surveil them at close range and he meant to take advantage of it.

He recognized Bernard, of course. Several others he remembered from the bus trip from Fort Bragg, including the mustachioed one who was such a peacock. The man should have accompanied him to the clothing store across the way, Bakr reflected. At least that way one of them would have enjoyed the experience.

Only three of them gave him concern. Of those, Bakr sensed that the oldest of them was the least to be concerned about, at least for the moment. He was a warrior, seasoned by sun and weather, but it was hard to tell much about the man, as he shrouded himself in a constant veil of smoke. What Sayid Bakr *could* tell was that while the man might be a dangerous opponent on the battlefield, he was not one who lived his life on the edge, in the shadowy side of the military world. The other two did. In a situation like this, the older soldier's battle senses would not be on alert.

The woman sitting next to Bernard was a different story. While for all intents and purposes she was enjoying herself with the rest of the party, Bakr noted that the woman only nursed her drink, and while doing so she constantly scanned the room. Twice she'd nearly made eye contact with him as he watched.

It was the third who made Sayid Bakr tread carefully. He was not physically overbearing in appearance, but there was something about him. Twice Bakr had turned to glance toward the table . . . and the man had been staring at him. It was as if he had a sixth sense that something wasn't quite right about Sayid Bakr, despite his new wardrobe. It had taken all of Bakr's discipline to let his gaze slide over the man to the television in the corner, to not lock eyes. But ultimately the dangerous one had lost interest in him. The Iraqi knew, deep down, that his cover had not been blown. This one was merely careful every second of his waking life. No one was above suspicion; there was no time for relaxation. The man lived on the razor's edge always. Bakr catalogued everything he could about the one the others called Cobb, because he had a feeling that ultimately, they would meet again.

Business had slowed and the waiter who'd been tag-teaming with Nicole, sensing she and Stuart had hit it off, took care of the remaining downstairs customers so the two could have a few minutes to see what, if anything, was going to develop before the end of the night.

"Look . . . ," Nicole began, speaking in a mesmerizing accent that spoke of both upstate New York and years spent in Texas as a young wife, finally seasoned with just a hint of the soft lilt made famous by North Carolina women over three centuries.

Mike Stuart's chin rested on a fist as he leaned against the bar. "I love your voice," he said.

"And I like yours. . . ."

"No, really. Yours is amazing. Mesmerizing even."

Nicole smiled, displaying an endearing space between her front teeth. "I'm so glad you like it. Now . . ."

"Your eyes, too. What color do you call that? They're not really hazel; almost yellow. . . ."

Nicole stomped her foot. "Will you *shut up* for a minute?"

Mike Stuart jumped. "Sure."

The young woman shook her head, more to herself than to Stuart. "Look, I don't usually do this—my God, I *never* do this—but, would you like to come over to my place? And don't get that funny look in your eyes, Sparky. I mean, come over, get to know each other a little better—*that's all*."

Stuart shook his head up and down for a few moments and then realized he should probably say something. "You bet. That would be—nice."

The girl smiled. "Okay. I'm clocking off, so if you want to follow me . . ."

The captain shook his head. "I'm afraid I can't. I came with those guys," he said, gesturing to the table full of Tommy team members behind him. "And I'm sure the prick in charge, following our earlier conversation, would no-go it."

Nicole looked toward the table Stuart had indicated. "Oh God," she said, recognizing Cobb.

Stuart sighed in frustration. "I knew from the way he was talking that there was something between you two."

"Shut up," Nicole said, taking off her apron and exiting from behind the bar. She took Stuart's hand. "Come on, I'll handle this."

As they approached the table, Cobb watched them from behind hooded lids.

"If I promise to have the young captain back at the bunkhouse before the sun comes up, do you have a problem with that?"

Cobb was silent for several long moments, but finally nodded. "The old compound. Call me when you're on the way in and I'll clear it."

Without another word, Nicole turned on her heel, pulling Mike Stuart with her toward the stairs. As they reached the first step, Stuart pulled up short. "Will someone please tell me what's going on? What's up with you two?"

Nicole turned and continued up the stairs. "Cobb is—was—my father-in-law."

Mike Stuart slapped his free hand to his head, everything suddenly clear. "Great. Just fucking great."

As the main party prepared to head upstairs to their vehicles, Cobb glanced to the corner where the man who'd caught his attention earlier had been sitting.

Other than an empty soda glass, the table was empty. He reached behind his head and scratched his neck. *Nothing,* he thought. *It was nothing.* But he turned and looked into the corner again.

The wind sighed through the pines in the hour before sunrise. Alone at the edge of the compound's pool, Clive Bernard had pulled off his ever-present Havaianas and set them aside. He stared into the backlit water as his feet made slow circular patterns in its depths. Though the pool was heated, the cooler temperatures of autumn had lent it a chill. Still, Bernard found it relaxing to feel the waters between his toes. Chilly though it was, the water was still a hell of a lot warmer than the Pacific off the coast of his boyhood home in northern California. As he stared, his face gave no indication of how his mind was racing. His life had changed so much in the past week. He still couldn't believe it. Had it really only been a week? His shoulder-length blond hair swayed, brushing the top of his shirt's collar as he shook his head in disbelief. Only a week.

"Mind if I join you?"

Bernard started, but then settled when he recognized Sarah Hunter. "Did you really have to do that?"

"What?"

"Scare the living shit out of me."

Hunter laughed. "You tried to get away from me, didn't you?"

"No, I tried—successfully I might add—to evade that big lug O'Sullivan. He was the shadow on watch and you don't see him here, do you?"

"Who do you think told me where you were? He was outside the building watching you from the time you left until I walked down."

Bernard shook his head. "You know, you two can take a break now and then. I'm more than confident in the abilities of Cobb and his crew."

Hunter shrugged. "As am I. But . . . orders."

"Orders." The word had come out like a grunt. "The iron shackles of duties and oaths."

Sarah Hunter bent and held something decidedly colder than the pool's water against his leg. "Corona?"

"Muchas gracias." Clive Bernard smiled as he accepted the beer and took a sip. "But before breakfast, Sarah? You're beginning to surprise me."

Staring at an eastern skyline that was only beginning to take on the deeper darkness that precedes dawn, Sarah Hunter shrugged. "I prefer to think of it as post-dinner as compared to pre-breakfast."

Bernard raised his beer and clinked it against Hunter's. "Cheers. I love a woman who knows how to rationalize."

Hunter rolled her pants legs above her calves, removed her shoes, and took a seat next to Clive Bernard.

He tried to warn her. "The water's just a little . . ."

"Jesus!" exclaimed Hunter as her feet entered the pool. "That water's freezing!"

". . . cold," finished Bernard.

For the next few minutes they sat in companionable silence, the doctor threading circles in the water, Hunter with her feet, now clad in socks, tucked beneath her.

Finally Clive Bernard grinned lazily. "So. You packing heat?"

"Heat?"

"You know, a piece . . . a gun."

"Do you always ask ladies such personal questions?"

Bernard shook his head. "No, but something's poking me in the side. I shudder to think what it could be if it's not a pistol."

Hunter smiled but remained silent.

"I'll bet you like red meat, too, don't you?"

The MP smiled. "Yummy."

The sky to the east had begun to lighten when an owl sounded from the nearby forest. Both looked in the direction of the bird's call.

"Probably one of Cobb's men giving the 'all is well' signal," said Bernard with a straight face.

"Cobb's not that bad, Clive. And I can tell that he's kind of growing on you."

Bernard turned to look at her. "The man is insufferable."

"And yet . . ."

Clive Bernard gave up. "And yet . . . yeah, I kind of like the dude. Damn his black soul to hell."

Sarah Hunter giggled.

"You know," said Bernard, "I think that's the first time I've heard you sound like a real girl."

Hunter frowned. "What the hell is that supposed to mean? And remember . . . I might be packing."

Bernard ran a hand through his hair, pushing back a few stray locks that had fallen across his eyes. "It doesn't mean *anything* other than it's nice to see you relax for once. At this rate, you're a heart attack waiting to happen. Early to mid-thirties is way too young to worry about that kind of thing."

"Thirties? I turned forty a month ago, Clive."

Bernard turned and studied his guardian angel. "No shit? Well, I might have to adjust my age standards."

Hunter shook her head in exasperation and stood. "You do know how to ruin a nice moment, Dr. Bernard," she said, gathering her shoes. Turning, she walked toward the dormitory.

Bernard frowned. "Hey," he called at Hunter's retreating figure. She kept walking. Turning back to the pool, he kicked hard and made a splash worthy of a twenty-pound catfish sounding. "It was a joke," he said in a voice too low for any but himself to hear.

Dumbass, thought Bernard, kicking out at the water again and watching the ripples multiply and roll across the surface of the pool. *You could indeed fuck up a wet dream, Clive.* Give him a woman in her early twenties and he was a silver-tongued devil, but someone like Sarah Hunter . . .

He thought about his last conversation with Nigel, just before his brother had deployed for Desert Storm over a decade earlier. Clive Bernard had phoned from Sydney, recently returned from a walkabout in the Australian interior, where he'd hoped to learn the secrets of the Aborigines' virility. He'd had an inspiration to cross-pollinate his findings with the Tantric techniques he'd brought with him from India.

After he'd explained the concept to his brother, Nigel had laughed. "I love you, Clive," Nigel had said, the static a half world between them audible across the overseas line. But the laugh had died after a few moments and it was his brother's next words that came to Bernard now. "But you know . . . someday you're going to have to grow up, man."

After word of Nigel's death, Bernard had tried to do as his brother advised. But he realized now that he'd only done so on certain levels. His taste in young women had continued. If someone closer to his own age—no matter how attractive—expressed interest in him, he always managed to somehow sabotage the relationship before it had a chance to begin, Sarah Hunter being the latest example. Having an adult relationship, he reflected in the throes of his self-analysis, would have been too much like *becoming* an adult, something he'd avoided thus far, at least on an emotional level. And then there was the hair, the hemp, and the flip-flops. *Man,* he thought, *I am an asshole.*

But he had an opportunity, here in the deep pines of North Carolina's sandhills, to change all that. To purge himself of the obsession he'd harbored since his brother's death by helping men like his brother, mechanized warriors. And maybe, just maybe, to let his brother see that he'd actually heard his words that last night.

Clive Bernard stood and killed his beer. "But I'm

not losing the Havaianas, man," he muttered. "No need taking this growing-up gig to nutty extremes."

Nicole drove through the interior gate and pulled to a stop next to the administrative building. She placed her hands on the steering wheel and stared straight ahead. "I can't believe I slept with you the same night we met." She shook her head slowly from side to side in denial. "I'm such a major *slut*."

Stuart laughed and reached a hand behind Nicole's head, gently rubbing the tension from her taut neck. "You are *not* a slut."

She wouldn't be consoled and slapped his hand away. "Am so."

Mike Stuart chuckled and crossed his arms across his chest. "All right then, have you ever done anything like this before?"

"No," she replied flatly. She turned to stare at him. "Have you?" she asked, raising an eyebrow.

"This isn't about me. But you see my point. You never did anything like this, so . . . you're not a slut. Hell, you're not even *sluttish*."

Nicole rolled her eyes and tapped the steering wheel. "Sluttish? Is that a word?"

Stuart shrugged. "I think so. If it's not, it should be. Definitely applies to enough people to qualify."

"How so?"

The captain cocked his head. "Well, if I had to put numbers to it . . . if you sleep with people you're meeting for the first time on a regular basis—classic slut. If you do it once a month or so—you're slut*tish*."

Despite herself, Nicole laughed. "Your rationale is flawed. A slut would lie to you, genius. Tell you that she didn't do it on a regular basis with guys she's meeting for the first time, when she's really scrogging left and right with anything that moves."

Stuart shook his head. "She might. But she wouldn't feel as badly as you do right now."

"You know, I can't help but get the impression

that—and please correct me if I'm wrong—but you're really talking about women. What about men?"

Mike Stuart grinned. "That's easy. We're all sluts."

Sighing deeply, Nicole shook her head. "What was I thinking when I started talking to you tonight? I should have known better. All-American good looks, charming."

"I couldn't figure it out myself," replied Stuart with a smile. "Especially after Cobb told me what a smart young lady you are."

Nicole cringed, thinking about Cobb for the first time in hours. "Speaking of the devil, I hope you're not in trouble."

"Trouble?"

She nodded. "He can be a little—overprotective."

Cobb. The man was quiet, but the young officer had seen enough of the world to know a bad dude when he saw one. He shook his head. *Stuart,* he thought, *you do have a way of working yourself into situations.* Not as bad as Dillon, another fine Irish lad, but bad enough to get him in trouble every now and again. Still, there was something about this woman that . . . *shit,* he couldn't pin it down with words. What he *did* know was that he wanted to get to know her better; maybe a *lot* better. That was something he normally didn't want to do when he met nice-looking women while out and about. Relationships tended to complicate his already complicated life. But Nicole was different from other women he'd met. How, he couldn't exactly put his finger on, but different she definitely was.

Another set of lights popped on from the building, pinning the two young people in their seats.

"Daddy knows we're home," said Nicole in the lightest voice she could manage.

As a shadow emerged, Stuart leaned over the Jeep Cherokee Sport's center console. Nicole, staring at the dark shape beginning to take on the form of a man, tried to pull back. Stuart managed to catch the corner of her mouth in a chaste kiss. "You'll miss me?"

She smiled weakly and pushed him back. "Yeah. Sure I will. Just try to live through the next five minutes and we'll have a chance, Sparky."

Stuart smiled . . . until he felt the door at his back open. He turned.

Cobb, an amused smile on his face, squatted to look at the vehicle's occupants. "So, did you two have a pleasant evening?"

The sarcastic delivery escaped neither of the passengers. Nicole managed a crooked smile that didn't convey much. Mike Stuart managed a gulp and a nod, but the guilty look on his face said it all.

"So," continued Cobb without missing a beat, "when's the wedding?"

"We-*wedding?*" croaked Stuart.

"Coobbbbb," hissed Nicole through clenched teeth. "Cut it out. *Now*."

Cobb belted Stuart's bicep good-naturedly, but with enough force to leave a bruise. He smiled, but it didn't reach his eyes. "I'm kidding, Captain. Just kidding."

Mike Stuart stepped from the car, forcing Cobb to his feet and backward. "You know, Cobb, you're starting to piss me off."

The man facing Stuart smiled and cocked his head. *"Really?"*

Stuart sneered. He might get his ass beat, but *by God* he'd been outnumbered by the Iraqi Republican Guard and outgunned by a horde of Russians and lived to tell the tale. He did *not* have to take this shit. "Yeah. Really."

Cobb dropped his hands to his sides and relaxed. "Take your best shot, kid."

Mike Stuart had been raised in New York City's Hell's Kitchen—the bad part of the neighborhood, at that. You didn't back down from fights, not when they came at you like this bastard was doing. It was go time.

"Mike!" screamed Nicole, reaching uselessly across the console. "Don't do it! You don't . . ."

But it was too late. Stuart's right hand was bunched and he was swinging from the hip. He felt his fist collide with Cobb's jaw and followed all the way through, keeping the weight on the balls of his feet. Returning to a ready position, he saw to his dismay that Cobb remained on his feet. The older man was rubbing his jaw and smiling.

"You know, you pack a pretty good wallop, kid." He spit out blood and his smile broadened. "Now it's my turn."

Nicole banged in frustration on the passenger seat, leaning as far as she could toward the object of her wrath. "Cobb, you son of a bitch! Don't you do it!"

Mike Stuart was vaguely aware of the right hook that connected with his jaw. After that he was aware of nothing. Cobb caught the young officer as he was falling toward the ground, catching him beneath the arms.

"Damn you, Cobb," said Nicole, spent of emotion at last. "You're not my father."

This time Cobb showed a real, yet sad, smile. "Hell, I know that, Nicky . . . but I wish I were."

He threw Mike Stuart easily across a shoulder and turned toward the dormitory. He paused after a few steps and half turned, calling over his shoulder, "For the record, I kind of like this one."

Bakr barely made it into the compound before the gate closed behind the departing vehicle. He looked at the sky as he crouched in the darkness, unmoving. While still dark, the night's shadows were beginning to thin. The Iraqi glanced at the luminescent hands of his watch and shook his head in frustration. It was later than he had intended.

He had almost decided to change his strike time after the team's unforeseen foray into town. But as he'd already done the legwork and packed his equipment for a hit tonight, he decided to at least go as far as the camp's perimeter. At worst more intel couldn't hurt his chances. If he was fortunate, he'd be offered an opportunity to complete his mission. But now he was weighing the mission's chances of success following the disaster that occurred while he made his way along the infiltration route he'd planned earlier in the day.

The route had indeed been a good one from the standpoint of avoiding electronic detection. What he had not counted on was a variation in the patrols. He and one of the guards, also dressed in black, had practically run into one another in the woods two hundred meters outside the compound's inner fence. Bakr had struck swiftly, disarming the guard of the Heckler & Koch assault rifle he'd been carrying. At that point the man had pulled a knife and crouched. Bakr had smiled because a silent battle was much to his preference at the moment. Ten seconds later, as he wiped his knife clean of blood on the guard's pants leg, he weighed his chances. To leave now, or carry on? He might as well press, he'd decided. Within a short time, the missing guard would be located and the Americans would know someone had penetrated deep into their security zone. His chances for a successful second incursion would be lowered exponentially.

Five minutes later he'd crouched outside the fence, watching the compound. He knew the window that would grant him access to Bernard's bedroom. He felt the lump of the satchel charge in his pack. It was a cool evening and he hoped the good doctor would have the window open. If not, Bakr had the tools to quietly do the job and drop his package. Soon Bernard's sleep would be forever uninterrupted. A similar but significantly larger package for the server farm rested in the pack as well. He'd emplace that one first, with enough cushion on the timer to ensure it didn't go off before he'd completed his primary task, Ber-

nard. As he had been laying out his tools to disable
the fence's motion detection system and cut through
it, movement from a corner of the compound had
caught his eye. He'd pulled out his night-vision goggles
and taken a closer look—the woman who'd been sitting next to Bernard earlier at the pub. She was coming from the area of the pool and did not look happy.

Sayid Bakr watched her enter the main building and
slam the door behind her before turning his attention
to the pool as he heard a soft splash. Allah was good,
the Iraqi mused, but he could not be that good to him
this night . . . but no, there he was. Clive Bernard sat
alone beside the dark water, lost in thought.

In his mind the terrorist—though he did not think
of himself in such terms—quickly altered his plan to
take advantage of this unexpected boon. He fingered
the knife that was still warm from the guard's life-
blood. Yes, sometimes simple was best. He'd just finished disabling the fence and had lifted his wirecutters
to penetrate the chainlink mesh when he heard a vehicle and saw the main gate rumble open. Seconds later
the Cherokee had pulled onto the compound's
grounds. Bakr could not see the vehicle's occupants
but he recognized the man Cobb as he came out
through the front entrance. The Iraqi waited. What
followed was mildly entertaining, but Bakr wished it
would end. His window of opportunity was rapidly
closing. It would be light soon, and he didn't know
how much longer Clive Bernard would remain at the
pool. The ex-commando made the most of the altera-
tion by using the time to cut a gap in the fence.

Finally Cobb had carried the unconscious man Bakr
now recognized as one of the American officers into
the building, and the Cherokee, after sitting stationary
for almost a full minute, pulled to the gate. Seconds
later it rumbled open. Not one to question a second
gift in one night, Bakr had hastily shouldered his
equipment and sprinted along the fence line to the

gate, rolling into the inner compound just ahead of the closing gate.

Cobb carried Mike Stuart to his room and laid the young captain on his bunk. He stood silently next to the bedside and looked at the officer. But his thoughts were of Nicole, of his grandson—and finally of his own son. He had been honest with his ex-daughter-in-law when he'd told her he wished she were his child. Despite the hurdles life had dealt her, Nicole had not given up. She had worked, fought, and lived to make a better life for herself and her son.

Cobb had long ago given up on his own son, much to his quiet sorrow. While he felt some amount of anguish for the part he'd played in the boy's problems—primarily not being around to help shape the man the boy would become—he was also honest. Each man was responsible for who he was. Cobb knew men who'd come from less than perfect backgrounds and yet still managed to accomplish much with their lives. The military was full of people from the inner cities of the U.S.'s metropolises, neighborhoods that resembled war zones more than Main Street, USA; from foreign countries that denied them basic freedoms; and worse. His son, someday, would face himself in a mirror and realize his life was his to do with as he wished and that whatever he ultimately became was up to him. Maybe there was still time, Cobb thought. Maybe. He hoped so.

A vibration on his hip broke Cobb's reverie. Looking down, he recognized the number on his pager. An overseas call from a contact he'd phoned a couple of days ago. And the caller had appended a "911" suffix to the end of the number.

Cobb quickly moved toward the security center and returned the call via one of the center's secure telephones. He donned a combination earpiece/boom-mike headset as the call went through and watched the communication console's plasma display. The icon indicating the near end—the phone Cobb himself was dialing from—was a solid green; secure. The far end's icon was a steady red until the caller picked up, and then it changed to yellow and pulsed on and off for three seconds, at which point it, too, went green, indicating the call was secure from both ends.

"Ja," was the only word spoken from the Munich end.

"You have something for me, Hans?" asked Cobb, reaching to rub the back of his neck.

The German's voice, a deep baritone, belied the man's height of just over four and a half feet. "Yes. My apologies for taking so long to get back to you, Cobb, but I was in Berlin for a briefing."

"That's all right. Thanks for getting back with me." Cobb paused. "The spike was from one of your FIS boxes, correct?" On a hunch, Cobb had sent the electronic anomaly recorded by the security system's scanner to Germany two days earlier.

Hans, a.k.a. "the Gnome," hesitated before answering. While he and Cobb worked for governments friendly to one another in the larger scheme of things, the relationship between the two world powers had been sorely tried since the 1990s. Still, he and Cobb held a grudging respect for one another's abilities in their respected fields. Hans grunted a laugh. Too bad Cobb wasn't German. The *Bundesnachrichtendienst* could certainly use his services, which was the primary reason the Gnome tried to stay in the American's good graces . . . much better to have him on your side than against you.

"How did you know it was one of my devices, Cobb? Their existence is known by few, even in the dark circles through which you and I dance."

"Shit," muttered Cobb, "I knew it."

The Gnome's voice was apologetic. "We did not realize one was missing until your call. A small shipment en route from Munich to . . . well, the destination does not matter. Suffice it to say, an inventory on the receiving end following your call turned up short by one device."

"Do you know what happened to it yet?"

Cobb had long ago become accustomed to the diminutive German's pauses prior to answering direct questions. He was a man who liked to savor the ramifications of each possible response. "We have a few leads. I would expect I'll have an answer within twenty-four hours."

Cobb unconsciously reached back and rubbed his neck. "Can you at least tell me the method of shipment?"

The Gnome considered the question. "It was shipped . . . overland."

"Fucking great, Hans," said Cobb tightly. "So the transportation either had wheels or it rode on the rails. I need more than that, dammit."

"Why?" asked the German, perplexed. "What possible good would the knowledge do you?"

A pause. "I'm not sure," Cobb finally answered in a quiet voice. "But I *need* to know."

Hans considered the request. The answer gave away nothing that Cobb couldn't find out with a few phone calls. "We have a small fleet of buses, fifty-eight passenger coaches disguised as tourist buses, with most of the seats removed. We use them to ship cargo discreetly within Germany's borders."

Cobb considered why he'd wanted to know the answer to that question so badly. He couldn't say. The German inventor was correct; the fact that they were shipped via bus told him nothing. And then Cobb's internal alarm system began clanging. "Thanks, Hans," he said shortly. "Please let me know what you find out."

"Very well, and Cobb . . . Cobb?" But the connection had already been broken from the other side of the Atlantic. The diminutive German shook his head and laughed quietly, shaking his head. "Good-bye, Cobb. As always, a pleasure speaking with you."

With reluctance Clive Bernard stood and slipped on his Havaianas. "Well, Bernard," he said to himself. "Tomorrow's a new day. Ready or not, it's finally time to start acting like a grown-up."

"Do you always do that?"

Bernard started for the second time in the past hour. He slowly turned toward the voice. The speaker stepped forward from the shadows, exposing himself to the muted light surrounding the pool area. Clive Bernard didn't recognize him, but something told the scientist that the man was not a guard. "I'm sorry," he said slowly, stalling for time to think. "Do I always do what?"

"Talk to yourself," said the stranger. "That is not a good sign for someone in as elevated a position as yourself."

The man's English was nearly flawless, but underlying it was an accent that Bernard couldn't quite place. "Look, man," he said. "Exactly who *are* you?"

A slow smile crossed Sayid Bakr's face, and for the first time Bernard saw the small fires of madness dancing in the eyes. "*Who* I am is not really important. *What* I am is your immediate concern."

"And . . . *what* are you exactly?"

Bakr reached to his hip and pulled a large knife from its sheath. "An instrument of retribution."

Bernard stared at the blade as light danced along its edge. He took a step backward and swallowed hard. "Man, I don't even *know* you. So . . . why would you want to kill me?"

Bakr walked forward. "There is no further use for words, Dr. Bernard, and you would not understand anyway. You see, this is not about you. . . ."

A crack and a burst of flame shattered the predawn darkness and Sayid Bakr staggered sideways.

"Move it, Doctor!" yelled Cobb. He was halfway to the pool and sprinting, a Glock 9mm in hand and still aimed at the intruder. "Get back to the building! *Now!*"

"You got it," mumbled Bernard. The only sound after that was the rapid flip-flopping of his sandals as he ran for safety.

Sayid Bakr backed toward the gap he had minutes earlier cut through the fence as an escape route. He could feel the clock ticking down. The gunfire would have more security personnel closing on his position within minutes, if not sooner.

"Drop the knife," said Cobb, stopping ten feet from Bakr. "Face down on the ground, arms and legs spread. Now!"

Bakr shook his head and grimaced. The shock of his wound was passing and the pain was beginning to set in, a dull throb. It felt like the bullet had only given him a deep graze along his right shoulder, but he had definitely lost some functionality. "I am afraid I cannot do that, Mr. Cobb."

Cobb stared at the intruder, recognition suddenly lighting his features. "You were at the pub."

The Iraqi took a slow step backward. He nodded. "But, how did you know I would be here tonight?"

"Bus."

"Ahhh, I see," said the Iraqi. "And I thought I had pulled that portion of my mission off with such success."

"You did," Cobb replied, the Glock locked onto the center of Bakr's chest. "Now then, I said drop the knife and grab some dirt. Otherwise I'll drill you where you stand."

Slowly Bakr's fingers relaxed and he let the knife drop. He reached toward a breast pocket on his utility vest.

"Don't do it," said Cobb through gritted teeth. "I'd prefer to have you alive, but dead is fine by me."

Bakr gritted his teeth and forced a smile as another

bolt of pain shot through his shoulder. "If I may . . . ," he began, reaching only an index finger and thumb into the pocket.

"Slow-ly," said Cobb.

Bakr nodded. He withdrew a black plastic remote. A small red light pulsed on its front display. "I believe we are at an impasse, Mr. Cobb," he said.

Cobb's expression never changed, his eyes didn't blink. "If you've got something to say, say it," he spat. "I'm getting bored."

Bakr nodded. "There is a rather large explosive device planted on your compound." He held the device away from his body. Cobb could see that one of the man's fingers was poised over a button. "If you shoot, I promise you, I will retain enough strength to detonate the device."

Cobb eyed the Iraqi down the length of the Glock's barrel, arms extended, head tilted slightly to the right.

"I know what you are thinking, Mr. Cobb. A nice clean headshot would preclude my detonating the device." Bakr smiled again. "If that pistol aligns with my head, I will consider that the same as shooting me. So . . . what is it going to be?"

Cobb's eyes remained locked down the line of his arm and the pistol that was its extension. "I say . . . I don't negotiate." A slight twist of his body to the left and the 9mm roared once, hitting the remote dead center and taking the finger that had been poised above the button with it.

The Iraqi, already beginning to weaken from loss of blood, spun to the ground. Keeping the Glock on him, Cobb advanced slowly. And then Sayid Bakr moved. Having landed atop his knife, he lifted his body and flung the blade on a line for the advancing American. Cobb just had time to note the scorpion-and-dagger tattoo on the man's forearm before firing off two rounds, but the four inches of steel buried in his right thigh threw off his aim. As the American staggered, Bakr rolled backward and disappeared through the fence line.

"Dammit," muttered Cobb, scanning the forest beyond the camp's perimeter. He reached for his radio. "All personnel, we have an intruder. He has escaped through a section of the northeast fence line. He's armed with at least a knife, maybe more. If you see him, do not attempt to apprehend . . . shoot to kill. Acknowledge, over."

As the security zone personnel finished responding the radio went quiet. Cobb noted that two stations had not yet reported. *"Damn,"* he said. He didn't bother calling the noncommunicative stations again. He knew his men. If they'd been able, they'd have answered the call. For the moment, the best he could hope for was that they were alive but incapacitated. But an inner voice told him otherwise. He activated the radio again. "Base, get the canine bomb unit moving. I think we've got a package on the grounds." He looked down at his leg and the knife protruding from it. Blood had already saturated the leg of his trousers and began filling his boots. "And send a medic to the pool, I'm feeling a little under the weather." And then things began spinning and Cobb found himself falling toward the ground. Someone caught him under his arms.

"Easy there, Cobb," said Clive Bernard, grunting at the strain. "I've got you, man. Let's just sit down, all right?"

Cobb grimaced as the scientist eased him toward the ground. "I thought I told you to get out of here," he said.

"I tried," Bernard said. "But, you know, I felt kind of bad leaving you like that. So, halfway to the building, I turned around and came back." Despite the circumstances, a laugh escaped Bernard. "That was quite a shot. How did you know it wouldn't detonate the explosives?"

Cobb grunted. "I didn't. But I don't like being blackmailed."

"Rest easy, my friend," said Bernard, though Cobb couldn't hear him. Bernard turned toward the sound of the medic team scrambling from the dispensary. "Over here, dammit! Hurry it up!"

Cobb came awake with a start three hours later and reached for the Glock that normally rested in an extended holster down his right side.

"Easy, old man," said a woman's voice.

Cobb turned and saw Nicole sitting next to his bed, her eyes red from crying. "Nicole? What are you doing here?"

"I called her," said a male voice.

Cobb turned to the other side of his bed. Mike Stuart grinned at him. Cobb grimaced in return.

"What are you trying to do?" asked Nicole, a note of anger in her voice as she wiped her eyes with the back of a hand. "Get yourself killed?"

Cobb had begun turning back to Nicole's side of the bed as a wave of dizziness hit him. He felt like a drunken tennis judge. He blinked twice. "What? No. There was a . . ."

"I know that!" yelled Nicole. "Don't you think I know that? But you . . . you aren't getting any younger, dammit, Cobb! And . . . and you've got a grandchild to think about! What would he do if something happened to you, the only male figure in his life?!"

"Well . . . ," Mike Stuart began.

Nicole and Cobb shouted in unison, "Shut up!"

Stuart raised his open palms in front of him. "Hey, I was just going to say—"

"Stow it, lover boy," interrupted Cobb.

Stuart grinned. "I just want you to get well quickly, Cobb. When I get another shot at you, I don't want there to be any doubts over the outcome because you were a little incapacitated."

Cobb began to reply when Nicole lashed out again. "Mike! Out! You're not helping."

"Okay, okay," muttered Stuart, retreating to the door. Before he left, he turned to Cobb and extended his index finger and thumb in a pistol gesture, and then squeezed his thumb twice and winked. "I'll be seeing you around, old man."

"Why you . . ." But Cobb was talking to Stuart's back.

"You listen to me, Cobb," said Nicole. "I want you to retire. Now. Tonight. Do you understand?"

The ex-operator tried to sit up and winced as the fresh stitches in his leg pulled tight.

"Lay down, you stubborn old goat."

Cobb flushed. "Look, I'm not even fifty years old. I'm getting a little tired of being called old."

Nicole's expression softened. "Listen, Cobb, please. . . ."

He shook his head. "I can't do it, Nicky. Not now. At least not until I see this project through."

"What's so important about *this* project? It's always something—why is this so different?"

Cobb didn't reply, his face sliding into a mask of neutrality.

Nicole threw her hands up in frustration. "Okay, fine. I know that look. The same one you used to use when I asked where you were going and when you'd be back just as you'd disappear for weeks or months. But why can't they do it without you? The military *will* have to get along without you one of these days, you know, difficult though it may be for them."

"I realize that," said Cobb, but Nicole could see she'd struck a nerve.

"Just get out *now*," she implored. "Please? For *me*?"

It took all of Cobb's inner strength to speak over the knot that had formed in his throat. "Nicole, you know . . . how I feel about you. But I can't quit. Not yet." He shook his head, thinking of the man he'd faced earlier. "This guy, he's special. And he'll be *back*."

Nicole was surprised by the statement and felt a shudder of apprehension run through her. "How did you know he got away? We just found out a few minutes ago."

"Because I recognized the type. He was good. *Very* good." The security man turned toward the door and yelled for the night shift supervisor. Thirty seconds later the man stood before him. "How many men did we lose?"

The supervisor looked at Nicole, then back to Cobb.

"Don't worry about her. Answer the question."

"Three," the man said. "Two were taken out as he made his entry. One on the way out."

Cobb nodded as he digested the information. It could have been worse. "And the explosives? Did we find anything?"

"Yes, sir. Five pounds of Semtex at the server farm building." The night supervisor, a man with plenty of experience in the world of plastic explosives, ran a hand through his hair. "He may have had a detonator, but he'd also set a timer. We found it with less than a minute remaining before cook-off. Simple rig, so we got her shut down quickly."

Cobb knew what five pounds of the Czech equivalent of C4 plastic explosives would have done to the project's efforts. "That was cutting it close."

The other security man nodded. "Roger that."

"Any trace of the bad guy?"

The man shook his head. "Other than a few blood trails, negative." And then the guard's face brightened. "We did get a piece of good news tonight, Cobb."

"What?"

"The ODA that went into Iran after our two soldiers . . . they made it out. They're en route back to the States as we speak."

"Losses?"

"The team came through clean. Apparently the NCO taken with the major, he didn't make it."

Cobb nodded. In his world, you knew you could never get everyone. All you could do was make the bastards pay. "Any word on the vehicles?"

The man shook his head. "Other than what we'd already heard, that they'd made it through the Persian Gulf, negative."

Cobb nodded and laid his head back drowsily on his pillow. "All right. Thanks for the report. The vehicles will show up. And when they do . . ." As his eyes began to drift closed, he sat up. "Nicole . . . where's my gun?"

"What in the world do you need with . . ."

"Please."

Nicole walked to the corner of the room and brought the Glock to the bed, handing it to Cobb.

The night supervisor looked at the gun and frowned. "What's that extension along the slide?"

Cobb grinned sleepily. "A new piece of kit some friends wanted me to try out for them. When you're clearing a building, sometimes photos are a good thing for post-op analysis. But your hands are kind of busy at the time." He fumbled a moment with the inch-long, thin piece of fiber optics running along the Glock's slide, then popped it loose and handed it to the supervisor. "Digital camera. Not great for anything past twenty meters . . . but that was plenty for tonight. I should have several decent pictures of this guy. I want to know who he is—soonest." Then Cobb passed into darkness once more.

Chapter 21

The Circle of Life and Assorted Musings

Institute for Plant and Seed Modification Research
Third Subterranean Level, Infirmary
Karaj, Iran

Sergei Sedov hung up the phone at his desk. Despite everything that had gone wrong this night, not to mention his aching back from the fall down the airshaft, finally some good news.

A shadow crossed his desk as someone entered the small office. "You have a great deal of explaining to do, Colonel Sedov," said the Ayatollah Khalani. It was all that the holy man said, but the anger that suffused his features said the rest.

"Holiness . . . ," Sedov began.

"I will tolerate no further failures, Colonel," said the cleric, staring at the Russian with his dead eyes. "None."

Sedov rose on shaky legs. "Security of this facility is not my responsibility," he said coldly. "Thus *I* have not failed, but rather your incompetent guards failed. And somewhere your internal security failed as well, because only an insider could have given the Americans the information necessary for them to enter the institute the way they did."

Reluctantly the Iranian leader nodded. "Yes. One

of the institute's employees gave the Americans the information they needed." His eyes hooded. "He will not have the opportunity for future treachery."

"If it makes you feel better, the American sergeant gave us the codes last night. Thus we have everything we need to crack the secrets from the systems."

"Where are the M4X1s now?" asked Khalani.

"They were here for a short period tonight, but I decided to have them diverted to a new location."

Khalani frowned. "Did it occur to you, Colonel, to consult with me before making such a decision?"

Sedov rubbed a hand across his suddenly tired eyes. "Most Exalted One," he purred, "you hired me for one reason and one reason only: I am your best chance for success in this endeavor. So why do you insist on second-guessing every decision I make?"

"Colonel . . ."

The Russian held up a hand. "Please, bear with me," he said. "Do you really think it wise to bring the Franks systems to a facility that it is clear the Americans have infiltrated? How long do you think it would be before smart weapons began descending on the institute?"

"I told you, our security problem has been taken care of."

Sergei Sedov smiled. "Of course it has, Your Eminence. Of course it has. But I am a believer in that American saying . . . better safe than sorry."

The Iranian leader shrugged in surrender. "Very well, perhaps you are right. Where are they now?"

Sedov consulted his watch. "About halfway to their destination."

"Which is?"

The Russian told him.

"Is that wise? And what makes you think the Americans—"

"Please. Trust me." Sedov smiled a Cheshire grin.

Walter Reed Army Medical Center
Washington, D.C.

As Chris Dodd departed the hospital room, his brother Luke stepped off an elevator and walked to meet him. "How's he doing?" asked Luke, nodding into the room where Patrick Dillon reclined in a hospital bed.

The elder Dodd shrugged. "Considering everything he's been through, amazingly well. He's got a couple of cracked ribs, but other than a dozen or so bad bruises and some scrapes, that's about it."

Luke Dodd shook his head in disgust. "Sedov. He didn't want to mess him up bad until he got what he wanted."

The CIA director nodded. "That's about the size of it. And of course, he got exactly that in the end. So it's fortunate you guys got there when you did—for both the major and Mrs. Dillon's sake."

As if having heard her name, Melissa stepped from a break room down the hallway and approached them, two steaming cups of coffee in hand. "Gentlemen, how are you?" she said, smiling. But the smile was drained of enthusiasm, and the Dodds knew pressures other than just her recent captivity were likely responsible. She held up the coffee. "I'm sure he'd rather have a beer, but this is the best I can do for him at the moment."

Luke took one of the cups of coffee from her hand and, looking around to ensure no nurses were in view, handed her a plain paper bag. Looking inside, Melissa smiled. "Fat Tire ale?"

Luke grinned. "Still cold. And there's an opener in the bag as well."

Melissa shook her head ruefully as she entered the room. "You'll never get him out of that bed now."

"Luke?"

The younger Dodd turned. "Yeah?"

"Where'd you get the Fat Tire?"

"I'd really like to tell you, Chris . . ."

"But you're afraid you might incriminate yourself?" Luke smiled. "Something like that."

Reaching for the door, Chris Dodd pulled it closed to give the Dillons some privacy.

"So what's the plan now?" asked Luke.

Chris Dodd shook his head in frustration. "Well, for my part, I get to go to the White House and brief the president that not only do we not know where the M4X1s are, but that the Iranians have everything they need to reverse engineer them."

"Shit," Luke muttered vehemently, hanging his head. "All for nothing."

"You know better than that," said Chris Dodd, placing a hand on his younger brother's shoulder and giving it a squeeze. "You, Krieger, and that Special Forces team got two people out of a living hell." He squeezed again. "And we'll find those Tommies, I swear to God we'll find them."

Luke nodded. "Was sending Ted in your idea?"

Chris smiled before shaking his head. "Ted? Ted who?"

"Jesus," said Luke. "You are the king spook. Can't even give your brother a straight answer."

Chris nodded toward the bank of elevators and the brothers walked in that direction. "So," asked Chris, hitting the DOWN button, "do I have any Fat Tires left?"

Luke Dodd smiled. "Maybe a couple. But I thought you had to meet with President Drake?"

Chris shrugged. "So we'll take him one. He's probably going to need it."

"Luke Dodd asked me to give you this," said Melissa, handing Patrick Dillon the bag.

Dillon, a new leather eyepatch in place, looked into the bag, and smiled. "I mean this in a totally nongay way," he said with a straight face, "but I *love* that guy."

"Yeah," Melissa said and laughed. "I thought you'd feel that way. So give me one of those."

"These are *Fat Tires*. Your palate's not refined enough to appreciate either the boldness of its bite or the ever-so-subtle malty flavor." He smiled tiredly. "No offense."

"Shut up, Pat," said Melissa, taking two beers and the opener from the bag.

Dillon shrugged as he accepted a beer and took a long pull. "*God* but that's good."

Melissa took a swallow of her own and shrugged. "It tastes like Budweiser to me."

Patrick Dillon shook his head in exasperation. "Told you . . . unrefined palate. That's the kind of reason it would never have worked with us."

Melissa put her beer on the nightstand next to the bed. "Speaking of which, Patrick, we need to . . ."

"This isn't the time, Melissa," he said, leaning his head back on a pillow.

"Why not?" she asked. "If not now, after everything that's happened, when we both almost died . . . when?"

Dillon closed his eyes and shrugged. "Maybe never," he replied quietly. "But definitely not until after I get back from Bragg."

"Patrick Dillon, you are *not* going to Fort Bragg," said Melissa hotly. "You think I don't know what's going on down there? Bill Jones, Dave Barnett, Mike Stuart . . . they're putting a team together. And I have a pretty good idea where that team will be going." She beat a hand on her leg in frustration as she sat on the edge of the bed. "You've done *enough*, Patrick."

The stocky major shook his head. "No, I haven't," he said. "There are lots of guys who've done more. . . ."

"You don't get it, do you?" said Melissa. "You *really* don't. No one has done more than you, Patrick. *No one*. And yet you keep going back, marching to the sound of the war drums. They start beating and you can't help but move toward them. You've lost men, friends, an *eye*, for God's sake, and—" Abruptly she quit speaking.

"And my family?" finished Dillon in a quiet voice. "Are you going to blame that one on the military as well, Melissa?"

Melissa stared at him. "It didn't help, Pat. Maybe if . . . I don't know. But that's behind us, and you are not going to Fort Bragg or anywhere else. You're getting on a plane with me to Colorado and you're going to see your daughters, spend time with them, heal."

Dillon smiled sadly and shifted as his ribs began aching. "You're talking like a wife."

Melissa opened her mouth to reply, closed it slowly, thinking how best to reply. "Sorry," she said finally. "But someone has to speak for your children."

Dillon shook his head. "That was low, Mel. Even for you."

"It's the truth. Forget me, what about them?"

Keeping his head on the pillow, Dillon took another long pull of beer. "My girls know I love them. And unlike you, they have always understood that I am who I am and that it isn't a lack of love for them that causes me to go where I go, to do what I do."

"Pat . . ."

"They're my *friends*, Melissa. I can't watch them go after the vehicles I was responsible for." He shook his head in frustration. "And Tom? What about Tom Crockett, Melissa? Remember him?"

"Tom wouldn't want you to go back to Iran, Pat," Melissa said. "Don't try to pull that crap with me."

"It doesn't matter," said Dillon, his voice hardening. "I told that fucking Russian I was going to be back for him. That's a promise I intend to keep."

"But . . ."

"No more arguments, Melissa. This is what I do," he said, staring at the ceiling. "It's the *only* thing I do well." Another pull from the bottle. "And I do it so well."

"You've always been something of an arrogant bastard, you know that," Melissa Dillon whispered.

Dillon shrugged. "Maybe. But it doesn't change the truth of it."

"Don't be stupid," she continued. "You're so much more than . . . all of that."

"Melissa . . ."

"You're the best father I know. Your daughters love you dearly." She paused, then smiled. "And you were a great friend . . . and husband."

Dillon lifted himself painfully onto his elbows, for the first time raising his voice. "Then *why*, Melissa? Why for Christ's sake did you do what you did if I was such a *great fucking friend and husband? Why?!*"

A nurse stuck her head in the door, looked back and forth between Melissa and Dillon. "Is everything all right in here?" she asked.

Dillon smiled. "Just groovy."

"Well, you'll have to keep it down. This is a hospital. That means there are sick people here trying to rest."

The major nodded. "Yes, ma'am."

As the door closed Dillon's head swiveled to Melissa, the question continuing to hang in the air between them.

"Because I'm not perfect, Patrick," she whispered, staring at him with a sincerity that was almost too much for him. "We can't all be perfect like the great Patrick Dillon."

Finally she'd managed to shut him up.

Wiping suddenly wet eyes, Melissa Dillon took his hand. "I need to know, Patrick. Are you willing to . . . to try to work things out? To *try?*"

No reply.

"I need an answer, Pat. I can't go home without one."

Patrick Dillon took a deep breath and thought about everything that had happened in his life since returning from Iraq the previous year. And then he looked into Melissa Dillon's eyes. "I think you're an amazing person, Melissa," he said. "You're one of the most beautiful, intelligent women I've ever known. You can make me smile with a look, make me laugh at myself, even when I don't want to. You're a wonderful mother and a good friend to those you care about." Abruptly he quit speaking, taking another long pull from the bottle of Fat Tire.

"But . . . ?" she asked, tears sparkling in her eyes.

Dillon stared at the ceiling, refusing to meet her gaze. "But as a wife, you suck. I'm going to have to pass." He lowered his head to look into her eyes. "Give the girls my love and tell them I'll call soon."

Without a word Melissa stood and moved toward the door.

"You can leave the beer," Dillon said.

Melissa turned and moved back across the room, putting the bag in his lap. "You can be such an ass."

A tear trickled down one beard-stubbled cheek as the door closed behind her departing figure. Dillon drained the Fat Tire and opened a fresh one. "Don't I know it, darlin'," he muttered to himself. "Don't I know it."

Iranian Desert

George Greenfield beat on the stolen Peugeot's radiator from the shadow of the car's raised hood as steam poured from the engine compartment.

"Great," said the CIA officer. "Just freakin' great. First this piece of shit"—he held up the satellite phone that was picking up absolutely no signal and stared at it with hate in his eyes—"and now the car." He threw the phone as far as he could and it rattled to a stop amidst a pile of rocks twenty meters off of the roadway.

He turned to look south. The column of trucks continued to wind its way along the curvy mountain road, the last transport disappearing over a hill as he watched.

"What the hell," Greenfield muttered. He grabbed a bottle of water and a pair of Steiner binoculars from the passenger seat and set off in the direction of the nearest series of hills. "For all the good it'll do me." He stooped and picked up the useless phone as he passed it. "Sons of bitches in accounting would probably make me pay for the worthless piece of crap," he muttered.

Watch Floor
National Security Agency (NSA) Headquarters
Fort Meade, Maryland

The NSA has a name for itself: America's Code-makers and Codebreakers. Their glass-and-chrome high-rise headquarters employs more than twenty thousand people, including the crème de la crème of the nation's mathematicians and computer scientists, programmers—and hackers. One looks at the high-rise and attempts to understand how, despite its gargantuan size, the structure can house so many employees. The current theory on conspiracy Web sites estimates that over ten acres of subterranean space and corridors run beneath the Maryland base.

Its mathematicians contribute directly to the two missions of the Agency: designing cipher systems that will protect the integrity of U.S. information systems and searching for weaknesses in adversaries' systems and codes. They also exploit non-U.S. transmission signals for foreign intelligence and counterintelligence purposes that further American interests—something even U.S. allies at times find offensive.

The analyst receiving a transcript stared at his flat-panel display with a frown. Picking up his coffee, he took a sip and hit the PRINT button. Spinning away from the monitor, he retrieved the text from a laser printer hooked to his workstation and walked across the watch room.

"Have any fresh coffee?"

The other man didn't look away from his monitor. "Help yourself," he said distractedly.

"Cream?"

"Don't push it."

The analyst refreshed his cup. "I need you to take a look at something. It might be big."

"Originating location?" he asked, still looking over the report he'd just received.

"Iran."

The other analyst turned in his chair. "Iran? That's a coincidence," he said, taking the proffered sheet of paper. "I just received an interesting intercept from our Persian brothers myself. The boys tell me it was a bitch to crack, which is unusual for them."

"This one wasn't too bad. A little manipulation and we had it."

The second watch officer read over the report, then turned to read over the one on his computer screen again, confusion written on his features.

"You mind?" asked the first analyst, pointing at the screen.

"No, go ahead."

The analyst took in the screen's message, finally shaking his head. "This makes no sense."

The second man lifted the watch phone next to him and winked. "And I'm not giving myself a headache trying to figure it out. Time to push this up and let someone else figure out what's going on."

Office of the Director
Central Intelligence Agency (CIA) Headquarters
Langley, Virginia

"Sir," Chris Dodd's secretary called over the intercom, "you have a call."

Dodd looked over the stacks of reports he was wading through. "Can it wait?"

"It's your counterpart from Moscow, Mr. Director."

Dodd frowned. So far as he knew, Russia had been quiet. "Avel? How are you?"

Avel Gadalov, head of the Russian Foreign Intelligence Service, or SVR, was normally a merry man. He didn't sound merry this morning. "I have some rather unpleasant information, Christopher. We need your help."

Dodd listened in silence for a full minute. When Gadalov finished speaking, he shook his head. This month just kept getting better and better. He looked at the phone that linked him to the President of the United States twenty-four hours a day, seven days a week, and began mentally packing a bag. It looked like he was headed to Florida.

Tommy Compound
Fort Bragg, North Carolina

Cobb sat at the head of the conference table. Around it were the corps team members—Clive Bernard, Sue Kwan, Bill Jones, Dave Barnett, and Sarah Hunter.

"So what's so important, Cobb?" asked Bernard. "The testing on the M1A1s is going well, but we can't afford to waste . . ."

Cobb shifted uncomfortably on his leg. It had been almost two weeks since his injury and it was healing nicely, but it was still stiff if he stood for very long. He looked at Bernard and marveled at the changes that had taken place in the man since the night of the attack on the compound. It wasn't his outward appearance, but the scientist now took his duties seriously, immersing himself in his work. No doubts, no screwing around. It was a welcome change.

"Doc, you know I wouldn't have interrupted your schedule if it wasn't important," said Cobb simply. He depressed a button on the remote he held in his hand. A darkly handsome man in his mid-forties appeared on the screen behind him.

"That's the dude," whispered Bernard.

Sarah Hunter leaned forward. "I recognize him from the pub. He's the one you were so interested in that was in the back corner, isn't he, Cobb?"

"Yeah," said Cobb. "Sayid Bakr. Ex-Iraqi commando fighting under our Marine forces in the Sunni Triangle area of Iraq." Cobb shook his head. "Educated in the U.S., some call his work in the medical field brilliant. And he was one of the best fighters in the theater according to the leathernecks I spoke with this week."

"So why the hell is he trying to kill *me*?" asked Bernard, baffled.

Another click. Collapsed mosque.

"His wife and daughter were in there," said Cobb quietly. "An unfortunate incident in which an American tank crew was involved. Pure accident, but . . ."

Another click. Five heads lined atop a Humvee's hood, one with blond hair—Americans.

"I take it he kind of snapped?" said Bernard, swallowing hard as he looked at the handiwork of the man he'd been face-to-face with, nothing but a knife and a few feet of distance separating them. He felt the skin around his throat tighten as he continued staring at the row of heads.

Bill Jones lit a cigarette and inhaled deeply. "Cobb, what does this have to do with our current situation?" he asked. "Okay, now we know who he is, and we can make sure that no one remotely fitting that description gets near the compound. Hell, within twenty miles of the compound. But why show us all of this?"

Cobb shook his head. "Because I want to impress on all of you just how good this guy is . . . and how motivated. We're assuming he's working for the Iranians, but all we really know is that he will take any job he thinks he can pull off that strikes at vital U.S. interests. He blames us for the death of his family, and he's not going to give up."

"So you think he'll be back?" asked Jones as he watched beads of sweat appear on Clive Bernard's forehead.

"Oh, he'll be back," said Cobb quietly, clicking back to the original photo. He stared deep into the dark eyes of the man who'd become such a part of his life. "You can bet on it."

A knock sounded on the conference room door.

"Come," called Cobb.

A familiar figure walked into the room. The assembled project personnel scrambled to their feet, knocking coffee cups over.

President Jonathan Drake shook his head. "Why do I always seem to have that effect on a room?" Just returned from his Florida cattle ranch for two days of much-needed "vacation," Drake still wore jeans, a flannel shirt, and dirty boots. "Mr. Cobb," he said, reaching a hand toward the security specialist. "As always, good to see you."

"And you as well, Mr. President," said Cobb, taking the proffered hand.

Jones and Barnett exchanged a look. They would never unravel all of the mysteries of Mr. Cobb, they silently agreed.

Drake motioned for everyone to sit. As the team settled once more into their seats, two more men entered the room.

"Mr. Cobb, I believe you know Director Dodd of Central Intelligence. And his brother."

Cobb exchanged greetings with the two men. "Good to see you again, Mr. Director," said Cobb.

Dodd smiled. "So are you ever going to take me up on that job offer, Mr. Cobb? It still stands."

The ex-operator smiled but didn't comment, turning instead to the younger Dodd. "Nice to finally meet you," he said to Luke. "I'm a big fan of your work in Moscow."

Luke grinned. "And your exploits in South America—magic, Mr. Cobb, pure magic."

"Is anyone but me lima-lima-mike-foxtrot as to what they're talking about?" muttered Dave Barnett.

"Lima-lima-what?" Clive Bernard asked quietly.

Sarah Hunter patted his shoulder affectionately, having slowly warmed to Bernard again after seeing the changes in him over the past two weeks. "Lima-lima-mike-foxtrot, Clive. It means lost like a motherfucker, dear."

"Oh," said Bernard. "Yeah, well, I am definitely clueless on this Moscow and South America stuff. And knowing Cobb, I don't think I want to know, man."

Jones winked and nodded agreement as Jonathan Drake moved to the head of the table and leaned over it to address the team. "All right, at this point you're probably wondering why POTUS is in the middle of the North Carolina woods slowing down your progress on an important project."

Silence.

"The reason is because your timetable is about to be moved forward, people," Drake said quietly. "I'll leave it to Director Dodd to explain why."

Chris Dodd looked over the team of scientists and military personnel. He'd been briefed on what they'd accomplished in their short time together and it was nothing short of miraculous. But would it be enough? "We've located the missing M4X1s," he began simply.

"And?" asked Cobb for the group.

"And within a few days, Sergei Sedov will have all the information he needs from the Tommies."

"As in all the data necessary for another country to make their own M4X1-type systems?" restated Bernard. "Basically shaving decades off of their R and D efforts?"

"Exactly," said Chris Dodd. "We need those vehicles and all of the data assembled by Sedov and his team in Iran to disappear."

"The question is," said Drake quietly, turning to Jones, "is your team ready? Would your upgraded Abrams have a chance if we send you in now?"

Jones tapped out a cigarette. Looking at the president, he hesitated.

"Go ahead, Colonel," said Drake.

Jones smiled and disappeared in a cloud. "That's a good fuck—uhhh, sorry. That's a very good question, Mr. President." He shook his head, thinking of what would need to be done and the timeline involved. "The appliqué armor provided by Dr. Levy is working very well, at least in the testing we've completed thus far. The General Dynamics Shield missile-defense system is also looking good." The old warrior shook his head. "But, gentlemen, we don't even receive our M1A2-SEPs until tomorrow. We'll need at least ten days of testing before—"

"We don't *have* ten days, Colonel," Chris Dodd said.

"Why not?"

"We have reason to believe Sedov is setting the Iranians up for a fall. Steal the data and then sell it."

"To whom?" asked Bernard in confusion. "I thought the Iranians had given him a sweet deal?"

The CIA director looked at his commander in chief.

"Tell them," said Drake. "They're the ones whose tails will be on the line, so they need to understand what we're dealing with."

"We have intelligence indicating that Sergei Sedov intends to sell the M4X1 data to the People's Republic of China in eight days."

"Eight days," echoed Dave Barnett, but his mind was already moving, calculating what the team would have to accomplish to be in the area of operations and prepared to execute a near-impossible mission in eight days. "Daunting, but doable," he finally murmured to Jones. "Assuming we fly our mod kits in with us and have platforms waiting for us."

"Tell them the rest, Chris," said Drake.

Dodd frowned. "Mr. President, we don't know that—"

"Tell them."

Chris Dodd sighed heavily before continuing. "We also have reason to believe Sedov may have laid his hands on a nuclear device."

"Whoooaaaa, man," said Clive Bernard. "What's this nuke shit?"

"The Russians have a stockpile of one-kiloton weapons that were originally assigned to their Spetsnaz forces during the Cold War," Dodd continued.

"I saw something about this on *60 Minutes* a few years ago when the Russians thought they might have a problem following the collapse of the Soviet Union," said Sarah Hunter. "Size of a suitcase, no launch code protection—and they can be prepped for detonation by one man in less than a half hour."

"That's our baby," said Dodd. "In a large city, they could take out fifty to one hundred thousand people."

"Jesus," muttered Bernard. "But I don't see the connection between a missing Russian nuke—assuming Sedov has it—and the Franks system."

"The Chinese are being rather insistent that once they have the technology, they don't want the prototypes around for someone else to reverse engineer," said Dodd. "Let's just say it was a deal-breaking point with them."

"But even Sedov wouldn't . . . ," began Jones, and then he shook his head. "Yeah. Yeah he would."

"The ayatollah has no idea what's going on?" asked Cobb.

Dodd shook his head. "I almost feel sorry for the old bastard."

"Man, this *sucks*," said Bernard, louder than he intended. But the response was a general nodding of heads from around the room.

Jones stood. "Mr. President, we're going to need some information before I can tell you if it's even possible to attempt to go in by ground with our big boys."

Drake nodded. "Go ahead."

"The Abramses are too heavy to airlift to some remote field in Iran. That leaves us two options. First, we can truck them in, but that ain't very tactical, sir. Second, we can punch in on the fly across the border into Iran. And this is when I bring up the fact that the M1A1 has a range of around three hundred miles on its fuel tanks, depending on our speed and road conditions. So I really need to know what those road conditions are—that is, where we'll be entering Iran—and how far we'll be traveling. Sir."

Drake and Chris Dodd exchanged looks. Dodd took over. "You'll be entering from western Afghanistan and heading one hundred kilometers across the border. Terrain is hilly in places, but it'll support armored traffic."

"Water crossings?" asked Barnett.

"None," replied Dodd. "It's a straight shot."

"What kind of support can we expect?"

"You'll receive a full military briefing on the plane," said Dodd, "but I can tell you this much . . . there's going to be a lot of fireworks that will, we think, turn their eyes away from that part of their border. The NSA has been in on this one from the beginning and they have a few—let us say *gadgets*—that they want to try out."

"Sounds good to me," said Jones. "Where do we link up with our Abramses?"

"According to General Werner, a company of M1A2-SEPs are en route via tractor trailers to western Afghanistan now," said Dodd.

The colonel shook his head. "That won't work. We haven't had time to do any testing against the A2s. We'll have to go with A1s."

"But why? The tanks are practically identical," said President Drake. "Can it make that much difference?"

"Oh, yeah, man . . . I mean, Mr. President," said Bernard.

"How?"

"Sir," explained Jones, "while the M1A1 and the M1A2-SEP *look* like pretty much the same tank, there's a night-and-day difference when you begin going through their guts. The old Abramses are late-seventies and early-eighties technology, the SEPs are all circuit cards and microprocessors."

"I'll get the word to the chief," said Drake. "Count on it. Travel safely and know that our prayers are with you and your team, Colonel." Drake extended a hand.

Jones took the president's hand. "You make it sound like we're leaving today, Mr. President."

"You are," said Drake. "That's why I'm here. When I give people bad news, I prefer to do it in person."

Barnett was already on his mobile phone calling Mike Stuart, who was currently at the range in preparation for further testing of the Shield systems. "Mike? Get the boys together. Start packing everything . . . that's right, everything."

Drake walked toward the door, and then paused, turning. "So, you really think you can pull it off, Colonel? If you don't, say the word. I'm not big on sending my people on suicide missions just to say we did something."

"And I wouldn't volunteer my war dogs if that was the case, sir. There's being brave and having a can-do attitude . . . and then there's being stupid," said Jones. "My boys and I can handle the mission planning to get our maneuver force into Iran and carry out actions on the objective, the objective in this case being the Tommies. If it's possible, we'll find a way. But the rest—taking out the facility, the data stores—that's not exactly a tanker's lane, Mr. President."

Chris Dodd smiled. "Already a step ahead of you, Colonel." Before Dodd could explain, a man in jeans, hiking boots, and a navy pullover fleece jacket entered the room. All eyes immediately locked on him.

"Patrick," said Jones. "I don't recall putting out a call for one-eyed tankers."

"Forgive me for pointing it out, Colonel, but you're getting a little long in the tooth to try to stop me," said Patrick Dillon.

Jones frowned, then turned to Dave Barnett. Barnett shrugged and tapped his pipe out in the ashtray in front of him. "You know what a pain in the ass Dillon can be if he doesn't get his way. Might as well make a space for him, sir."

Bill Jones rubbed a calloused hand through his thinning hair. "Well shit, I guess I don't have much of a choice, do I?" The big tanker lumbered to his feet and walked to the doorway in which Patrick Dillon stood. The younger man looked pretty good, he thought; a little thinner than when he'd last seen him, more silver in the hair, a few scratches on his face. Jones looked closer—yes, the single, piercing blue eye . . . there was something new there. Not fear. Haunted might be the word he was looking for. And determination, that was there as well.

Jones wrapped his arms around the major who'd worked for him for so long and through so many battles. "Good to have you home, son. Damned good," he whispered in Dillon's ear.

"Good to be home, sir," said Patrick Dillon quietly. He looked over Jones's shoulder and blinked. "Uhhh, hello, Mr. President."

It was midnight by the time the team, the cargo trucks hauling their equipment and personal gear, and over a dozen Hummers manned by MPs behind .50 caliber machine guns drove onto Pope Air Base adjacent to Fort Bragg. In front of them were two C-17 Globemaster III cargo aircraft. Dozens of floodlights made the loading area glow like a NASA pad the night before a shuttle launch. The ground combat soldiers ogled the big craft, each one hundred seventy-four feet long and with one-hundred-seventy-foot wingspans. The aircrafts' giant aft hatches were open and the watchful eyes of the two loadmasters, senior Air Force NCOs who knew exactly how much *their* aircraft could take on and how to properly ensure it didn't slide all over the place in mid-flight, were overseeing the upload of equipment.

Patrick Dillon turned to Jones after looking into the rear of the lead Globemaster. "Are those two Strykers I see in there?"

Bill Jones nodded. "Yeah, the command vehicle variants. The chief called me this afternoon after POTUS left. Said Merry Christmas. We can damned sure use them to help with command and control during the mission."

The Stryker CV weighed in at almost forty thousand pounds. Quick and agile on the battlefield, as proven in Iraq, the eight-wheeled armored vehicle could reach speeds of sixty miles per hour. The vehicle features a Force XXI Battle Command Brigade and Below (FBCB2) digital communications system, allowing communication between vehicles through text messaging and a map network, as well as with higher headquarters. The map displays the position of all vehicles on the battlefield, and the commander can mark the position of enemy forces on the map that can then be seen by other commanders.

"Sweet," said Stuart. "By why send two? Shouldn't one be enough?"

All heads turned toward him. "Do I need to spell it out, son?" asked Jones.

"Oh," the captain said. "No need."

A Hummer came tearing across the tarmac toward them, horn blaring, an Air Force security truck flashing blue lights right behind it. The big utility vehicle squealed to a stop next to the group of tankers. Clive Bernard hopped out of the Humvee and ran toward them, sandals flopping loudly in the still night air.

"Colonel, can you help a brother out? The guards behind me didn't want to let me through the gate."

"So how'd you get in?"

Bernard scratched his head. "Well, I kind of rammed the Hummer through the fence."

Dave Barnett laughed. "Doc, you're not on the manifest, so there's no way—"

"Listen, man," fired back the scientist as he pulled stray hair from his face. "We've still got some kinks to work out of the Shield systems *before* you go in. Who's better qualified to do that, Colonel, you or me? This is supposed to be a team, so let me do my job."

Jones held up a hand to the approaching SPs, who at the moment were reaching for their sidearms and eyeing Bernard as if he were a terrorist, which for all they knew, he was. "Easy, boys. There's been a mistake. The man is with us."

Chapter 22

Return of the Assassin

Cobb Residence
Southern Pines, North Carolina

Cobb sat back on his rocker and threw a tennis ball across the backyard. His three-year-old Rhodesian Ridgeback, Shelby, flew after it.

The house sat back against several acres of woods that Cobb had slowly purchased over the years. He liked the feeling of seclusion the additional land gave him.

What the home lacked in size it made up for in character. Each time he'd returned from some remote corner of the world, especially after Ruth's death, he'd reworked a section of the house himself, as though through repairing the structure he was somehow making needed repairs to his soul. He'd begun with the floors a few years ago, ripping out the carpeting and reconditioning the hardwood floors hidden beneath until they glowed dark and rich. He'd then focused his efforts on the kitchen, removing the cabinets and building his own, one nick of the Skilsaw at a time, and replacing them; new appliances were next, and then replacing the linoleum with slate tiles. He'd continued throughout the house, his final renovation being the addition of a sunroom with a natural stone fireplace. From this glassed retreat he could see deep into the back of the property, watch as waterfowl landed on the small lake, or deer eased themselves from the woodline to enjoy one of several salt licks strategically placed along the woodline. As old habits died hard, Cobb had long ago installed a state-of-the-art security system.

Nicole rocked in silence as she watched Shelby retrieve the ball and bring it back to Cobb, dropping it in happy anticipation at his feet. "You're useless," Cobb said to the dog.

Bark. *Throw the damned ball.*

Cobb threw the damned ball, then he turned to Nicole. "What is it, Nicky?"

"What do you mean?"

"You wouldn't have asked me to meet you here if there wasn't something on your mind, sweetheart."

She blinked rapidly. "Can't I . . . can't I just want to see you every once in a while? I mean, you stay so wrapped up in your latest project that I never get a chance to . . ."

"Nicole."

"What?"

"Talk to me," said Cobb quietly. He stared into her eyes as he bent forward and took her hands in his own. "Talk to me."

Bark.

Cobb turned to Shelby and favored her with the look he generally saved for his direct action targets. The dog's tail went between her legs and she stalked to the end of the deck and collapsed into a discontented heap, staring at Cobb in silent accusation.

"It's that damned tanker, isn't it?" said Cobb into the silence.

"What? No . . . no, it's got nothing to do with Mike," Nicole stammered.

Cobb sat back in his rocker and folded his hands across his midsection. "You're pregnant." It wasn't a question.

Nicole shook her head in disbelief, saying nothing for a few moments. Then she looked at Cobb. "God, but you're scary good."

Cobb looked away for a moment, then back. "How did it happen?"

His former daughter-in-law favored Cobb with a blank expression. "You're kidding, right?"

"No . . . I mean, weren't you using . . . protection? I mean, you're a bright girl, Nicky, and . . ."

"Cobb, have you ever read those 'ninety-nine point whatever percent effective' words on the back of boxes?"

Cobb frowned. "Oh. Lucky you, huh?"

"Yeah. Lucky me."

"Does the kid know?"

She shook her head. "No, I haven't told him."

"Are you going to?"

"This isn't about *him*. It's about me and how *I* want to handle the situation," she said. Then, more to herself than to Cobb, "It's *my* life, dammit."

The security man cleared his throat. "Don't you think he has a right to know?"

"Why?" Nicole asked. "What good would it do to tell him? Do you think he's going to propose? That he's not really going to go away soon? Or maybe he'll leave the military and settle down here in North Carolina with me."

Cobb's eyes hardened. "How did you know they were leaving?"

Nicole laughed. "See, I *have* learned a thing or two from you over the years." She shook her head. "I didn't know. Not for certain." A hopeless expression took hold of Nicole's normal smile. "Not until now."

"Nicole . . . he's already gone, sweetheart. Left last night."

"But . . . where? When will he . . ."

A sad shake of the head. "You know better than to ask, darlin'."

"Yeah."

Cobb sighed. How his son could let this one get away was beyond him. "Why don't you and Aaron move in with me for a while?" he asked. "If you give up your apartment, you won't have to work, or at least not as much. Finish school and take some time to think about what you want to do."

In the past, his former daughter-in-law had always turned down offers she deemed handouts. But he could tell she was considering this one.

"To be honest," he said, "I could use the company."

Nicole smiled as the first tears spilled. "Why, Cobb, I do believe you're starting to become a softy in your old age," she said.

Cobb's lips tightened. Nicole, knowing how hard that last admission was for him to make, took his hand again. "It's a kind offer. I'll seriously consider it, okay?"

Cobb nodded. "Sounds good."

They both knew that, in their own way, they'd just agreed on the arrangement. The rest was semantics.

Cobb stood and walked toward the glass door leading into the kitchen. "I'm going to grab a beer. Can I get you anything?"

"Sure, I'll have one with you."

"How about some nonsweetened iced tea? Or ice water?"

"Cobb . . ."

"Or a nice glass of milk?"

"Listen," she said with a note of annoyance in her voice. "I'll have *one* beer. But if you're going to handle me with kid gloves every time I'm around, then—"

Hands up. "Okay, okay." He disappeared into the house.

Nicole turned her attention to the lake. What was she going to do? What could she really expect from a guy she'd known for such a short period of time, no matter how clear it was that they were great together? She put her head in her hands. How had she gotten herself into this *mess* just when she'd been on the verge of straightening out her life?

A low growl from across the deck caught her attention. Shelby was staring into the kitchen, and the natural line of fur along her spine that was a characteristic of the Ridgeback breed was more pronounced than usual.

"What is it, girl?" asked Nicole, not yet concerned. As always, Cobb had turned the security system on as soon as he'd closed the front door behind her. The man was cautious to a fault. She got up and walked to the sliding door, sliding it open several inches. "Cobb?"

No answer. Mild panic now. *No,* she told herself. Not only was the alarm system activated, but Cobb was able to take care of himself better than any man Nicole knew.

Pushing the door open a few inches more, she stepped into the kitchen. Sliding the door closed, she gave the upset Shelby a "ssshhh" signal and walked toward the sunroom. There she saw Cobb lying unconscious on the floor, a strange man sitting on the leather ottoman next to him. The man didn't look up. He sat silently, a silenced pistol pointed at Cobb's head, watching him.

Nicole slid back toward the kitchen. Every room in the house had a weapon of some type hidden away. In the case of the kitchen, Nicole knew a 9mm Browning High Power automatic lay waiting just beneath a pile of hand towels in the top drawer nearest her.

Though the man continued observing Cobb as Nicole backed away, the pistol in his hand swiveled in her direction. "Please, come over here," the man said quietly.

Nicole froze.

The man finally turned his dark gaze upon her. "Come here *now*, or I promise you—he is dead."

Nicole walked slowly toward the pair and knelt next to Cobb. "What do you want?"

"I must kill him," the man said simply.

"But why?" Nicole asked. "What has he done to you?"

The shadow of a smile crossed the man's features

for a moment, but it was gone now. He held up his left hand, the middle digit of which was too short by half and heavily bandaged. "Other than this? Nothing."

"Then why?" Nicole asked, leaning protectively over Cobb. *"Why?"*

"He is the primary obstacle in keeping me from my assigned mission," said Sayid Bakr. "He therefore must be neutralized."

Something struck Nicole as odd. If this man had wanted her father-in-law dead, he could have killed him and left before she'd ever returned to the house. Instead he'd simply been staring at Cobb when she entered.

"You don't want to do it, do you?" she asked quietly.

"I must," he said.

Nicole was afraid to say anything. So long as the man did nothing, she would do nothing.

"He is your father?" Bakr asked finally.

"What? Why do you ask?"

"I heard you talking on the porch."

Nicole thought about the question and finally nodded. "Yes," she said. And for the first time she realized that *was* what Cobb was to her. "He's my father."

Sayid Bakr nodded. "I, too, had a daughter."

"What . . . what happened to her?"

"She died," he said simply.

"I am so sorry," Nicole said into the ensuing silence. "I . . . I have a son. I can't imagine what it would be like to lose him."

The Iraqi nodded. He slowly lifted the pistol until it was leveled once more at Cobb's head. "Please go into the next room, miss. Do not do anything stupid, as I do not want to harm you." He glanced at her for a moment. "But I will if your actions put my mission in jeopardy."

Nicole lowered herself slowly, until her body was between Sayid Bakr's pistol and Cobb's head. "I will not let you do this. If you're going to shoot him, then you're going to have to shoot me to get to him." She stared into Cobb's face, refusing to look at the pistol whose weight she could almost feel like a weight at the back of her neck.

"You would die?" The voice was quiet, curious. "Even though you carry another life within you? For no reason?"

"For no reason?" Nicole asked, still not looking up. "How about because I love him? Do you know what that is—love? Do you *remember*?"

Silence.

Nicole closed her eyes, accepting what was about to pass. She had few regrets. But somewhere the final question came to her. "What do you think your daughter would do if it was you on the floor with someone pointing a gun at your head? What would *she* do?" Several interminable seconds passed. Finally, not able to take the strain, she opened her eyes. She and Cobb were alone.

Chapter 23

Release the Hounds

Phase Line Husky (Line of Departure)
150 Kilometers Southwest of Farrah, Afghanistan
Day 8

Patrick Dillon stared west at the expanse of open, rocky ground through his night-vision goggles, the feel of the Abrams vibrating beneath him as it idled reassuringly after his decade spent on the system. Somewhere between his current position and the next rise of high ground ten kilometers to his front was the Iranian border. A hundred kilometers farther were the Tommies whose secrets he was intent to see did not fall into the hands of the Chinese. He already didn't trust the bastards, and he'd be damned if one day he had to fight the bastards mounted in the machine he helped make a reality.

As he waited for word from Jones to move out, Dillon marveled at the events of the past year. He'd lost so damned *much*, and then, after everything, had the opportunity to get much of it back—an opportunity he would have welcomed not long ago. He shook his head and scanned the horizon again, forcing thoughts of Melissa and the girls from his mind. He'd deal with that one when it wouldn't get him killed; tonight there was only the mission. Dillon smiled and rubbed a hand along the rough texture of the main battle tank he knew so well. Here, heading to battle, he felt at home and at peace for the first time in months. He knew some would call that strange; Dillon didn't question the irony.

Next to him, his loader, a sergeant named Fortin who'd signed on from the schoolhouse at Fort Knox but whom Dillon didn't personally know, popped out of sight into the turret interior. The major had to admit it was a strange company. Jones had definitely put the call out in the right places. Only a group of tankers as savvy as those he'd met over the past week could come together and gel as quickly as the War Dogs, as they'd come to be known.

Staff Sergeant Randy Bickel popped through the hatch. Dillon couldn't help but smile. He should have known his gunner of the past two wars wouldn't miss an opportunity such as Jones had offered. The man was the best natural tank gunner Dillon had ever seen, and the major had been ecstatic to see such a familiar and trusted face on meeting the team at Bragg. While Bickel had thrown his arms around his former commander in a gesture of genuine affection on seeing him a week ago, he had been less than happy that Dillon's addition meant he'd be moving from a tank commander position back to a "lowly" gunner's station. But Dillon knew Bickel's disappointment was tempered by the fact that he would much rather be shooting than hanging out atop the tank directing the rest of the crew.

"So what's the deal, sir?" Bickel asked, pulling off his CVC helmet.

Dillon lifted the left side of his own helmet over the top of his ear so he could hear his gunner and the radio, and then pulled a can of Copenhagen from a zippered pocket on the side of his Nomex combat vehicle crewman jumpsuit. "Standing by. We'll jump when Jones says jump."

The veteran gunner ran his hands along the rows of translucent brown tiles covering the tank's exterior. "You sure this shit's going to work?"

The major grimaced. "The leader in me should ensure you that it will, but we've been together too long, Bick. Truth is, I have no idea."

"Encouraging."

Dillon smiled. "Hey . . . Jones and Barnett, along with Captain Stuart, did some testing with a plasma cannon shipped to Bragg. They seemed pretty happy with the results." The smile disappeared. "But all the same, we'll keep this baby moving and make ourselves as difficult to hit as possible . . . they don't hit us, no worries."

"Good plan."

"I knew you'd like it."

"All Dog Elements, Dog Six, move out, time now. Six out."

"He's singing our song," said Bickel, dropping into the turret and disappearing as he moved forward to his gunner's station.

"Yep," said Dillon. "Looks like it's time to do that dance one more time." He keyed the switch on his CVC to activate the tank's intercom system. "Crew report."

"Driver ready."

"Loader ready, sabot loaded."

"Gunner ready," called Bickel. "Sabot indexed."

"TC ready," reported Dillon to the crew. "Driver, move out. Stay one hundred meters behind the Stryker to our front. Gunner, pick up a scan." He leaned back in the turret and lifted his good eye toward Iran. *God help me,* he thought, *but I do love this shit.*

White House Situation Room
Washington, D.C.

Jonathan Drake stared at the electronic board mounted to the paneled wall in front of him as a series of blue icons proceeded slowly across the airspace of northern Iraq. The icons represented a flight of F-117A Nighthawk stealth aircraft. Though the aircraft would already be practically invisible to Iranian radar, the Pentagon wasn't taking any chances.

The president shifted his eyes east. Ahead of the Nighthawks and already over Iran, large numbers of Navy EA-6B Prowlers were opening a lane for the 117s. Primarily used in the SEAD—suppression of enemy air defenses—roll, the Prowlers were jamming the signals of Iranian early-warning radars. Several of the missile sites beneath them had already found out the hard way over the past few minutes that locking on the 6Bs with their tracking radars in order to engage the approaching threat was a serious mistake. Upon detecting tracking systems illuminating the early-morning skies—it wouldn't be dawn for another hour—the Prowlers unleashed HARM missiles that guided on the radar sources, riding the beams all the way to the ground and rendering the site and its occupants so much rubble. But the Prowlers weren't the first American ships flying to battle.

Drake watched as the leading blue diamonds closed on their target: a formerly abandoned airbase in the vicinity of the northern town of Tabriz. "How soon before the Tomahawks reach their target, Tom?" he asked General Werner, the Chairman of the Joint Chiefs of Staff and his ranking military advisor.

The beefy general grunted. "I would say anytime. . . ."

"We have impact," called one of the Air Force officers monitoring the air battle.

"How soon before we know the damage?" asked Drake.

Werner looked at the digital clock over the display. "We'll have a high-altitude platform beaming us back a battle-damage assessment report within the next ten minutes, sir."

Every man and woman in the room knew it would be significant. The BGM-109 cruise missiles, launched earlier from four Navy fast attack subs in the Persian Gulf, had a range of over a thousand nautical miles—

more than enough for the boats to range their targets in this instance. They carried a mixture of munitions, some of the eighteen-foot, terrain-hugging missiles carrying a payload of combined-effects bomblets that would rend soft targets into tatters, others one-thousand-pound warheads that could, and would, cut deep into hardened facilities. Some of the Tomahawks didn't make the full trip to Tabriz; instead they were targeted against high-priority radar sites before the Prowlers ever crossed into Iranian airspace. Their brothers continued droning on, fast enough that they'd shortly be over target, slow enough to be seen by the naked eye if it had been daylight.

A few minutes passed. "We have imagery, sir," said Werner, stepping across the room and handing Jonathan Drake a folder.

Drake opened it. The destruction of what had been dozens of reinforced buildings was almost too much to absorb. But that wasn't the worst of it. The high-resolution photos showed in excruciatingly vivid detail the state of the Iranian forces who'd recently occupied the facility. And the F-117As with their two-thousand-pound precision-guided payloads hadn't even arrived on the scene.

"My God," Drake breathed.

"Yes, sir," said Werner.

"Is it really necessary to continue with the mission, Tom?" asked the president.

"Sir," began Werner. He stopped, staring at the images of the carnage in Tabriz. He shook his head sadly. "Sir, it's critical if we want to give Jones and his men their best chance for success."

Drake nodded. "Very well."

**M4X1 Research Facility
Eastern Iran**

Sergei Sedov was already counting the funds from the Chinese that would soon be filtering into the several

Swiss and Caribbean accounts he had established. For once in his life, he would answer to no master, be in full control of his own destiny. He looked about the barren facility housing the world's most sophisticated ground combat systems. *My God but this nation is a wart on the ass of civilization,* he told himself. He could not wait to leave it—and leave it he would. Very soon. He sat down in front of the monitor connected to his private workstation. From this terminal he would send the data red China wanted so badly once he confirmed the transfer of funds. His fingers worked over the keyboard, ensuring the data was ready. The timeline was a short one once his plan went into motion.

For the right price, one of the Iranian I.T. personnel had set up a file transfer protocol, or FTP, link with Sedov's contacts. This was a secure method of transferring files over the Internet from one computer to another, in this case from his to a server located at one of the Red Army's military research plants in China's Shandong province. Once the transfer of data was complete, the link would be collapsed from both ends. Sedov smiled. Too bad the tech had to die, but he made the mistake of giving clear enough instructions for how to accomplish this collapse that he was nothing more than a loose end; and loose ends must needs be clipped before they have an opportunity to unravel.

Switching views, Sedov scanned the offshore account activity in real time . . . yes. The balances in the accounts were rolling up, now into six figures each and continuing to escalate. Another five minutes and he would FTP the data, activate the device in order to appease the Chinese—not that the idea of a large crater and radioactive cloud over this turd pile bothered him—and fly out before the device detonated.

"So I understand that we are doing well with the project?"

The Russian froze. That serpentine voice. Here. He turned slowly. "Holiness," he said, recovering quickly from his shock. "What a pleasant surprise." He frowned. "But I thought we agreed, the less traffic between Tehran and the facility . . ."

"I thought it time I take a personal look at what all of the money we have paid you is buying my nation," said the cleric. He looked at Sergei Sedov as if the Russian was an insect under a magnifying glass. "Do you take issue with that, Colonel?"

The sound of running feet preceded the arrival of one of Sedov's military aides. "Colonel . . ." The soldier froze at the sight of the Ayatollah Khalani, having never seen his nation's spiritual—and feared—leader in person. He began to fall to his knees.

"Go on, man," said Khalani, irritated. "State your message."

"Yes, Father . . . it is Tabriz."

"What of it?" asked Khalani. "Be clear or be dead."

"It is . . . *gone*," stammered the aide. "It was hit by several massive strikes minutes ago."

Sergei Sedov nodded. "Leave us."

The officer gratefully backed out of the room.

"The men and material you moved into Tabriz had better be worth it, Colonel," said Khalani. "The cost was enormous."

"The cost will prove insignificant, Holiness," the Russian said. "Do you think the Americans would have struck with enough firepower to completely destroy the base in Tabriz if they did not believe their vaunted M4X1s were there? To have any chance of dealing total destruction of the combat systems conventionally, they would have to use a massive air strike—and they *did*." He looked toward the ceiling and clasped his hands behind his back. "They took the bait, Holiness. You can point to the humanitarian supplies you were stockpiling in Tabriz, a fact that can easily be established when the world's press investigates the site, and turn the anger of every nation on the face of the planet against the Americans." He laughed. "Yes, this will keep the U.S. busy for a long time. It will make their strike against the Chinese embassy a few years ago look like a small mistake."

"It sounds like a good plan," said Khalani. "But with you, things never seem to go according to plan."

The Russian smiled. "What could happen now?" he asked. "But let us celebrate, O Most Holy of Holies. I'll give you a tour of the facility—how would you like that? I will be but a few more minutes here. Perhaps you would like some refreshments after your journey? And then I can meet you in the main hangar in"—he looked at his watch—"let us say twenty minutes?"

The cleric nodded, but it was clear from his expression that Sergei Sedov's concern for his comfort was not going unquestioned. "Very well," he said. "Twenty minutes."

Alone again, the Russian wiped the thin film of sweat that had formed on his upper lip and walked back to his terminal. The transaction was complete. Closing the screen, Sergei Sedov brought up the FTP application and initiated the transfer of the Franks Combat System data to China. He frowned. Digital information should have been flowing, but nothing was happening.

Khalani's words returned, floating just beneath his consciousness: *"With you, things never seem to go according to plan. . . ."*

Sedov looked into a corner of the room toward the closet containing the nuclear device. *Not this time,* he swore. He had come too far. But as a chill ran along the Russian's spine, he understood the saying about how it felt when someone stepped on your grave.

His aide ran into the room again. Sedov spun, not giving the man time to report. "Get the M4X1s manned!" he yelled. "I want them moving in five minutes!"

The Iranian officer saluted and moved out. Sedov, knowing something was very wrong, began downloading the contents of the data file containing the Franks information onto a separate, detachable hard drive. As the data began transferring, he glanced at the Zodiac he'd taken from Patrick Dillon. "Yes. There is just time."

Proceeding to the closet, he opened the door and initiated the timer on the nuclear device. A red three, followed by three red zeroes, flashed twice, and then changed to a two, a nine, a five, and a nine. . . .

Watch Floor
National Security Agency (NSA) Headquarters
Fort Meade, Maryland

The two watch officers were back, having wanted to be in on the operation, as they were the first to understand what the Iranians and the Russian were about. But tonight they were watching, not participating. The atmosphere was akin to a sports bar just before the Super Bowl kickoff. A lot of the Agency's employees who knew what was about to occur had found one reason or another to assemble in the Watch Room and stare at the giant plasma display dominating the north wall.

"Pass the cashew chicken," whispered the officer who'd received the first message a week earlier.

His partner complied, dipping an egg roll in a small dish of sweet and sour sauce, and took a swallow of Coke from an NSA coffee cup whose lettering read: *NSA: If You Know . . . We Know.* The cups had become a very popular item in the headquarters after the leadership confiscated the majority of them, afraid someone's idea of a joke wouldn't be popular with the increasingly paranoid—perhaps for good reason—American public.

As they chewed, a bright white light bloomed over eastern Iran.

"There it goes," said the first officer. "Man, look at that blossom."

The other man nodded. "Nothing will be getting in or out of there for a while, that's for sure."

A satellite with a very special payload, a payload all but a very few NASA insiders thought was a radar system designed to measure the encroachment of global warming into the waters of the south Atlantic, had hummed to life. In space, nothing could be seen. But the satellite was pouring out a beam of white noise the likes of which had never been seen. Every five seconds it pulsed, pulling from solar cells that had been building up their storage capacities for the six months the satellite had been in orbit.

"How long will it be able to maintain the blanket?" asked the second officer, watching the screen as he opened a fortune cookie.

"About an hour, then the cells will have to be recharged."

The other man looked down as he cracked open the cookie. He extracted the small piece of paper. *Your influence will be felt by the masses,* it read. He popped half of the fortune cookie into his mouth and pocketed the message. "They have no idea," he said with a smile.

Chapter 24

A Little Less Conversation

Phase Line Doberman
Eastern Iran
Dawn

The night-vision goggles fell to Dillon's chest, held by a cord around his neck. The sun was rising behind the formation, a bloodred sun that lent an eerie quality to the terrain in front of him. Eerie or not, thought Dillon, at least he could see.

"Dog elements, Dog Six," called Jones. *"The lights are about to go out and we will be operating by hand and arm signals after that. Tighten it up to a seventy-five-meter separation . . . stand by."*

"What's up with that?" asked Bickel. Dillon had decided to put his entire crew on the command push so they could hear what was happening within their small unit. In battle, knowledge is power and time can save lives.

"Don't know," Dillon said from the cupola, pulling a pair of Ray-Bans into place to cut the glare. "But I don't like the sound of it."

No sooner had the words passed his lips than the Shield antimissile system's warning signal sounded in the Abrams's turret. *"Missile launch,"* announced the smoky female voice General Dynamics' system designers had decided to go with. *"Two thousand meters."*

"Fuck!" yelled Dillon, locking himself into place in

the cupola and pulling the boom mike of his CVC helmet to his mouth. "Driver, hard right track!"

As the seventy-ton tank veered to the right, a rooster tail of sand and rock spewed to the left.

"All Dog elements, Dog Three!" called Barnett. *"Airborne warning systems report we've got multiple tracked vehicles to our front! Appears to be a mechanized infantry battalion. Deploy into line formation!"*

Sweat poured from Dillon's face as he looked to his front. Pulling an OD green handkerchief from where he had loosely tied it to the .50-cal mount to his front, the major lifted his Ray-Bans and wiped his eyes, cursing silently. Jones was in one Stryker, Barnett in the other. They'd decided to position themselves in the center front of the fourteen upgraded Abramses, despite his and Stuart's arguments that they didn't have the armor protection the M1A1s provided. No way they could survive a direct hit by an ATGM.

"Monk!" yelled Dillon into his CVC boom mike to his driver. "Get this fucker in front of those Strykers now!"

A guided missile sizzled over the Abrams as the driver responded, dropping in its wake a wire hot enough to singe the hair from Dillon's forearm. The major knocked the wire to one side and patted the arm down as he felt the sting. He didn't know much about his new driver other than that the guy was a man of few words—he hadn't spoken at all other than to reply to direct questions, and then only as much as necessary. The word on the street was he'd once been in a seminary, but he'd left when the last war with Iraq started, feeling God had called him to arms. All Patrick Dillon knew was that the son of a bitch could *drive.* Thanks to his maneuvering—and maybe the Shield system, Dillon wasn't yet a true believer in the technology—their tank was unscathed.

"Nice driving, Monk," Dillon said into his boom mike, expecting no response.

"All praise and glory to him," came the soft reply.

Dillon blinked, at a loss for words at the unexpected response. When under fire, a tank crew's intercom is normally bedlam; Dillon's tank was silent. Then the major's Roman Catholic upbringing kicked in. "Fucking ay," he finally said, pulling out the St. Michael medal he wore on a leather string around his neck, kissing it, and thinking of the words engraved on the medallion. *St. Michael, Protect Us.* "Whatever works." Glancing at the red sky above him, Dillon smiled weakly at the heavens before turning his face once more to the battle before him.

Reaching to where he'd lashed his binos the night before, Dillon pulled them loose and looked toward the series of hills two kilometers to the west. "Bick, what have you got?!"

"I'm already on it!" yelled the gunner. "I've got multiple Type Eighty-sixes, ten o'clock to two o'clock! Range, one-nine-hundred meters!"

The team had received a thorough briefing on what, if any, Iranian armor they'd see between their jump-off point in Afghanistan and their objective. The Type 86 was a Chinese-manufactured version of the Russian BMP-1 infantry fighting vehicle. It featured a 73mm main gun and a Sagger antitank guided missile system. It looked like they'd decided to hit the invading Americans as quickly as possible from their position on the high ground with their ATGMs, knowing the 73s would do the American heavies little harm. The same couldn't be said for the command and control vehicles manned by Jones and Barnett.

"Kick it in the ass, Monk!" Dillon yelled. "Get in front of those fucking Strykers!" Dillon keyed the command and control frequency. *"Dog Six, Dog Three, this is Dog One . . . slow down! Let us get some armor in front of you!"*

Nothing but white noise. *Fuck,* thought Dillon. They were in the comms blackout. Dillon looked to his left. Mike Stuart's tank had pulled alongside his own, his thoughts running parallel to Dillon's. Stuart threw his right arm forward and pumped it back and forth repeatedly, acknowledging they needed to move forward as quickly as possible. Dillon gave him a thumbs-up. He didn't bother relaying the signal to his driver; from the feel of the mammoth beneath him, Dillon knew Monk was going full throttle.

"Permission to fire!" yelled Bickel. "I've got two of the bastards pulled forward to engage!"

Dillon debated firing from behind Jones and Barnett. An errant 120mm round would destroy either of the Strykers. But the enemy vehicles were on the high ground forward of the two friendlies. More, he had Randy Bickel as a gunner. "Fire and adjust!" Dillon yelled, giving his gunner discretion to engage and to continue engaging at will. At this point, he himself would only get in the way.

"On the way! And keep loading HEAT!" yelled Bickel, depressing the firing trigger on the Abrams's Cadillacs. His message to the loader—*We've got a lot of soft armor out there, so every time I fire, throw a HEAT round into the breach.* The more valuable sabot rounds would be saved for tougher prey—like the Tommies.

The tank bucked beneath Dillon, rattling him in the cupola like a pinball for a moment, and then entered a thick cloud that smelled heavily of cordite. Dillon could picture Bickel below in the turret, forehead pressed tightly to his gunner's brow pad, straining to see through the cloud to check his work and get on the other Type 86. "Target!" yelled the gunner.

Dillon saw a cloud of black smoke on the hilltop at his twelve o'clock. He looked to his left and saw Stuart's tank belch flame. Scanning quickly to the front, he saw a flash of metal on metal as the depleted-uranium sabot hit an Iranian vehicle two hundred meters to the left of the one Dillon's crew had destroyed. Within two seconds the Type 86 ignited and black smoke rolled out of it.

"On the way!" announced Randy Bickel, his reticle on the second vehicle to their front and a firing solution in the Abrams's onboard computer. Monk continued to push the big Abrams through the aftereffects of the shot, giving his gunner a look at the target as rapidly as possible. "Target!"

The other modified M1A1 heavies were engaging now and smoke began to darken the horizon to the west as Dillon and Stuart moved past the Strykers. Dillon looked to his right and saw Dave Barnett smiling—actually fucking *smiling*. The lieutenant colonel threw Dillon a wave . . . and then his Stryker was obscured in a blast of flame and smoke. The rolling pressure wave threw Dillon into the left side of the turret with enough force to reinjure his mending ribs. *"Dammit!"* he breathed through gritted teeth, watching as the Stryker fell behind, stopped in its tracks, as Dillon and his own crew tore westward. "Dammit," he whispered again. "Dammit, dammit, dammit."

"What's wrong, sir?" asked Bickel, concern in his voice.

"Nothing," replied Dillon over the intercom, his voice tightening as he compartmentalized the loss of Barnett to be revisited at the proper time and place. "Keep moving."

Ten minutes later the War Dogs were a kilometer past the remains of the Iranian battalion, and they weren't happy. Within the next three seconds, two things happened: they saw the Iranian base in the distance . . . and the Tommies moving toward them, rapidly moving to a line formation and stopping to engage.

"Bick," said Dillon tightly, "what do you have for a range?"

No hesitation. "Five thousand meters!"

Too fucking far, thought Dillon. "All right, Bick, double-check the Shield system. Monk . . ."

"Yes, sir?"

"Do what you do best, my friend," said Dillon. "Keep us alive."

"I tell you the truth, if you have faith as small as a mustard seed, you can say to this mountain, 'Move from here to there' and it will move," said the driver in a humble voice.

"What the fuck does that mean?" asked Bickel, his fingers flying over the Shield system's control box. "Shield's up!" he announced, his face flying back to his gunner's sight.

"Matthew," answered Dillon, surprised he remembered the verse. "Book of Matthew."

Across a narrow valley the fourteen Abramses spread out, by SOP seeking out the vehicles in their assigned areas of fire.

"Range!?" yelled Dillon.

"Three-nine-hundred meters!" returned Bickel. *"Permission to engage!"*

"Missile launch warning, three-eight-hundred meters," called the smoky bitch.

"Stand by," said Dillon from his position in the cupola, his voice quiet, mesmerizing the voice his high-strung crew needed at the moment. "Steadddyyyy . . ."

"Three-five-hundred meters!"

Dillon could see a Sagger en route toward their tank. Monk, also able to see the incoming missile from his vantage, veered right at the last moment and the ATGM flew harmlessly to the right.

But the sky was filled with the black, wire-guided specks. It was too late as the crew saw another missile in the final leg of its flight, headed directly for them. At the last second, the Sagger, for no apparent reason, flew upward toward the sky.

"Fucking Shield . . . it works," muttered Dillon. *"Fire, fire sabot!"* he called out, giving his gunner direction to release the HEAT round still in the breech and for the loader to begin loading the big tank-killing sabot rounds as soon as the first round was launched.

"On the way!"

The other Abramses, all speeding across the desert at almost forty miles per hour, began engaging the

Tommies as ATGMs flew through the sky around them. Most missed. But two of the Abramses skidded to a halt, flames beginning to lick from their turrets.

"Sensing!" yelled Dillon, his binos to his face, trying to see the effect of the HEAT round on the Tommy that had been their target. As the HEAT rounds took a higher trajectory, the Abrams was clear of its cordite shroud in time for Dillon and Bickel to both see impact as the big 120mm shell reached the bottom of its arching trajectory.

"Fuck," breathed Dillon, dropping the binos from his eye.

"The son of a bitch bounced off!" yelled Bickel. "It fucking *bounced off*!"

"All right, keep it together!" said Dillon tightly. "That was a HEAT round. What did you expect, a kill?" But he was rattled himself, never having seen anything like that.

"Sabot's up!" called the loader.

"All right, Bick, remember what Doc Bernard told us," said Dillon. "If it's a frontal shot, aim for the line representing the junction of the turret and the hull, just below the gunner's doghouse."

Sweat dripped from between Randy Bickel's eyes as he lased the sweet spot, an infinitesimally small target when cruising at speed across the desert on a tank. He lased. Three thousand meters. "I'm on," he said quietly into the intercom as the firing solution illuminated in his sight picture.

"Fire!" called Dillon.

The sixty-eight-ton Abrams rocked and kept moving.

It was Monk, from his position forward, who first saw the result. "Praise his name."

"Target!" yelled Bickel. "That's a fucking kill!"

Dillon had the binos to his face once again. There was no giant fireball reaching toward the sky, but the M4X1 was smoking. The best indicator was that the Tommy's crew was clearly visible evacuating the vehicle. "All right, Bick, good work. Now pick another target."

"Oh, shit," said the gunner. "One of them's got a line on us! Sir, drop into the turret! *Now!* I'm engaging. . . ."

One thing Patrick Dillon had learned over the years: when a good NCO tells you to do something "now," don't argue. Within a second his body slid into the turret's interior and he sat on the tank commander's seat. He grunted as his reinjured rib cage jolted from the drop.

Then the giant Abrams shuddered and Dillon and his crew were thrown hard against the unforgiving steel of the turret.

Dillon shook his head after a moment, dazed. Feeling an odd sensation in his mouth, he moved his tongue around a tooth barely dangling by some bits of flesh. Reaching up, he ripped it from its tenuous hold and dropped it to the floor, spitting blood. "Crew report!"

"Driver's up, all indicators green," came Monk's calm voice.

Dillon looked to his left. His loader, a sergeant from the M1A2-SEP new-equipment transition team at Fort Knox, was shaking his head to clear it. Not able yet to speak, he gave his tank commander a thumbs-up in the dim blue lighting. "Loader's up!"

"Gunner's up," said Bickel. "And gunner's *pissed.* On the way!"

The big 120mm breech slammed backward, sending its sabot payload streaking in the direction of the offending Tommy.

"Give me an up, loader!"

The sergeant was in the process of ramming a fresh forty-pound sabot round into the gaping breech's empty maw. As the breech closed, the loader hit the arming switch and threw himself against the side of the turret to get clear of the coming recoil. *"Up!"*

"On the way!"

The Abrams roared. Silence for two seconds, then, from the driver's compartment, "And those works done in his name shall be blessed."

Dillon clambered up to get a view from outside the turret, never feeling fully in control of his steel beast from the confines of the turret. "I take it that's a kill?" he asked as he breathed in the fresh air of the Iranian high desert and reached for his binos.

"Roger that," said Bickel, laughter tingeing the edge of his voice despite the circumstances. "I'm searching for another target."

Dillon took a quick survey of the situation, doing the battlefield calculus in his mind. Still over three thousand meters out, the Tommies had a definite advantage with their newer main guns, missiles, and stationary position. The Shield systems and appliqué armor designed by the Israelis were doing their jobs, but the mass of firepower arrayed against them was beginning to tell. Thus far three of the M4X1s were down, leaving eight. But the War Dogs in their Abramses had already lost five of their vehicles. Dillon saw a brave crew of medics—two M1133 Stryker MEVs had attached to them the day prior—already moving forward to see what, if anything, could be done for the damaged vehicles' crewmen. The Abramses themselves were abandoned. The bottom line on the field was that, by the book, an attacker needs two-to-one odds to have a fifty-fifty chance of winning against an opponent in a hasty defense. In this case, the War Dogs outnumbered their opponents by only one vehicle, and they were also outmatched in the technology department. The friendlies could definitely use some . . .

Overhead and moving east, Dillon saw the unmistakable flash of a guided Hellfire air-to-ground anti-tank missile. Another of the Tommies blossomed where the missile met it at endflight, blowing skyward in a shower of sparks and metal as the Hellfire's warhead impacted on the vehicle's most vulnerable position, its thin top armor.

Captain Kristy "Thumper" Milner scanned her instrument panel, the battlefield, and the positions of the other seven OH-58D Kiowa Warriors of her company. Milner commanded D Company, 1-82nd Aviation Brigade, part of the 82nd Airborne Division out of Fort Bragg. Her D Company Timberwolves had sped across the border into Iran as the sun was rising. It looked like their timing was perfect. They'd caught the Iranians unawares and had already destroyed three of the stolen Tommies.

"Wolves, Wolf Six," Milner called, holding her ship slightly back in order to better command and control her elements. "Remember the Tommies have Stingers, so stay alert for launch. . . ." And then Kristy Milner remembered the comms blackout. All she could do was hope her crews kept their briefing on the Tommies' capabilities in mind rather than fixating on fighting the ground fight.

As if in answer to her attempted warning, flashes of light from the Tommies barely preceded the missile warning indicators aboard the Kiowa Warriors. The D Company pilots immediately took evasive maneuvers, breaking the locks on the majority of the Stinger ground-to-air missiles before they could home in on their target heat sources. But two of the aviators attempted to hold track on their targets a little too long, wanting to give their Hellfires time to go final on their targets. While one of them succeeded in destroying another M4X1, seconds later both ships leaped into the sky twenty feet before dropping to the ground in fiery balls of destruction.

Milner grimaced in anger and frustration. Checking her fuel status, she knew that she couldn't give the tankers much more time and still make it back into Afghanistan. She joined the fight proper, determined that the time the Timberwolves were on station would be time well spent.

M4X1 Research Facility
Eastern Iran

John Bertetto turned, yelling into Jack Kelly's face from the cockpit of the MH-60K in an attempt to be heard over the rotor blades and the scream of the big helo's two General Electric T700 turboshaft engines. "Okay, you fuckin' listen to me, pork chop! We just went into total fucking communications blackout, so I ain't gonna be able to call and tell you time's up! You got fifteen fucking minutes! Are you clear? *Fifteen* minutes!"

Kelly leaned forward, frowning. "Did you just call me *pork chop*?"

"Can we get moving, please?" said Luke Dodd, jumping from the helo's open door and joining the other team members already on the ground. Dodd had been added to the mission in a joint White House, Pentagon, and Central Intelligence Agency decision for one reason: at this point, they had to assume that Sergei Sedov had a one-kiloton nuclear device in his possession and that the crazy Russian bastard was going to use it. If he hadn't started the countdown yet, odds were he would as soon as he heard bullets flying and realized his communications to the outside world were dead. Given that situation, the Agency wanted representation on the ground.

Bull Dell, crouching at Kelly's side, was nodding his head up and down vigorously. "He did, Sonny!" Dell yelled into Kelly's ear. "Son of a bitch called you a pork chop!"

"Okay, okay," said Bertetto, rolling his eyes. "Forget the fucking pork chop comment. You got fifteen minutes! There's a potential nuke in there somewhere and I ain't hangin' around any longer than necessary.

You clear?" He pushed a finger into Kelly's thick chest for emphasis. *"One-five minutes!"*

Kelly was about to bend the errant finger backward when all three men turned toward the east and the unmistakable sound of tank cannons.

Kelly and Dell joined the rest of the ODA without another word as the team completed deplaning from the Nightstalker birds.

"One-five, pork chop!" yelled Bertetto at their departing figures. "Nukes," muttered the captain to himself as he turned back to his displays. "I fuckin' *hate* nukes. No fuckin' elegance to the bastards."

"What?!" yelled his copilot.

"Just watch the fuckin' clock, asshole!" yelled the captain.

As rehearsed on the Urban Recon LIDAR system, the team headed toward the entrance closest to the research section of the facility. Suddenly Lurch Purdue spun and went down, holding his leg. A split second later the area around the team erupted in fire.

Dropping to the ground, the team returned fire in the direction of four guards manning the roof of the building toward which they'd been moving. A single boom split the morning sky and one of the guards' torsos fell from the wall. His lower body remained standing for a second before following its upper half to the ground. As the guards hesitated, looking for the source of this new danger, one of their members' head disintegrated in a red explosion as another boom echoed from the distance.

Jack Kelly turned and pulled a set of field glasses to his eyes. Two kilometers to the north, on top of a piece of high ground, Kelly barely made out what he at first thought was a jumble of debris and rocks. Then an arm was pointing from beneath what the captain now recognized as a gilley suit, gesturing for the team to continue moving.

"All right, let's go. Someone's covering our ass, so let's take advantage. Betty, take care of Lurch. Catfish, give him a hand. Get to the building as quickly as you can, we'll cover you."

No further words were necessary as the team leaped into action, firing covering shots at the top of the building as their unknown benefactor took down a third guard.

"Dude has *got* to have a Barrett," Bull Dell said to Kelly as they ran across the open ground, referring to the Army's big .50 caliber long rifle. "Distance looks to be over two klicks."

"I didn't think its range went much past fifteen hundred," said Kelly, his back hitting the wall next to the door they intended entering.

Dell hit the wall on the other side of the door. "Depends on the man behind the scope," he said.

On cue, the Barrett boomed a final time. A body dropped at their feet, a hole the size of a basketball punched through what used to be the guard's stomach. The eyes were open wide, as if the Iranian's last thought had been one of surprise that anything could leave such a wind tunnel through his anatomy.

"Damn," said Dell, assessing the damage. "We *gotta* get one of those."

Sprinting down the hill with the Barrett, Cobb jumped into the GMV, where Krieger waited in the driver's seat. The GMV, or Ground Mobility Vehicle, was a specially designed and reinforced Hummer built to Special Forces specifications. Used extensively by Green Berets throughout Iraq and Afghanistan, the GMV had proven itself a workhorse within theater. "All right, kid," he said. "Show me I wasn't wrong to let you talk me into making the trip; I want to beat those guys inside that building."

Rolf Krieger smiled and floored the gas on the big Hummer.

As the rest of the team formed up, Kelly saw the pile of debris on the distant hill stand and then disappear down the backside of the high ground. "Boom, Crapper . . . get us in there!"

The two demo men came forward and checked out the door; roughly two and one-half inch wood. Standard handle and lock set, standard hinges.

"Easy breach," said Taylor, then he felt eyes on the back of his neck. He turned.

Dell stared at him, one eyebrow raised.

"I'm all right, dammit!" he said to the big warrant. "I told ya, as long as I'm doin' something!" Turning his back to Dell, Taylor raised a semiautomatic Benelli M4 Super 90 12-gauge shotgun to his shoulder. The engineer glanced at Boom Eastbrook. Eastbrook nodded.

"On three," said Taylor. "One, two . . ." The sergeant fired two loads in rapid succession through the door, one each through the upper and lower hinges from a distance of roughly one inch, and spun out of the way after kicking the door into the room. Dell and Kelly each tossed in flash-bangs, and the team turned from the opening. Two seconds later light and noise enveloped the shattered doorway and the team poured through the breach.

"You're fired," said Cobb, holding on for dear life as the GMV slid to a stop one hundred meters from the Iranian military complex. "The team's already in and now you've stopped the vehicle. Why?"

Krieger pointed off into the distance toward the base's airfield. A pilot was prepping a small twin-engine airplane, the only aircraft presently on the field. And a man with a strange, limping gait, carrying a backpack over his shoulders, was running as quickly as he could toward the aircraft. "Does he look familiar to you?"

Cobb threw a set of binos to his eyes. "Sergei Sedov. And it looks like he's in a hurry to get out of here." Without lowering the binos, he hooked a thumb over his shoulder at the weapons storage rack built into the toughened Hummer's rear floorboards. "You know how to use one of those things?"

While a variety of weapons and missiles were in attendance, Rolf Krieger didn't need to ask which the ex-operator was referring to. "Yes." Reaching into the rear, the big scout pulled a Javelin Command Launch Unit housing the system's trigger mechanism and integrated day-night sighting device. He gave the unit a quick once-over. Satisfied, he grabbed a missile launch tube and had the system assembled in a few seconds, activating the battery as the final step. Stepping away from the vehicle, Krieger sighted on the aircraft. Over a kilometer away, he judged, but well within the Javelin's range of two-plus kilometers. Making a mild correction, the lieutenant activated the unit. There was a second of noise and smoke, and then the missile was away.

Sergei Sedov's legs were past mere pain. They were in agony. But with no other choice, he continued running. He was tempted to drop the backpack, but he knew it was the one thing he could *not* drop. Glancing at the Zodiac strapped to his wrist, the Russian grimaced. Twenty minutes. Not long, but long enough. He smiled at the thought of that bastard Khalani sitting atop a ticking nuclear device. There was a certain poetry in the image.

Then Sedov was tumbling backward, his eyebrows and other exposed hair singed, his ears roaring. He sat up on the tarmac and looked toward the waiting aircraft. "No," he said, the word barely audible. "Nooooooo!" The plane was a flaming wreck. Sedov shook his head in despair, knowing he couldn't turn off the nuclear device if he wanted to. He'd damaged the timer unit beyond repair before leaving the facility, safe in the knowledge that he would be long gone when the countdown reached zero.

As he listened to the flames crackle, Sergei Sedov almost gave in to crushing defeat. Almost. Then something strange happened. He noticed the silence to the west. Until only a few moments ago, the sound of armed conflict had filled the mouth of the valley where the M4X1s had met the American force—and it *had* to be the Americans. Sedov gave them due credit; he had truly believed the U.S. to have fallen for the Tabriz ruse. He had been wrong. It was a mistake he had lived to learn from, however, so the situation was not without its positive side. But the silence . . .

Reaching into his backpack, the Russian pulled out a set of field glasses and looked west. He could not believe his eyes. An odd-looking group of Abramses was closing on the Franks systems. In the sky above them hovered several of the American Kiowa Warrior helicopters. His cherished M4X1s . . . all were smoking and belching flame. He looked harder through the glasses as movement caught his eye. No, not all of them. All *but one*. Its driver was taking it away from the battlefield as quickly as he could . . . straight toward Sergei Sedov.

Patrick Dillon pulled the CVC helmet from his head and laid it atop the .50 caliber machine gun located in front of his cupola. Grasping the sides of the hatch, he pushed himself out. Walking along the top of his turret, he hopped to the hull, landing next to the driver's hatch, and then onto the ground.

Monk lifted himself from the driver's hole to stretch. The normally sedate soldier for the first time saw the unbelievable devastation wreaked on the field in such a short period of time. His jaw dropped in disbelief. "Holy shit," the former seminarian uttered, eyes blinking rapidly. "We did this? Holy *shit.*"

Dillon raised an eyebrow in mild surprise. "Amen, brother," he said, looking at the burning hulks, many of whose onboard ammunition continued cooking off in the flames, breaking the silence of the otherwise calm morning. "Amen."

As Dillon stood, enjoying the sun and the peace for a few moments, the roar of rotors and prop blast settled over him. Looking up, Dillon saw the lead OH-58D hovering nearby. The pilot was visible in the cockpit. She smiled and gave Dillon a thumbs-up signal. Dillon, despite his fatigue, couldn't help returning the smile. Holding up a thumb, he followed with a quick salute. That lady and her Kiowas had come through in a big way. And with that pixieish face he spied through the canopy glass, Dillon saw she was actually kind of cute. Maybe the armor community needed to rethink its no-female policy; it might make things more interesting for all concerned. With a final waggle, the Kiowa was away and headed back toward Afghanistan, her remaining birds in trail.

Mike Stuart joined him a minute later as Dillon pulled a tin of Copenhagen from his Nomex coveralls.

"You know," said Stuart, his voice tired and his face dusty. "If you could keep up with your shit, it would have saved us a lot of trouble."

Dillon chuckled, but that just caused pain from deep within his rib cage, so he bit it off short. "Fuck you, Mike," he muttered.

Stuart nodded.

"Did you see what happened to Barnett?" Dillon finally asked as the silence stretched.

Stuart didn't look at him, instead staring at a fixed spot on the eastern horizon. He nodded.

Dillon nodded in return.

And then the men were enveloped in a cloud of smoke. "Good work, gentlemen," said Bill Jones, stepping between the two tank officers and wrapping an arm around each of them. "But we ain't done. Comms are back up and we've got to get busy. Mike, I want you and a couple of crews to secure this area. Get the Iranians still alive gathered into one place and allow them to tend to their wounded. I'll have a couple of trucks from the base sent up with their own drivers. I want them moving as far and fast from here as possible in the event Sedov's little toy goes off.

Once they're moving, meet us in the vicinity of the main building. The birds are already standing by."

"Why don't we just take the Iranians with us?" asked Stuart.

"Not enough room on the helos," said Jones. "But we can give them a chance. They may be the enemy, but they're soldiers and they were following orders."

Jones turned to Dillon. "Patrick, you're my new second in command. Gather up the remaining crews, have them mount up, and follow me to the main building. The Special Forces team has it secured and apparently there's some bad news."

"What?"

"No Sedov. And the hard drives have been removed from all of the computers."

Dillon spat in disgust. "Shit. So he's got the data?"

Jones nodded. "Looks that way."

Something in the distance caught Patrick Dillon's attention. "Hey, boss," he said to Jones, "can I borrow your binos a second?"

Jones handed him a pair of Steiners.

"Sir, can you do without me for a few minutes?"

"What is it, Patrick? We don't have long, son."

"Trust me, sir."

"All right," Jones said. "You've got five minutes."

Dillon nodded and hopped onto the front slope of his Abrams. He paused, pounding on the driver's hatch. "Get her going, Monk."

A minute later and the Abrams began moving to the east. As he moved past Jones, Dillon tossed Jones's binoculars back to him. The colonel put the glasses to his eyes and frowned. "Shit."

"What is it?" asked Stuart.

"Sedov," said Jones. "The son of a bitch is going after Sedov. And Sedov's in the last Tommy."

Cobb and Krieger entered the building. Kelly quickly briefed them on the status. "The building's secured. We rounded up all the Iranians and put them in trucks, moving them west."

"The Tommy data?" asked Cobb.

"Someone's pulled the hard drives," said Luke Dodd. "My guess is Sedov, who himself is missing. When everything began going to hell, he probably tried to send all of his data to the Chinese electronically. Seeing he couldn't, thanks to our friends at that *other* national agency, he likely grabbed them as his insurance policy." Dodd grinned. "The Chinese can be extremely unpleasant with those they consider deal breakers."

"He is on the airfield," said Krieger. "But he's not going anywhere." Then he remembered something. "He had a heavily laden backpack. Probably the hard drives."

"We need them," said Kelly. "Part of our mission is to ensure that the M4X1 data doesn't fall into the wrong hands. And speaking of missions," Kelly said, looking at Cobb. "Who are you and what are you doing here?"

"I'm Cobb."

Kelly looked surprised as he stared at Cobb. "I always thought you'd be bigger."

Cobb shrugged. "I get that a lot."

"But why *are* you here, Cobb?" asked Luke Dodd. "My brother and the SECDEF lose all faith in myself and Captain Kelly, send you in as an insurance policy?"

Cobb shook his head. "Different target. The location was coincidental." As he finished speaking, movement at the top of the stairs caught the ex-operator's eye. Without giving anything away, he nodded upstairs. "What's up there?"

Kelly shrugged. "Sedov's office. His personal computer. We've rigged it all, along with anything else on-site that might contain useful project data, with incendiary devices. We start the timers before we take off."

Cobb nodded. "I want to take a look around."

"Roger," said Kelly. "Help yourself. But the birds are taking off in five. And the prick in charge of them will leave with you or without you."

Krieger began to follow Cobb. Cobb held up a hand. "No, you stay here."

The scout frowned, but nodded. Cobb had offered to take Krieger with him when the scout was stranded at Bragg after the War Dogs had pulled pitch. He'd told him he normally operated alone, but that he might need help with this one. Krieger had a feeling the man *never* needed help and had merely felt sorry for him. But after spending several days together, Krieger still didn't know what Cobb's mission was. All he knew was that the man had a piece of paper in his pocket that got him whatever he wanted from whatever government agency he asked. Only once had Krieger caught a glimpse of the document, and he knew a presidential seal when he saw one.

Moving up the stairs, Cobb pulled his Glock from the leg-rig extension along his right thigh. Entering the office, he saw no sign of life. He spotted what looked to be a storage closet. Walking slowly and distributing his weight evenly on the balls of his feet in order to make no sound, he approached the closet door.

One minute later Cobb ran for the top of the stairs. "Out! Everyone out! The device is armed and there's only ten minutes left on the timer!"

"Christ," said Luke Dodd, looking up the stairs toward Cobb. "Can't we stop the countdown?"

Cobb shook his head. "No. Sedov damaged the timer once he initiated."

"Get moving!" Kelly yelled to his team. "Forget the incendiaries, they would just be overkill at this point. Bull," he said, grabbing the big man's arm. "Get on the horn and let Colonel Jones know what's going on. We need everyone on those birds and moving."

Bull Dell nodded solemnly. "You got it, Sonny."

It was a race. None of the men knew how far was a "safe" distance from a one-kiloton nuclear explosion, but they knew it was going to be a near thing. At this point, every second counted.

The driver of the M4X1, recognizing Sedov, pulled to a stop when he saw the Russian waving him down from the airfield. "What happened here, Colonel?" asked the Iranian, taking in the burning aircraft and Sedov's own disheveled state. "Are you injured?"

Pulling his sidearm, the Russian pointed it at the driver's head. "You will do exactly as I tell you—is that clear? I do not have time for questions."

The driver swallowed. "Yes, Colonel."

Being careful with the contents of the backpack, Sedov climbed atop the Tommy and lowered himself into the commander's position. In order to do so, he had to dislodge the dead vehicle commander and stack his body atop the gunner's. He hated that he didn't have time to make the driver remove them, but time was the one commodity he was dearly short of. Pulling on a crewman's helmet, he activated the intercom system. "Can you hear me, driver?"

"Yes, sir."

"You will begin driving east as rapidly as possible, attempting to reach the mountain passes. You do not stop for anything. Am I clear?"

"Yes, Colonel."

"If you fail to follow these instructions, I will kill you. Do you understand this as well?"

Sedov could almost hear the man swallow heavily before answering. "Yes, Colonel. I understand."

"Very, well. Then *drive.*"

"Bick," Dillon said into his boom mike. "Keep your hands off of the Cadillacs. This one is mine."

"Roger that," said Randy Bickel, knowing when it was pointless to argue with his tank commander. "She's all yours."

Dillon thought about his promise to Sergei Sedov. *By my hand. And now it will be painful.* He was sure the Russian had thought the words empty threats. His mistake.

"Dog One, Dog Six," called Jones.

"One," answered Dillon shortly, his eye to his sight extension as he lased the Tommy for range.

"I need you back here, time now."

"Sir . . ."

"Patrick, that's a fucking order, son," snapped Jones. *"We've got a nuke ticking down. If you want to kill yourself on a personal quest for revenge, that's your option. But you've got a crew with you. Is the Russian worth their lives to you?"*

The old bastard knew how to hit him where it hurt, Dillon reflected. Looking to his right, Dillon saw the Black Hawks of the 160th SOAR uploading passengers. Two hundred meters away, at most. While he'd like to have moved closer, this would have to do.

"Stop the tank, Monk," Dillon ordered.

The Abrams ground to a halt. Dillon sighted carefully. "From my position . . . on the way."

The breech reared backward and cordite fumes filled the turret. "Give me another sabot!"

"Last round, sir!" announced the loader. "Up!"

"On the way!" The M1A1 rocked again.

Patrick Dillon watched through his commander's sight extension as the Tommy ground to a halt, smoking. Then he saw Sergei Sedov hop from the M4X1's commander's position and begin sliding to the ground. "That fucker's got more lives than a cat," Dillon muttered. "All right, everyone out!"

Dillon had already disconnected his CVC helmet and was sliding down into the driver's compartment vacated by Monk.

Bickel squatted above him on the tank's front slope. "What the hell are you doing, sir?"

"Bick . . . listen carefully, as this is an order: Get these men to those choppers *now*."

"But, sir . . ."

"*Now,* dammit!" Dillon yelled. Seeing the stricken look on his gunner's face, Dillon softened his tone. "Randy, I'm responsible for them. Please . . . do this for me, all right?"

The sergeant nodded once, his eyes glistening despite his best efforts. "Roger that, sir." He saluted smartly. "See you on the high ground."

Dillon returned the salute. "Roger. On the high ground."

Sergei Sedov was a dead man walking and he knew it. He'd become his own executioner. Still, something about the human condition made him try to put distance between himself and the device that was about to destroy him. He heard a noise behind him, a bansheelike scream he was all too familiar with. He turned and saw the Abrams screaming across the desert toward him, rooster tails of sand high in the air in its wake.

For a moment Sedov thought that, despite the fact that this was an enemy vehicle, perhaps it would somehow be his salvation. Perhaps they wanted him as a prisoner. Sedov knew himself well enough to understand that he would tell the Americans whatever was necessary to save his life. Then he saw the face staring at him from the driver's position. It was the one-eyed madman, Dillon, and he was not slowing down. Sergei Sedov began running faster than he thought possible, given his disabilities. For the first time he could remember since achieving adulthood, he screamed in pure terror.

Dillon almost felt sorry for the pathetic figure fifty meters in front of him. Sedov had thrown aside his backpack in an all-out effort to live. The man looked like an animated scarecrow, his legs moving in an oddly disjointed cadence to his flapping arms.

Sedov went sprawling face-first into the hard desert

scrabble. For a moment Patrick Dillon hesitated. He remembered the scores of men from the previous war, unarmed men that the Russian had ordered killed. He remembered Melissa, how close his daughters had come to losing their mother, and what the animal had planned for her. He remembered Tom Crockett. Bending his wrists back as far as they would go on the throttles, Dillon picked up speed as he centered the sixty-eight-ton Abrams's right track on his target.

The last thing Sergei Sedov remembered before opening his eyes was the scream of the M1A1's turbine as it accelerated and a shadow passing over him. Now all was silence. He smiled briefly at the realization that he felt no pain. Once more the American had spared him.

"I wouldn't be laughing just yet," said a familiar voice at his shoulder. "You thought you looked fucked-up before? You should see yourself *now.*"

"*You,*" Sergei Sedov tried to say. But the word sounded as though it came through so much bloody froth.

"My guess is your spine is mush, which explains the lack of pain," said Dillon conversationally. "Frankly, it's a miracle you're still alive. But let me help you share the moment with me." Grabbing the Russian's hair, Dillon pulled Sedov's head up so that he could survey his body.

A strangled scream escaped the Russian's throat. The pressure exerted on his midsection by the Abrams had crushed his abdominal area to a pulp roughly one-half inch thick. The ends of his boots had blown off his feet when the internal pressure brought to bear on his body needed an outlet, exploding all of his toes and fingers like overcooked sausages. "Plu-please," gargled Sedov, his eyes begging. "Please. Kill . . . me."

Dillon let the head drop back to the desert floor. "Oh, I *have* killed you, Ivan. Make no mistake about that." Pulling his field knife from the scabbard at his

side, Dillon cut the black nylon Rhino band securing
the big SeaWolf to the Russian's wrist. Putting it to
his ear, he heard the purr of the Swiss components
and smiled. "You believe that, Ivan? Still running like
a top." But when he looked into Sergei Sedov's eyes,
they held only the blank stare of eternity.

Cobb was the last man to board Bertetto's MH-
60K. "It's about fucking time . . . ," the aviator began.
One glance into the newcomer's eyes and the captain
decided to cut off further comment. "Well, all right,"
he finished weakly. "Everybody get strapped in."

"We've still got a man out there," said Jones over
the intercom. "He's to the east, along the exfil route.
I need you to stop and—"

The captain began tapping on his watch. "Sir, if you
want to live, and you want my boys and me to live,
we got no fuckin' time to be dickin' around!" And
then they were in the air, wheeling toward Afghanistan and safety from the nuclear fireball simmering
behind them.

"There he is!" yelled Jones, pointing to the ground.
"Next to the M1!"

Bertetto began to speak, but he found himself staring at the business end of a 9mm pistol. "Get us down
there, pork chop," said Jack Kelly softly.

"It ain't like you need that fuckin' thing!" Bertetto
said. "I was fuckin' goin'!"

Thirty seconds later, Dillon and a very frightened-
looking Iranian soldier, the Tommy's driver, were
loaded aboard. Jones noted the soldier stayed as far
away from Patrick Dillon as possible, given the confines of the aircraft.

"What happened down there, Patrick?" he asked.
"That kid acts like you're the devil himself."

Dillon merely shook his head as he lay back against
his seat.

"Sedov?" asked Jones finally.

"Dead."

"I hate to ask, but the past being what it's been . . . you're sure?"

Dillon kept his eye closed. "Oh yes."

Jones nodded. He noted the backpack at Dillon's feet. "What's in the bag?"

Dillon grinned tiredly. "A little gift for Doc Bernard," he said.

Krieger sat silently next to Cobb. Finally, he had to ask, "Did you accomplish your mission?"

Cobb shrugged. "Not yet. But soon."

"Should I bother asking what the mission *was*?"

Cobb thought about the question. "This is a great nation we live in, Lieutenant. And despite what the liberals in our country, the European Union, and a lot of enemy states say, all in all we really are the good guys. We try to do the right things for the right reasons." He paused, selecting his wording carefully. "But there is evil in this world, true evil. And sometimes, in order to defeat this evil . . ."

"We must become evil ourselves?" finished Krieger.

"I wouldn't go that far, but to an extent . . . yes. We have to do things we normally wouldn't do. Things we find distasteful. We have to fight fire with fire."

"And when such times arise . . . you are that fire?"

Cobb smiled.

The Ayatollah Khalani stared at the device ticking down before his eyes. From his position tied to Sergei Sedov's chair, he could see how much time he had left in this world—not long. He could also see the hastily scrawled note taped to the device. It read simply, *For crimes against the United States of America and her people, you have been found guilty. Sentence—death.*

And then the red digital numbers reached zero.

The big Black Hawk had barely cleared a third mountain pass when the aircraft lurched violently and the interior lit up like noon in the park on the Fourth of July. "Hang on! And keep your eyes closed!"

Dropping the helo low in an attempt to miss the worst of the nuclear winds blowing outward from the device behind them, the aviator flew like he'd never flown. The airframe felt as though it were twisting apart in his hands, but he somehow managed to keep it in the air, feathering the controls where possible, handling the cyclic and pedals with pure brute force when necessary. "Mother *fuck!* I hate nukes! Fuckin' *hate* 'em!" he yelled.

An hour later, spewing hydraulic fluid like blood from numerous hoses and with smoke billowing from one engine, John Bertetto set the big bird down at a remote American camp in central Afghanistan.

As a team of mechanics swarmed over the helicopter, the crew chief helped the passengers unload.

Bertetto stayed in his seat, staring out of the windscreen, physically and mentally too exhausted to move. He felt a hand on his shoulder.

"Nice fucking flying, pork chop," said Jack Kelly, extending a hand.

The stocky aviator winked as he took the hand. "Nothin' fuckin' to it," he replied. "Piece of fuckin' cake."

As Jones and Stuart walked toward the camp's field hospital to check on their men, Dillon turned his wrist out of habit to check the time, then remembered the Zodiac. Reaching into his pocket, he pulled it out. He'd loved this watch. Now it seemed somehow . . . distasteful . . . to him. He knew he couldn't wear it again. Ever. He handed it to Stuart.

"I want you to have this, Mike," he said. "Replace that beat-up G-Shock you've been wearing forever and maybe some chick will actually talk to you."

Realizing what he held, Stuart attempted to return it. "I can't, Pat. I know how you feel about your watches. . . ."

"Timepieces," corrected Dillon. "A quality watch is a *timepiece*."

"Whatever. I can't accept it."

"Mike, we've been through a lot together. I want you to have it, okay? Besides, I've had my eye on an I.W.C. Aquatimer."

Mike Stuart shrugged. "All right. Thanks. What happened to the strap?" he asked.

"Shut up, you fucking ingrate. They cost less than twenty bucks, buy another one."

"You two," called a familiar voice. "Over here."

Jones stood next to two other figures in the gathering darkness. As Dillon and Stuart approached, one of the figures struck a match and began puffing vigorously on a pipe.

"You're alive," Dillon said slowly, walking to Barnett and wrapping an arm around his old battalion commander. He pulled back to arm's distance. "But I saw—"

"What you *saw* is how effective the fire suppression system of the Stryker is, Major." Dave Barnett grinned, face aglow from his pipe. "Don't get me wrong. I'm a little singed. But I wouldn't be here at all if someone hadn't pulled my unconscious ass out of the vehicle before it went up."

"Ahhh, man. It was nothin'," said the second figure. Although the man was clad in Nomex coveralls like the rest, his hair was pulled back in a ponytail.

"You were on the Stryker, Doc? What the hell for?"

"Stowaway." Clive Bernard grinned. "And the colonel here's already chewed my ass—and put me in for a medal—so let's just drop it."

"But *why*?" asked Stuart.

The lanky scientist hesitated. "When I saw you guys leaving, carrying all of this equipment that I'm telling you will save your lives, but having no real idea whether it would or not . . ." He paused, thinking. "I don't know, man. I just felt kind of like an asshole. So . . ."

"I'm going to have to be much more vigilant," finished Sarah Hunter as she joined the group and placed her arm through his. "You're not leaving my sight from here out."

"Yes, ma'am," said Bernard. For once he was smart enough to shut his mouth.

Chapter 25

Cielo Vista Ranch
Big Horn Mountain Range, Wyoming

"It is good to have you home again, Señor Luke," said Enrique.

"Good to be home, old friend," said Luke.

The season's first snow had fallen and the two men wore heavy, lined jackets and gloves as they leaned against the corral's top beam, their hats pulled low on their heads to keep out the chill wind. They stared at the black Morgan across the open ground. Malvado's breath came in ragged snorts of steam as he stared at the men.

"Why don't you come to the house, let me make you some breakfast before you begin with that evil creature?"

Luke shook his head. "He isn't evil, Enrique. Spirited."

"Yes, spirited with an evil spirit," replied the foreman, making the sign of the cross. "It is your life, Señor Luke. I am only saying, why not end it on a full stomach?"

Luke walked to the railing and lifted his saddle. "I'll be up directly. I've been away too long and me and Mal need to get to know one another again."

"*Sí, sí,*" said Enrique, walking away and continuing to mutter about demons, curses, and death as he made his way along the path to the main house.

As Luke approached the horse, saddle in hand, Malvado stood his ground. The only sign that he was in the least agitated were the few short jerking motions of his thick neck and a slight roll to his eyes.

Luke placed the saddle on the top rail of the fence next to the Morgan. Reaching up, he gently caressed the side of the big black's face. "Yeah, you remember me, all right. It's just a matter of getting to know each other again."

"Is that all it takes?" asked a voice from behind him. Luke froze. He turned very slowly, not wanting the dream to end.

"Natasha?"

Natasha Khartukov smiled as she shivered in the early-morning cold, her black leather jacket a wonderfully effective and stylish overgarment in Manhattan, but not quite sufficient to the task in the shadows of the Tetons.

As Luke Dodd stared, a frown crossed Natasha's face. "Aren't you happy to see me, Luke? I can go, if that is what you want."

Luke dropped the blanket he'd been about to place on Malvado's back and walked toward Natasha. Before reaching her, he stopped short. "But what about . . ."

Natasha threw herself into his arms, burying her face in the thick lining of his jacket. "Luke, I am *here*. And, if you will have me, this is where I want to stay."

Southern Pines, North Carolina

"Nice place you have here, Pops," said Mike Stuart from his chair on Cobb's deck.

Cobb, with apron in place over his jeans and T-shirt, interrupted the flipping of steaks on his oversized charcoal grill long enough to point them at Stuart. "Watch it with the 'Pops' shit, pup," he said. "You ain't married yet."

Nicole walked out onto the deck. "Are you two having a nice talk?" she asked.

Stuart grinned over his Bass ale. "Oh, yes. Cobb was just telling me how much he looked forward to me becoming part of the family."

"Why, Cobb, that's so sweet," Nicole said, giving the ex-operator a hug.

Cobb glared at Stuart over Nicole's shoulder.

Stuart grinned back at him.

Nicole pulled back and turned, handing Stuart a box. "I meant to show you this earlier. It came in the mail today."

Opening the box, Stuart saw it was a silver baby spoon. He frowned. "Who sent it?"

Nicole shook her head. "There wasn't a return address."

"Let me see it," said Cobb, stepping forward. Taking the spoon, he examined it closely.

"The engraving is nicely done," she said as Cobb stared at the spoon. "But I don't understand what it means."

"What was it?" asked Stuart. "I couldn't make it out."

"A scorpion," Cobb said, looking up slowly. "A scorpion with a dagger."

Raleigh-Durham International Airport
Raleigh, North Carolina

Patrick Dillon had already been through the security checkpoints and was now looking through the window at the plane he was supposed to be aboard.

The public address system sounded. *"Last call for Southwest Flight twelve-sixty with service to Colorado Springs and Denver. This is your final call."*

Dillon looked down at the boarding pass, lost in thought.

"Can I help you, sir?" a uniformed attendant asked from the gate. "If you're going to board . . ."

Patrick Dillon looked up, disoriented for a moment. "I'm sorry . . . what did you say?" Then he understood. Tucking the boarding pass into a pocket, he shook his head. "No, but thanks anyway." And he walked away from the gate.

⊘ SIGNET

BESTSELLING AUTHOR
MICHAEL FARMER

TIN SOLDIERS
A Novel of the Next Gulf War
0-451-20905-2
An alliance with Iran reinvigorates the Iraqi
military. To prevent a total conquest of the
region, a U.S. Army Heavy Brigade must stand
against Iraq's greater numbers and updated
technology—while the locals are bent on
grinding the small American force into the
ancient desert sand.

IRON TIGERS
A Novel of a New World War
0-451-21262-2
In the wake of the second Gulf War, the Middle
East is in turmoil and a new communist leader in
Russia has vowed to return his country to its
former power. He's allied himself with the Saudi
prince and is poised to assert military power with
a sudden act of aggression. It's time for the
tanks to roll.

Available wherever books are sold or at
penguin.com

S788

Military action from
JOHN MANNOCK

"John Mannock gives readers a compelling and
stereotype-breaking story...With a
combination of action, war, love and betrayal."
—Soundings

IRON COFFIN
0-451-21140-5
Far below the surface.
Far from the Fatherland.
And too close to the enemy for comfort.

THE SEN-TOKU RAID
0-451-21440-4
Underwater Demolition Team operative
Lieutenant Charlton Randall and his crew must
destroy a sea base of subs aimed at
Washington, D.C.—or die trying.

Available wherever books are sold or at
penguin.com

s114

ONYX

CHRISTOPHER HYDE

"Hyde's storytelling is PURE GENIUS."
—*New York Daily News*

THE SECOND ASSASSIN
0-451-41030-0

THE HOUSE OF SPECIAL PURPOSE
0-451-41108-0

AN AMERICAN SPY
0-451-21489-7

Available wherever books are sold, or
to order visit penguin.com

S630

Penguin Group (USA) Online

What will you be reading tomorrow?

Tom Clancy, Patricia Cornwell, W.E.B. Griffin,
Nora Roberts, William Gibson, Robin Cook,
Brian Jacques, Catherine Coulter, Stephen King,
Dean Koontz, Ken Follett, Clive Cussler,
Eric Jerome Dickey, John Sandford,
Terry McMillan…

You'll find them all at
penguin.com

*Read excerpts and newsletters,
find tour schedules and reading group guides,
and enter contests.*

Subscribe to Penguin Group (USA) newsletters
and get an exclusive inside look
at exciting new titles and the authors you love
long before everyone else does.

PENGUIN GROUP (USA)
penguin.com/news